THE LAND BEYOND THE MOUNTAINS

THE LAND BEYOND THE MOUNTAINS

Janice Holt Giles

With a Foreword by Dianne Watkins

The University Press of Kentucky

Published in 1995 by The University Press of Kentucky

Scholarly publisher for the Commonwealth,
serving Bellarmine College, Berea College, Centre
College of Kentucky, Eastern Kentucky University,
The Filson Club, Georgetown College, Kentucky
Historical Society, Kentucky State University,
Morehead State University, Murray State University,
Northern Kentucky University, Transylvania University,
University of Kentucky, University of Louisville,
and Western Kentucky University.

Editorial and Sales Offices: The University Press of Kentucky
663 South Limestone Street, Lexington, Kentucky 40508-4008

Library of Congress Cataloging-in-Publication Data

Giles, Janice Holt.
The land beyond the mountains / Janice Holt Giles ; foreword by Dianne Watkins.
p. cm.
ISBN 0-8131-1936-7 (cloth : alk. paper). — ISBN 0-8131-0848-9 (paper : alk. paper)
1. Wilkinson, James, 1757-1825—Fiction. 2. Kentucky—History—To 1792—Fiction. I. Title
PS3513.I4628L3 1995
813'.54—dc20 95-24117

This book is printed on acid-free recycled paper meeting
the requirements of the American National Standard
for Permanence of Paper for Printed Library Materials.

TO

PANSY WILCOXSON PHILLIPS

"But here's the joy; my friend and I are one."

FOREWORD

Cartwright's Mill is an entirely imaginary place. But if I look out the big window in my living room the Green River valley outstretched before me has much the appearance of the valley in which Cassius Cartwright settled; and while the inhabitants of Cartwright's Mill are wholly imaginary also, my neighbors are the descendants of just such people. All the other people in this book are real.

General James Wilkinson is one of the most elusive, enigmatic, and controversial figures in American history. John Randolph of Roanoke called him a "finished scoundrel." Washington Irving wrote of him as "the admirable trumpeter." Two of his biographers took advantage of these epithets to find titles for their books. A third called him, simply, "the tarnished warrior."

There is no doubt he was deeply tarnished. There is no doubt he intrigued all his life, ruthlessly, selfishly, without conscience. He was vain, pompous, jealous, and ambitious. Yet the man was charming, brilliant, likable, and to the end of his life he was able to retain warm relationships with incorruptible men in high places of government. He was for thirteen years a pensioner of Spain, holding most of that time a commission in the United States Army. His loyal friends, and they were many, maintained that he used this connection with the Spanish to work actively against them. Opinion remains divided on that point to this day.

His lifelong dream of empire in the west did, however, result in focusing attention upon it, and as commander of the Army he was able to map and explore, in expeditions under Zebulon Pike and his own son, James Wilkinson, Jr., many of the rivers and mountains in the southwest. Thomas Jefferson seems to have been aware of many of Wilkinson's schemes, indeed strangely sympathetic to them, and while he gave no official sanction, he certainly did nothing to restrain them.

It has grieved me that I could not follow Wilkinson to the end of his life, but this book has had to be concerned only with his intrigues in Kentucky. I have drawn from his *Memoirs,* his biographers, general history, and in particular from a Ph.D. dissertation by Percy Willis Christian, "Wilkinson and Separatism." I am indebted to Miss Elizabeth Coombs, Librarian of the Kentucky Building Library of Western Kentucky State College at Bowling Green, Kentucky, for calling this manuscript to my attention.

I have also leaned heavily again on the Ph.D. dissertation of Dr. Charles W. Talbert, "The Life and Times of Benjamin Logan," for authenticity as to the general situation in Kentucky at this time. From long familiarity with his work I am of the opinion that where Kentucky history is concerned Dr. Talbert is well-nigh infallible. I am deeply grateful to him once more.

I owe much to Miss Frances Coleman, Mr. G. Glenn Clift, Mr. Charles V. Hinds, all of the Kentucky Historical Society, for help rendered patiently.

Mr. Allan M. Trout, columnist and news reporter for the Louisville *Courier Journal,* a resident of Frankfort, Kentucky, directed my attention to a small pamphlet on the history of Frankfort which he had in his library. This was most helpful in tracing Wilkinson's activities in founding Frankfort. I thank Mr. Trout heartily both for his interest and his help.

I am, of course, wholly responsible for my own interpretation of all facts discovered.

J. G.

Spout Springs
Knifley, Kentucky
February 10, 1958

FOREWORD TO 1995 EDITION

"Some fabulous things have happened on the frontiers of our country and all I have to do is hit upon an especially vivid piece of time and place and build a story into it," explained Janice Holt Giles of her inspiration for writing a series of historical novels she began in 1953. Professing a personal love for history and an intrigue with the opening of the West, Giles embarked on an ambitious project of developing a succession of stories that would trace the westward expansion "in such a way as to make history more interesting for the general reader, and hopefully, more useful to the students of American history."

"History itself is the creative part," Giles stated, "and the author simply grafts some fictional characters onto the history and moves them through the historical plot of figures and events." While reading a biography about General James Wilkinson, Giles discovered the story idea for *The Land Beyond the Mountains* (1959), fourth in the series that included *The Kentuckians* (1953), *Hannah Fowler* (1956), and *The Believers* (1957), and would eventually comprise nine titles.

The Land Beyond the Mountains recounts the Spanish conspiracy in which General James Wilkinson secured a trade monopoly on the Mississippi River from the Spanish authorities. He sought to detach Kentucky from Virginia as well as the United States in order to create a vast western empire with himself as the "Washington of the West." Using the intriguing Wilkinson as the main historical character, Giles introduced the fictional protagonist, Major Cassius Cartwright, to infuse new blood into the Fowler and Cooper genealogy of the preceding novels that would carry the generations forward as the families continued their settlement of the American West.

Young Cass Cartwright, narrator of *The Land Beyond the Mountains*, is a wealthy, educated Virginian who has crossed the mountains into Kentucky to establish a settlement of his own on the Green River. Cartwright meets the already notorious twenty-six-year-old Wilkinson while on a business trip to Philadelphia. Wilkinson soon solicits Cartwright to become his partner in shipping goods to Kentucky and opening the first mercantile store in Lexington.

During the same eventful trip to Philadelphia, Cartwright, by assignment and by chance, encounters two women: Rachel Cabot, a young Quaker woman whom he sadly must inform that her husband has died at the cruel hands of Indians; and Tattie Drake, a scrawny fourteen-year-old waif attempting to assist a drunken sailor to his room at the tavern in exchange for her supper. Homeless and penniless, Tattie turns up later among a boatload of girls secured for marrying the "lonely, woman-starved males of the Kentucky wilderness." Recognized by Cartwright, Tattie is rescued and sent to Cartwright's home, where she would have a room of her own and the care of his servant, Sheba. Both Rachel and Tattie are later to compete for Cartwright's romantic attention.

"I love this little Tattie," Giles wrote in *Around Our House* (1971). "She is small, sprightly, uncouth in many ways, but teachable with a good mind. I mean for her to become the other strong grandmother in the series and bring her bawdiness and rough sense of humor into the line of Fowlers, who without this foil would be too serious and too silent."

Cass Cartwright peoples his settlement on the Green River with four Shenandoah Valley families who have lost their land through worthless claims. Among the colorful group of personalities are a blacksmith, a granny woman, and a small, hunchback man, Jeremy Yardley, who quickly becomes Cartwright's closest friend. The everyday tasks of the diverse tenants of Cartwright's settlement provide flesh for Giles's full-bodied tale about the new land west of the Appalachians. The author is at her best when describing the early Kentucky folklife which she has seen from personal experience and observation of rural northern Adair County, Kentucky. It was here in a tradition-saturated environment that she moved with her husband Henry in 1949 and practiced many of the old ways.

In *40 Acres and No Mule* (1952) Giles confessed contentment at having spent some years as a member of this rural society before it began to change. "I am glad I saw it lit by kerosene lamps and warmed by woodburning stoves," she wrote. "I am even glad I made use of an outdoor privy and walked a dirt road. I am glad I helped spring-pole a well and raise a tobacco crop." She knew firsthand "the smell of wood smoke as thin tendrils from fresh-laid fires spiraled out of the chimneys," the smell of meat roasting, of bread baking, of stews simmering, and the "acrid smell of stock, heavy and sweaty and animal" from "stables and stalls back of the houses."

In 1957 Henry and Janice purchased several old log houses made of hand-hewn timbers to use in constructing their home on the seventy-six acres they purchased in Spout Springs Hollow, a story the couple later related in *A Little Better than Plumb* (1963). Work on the house began in September at the same time Janice began writing *The Land Beyond the Mountains.* Giles locates the mythical Cartwright's Mill in the Green River Valley and patterns the setting after her surroundings in Spout Springs Hollow. Although not a Kentuckian by birth, Giles skillfully mines the soft-spoken language of her husband's homeland for authenticity in the settlers' speech. Rather than belaboring the vernacular, the author gives the flavor of the language through recurring colloquialisms, such as the ficitional scout Tate Beecham's description of General Wilkinson as "overbearin' an' vain an' in my opinion he's mostly breath an' britches."

Giles portrays Wilkinson as he was in reality: an intelligent man of intrigues who was egotistical, shrewd, ambitious, deceitful, conceited, and a charmer capable of treason. Cartwright soon learns that lending money to the flamboyant general, who lives like a man of great wealth, is like "throwing corn to geese." Cartwright continually rallies fellow Kentuckians and convention delegates at Danville to defeat Wilkinson's scheme. Early on, he realizes that "the whole future of Kentucky might be altered by this one man. He could well be their savior and their good friend, or their worst enemy." In reality, Wilkinson's plot might have succeeded had it not been for the loyal determination of hardy frontiersmen like the fictional Cartwright. He represents any one of the honest, dedicated men who tirelessly and valiantly sought Kentucky's statehood.

Five months from its beginning, the manuscript of *The Land Beyond the Mountains* was mailed February 10, 1958, with a letter stating, "Here it is—all of it; finished, done, the end! As usual I'm worn to a nub—so very tired I feel as if I could barely lift my hand." The publishing date for the book was set for March 4, 1959. The following day Paul Brooks, editor at Houghton Mifflin, sent the author a telegram to share the news: "OFF TO A GOOD START WITH ADVANCE SALE OF OVER SIX THOUSAND COPIES."

In his introduction to her last publication, *Wellspring* (1975), Brooks wrote, "A book editor can know no greater satisfaction than to be associated, over a long period of years, with a literary craftsman like Janice Holt Giles. The short pieces presented in this volume give some idea of the versatility, the wide range, and the authenticity of [her] work. There is a great variety of mood and setting; one of her greatest strengths as a writer is her sense of time and place."

That the University Press of Kentucky has chosen to reprint *The Land Beyond the Mountains* and other Giles titles is testament to that accolade. Janice Holt Giles's unique style and extraordinary talent have earned the continual popular readership of her books. Her ability to make her characters live and walk through the pages of history is a gift that will endure in the historical novels that celebrate Kentucky's heritage.

—DIANNE WATKINS

CHAPTER 1

His heels drummed a quick, descending tattoo on the bare boards of the tavern stairway. The gabble of voices in the taproom stopped at the sound and, as if swiveled by the same mechanism, every head at the tables turned to look at him. He nodded pleasantly, but briefly, as he passed.

In the dimness of the room the men saw a long-boned man whose polished shirt front gleamed whitely and whose fine blue cloth coat sat elegantly on his shoulders. They saw that his clubbed hair was tied with satin and that the ruffles at his wrists were lace. He walked to the bar and rapped his knuckles in front of the wicket, the clicking of his heels dulled now by the sawdust on the floor.

"Azariah's to the kitchen, sar," one of the men called to him. "Ye want I should fetch him?"

He faced the man, his dark brows drawn together slightly. "Thank you kindly, Noah — perhaps you'd better. Ah . . ." he broke off, "here he is. Does the goose hang high, Azariah?"

A ponderously fat man, jowls hanging, eyes almost hidden in rolls of flesh, waddled through the door. "No, sar, Major. 'Tis a saddle of lamb."

"It smells like an excellent saddle. My mouth waters for a plate of it."

"Y'r sarvice, sar."

"No, Azariah, I haven't time. Besides I'm dining out. I'd like my horse brought around, please."

"Yes, sar, immejutly." The tavern keeper lifted his voice in a booming roar. "Zeke! You, Zeke! Bring the major's horse 'round."

The man winced at the roar and then laughed. "By God, Azariah, the angel Gabriel won't need his trumpet on doomsday if he has you at hand."

The fat man chuckled, all his chins quivering and his belly shaking. "No, sar, that he won't. I've a strength of voice, and no denying. Anything else, sar? A tot of toddy while you wait?"

"Not tonight. I'll wait outside, Azariah."

He turned away and strode briskly across the taproom to the door, flung it wide and stood in the opening, sniffing the sea-damp air of Philadelphia.

" 'Twon't be but a minnit, sar," Azariah assured him.

Over his shoulder the man replied, "It will be a good quarter of an hour and you know it. The fool is afraid of my horse."

"Yes, sar. I'm afeared of him meself."

The man laughed. "I'm dining with General Wilkinson tonight, Azariah, and I may take a bed with him also. I tell you so that if my bed has not been slept in tomorrow you'll not think Judah has thrown me and broken my neck."

" 'Twould be like the young deavil to try it, sar."

"He knows better than to try. No, Azariah, he's just nervous under strange hands. Goodnight, Azariah . . . gentlemen." He stepped outside and closed the door behind him.

The men at the table resumed their drinking, a newcomer among them jerking his head at the door. "Who's the macaroni?"

Azariah scowled at him. "He's no macaroni — not that one. He's no dandy. That's Major Cassius Cartwright of Kentucky." The tavern keeper leaned hard on the table on his broad, fat hands, pushing his nose almost into the newcomer's face. "That man, sar, was with General Clark on the march against the British forts in the Illinois country. And he's no milishy major, neither. He was Virginny line, though he's lately resigned his commission and taken up land in the country."

"What's he doing in Philadelphy?"

The tavern keeper's round red face stiffened coldly. "He's minding his own business, which is more than you're doing, my friend."

The man buried his face in the tankard of ale and the men around the table guffawed at his discomfort.

Outside, Cass Cartwright stood on the doorstep of Azariah Bates's tavern and waited for his horse. On this soft May evening of the year 1783 he was twenty-four years old. He was a big man, though there was no trace of awkwardness in his bigness. It was as if he had grown up easily, bone and flesh knowing their needs until, in maturity, they were each a perfect complement of the other. You would know, looking at him, that here was a man whose body was swift, tough, obedient, disciplined and trained. You could not imagine it refusing, by illness or fatigue, any demand placed upon it.

The hard, dark planes of his face were good and the deep-socketed gray eyes were steady and direct. They had had need to be. For six years, since he was eighteen, he had been in service on the western frontier.

In the week he had been in Philadelphia he had caused something of a sensation. With letters from Jefferson, he had been received into the homes of the most prominent men. He had been seen in the company of several congressmen, and rumor ran high as to his business. It was thought to be political, and it was known to be mercantile. He had made no secret of the fact that he was buying flour to ship back down the river.

He had caused a sensation among the ladies of Philadelphia, also. Among themselves they whispered about him. "He is not really handsome," they told each other. "His jaw is too long and his skin too swarthy."

"His mouth is wide, also."

"And many men have black hair and cool gray eyes."

A knowledgeable matron summed it up for them dryly. "He is from Kentucky, he is wealthy, he is unattached, and he looks like a buccaneer."

The ladies had been destined for disappointment. Though he had charming manners, though he wore elegant clothing, though he spent money freely, he pursued none of them. At the routs and balls he danced dutifully with them, but he whispered no sweet nothings in their ears; he asked none of them to take the air on the gallery with him; he squeezed no waists and he escorted none to supper. He was most provoking, this Kentuckian. The only subject upon which he waxed eloquent was that western country itself. "To hear him tell it," young Nellie Cameron said, flouncing angrily because he had ignored her charms, "the place is little short of paradise. Everyone knows it is nothing but a wilderness inhabited by savages."

"But very charming savages if they're all like him," her sister teased slyly.

"Fiddlesticks," said Nellie, tilting her chin. "He's too dark. He looks like a savage himself. The female barbarians out there can have him, for all of me."

"Doubtless they will," her sister said, dryly, "doubtless they will."

The twilight was deepening now and a few yellow gleams from candlelighted windows were making golden squares on the old cobblestones of the street. The busy, broiling, fermenting activity of the day had died away, and as the salt damp blew in from the harbor, the sounds to be heard were all homey and domestic sounds. Women called to their children. Doors were closed, with sharp clicks, against the quick chill of the fast-falling night. Well chains rattled as water was drawn and armloads of cooking wood, brought in for the night, dropped on porch floors clatteringly.

The smells were different, too, now. There was the smell of wood smoke as thin tendrils from fresh-laid fires spiraled out of the chimneys and drifted, a paler blue than the twilight, upward. The smell of suppers cooking seeped through the closed doors and windows and mingled with the odor of the smoke; the smell of meat roasting or broiling, of bread baking, of stews simmering. It was a rich, savory smell. From stables and stalls back of the houses came the acrid smell of stock, heavy and sweaty and animal. Overlying all the smells, though, and stronger than any was the wood-soaked, ropy, tarry, salty smell of the harbor. Cass drew it in through his nostrils and thought you could always tell a port town, even if you were blind, by the smell of the harbor. In all Philadelphia, it was the smell he liked best.

He leaned against the wall of the tavern, patiently. It would take that boy of Azariah's a timeless time to saddle and bring round the big sorrel stallion. The animal was young and nervous, fidgety to stand, and the boy was, as he had said, afraid of him. He made himself comfortable, hitching his big shoulders lazily against the wall, propping one foot on the mounting block. He flicked a speck of dust off his shoe, settled the ruffles of his sleeve and chuckled. He was just as glad that Benjamin Logan, or William Tye, or David Cooper, or any of his other friends back home couldn't see him right now. He'd have a fight on his hands if they could. They'd whoop and holler and yell dandy at him if they could see him in this blue cloth coat and in these pale tan britches. They'd finick and scamper to show how a dandy walked and talked and fidgeted his lace ruffles, and nothing would please them more than to take them off his back, piece by piece, and rub his nose in the dirt. They had an inherent distrust of fine clothes, those Kentuckians. Their own buckskin and linsey-woolsey were good enough for anybody, they thought.

Well, they would never see his blue cloth coat and his lace ruffles. He had left in buckskins and he would return in them. But here in Philadelphia he had felt his mission so important that he had done his best to make a good impression; to let the Congress and Mr. Jefferson's friends see that they were not all ruffians and scum on the western waters.

He thought about that mission. They were in a bad way in Kentucky, and the people were beginning to feel abandoned by both Virginia and the Congress of the Confederated States. When the war had ended Virginia had voted to cede all those lands north of the Ohio River, which George Rogers Clark had won for them from the British, to the new nation. Promptly the Congress had barred further settlement there and what was worse, they had barred the Kentuckians from taking the offensive against the Indians who, still armed and provisioned by the British forts not yet evacuated, continued to harry them.

The Congress said they could call out the militia only to defend themselves, within their own borders. They must not cross the Ohio on the north, or the Tennessee on the south, to invade the Indian towns in retaliation. By long experience the Kentuckians had learned that retaliation, swift and punitive, was the only thing the Indians understood and feared. And having quickly learned the state of affairs, the Indians were prompt to seize the opportunity. Never before, not even when the country was first settled, had the Kentuckians been so constantly harassed. Every boat coming down the Ohio had to run a gauntlet of ambushes. The Wilderness Road, which bridged the mountains for the land travelers, had become a death trap. No homestead, however far from the borders, was safe from quick, horrible attack. Almost as many people had been killed in the year just past as had been killed in all the years of settlement. And, to make matters worse, in the terrible battle fought at the Blue Licks the summer before, many of the leaders, the experienced militiamen and Indian fighters, had been killed. Feeling helpless, their hands tied, they had sent petition after petition to the Virginia Assembly and to the Congress itself. "If we may not take the offensive," they said, "send us troops who can."

Virginia, abiding by the congressional proclamation, said they were helpless to aid. No Virginia troops could be used for invasion of national lands. The Congress sent pretty, meaningless phrases. "We intend to treat with the tribes and obtain a peaceful settlement."

"Treat!" the Kentuckians said. "When have treaties ever been worth the paper they were written on! Send us men with guns, or let us use our own."

When he had learned that Cass was coming east on private business, Benjamin Logan, the head of the Kentucky militia, had come to him and said, "Cass, you lived neighbors to Mr. Jefferson in Albemarle County, didn't you?"

"Yes," Cass said, "I've known him all my life."

"Well, go by Richmond and see him. Talk with him. Tell him the conditions in the country. Tell him either we've got to be helped or the Congress has got to let us help ourselves. We can't go on the way we are. Tell him how many people we've lost this year. Make it as strong as you can. Tell him it only needs a spark to set off a fire of dishumor that could lose this country, not only to Virginia, but to the nation itself. Our people won't sit here and lose their lives and their stock and their homes, abandoned and left helpless, much longer. There is more discontent than those in the east know about. Tell him what you know, Cass, what we both know, and ask him to use his influence to bring about an easing of our situation."

Cass had ridden Judah over the mountains and had found Mr. Jefferson, not in Richmond, but at his estate, near Cass's own home, where he seemed interminably building on the fine mansion on the hill. He went over again, now, the conversations they had had, heard his own voice forming the words the Kentuckians were saying with such vehemence. He recalled that he had leaned forward in his eagerness to be understood. "Sir, if we are not to be allowed to protect ourselves, then the Congress must send an army into that country to protect us. We have petitioned them, to no avail. We have petitioned Richmond, to no avail. No man, not living in that country, can imagine the difficulties. It is hard to understand why the Congress does not act."

The tall, slender, lean-faced man had listened to him gravely, but in the end a small smile had stretched the thin mouth. "Perhaps it is difficult, also, Cass, for your people to understand the problems of the Congress. We have won our independence. We have become a nation, but what kind of nation we are yet to be has to be determined. Do you know that the powers of the Congress are almost wholly limited to the right to treat with foreign countries? It is, after all, only a federation of states which they represent, and the states are very jealous of their rights. Federal government? We have none yet. It remains to be designed. Another appalling fact is that the Congress has almost no funds. Since the war and the generosity of the people are simultaneously over, where are they to turn for funds? Taxes? They have not the right to tax. They are operating from hand to mouth until we do have some kind, some sort of central government. Another dread fact is that the great European empires, any one of them, is ready to leap at our throats, to begin another war if need be, to regain what they have lost. The Congress must steer a narrow channel between Scylla and Charybdis to keep from foundering on the rocks of new wars. We are weak, we are struggling, and we are well-nigh bankrupt.

...8...

"Now, you ask — why doesn't the Congress do something for you? And your needs *are* great, and your position *is* delicate. But you must see the position — almost embarrassingly the new nation finds itself composed of not only the thirteen colonies here on the Atlantic coast, but of a vast land beyond the mountains, stretching to the east bank of the Mississippi and from the Great Lakes to the Floridas. Except for a few struggling settlements, it is Indian country."

"We are well aware of that, sir," Cass had said. "But we have heard that in the east there is much talk against aiding those settlements, that there is even a will to check them. We have heard that it is thought by some prominent men that continued settlement will impair the resources of the colonies; that it will enfeeble the nation; we have heard it said that we are but white savages and that in time we shall become more formidable than the red ones!"

"There is some truth in what you have heard, Cass. Some men are saying those things, and if you are just you must understand that there is some truth in what is being said. Your western settlements, especially if they continue to grow unchecked and undisciplined, *will* enfeeble the nation to some degree. What you are asking now would be a tremendous drain upon it. But I do not agree that we must not run the risk."

"We are a part of the nation, sir," Cass insisted stubbornly. "We are a part of Virginia and you cannot deny . . ."

"I do not deny anything you have said. I know it is true. And the Congress knows it is true, also. But it will take time, Cass. It may take a long time, and your people must make an effort to be patient."

Bitterly Cass had said, "It is hard to be patient, sir, when it is your home that is burned, your family that is murdered, your stock that is stolen."

"I know. I will do what I can. I will give you letters to my friends in Philadelphia. Tell them your story, my friend, as eloquently as you have told it to me. It may have some influence." He had smiled encouragingly and then continued. "Is the disaffection to Virginia growing among the inhabitants?"

"Yes, sir, I'm afraid it is. There is a growing feeling that we would do better to separate ourselves from Virginia and become a free and independent state."

Thomas Jefferson had looked thoughtful. "The separation from Virginia will come in time, and it is right that it should. You are too far from the seat of government. My great fear, however, is that the country will not wish to become a free and independent *state,*" he emphasized the word, "but a free and independent country . . . that it may even attach itself to another loyalty, and that would be disastrous in my opinion. We must not lose the west, now that we have won it."

"Sir, the opinion of stable, loyal men is that when, or if, we are separated from Virginia we must immediately become a part of the union."

"It would be well," the older man mused, "if Virginia makes certain of that. Well, sir," he said, briskly rousing himself, "I shall write those letters for you, now, if you will excuse me."

Cass had taken time, then, to visit his parents. His father's estate, nearby, was not as extensive as Mr. Jefferson's, but it was perhaps more lucrative because he gave it all his time and thought. Cass had always known his father was wealthier than most of his neighbors and he had had reason to be thankful for it in the advantages of background, education and opportunity it had afforded him. It had not prevented him, however, from following his own desires. He had had no wish to follow in his father's footsteps. As the oldest child, however, and the only son, the knowledge that the estate would one day be his gave him an added security in launching out in his own life. Kentucky was his home and he never meant to live anyplace else; but the income from the estate, or its sale, would be buttress to his own affairs.

From his parents', he had ridden on to Philadelphia. He had presented his letters to Mr. Jefferson's friends, he had told his story, but he did not think it had done much good. Mr. Jefferson had been too correct in his reasoning. However, a Kentuckian had talked with them, and that was something. They would remember, at least, that a Kentuckian had troubled himself.

His mind wandering from congressmen and their problems, he began wondering again, as he had done several times since he had received the invitation, why he was being asked to dine at General Wilkinson's. Vaguely he knew that the general was retired from the army and was breeding horses on his big farm, Trevose, near Bristol. Even more vaguely he knew that he had been a brigadier general in the Continental army, had been with Gates at Saratoga, had been with Washington at Trenton. But Mr. Jefferson had not given him a letter to the general, and the general had not been present at any of the conversations he had had with the men to whom he presented his letters of introduction. The invitation to dine with the Wilkinsons had come yesterday, by way of a note delivered to him at Azariah's. "I think we have a mutual friend in Mr. Jefferson," the note had said, written in a bold, black hand, "and can be of mutual advantage to each other. I am much interested in your country. Dine with Mrs. Wilkinson and me at eight tomorrow night, and since the distance from the city is some six miles, it is our hope you will agree to take the night with us also."

Well, he thought, putting it aside, I shall soon see.

A heavy, ponderous, clanking noise came from down the street and Cass turned to see what was causing it. An ancient, decrepit old cart, drawn by an equally ancient, decrepit old horse, was turning the corner. It was heavily loaded with firewood and it jolted and lurched over the cobblestones, its wheels leaning perilously inward and wobbling with every revolution as if they were going to quit and fall in the next time over. It was their iron rims, jouncing and ringing on the street stones, which made the clattering, banging noise.

At the horse's head an old man, capped and whiskered, and almost as rickety as the horse or the cart, hobbled along, screeching profanity and threats with every step. "Goddammee for a lazy bag of bones! Git along, thar, or I'll put a musket ball through yer brains. Giddap, Jep, keep a movin' thar, or I'll whup the skin offen yer lazy carcass."

Cass watched them come up the hill, amusement stretching his mouth. He wouldn't have wagered a farthing that the cart, or the horse, or the old man could make it to the top, but he thought if it were possible the scorching the old man was giving the horse might do it. He noticed, though, that for all the oaths and for all the threats, the whiskery old fellow never laid a limb on the horse. Instead he limped along beside him, yelling at every step, but one hand was kept encouragingly on the animal's head. Cass grinned. He had seen other men curse the thing they were fondest of. He remembered a corporal who had never saddled General Clark's horse without turning the air blue around him, but who would have laid out any man who offered to touch him. He thought what he was hearing now was that kind of affectionate profanity, but it was a blue-streaked, lightning-forked profanity just the same.

From across the street, then, out of the shadows, a voice was lifted in a rumbling song. "Oh, my Annie was a bonny gel, and oh, I loved her true . . ." A drunken seaman, leaning heavily on the shoulders of a girl, lurched out of the shadows and reeled and almost fell into the street. Cass heard the girl cry out and saw her stumble under the weight of the big man who was almost helpless with drink. He saw her try desperately to straighten him up, saw her push and shove at him with both hands, arrange his arm about her shoulders again. "Now, sir," she said, pleadingly, "ye'll have us both in the gutter and the watch takin' us in. Don't be stumblin' all over the street. I'll have ye to the tavern in a minnit, do ye but lift yer feet a little. It ain't far, now, jest across the road. Come on, sir, ye're doin' master good."

She wheedled and cajoled, his heavy weight making her sag, and she edged him carefully onto the cobblestones. The seaman, queue loose, hair awry, jacket rumpled under his arms, took another step or two, lurched uncertainly, hesitated and stopped, flailing the air with his free arm. "Oh," he lifted his voice in lugubrious song, "she was my Annie, but she lived beyond the blue . . ."

"Come on, sir," the girl begged, her eyes going longingly to the lighted windows of the tavern, "ye can sing when we get to Azariah's. We got to git to Azariah's now. It's jest a little piece across the road. Start walkin', now. Don't jest *stand* there."

The man stood, weaving, sweat running down his broad, red face, his hair hanging in his eyes, his arm heavy across the girl's shoulder. "Ye're a good gel, Tattie Drake," he said, his voice rough, the words slurring together, "ye're a fine gel to be leadin' me to the tavern. I'll buy yer supper fer it. I said I would and I will . . . and a noggin of rum. I got me pay here along of me, and I'll make it ring on Azariah's counter fer a good hot supper for ye. Ye're a fine gel, Tattie Drake."

His head lolled dangerously and the girl jerked at him despairingly. "Name of Jesus, come *on!*"

Cass had almost forgotten the cart, but it crested the hill just then and the seaman, pulling himself together for another effort, spied it and straightened to attention, peering, trying to lift one soggy arm to point. "Whut's that, Tattie Drake?"

"It's nothin' but a wood cart, sir. Never mind it. Start walkin', now, so's we can git to the tavern."

"Need some wood, Tattie?" the man asked, maudlinly, trying to look into the girl's face and almost falling in the attempt, "need some wood? Goin' to be a cold winter, Tattie. *I'll* git ye some wood."

He gathered his feet together in a magnificent effort and started toward the cart. The girl clutched at him, crying, "No, no, sir. Leave it be!" but his momentum carrying him forward a few feet, he eluded her. Then his legs tangled ludicrously and he fell heavily against the wheel of the cart, swaying it tipsily. Cass thought the entire load of wood would collapse on him. The old man danced in sudden anger and yelled shrilly, "Take keer, thar. Take keer. Ye'll overset the load. Mind whut ye're doin', fool!"

The girl, left behind, stood with her hand over her mouth and watched as the seaman lay where he had fallen, overtaken with drink, stretched out and already beginning to snore. The old man ran with surprising sprightliness around the back of the cart and kicked the sailor vigorously. The man moved sluggishly, then settled himself more comfortably, snuggling his face against the filthy cobblestones. "Drunk as a fiddler's bitch," the old man quarreled noisily. "Scum, ever' one of 'em, sea scum. Make port and git drunk."

He kicked the seaman once more, then went back around the cart to the horse's head. "Git movin', Jep. Damn yer blind eyes, git movin' 'fore some other whoreson wrecks my load." He laid a gentle hand on the ancient animal's head and tugged him on. The horse, without hesitation, moved forward at a shambling gait that pulled the cart behind him at a snail's pace, and the old man, rickety and frail-looking again, wobbled weavingly along, shrilling oaths at every step.

Invisible himself, because of the growing night, Cass saw the girl approach the seaman when the cart had passed. In the light from the tavern window he saw that she was very young, fourteen, fifteen, certainly no older. She was a thin little waif, flat-chested, bony, hardly larger than a child. Her face was heart-shaped, the chin pointed, but it was so scrawny that it looked half starved. Out of it her eyes stared at the seaman. Cass saw that her arms, under the ragged shawl clutched about her shoulders, were like sticks they were so thin. An untidy mop of hair hung over her forehead and he saw her swipe it back with one hand as she bent over the sailor. Her dress was threadbare, fringed and frayed around the bottom, and slick with dirt and grease. She had on shoes, but they were rough and so much too big for her that they scuffed on the stones as she crept closer to the drunk man. From such shoes her legs went up straight and birdlike, with little flesh to round into healthy curves.

She crouched over the seaman and shook him. "Wake up. Wake up, sir. Ye can't lie here in the road. Ye'll git run over. We're most to the tavern now. Come on, sir, git up!" She tugged at him and strained back to lift him off the ground, but the man was a dead weight, inert and slack, and when she released him he slumped back as limp as a wet rope.

Cass watched, wondering what she would do next. She straddled the man's body and tried once more to lift him up. "Sir, ye'll have to git up. Ye'll have to help me raise ye. Cain't ye hear me, sir? Git up!" Suddenly she released him and stepped to one side, kicking at him viciously. "Oh, name of Jesus, why'd ye have to fall down! Why'd ye have to swill all that rum! Why'd ye take notice of the cart! Why'd ye have to be such a pig!" She leaned over and poked and pummeled him with her fists, her hair flying about her head. "Ye promised me a hot supper, ye goddamned sot, and ye never kept yer promise. Ye said I could have all I could eat if I'd lead ye to the tavern, and here ye be, stretched out in the road like you'd been clumped over the head. God's blood, I'd like to clump ye one myself!" In a spasm of fury and rage she began to pound him with her clenched fists and to kick at him with her rough shoes, blistering him all the time with her guttersnipe tongue.

In the shadows, Cass watched, amused by her temper, not at all shocked by her language, and more than a little sympathetic with her disappointment. Evidently the seaman had realized he was too drunk to get to the tavern and had promised her a meal if she would lead him there. By the looks of her, she badly needed it, too. Moved, impulsively, he straightened, but before he could step into the light, a shoe flew off the girl's foot, sailed through the air in his direction and he ducked back against the wall to dodge it. It fell harmlessly at his feet.

Without looking up to see where her shoe had gone, apparently not even missing it, the girl continued to berate and beat the seaman; then suddenly she left off, stood crouching over him, gnawing one fist, her shoulders shaking with harsh sobs. Just as suddenly, Cass saw her glance around furtively, bend again quickly, and he saw that she was going through the man's pockets. He leaned back against the wall, grinning. That one could take care of herself, he thought. He heard the clink of coins and watched the girl tuck the money safely under her shawl. When she had finished she looked about, as if searching, now, for her shoe.

Squeamishly, with two fingers, Cass picked it up and advanced toward the girl. Hearing him, she swirled suddenly, caught in the light, naked, desperate, terrible fear sweeping over her face. It startled him. He had not thought to frighten her. She started to run but he caught her. She squirmed and twisted in his clutch, but after one grieving moan she struggled silently. She was like an eel in his grasp, wiggling and worming under his arms, behind him, between his legs, kicking, scratching, clawing and trying to bite. Finally he was able to catch both her arms behind her and hold her firmly. "Be still, you little fool," he told her, "I only meant to return your shoe."

"Name of God, why didn't ye say so?" she snapped at him. "I thought ye was the watch."

He released her and pointed to the shoe, lying where he had dropped it. " 'Tis a wonder you've not aroused the watch, pounding and kicking and screeching so."

She flung back her hair and slipped her small foot into the big shoe and bent to latch it. Straightening, she looked up at Cass with sullen eyes. "Where was you, to be seein' so much?"

He pointed at the tavern wall. "It would be wiser," he said, "if next time you turn thief you pick a darker spot."

Quickly she began to deny it. "I never stole . . ."

"Don't lie. I saw you."

She drew in her breath, but her head went up. "He promised to buy me a supper if I'd bring him to the tavern. I kept my bargain, or I would've if he hadn't been such a sot. I brung him here, and he was a tedious load. Then he went and laid down on me. What do ye aim to do? Turn me in?"

"No. It's nothing to me if he lost his pay. If you're going to pick pockets, though, you'd better be more careful. Someone *will* turn you in."

"What did ye want of me?" Her voice was sulky.

"Why, nothing. Your shoe was flung at my head and I merely wanted to save you the trouble of searching for it."

She eyed him suspiciously and muttered something under her breath.

"What?"

"I said I could've found it 'thout your help."

"Well, that's thanks for you! Did you get enough off the sailor to make it worth the risk?"

"It's none of yer business."

"You're right," Cass laughed. "Absolutely and entirely right. Well, goodnight, my dear. Go along with you now. Here's my horse."

The girl did not leave, however. She watched him mount his horse, gather up the reins and pull the big sorrel stallion around.

Before he could leave, she ran to his stirrup. "I do thankee, sir. I might of looked half the night, and been took up by the watch. I was still afeared of ye, sir."

Cass looked down at the small, peaked face turned up to look at him. "That's all right, Tattie."

"You know what I'm called, sir?"

"I heard the sailor speak to you."

"Yes, sir."

He lifted the reins, but the girl still held to his stirrup. "Would yer lady be needin' a washerwoman, sir, or a girl in the kitchen? I can wash real good and I'm a master hand at flutin', sir."

It occurred to Cass that she could do with a little washing herself. The odor that came from her was rank and sour, old sweat and old dirt, the smell of poverty itself. His voice was kind when he answered, however. "I have no lady, Tattie, and I am but a visitor in town."

"Oh." She turned loose of his stirrup.

The stallion was restive and jerked at the reins. Cass soothed him, swinging him away from the girl. "Aren't you bound out already?" he asked, when the animal was quiet again.

"No, sir, I'm not. I live with my uncle who's a cobbler over on the next street. But there's a houseful of them already. My aunt says I've got to find work to do or get out."

Cass envisioned the home, the girl, orphaned probably, thrust suddenly and unwelcome into an already crowded and poor household, made to be a slave in the kitchen, given the leftovers to eat, if there were any, sleeping very likely in a cold attic. He gave an angry twitch at the reins. It was an all too common story. Orphans, or for that matter anything helpless, poor and weak, had a hard time of it, especially in cities like this. Kicked about, they had to scrounge for themselves as best they could. And she was such a little, half-starved wench. He said, "I'll tell you, Tattie, I'll see what I can do for you. Maybe I can find some work for you to do with one of the ladies in the town. Come around tomorrow afternoon and I'll talk with you."

"Oh, sir, would ye? I'm good with mindin' babies and I can turn a roast on a spit so it browns even all over, and my wash is as white as a lady's skin. I'd thank ye to my dyin' day if you could find me something to do."

"I'll do what I can. Now, take this and get yourself some supper. Don't be flashing that sailor's money around in the tavern. It's likely Spanish piasters and will give you away. Tell Azariah I gave you the coin and said to give you a proper supper for it."

"Yes, sir." The girl caught the coin and tucked it in her fist. "What time tomorrow, sir?"

"Not before two. I'll need to make some calls in the morning."

"Yes, sir." She made an attempt at a clumsy curtsey, but her ragged dress caught in one of the big shoes and she went down on her knees. Cass forbore to laugh because even in the dim light from the tavern window he saw the cruel flush that crept up her neck and spread over her face. She picked herself up and fled across the road into the covering shadows.

She'll probably get a beating when she gets home, Cass thought, swinging the horse around. He hoped one of the matrons he had been so polite to could be persuaded to give her some work to do.

He put her out of his mind, then, and thought of the evening that lay ahead.

CHAPTER 2

The meal was over. The general's wife had retired and the two men sat before the hearth in the library, excellent brandy in their glasses, good tobacco in their pipes, and a small fire of chestnut logs burning to take the chill out of the evening.

Trevose, the general's home, was a gracious place. It was a spacious brick residence, sitting at the top of a slight rise from the road, the drive winding up between tall trees. When Cass rode up, the windows were all aglow with lights and he could see the tall, square outline of the front of the house. The general had met him at the door and a Negro servant had taken his horse.

Within, the rooms were in good proportion and they were furnished with elegance and grace. The drawing room was long, with a shiny, polished floor, scattered with deep-piled rugs. The furniture was French gilt and the chandelier was prismed glass. The fireplace was Italian marble. It was an elegant setting for the beautiful, gifted and charming Mrs. Wilkinson. The general explained to him that he had bought the place at a bargain. It had been the estate of a loyalist and had been attainted during the war, and sold. "I came by it," he said, "through the services of my brothers-in-law, Clement and Owen Biddle of the city."

Mrs. Wilkinson had been Ann Biddle. Cass thought the general was a little proud of his connection with the family, and perhaps he had reason to be. It was well known that Clement Biddle had been a close friend of General Washington and had served as his adviser on many occasions, and that the family were people of wealth and influence.

The dinner had been sumptuous. Turkey, ham, lamb and oysters had been served on a table draped with the finest linen, and they had eaten from thin china with the heaviest, most gleaming silver. Mrs. Wilkinson, in pale green watered silk, with a deep lace fichu, had been courteously thoughtful and hospitable. The general had been gracious, cordial, easy in manner and polite. They laughed often, the general and his lady, and seemed to share a common love of the good things of life, including this beautiful home, this good food, good wine and the good conversation that accompanied the meal. If the general was eloquent, with long, flowing, polished sentences, his lady was sparkling and witty. Cass had enjoyed the meal, had enjoyed the talk, but the purpose of the evening remained as much a mystery as ever. Perhaps now that they were alone the general would get to the point.

Over his glass Cass watched the man sitting opposite him. He was a short man, almost a little man. His face was round, bland and expressionless, full in the cheeks. The skin was quite clear, neither florid nor pale, and its smoothness showed his youth. His eyes were dark, an amber brown. They were also round and heavily lashed, but they were intelligent eyes, bright, open, frank and clear. He had a habit of dropping them when he emphasized a remark and then suddenly lifting them to fix steadily upon his listener. It could, Cass thought, take a man by surprise and confuse him. His mouth was full-lipped and red, slightly moist—and his chin was cut by a deep cleft. Cass imagined that he had been a pretty little boy and the pretty face of the child continued into the man, a little firmed, a little hardened.

He spoke with a very positive and certain manner, a little opinionated and pompous. He listened with deference, however, and in his polished, gracious manner made a guest feel very much at ease. It was evident that he thought well of his own opinions, and Cass thought he might be a little vain, from the care which he took with his clothing, but it was also evident that he was a man with a shrewd, keen mind, clever, and with a good knowledge of the general state of affairs in the nation. He had lost the thread of what the general was saying and he came back out of his thoughts to give him his full attention.

". . . they were as unruly and crude a bunch of fellows as I have ever seen." Cass remembered that he had been telling him of his first command. ". . . not a uniform in the crowd, undisciplined, untrained, uncouth. I was determined, sir, to change that at once. The regiment was ordered to muster the day I entered on duty; the company paraded, and I presented myself to take the command; but when I gave the order to shoulder firelocks the men remained motionless, and the lieutenant, stepping up to me, inquired where I was going to march the men. I answered that he should presently see but in the meantime he must consider himself in arrest for mutiny and 'march to his room,' which he did without hesitation. I then addressed myself to the company, sir, pointed out to them my right of command and the necessity for their obedience; I informed them that I would repeat the order, and if it was not instantly obeyed I should run the man nearest me through the body, and would proceed on right to left, so long as they continued refractory and my strength would support me. I had no further trouble but joined the regiment and marched to the parade of general muster. I was nineteen years old at the time, sir."

Thoughtfully Cass swirled the brandy in his glass. "When was that, sir?"

"In May of '76." The general laughed heartily. "You are trying to form some opinion of my age, are you not? I shall relieve you of the tedium of subtracting, Major. I am twenty-six years old."

He looked older than that; he looked nearer thirty-six, for the dark hair was beginning to recede, and the neck around which his tall collar formed a frame was short and when he forgot to hold his chin up, there was a definite crease of flesh under it. He was also beginning to have a slight paunch, though he was firmly sashed and carried it well.

"You earned your laurels at a very young age, sir," Cass said.

"I was a brigadier before I was twenty-one, sir. But the war made heroes of many extremely young men."

Cass wondered if he included himself among them. "You were at Saratoga with General Gates, were you not?" he asked.

"Sir, if I had not been with General Gates at Saratoga we should have lost the battle. With modesty I may say that I penetrated the moves of Burgoyne's attempt to flank us and that General Gates's orders to attack were made as a result of my investigation. He was a slow, vain, befuddled old man, however, and had I not perceived instantly, on the next morning, that he meant to direct the entire army in a frontal attack, which would have been suicidal, sir, the army would have been defeated and we should have had to retreat in disgrace. As it was, I persuaded him to allow me to reconnoiter in person. I found Morgan's command advancing through a fog, uncertain of where the enemy was and I was able to direct their advance. I found Learned's men in a very exposed and hazardous spot and ordered him to retreat. General Burgoyne himself said, after the surrender, that the decision not to attack on that particular front was one of the most adverse strokes of fortune in the whole campaign."

Cass might have taken this monologue as brag and boast had he not known it was true. The general had done exactly what he said, and Cass now remembered that General Clark, studying the strategy later, had said the victory was due to Wilkinson's alertness. "I understand you arranged the terms for Burgoyne's surrender, sir."

"I had that honor, yes, sir. During the negotiations I acted as General Gates's representative. I shall never forget it. I was a youth, in a plain blue frock without other military insignia than a cockade and a sword, and I stood in the presence of three experienced European generals, soldiers before my birth . . . yet the consciousness of my inexperience did not shake my purpose. I had suggested to General Gates that the terms of our proposals should call for unconditional surrender. The *general*," he emphasized the word with irony, "would have considered less and was fearful of our demand, but personally I had determined that I would not take less. General Burgoyne made every attempt to delay the proceedings, in a fond hope that General Clinton would come to his aid. I told him, sir, that he had the choice of dissolving the negotiations or giving an immediate answer. I granted them a truce of one hour for consideration, and then I walked away. I may confess now, Major, that as I turned my back on them I had some most uncomfortable sensations, for our troops were much scattered . . . the men had got the treaty in their heads and had lost their passion for combat, and what was worse, we had been advised of the loss of Fort Montgomery, and a rumor had just arrived that Esopus was burnt and the enemy proceeding up the river; but I had not proceeded fifty rods when Major Kingston ran after me and hailed me; I halted, and he informed me that General Burgoyne was desirous of saying a few words to me. He asked me for two hours to consult with his general officers. I sent word to General Gates that I was allowing the delay. At the end of the time, the British officers decided to accept the terms of the surrender and on the morning of October 17, 1777, it was my privilege to escort General Burgoyne to his meeting with General Gates, when the surrender was formally made. Firmness, sir. It is the only way to deal with men, whether they be friends or enemies."

Call it bluff, Cass thought to himself — call it cold, calculating bluff. And it worked. He had seen George Rogers Clark make it work, with the French in Vincennes, with the Shawnees, with the provincial troops, and even with the Virginia assembly. He had worked it himself. When the line was very thinly drawn, when there wasn't much but the wall at your back, that was the time to square your shoulders, keep your eyes steady, keep your voice cold and edged with iron — put on the mantle of authority, and it worked. Firmness, bluff, cold nerve, guts — the steady hand, the unwavering eye, the cool, inscrutable, demanding voice, admitting of no defeat.

Cass's opinion of the general went up a few notches. Pompous and vain this man might be, but he was no ass. You didn't get to be a brigadier at twenty-one without merit. You didn't outbluff British line officers without nerve. The man had the kind of brass and gall Cass admired. It was doubtless heavily mixed with ambition, but whatever kind of egotistical, parading fool he was in other ways, if a man had nerve and cool self-confidence men would always follow and believe in him. Cass granted him the right to a little preening of himself, for he was beginning to realize that just as coolly as he had confronted three British officers, he was drawing Cass a deliberate picture of himself — showing him the unconquerable, the shrewd, the wise, the experienced, the capable General Wilkinson. Taking a light from the coal the general extended in a pair of small brass tongs, Cass looked at him. What was he bluffing for now? What wall was his back against?

It came suddenly. When he applied the coal to his own pipe and got it drawing, he leaned back in his chair. "Major Cartwright, I am thinking seriously of removing to Kentucky."

Not by so much as the tremor of an eyelash did Cass betray any surprise. Actually he felt little. The general's note had indicated he wanted to discuss the western country with him, and Cass had privately decided it was one of three things. The general was speculating in western lands and wanted some firsthand information; the general had friends or relatives he wanted to get situated in Kentucky and wanted some aid in doing so; the general was interested in locating there himself. The house, however, and the lavish way the general lived had made him think it probably was not the latter. Was the general overextended? Was he living beyond his means? Drawing on his pipe and waiting a perceptible moment for the smoke to ring upward, Cass said quietly, "Indeed, sir?"

The general sat forward suddenly, as if about to divulge a confidence. "Yes. Since the terms of the peace have been made public . . . you are familiar with them, sir?"

"Yes, sir."

"Then you know that the western lands have been included in the treaty. That, sir," he said, abruptly standing, "is the most momentous clause in the entire treaty. That," he added, with a sweeping, dramatic movement of his arm, "gives our country the key to a whole empire that only lies waiting to be developed." He moved briskly across the room to a handsome mahogany desk, took from its center drawer a roll of parchment. "I am an amateur cartographer, Major. I became interested in topography when serving with General Gates and I have pursued it as a pleasant interest ever since. I have just completed a map of the North American continent, which I flatter myself is more accurate than any in the congressional archives. I should like to show it to you, sir."

Cass stood also. "I shall be extremely interested in seeing it."

When he stood beside the general Cass could look down upon the top of his head. He's very short, he thought. He's not more than five feet eight, if that. Cass himself stood six feet two, barefooted. But the military stance of the small man, the squared shoulders, the chest thrust forward, made him look taller. Like a banty rooster, Cass thought, grinning inwardly, and likely just as cocky.

The general unrolled the parchment and hung on the wall a truly beautiful map, lettered painstakingly and with clarity, the lines of the rivers and mountains inked in precisely, the known limits of the land and seas bounded accurately. It was a genuine and loving work of art, and without hesitation Cass said so. "It is a beautiful piece of work, sir. I never saw a prettier map."

"Thank you. I take great pride in all my topographical work. Now, Major, I ask you to bear with me a moment while I explain. Here, once, were the French, in Canada and down the Mississippi and the Ohio. Here were the Spanish, in the far west. Here were the British, on the Atlantic coast. That was the picture until the Seven Years' War. Then it changed. The French lost their holdings in Canada and the Ohio valley to the British, and rather than give up the Mississippi valley to the British also, they ceded it to Spain before the treaty. Momentous, that decision, Major." He laid a spatulate forefinger on the mouth of the Mississippi. "Here is the key to the continent. But it must begin to unlock here." He moved the finger up the broad line of the Mississippi to the Ohio, and up the crooked, wavering line of that river. "Do you see, my friend, why it is inevitable?"

Cass placed his own finger at Philadelphia, ran it slowly down the Ohio to its junction with the Mississippi, ran it down the Mississippi to New Orleans, paused, slid it across to Cuba, then made a wide arch back up the coast to Philadelphia. The general threw his head back and laughed. "Ah — it has not escaped you. Let's say you make up a cargo of flour here in Philadelphia, Major. You take it down river to New Orleans, exchange it for furs, ship the furs out to Havana and exchange them for sugar. The circle is complete when you sell the sugar in Philadelphia."

Since that was exactly what Cass was doing, and in all likelihood the general knew it, he thought he knew what was coming, and he must be the one to look sharp. "A few of us in Kentucky are aware of that, sir."

"Good." The general's voice altered, became sharper, crisper, as if he were already in command. "When you know also, as I do, the true reasons for the French and Spanish support in the late war, their jockeying for control in the west, their deep hatred and fear of Britain, and their preference to help a new nation into existence rather than see those western lands remain under the control of the British, the map simplifies itself and the lands of the Ohio country become the key to the empire. I propose," he announced, robbing his statement of nothing of its pompousness by rolling up the map at the same time, "I propose, Major Cartwright, to join you there to assist in developing the empire."

Cass took his seat again and observed, rather dryly. "There are many of the same idea, sir."

"Yes. I have no doubt of it, but not," he said, pouring more brandy in their glasses and resuming his own seat, "with my experience in military affairs, which your country sadly needs, and not, I flatter myself, with my understanding of national affairs, and probably not with my connections."

Cass waited. It was all true. The country could certainly use a man of military experience in their present sad state. Undeniably the general had a unique and thorough knowledge of the entire situation throughout the west. It was true, also, that he had important connections. He knew intimately nearly every important man in the country, had served under many of them, was well thought of by them. He would bring great influence into the west with him. Cass sat quietly, though inwardly his stomach was beginning to churn. The whole future of Kentucky might be altered by this one man. He could well be their savior and their good friend, or their worst enemy.

"Now, as to the actual purport of my conversation with you. I have sufficient backing to remove to the country and it is my thinking to enter the mercantile business."

Cass's wide mouth stretched into a grin. "That, sir, seems inevitable."

The general laughed with him. "Yes. Though I am also interested in taking up some land."

Swiftly Cass interposed. "Do you have a connection with any of the land companies, sir?"

"No, sir, I do not. I mean to steer clear of them. This is a private speculation."

"Good. We are not fond of land companies in Kentucky."

"I have no prejudice against them," the general said frankly, "save that on close inspection I have not found them to be as profitable as reported."

Cass saw the glint in his eyes and knew immediately that what the general intended was to take all the profit himself. Well, there had been many others with the same motive, many good men in the country who had made a considerable profit in the same way. He had himself. So had Benjamin Logan. So had Billy Whitley. The public estimate of a man was guided largely by the fortune he was able to accumulate. Any ambitious man hoped to accumulate a sizable one. It was entirely legitimate.

"My good friend, Thomas Jefferson," the general resumed, and by the emphasis on the name Cass understood that the general knew of his visit to Monticello, "a fellow member of the Philosophical Society and a man I esteem highly and have the honor to correspond with frequently, has told me that there is some disaffection in Kentucky, some discontent and murmurings against the present status. Is this true?"

Cass weighed the question. Since the general had the information, whether or not Mr. Jefferson had told him, he saw no harm in admitting it. "To some extent, sir. It is felt that we are too far from Richmond and the seat of government, too far from the courts, and too far from the military to count upon their protection and interest. As you know, sir, General Clark has recently resigned his commission, and the regulars which garrisoned Fort Nelson at the Falls have been withdrawn, except for a handful. The country is without military protection except for the militia."

"Who is head of the militia?" the general asked quickly.

"Colonel Benjamin Logan."

"I have heard of him. A good man."

"One of the best, sir."

"They have no redress for Indian attacks, I believe."

"None, save their own defense. Since the end of the war they are barred from carrying the attack into Indian country."

"I know. The Congress is a pack of imbeciles, sir."

"You have had experience with them?"

"Their conduct of the war was disgraceful," the general growled. Then he smiled and became candid. "It is necessary to know the true state of affairs in the country when one is proposing to stake his entire fortune there."

"I should think so, sir." Cass sipped his brandy.

A log burned through with a sharp crackle and dropped, the sparks flying up the chimney. The general stepped to the hearth and took a poker from the stand, juggled the log back into position. "I have some doubts," he continued, when he had taken his seat again, "as to where to locate a mercantile business. On the face of it, Louisville — you call it the Falls?"

"We call it the Falls."

"On the face of it, the Falls would seem to be the most strategic place. It is on the river and trade naturally follows the streams. However, I have heard much about an interior village . . . Lexington, I believe it is called. What is your opinion, Major?"

Cass rubbed his finger around the rim of his glass and studied the dark liquid within. "Well, sir, I was stationed at the Falls too long to retain any great love for the place. It is true it is on the river and General Clark has always held that it will become the most flourishing town in the country in time. He thinks it is inevitable."

"General Clark resides there, I believe?"

"He does. When he is in the country."

"Is there any other mercantile business there?"

"One general store has recently been opened, sir."

The general firmed his lips. "Where are you located, Major?"

"My lands are in Lincoln County, General. On the Green River."

"That's in the interior?"

"It is very much in the interior, sir."

"Do you mind telling me why you chose that situation?"

Cass leaned back. "I don't mind at all, General. As I said, I grew weary of the Falls. When I resigned my commission at the end of the war, I sold my pre-emptions there and when I had prospected the country sufficiently I decided upon some land bordering on Green River."

Unbidden there rose before him the memory of the river at that particular place, flowing with sweeping dignity in a long, broad curve, the high limestone bluffs towering massively on the far side. The lower edges of the cliffs were banked and massed with drooping ferns which were always dripping with damp, which were always cool and green and dark and always giving off a bosky, leafy smell. But in the blaze of morning sunlight the quartz in the upper reaches of the cliff, like diamond facets, gave off a thousand twinkling lights. In the evening, when the sun had set behind the bluff it threw an early twilight on the green water and set it to sparkling among the riffles. Slowly, as the night darkened, the shadow of the bluff lengthened to touch the slim trees along the river's edge and soften their young stiffness, until it swallowed them and merged with their own shadows to extend over the flat, reed-grown swale that stretched beyond.

In almost the exact center of the river there was a long island, willow-grown and strewn with whitened pieces of driftwood. Its pebbly beach was pitted by floods and small pools of green water lay quietly unstirred, placid in their separation from the river, waiting stilly for the freshet and the tide which would join them again with the mother water.

A quarter mile back from the river a shelf of land, ten, perhaps twelve feet high, rose abruptly, like a mesa, and extended flatly and unbroken up the valley. Here, in a druidical ring of ancient beech trees, Cass had built a two-story log house. Here he rose in the misty mornings and washed his face at the spring, which had its hidden source in a rock ledge at the root of the old trees. As still as the pools on the island it lay, a tranquil, leaf-floored basin, perpetually flowing, perpetually cold, perpetually clear.

A squeezing pang of nostalgia for the place struck him and he wished he could wake in the morning and look across the river at the strong, morning sun on the face of the limestone bluff.

He brought himself back, conscious of the general's waiting. He laughed. "I hope to encourage settlers to come my way, and perhaps to lay out a town there some day."

But the general had lost interest and Cass felt foolish discussing so personal a dream with him. He did not know why his tongue had become loose. He felt himself flushing and lifted his glass in embarrassment. The general was studying the fire. Suddenly he raised his eyes, in that quick motion Cass was beginning to expect. "Lexington, I believe," he said, "is in Fayette County."

"Yes, sir."

"Is there any business in Lexington yet?"

"There is a stockade, some mills and tanneries. There is no general store as yet."

"What is the land around the town like?"

"The richest in the country, sir. Well watered, limestone base, and fertile."

"How does it lie?"

"Rolling to level. It is the heart of the bluegrass."

"Should breed excellent horses." It was the farmer and horse breeder speaking.

"Some of the gentlemen located there are discovering that, sir."

"I suppose it's all taken up."

"Not all, but it's pretty well pre-empted."

"How does the land around the Falls lie?"

"Marshy and low. The air is miasmic and, I think, unhealthy. My men suffered constantly from agues and fevers. There was a disproportionate amount of illness in the company, and I believe it arose from the generally unhealthy situation."

"General Clark agreed?"

"General Clark believed it could be ditched and drained, but there has never been time to do it. The land is rich, but swampy."

Silence fell between the two men and into the quietness the hissing slide of rain down the windows was the only sound. The general raised his head from the contemplation of his gaiters and looked at the windows with surprise. "Why, it's raining."

"It has been raining for some time," Cass said quietly.

"You are more observant than I."

Cass forbore to tell him that his ears, his eyes, his entire body, had too long been attuned to every change of weather, terrain, movement, sound, for him ever to cease to be aware and alert. A man's life too often depended upon his awareness of such things. He had known when the rain began, some thirty minutes before, he also knew a southwest wind was blowing, but he had made no comment. It had not seemed necessary.

The general rested his eyes on him and looked at him steadily. "When do you return to Kentucky, Major?"

"The day after tomorrow."

"Can you postpone your departure for two or three days?"

"No, sir, I cannot." He made no explanation.

The general's gaze returned to the fire which was slowly burning itself out. Cass waited. He was growing sleepy and he would have liked to retire, but apparently the general had more to say. Cass wished he would say it, for his lids were beginning to droop. Then the man in the chair on the opposite side of the hearth raised himself a little in the chair and said, abruptly, "Can you raise five hundred pounds, Major Cartwright?"

Cass's sleepiness disappeared. So it was money. The general had funds, but not quite enough. "I could," he said, casually, "but I know of no reason to do so."

"Major, I shall be entirely frank with you. I think it would be to the good advantage of this new venture if someone familiar with that country went into this mercantile business with me. I have the backing of my wife's people, and of some friends, but more than funds I can see that someone experienced in the country, to give counsel and advice, would be helpful. If you can raise five hundred pounds, I should be delighted to offer you a partnership."

"On what basis, sir?"

"Full one half. If you put in five hundred pounds it would release my brother-in-law's funds to use in purchasing more land. This is a time for plunging deeply, not for finicking timidity. In all candor, sir, I should like to be able to take up at least fifty thousand acres. I cannot do it if I must use the funds available for the mercantile business."

Cass eyed the man and weighed his statement. Whether the general was aware of it or not, he had just confessed that he had no funds of his own at all. The wall at his back was the simple fact that his purse was entirely empty and that he stood thus, empty-handed, with only borrowed funds in his pocket, on the verge of a total commitment in a new country. As they said back in Kentucky, he liked to live high on the hawg, but the general's hog was just about gone. He was going to gamble and gamble heavily. A partner, just as willing to gamble, with just as much nerve as the general, might be able to come off very well with him.

He gave no intimation of what he was thinking, however. He got up and stood with his back to the fire. "General, this is a new idea, as you must know. I shall need time to think it over."

There was a sudden gleam in the general's eye, a greedy and triumphant gleam. Very well, sir, Cass thought. Have your triumph. We shall see in the end.

The general stood also. "Of course, my friend. You must take all the time you need to think it over. I am aware that it has come as a surprise to you. But I should like, if it is at all possible, to have an answer from you before I leave for Kentucky."

"When will that be, General?"

"Not before fall, or perhaps winter."

"I shall be able to give you an answer by then, I'm sure."

The general extended his hand. "May I be so presumptuous as to hope that I shake the hand of my future business partner? I do hope it, very much, you know, Major Cartwright."

I'll wager you do, Cass thought, taking the small, white hand in his own capacious paw and resisting the impulse to crush it with a great giant squeeze. I'll wager you do. You would have to do all this palavering over again, with someone far less promising, as you have taken the trouble to find out, if I don't become your business partner. He wondered whom the general had talked to about him. "I am honored, sir," he said, bowing lightly, "and now, if I may, I should like to retire."

"I have kept you too long," the general said, contritely, "but I found our conversation too interesting to break off. I shall light you to your room, sir. I venture to hope you will find it comfortable and that you will rest well."

At the door of an upper room the general handed him his candle, opened the door, glanced around to make certain the room was in order, then turned to him hospitably. "I believe you will find everything you need here, Major. Must you return to Philadelphia early, or shall we have the pleasure of your company at lunch tomorrow?"

"I shall not trouble you in the morning, sir. I shall be on my way at first light and I will breakfast at Azariah's."

"No, no. Mandy can give you breakfast."

"I wouldn't hear of it, sir. I shall take care to disturb no one. Please make my compliments to your wife and say again for me how delightful a hostess she is, and how very excellent her dinner was."

"She will be very happy to know you have thought so."

"Goodnight, General."

But the man turned in the door. "I should have proposed a toast, Major. The heroic age is over, and the day of the politician has dawned. We should have drunk, Major Cartwright, to the day of the politician. Goodnight, sir."

His candle flickered down the hall and slowly Cass closed the door upon it. The day of the politician. Somehow, it seemed to hold a threat.

CHAPTER 3

Cass was returning to the tavern.

He had spent the morning conscientiously seeing every matron he knew in Philadelphia, the wives of the men he had come to see, the women he had been so polite to, and he had not found anything for Tattie to do, nor anyplace for her to live. They all viewed her with suspicion, and in all honesty he could not blame them. Knowing more than he had told about her, he knew she was a poorer risk than they suspected. Blast and damn, he thought, what did I let myself get into such a scrape for! There's nothing to be done but to give the wench, if she comes (and he had a sudden bright hope she might not), some money. It's all that's left to do. He squirmed, seeing already the disappointment spread over her face when he told her he had failed. But perhaps with what she had lifted from the sailor and what he would give her, she could strike out on her own. He made himself put the whole thing out of his mind with that thought.

The street was slippery and wet with the rain which continued to fall in a sullen drizzle. Judah was picking his way carefully and slowly and Cass began to turn over in his mind what remained to be done before beginning his journey in the morning. He had yet to settle the details with the man he had hired to pack his load of flour over the mountains to Pittsburgh. He wanted especially to see the man's horses and make certain he knew his business. He had to call on the firm with whom he had dealt and make payment. He had a dozen letters to write and he had to make at least one more call.

He had saved it to the last because he disliked having to make it. The woman was the widow of a man who had been killed the winter before by the Indians. He had been in the country only a few weeks and had taken up land in one of the river valleys near St. Asaph's. He had come ahead of his family, intended to build some sort of shelter for them, to winter there and then to return to Philadelphia for them. It was Ben Logan who had thought the woman might like to have first-hand news of her husband's death, and that she might also like to have the three books that were all the Indians had left of her husband's possessions. Ben had written to her, of course, but letters were very uncertain, and Cass knew that he might well be the bearer of the first tidings. He dreaded the call.

He was brought out of his reflections abruptly when his horse slipped, stumbled, and almost went to his knees. "Whoa up, Jude. Easy, boy, these stones are slippery." He soothed the animal, which had flung up its head nervously and was whickering through its nose. He gave the horse a moment to recover, then tightened the reins. Uneasily the animal moved on a few steps and Cass knew immediately that he had cast a shoe. He dismounted to inspect the hoof and a passerby stopped to watch. "Cast a shoe, did he?"

"Yes. Is there a blacksmith near?"

The man pointed up the street. "Two squares up. Sam Doddridge."

"Thank you, sir."

When he reached the blacksmith shop there were half a dozen other horses hitched to the rail and the blacksmith was busy. He took time to tell Cass it would be an hour before he could attend to Judah and Cass prepared himself to wait. He did not want to leave the horse for a strange smith to work on.

An hour passed and Sam Doddridge seemed no nearer getting to Judah than he had in the beginning. Dismayed, Cass saw that it was after one o'clock. Tattie would be at the tavern at two, long before he would be able to get there.

He tried to think of some way to reach her, but he had no address save the vague one she had given him the night before.

He had better, he decided, send a note to Azariah and have him explain to the girl when she turned up.

A scrivener's shop was down the street and he went there, wrote the note, enclosed some money for the girl and paid the clerk sixpence to deliver it to Azariah. Having disposed of the matter as best he could, and unashamedly feeling some relief that he need not face the girl himself, he went on about his affairs when the blacksmith finished with his horse, and spent the entire afternoon at them.

At last, every detail of the journey settled to his satisfaction, the hour for departure arranged, all his bills paid, Cass made his way to the home of Edward Cabot's widow.

She was staying with her parents who lived in a narrow, two-story stone house on the edge of town. It was neat and orderly and the stone slabs which formed the steps were scrubbed almost to whiteness. A small boy, five or perhaps six years old, came to the door. The child gazed fixedly at him with round, brown eyes, one finger stuck in his mouth. Cass looked over his head down the hall, but no one else was to be seen. Returning his attention to the boy he asked, "Is your mother at home? Does Mrs. Cabot live here?"

A small nod was his answer, then from the back of the house a voice called, "Who is it, Edward?"

The little boy turned at the sound of the voice and fled down the hall. In a moment a slender, brown-haired woman came into the hall from a door at the back, tucking the ends of her hair under her cap and hastily arranging the folds of her fichu. "I am sorry, sir. Edward is a little young to be answering the door, but he was handy and I was . . ." She left off. "Thee has business with my father?"

It was going to be worse than he thought, Cass realized. The brown eyes with which she looked at him were so tranquil, so serene and untroubled, she could not possibly know that her husband was dead. The face was oval and pale-skinned, but it showed no marks of grief. She had the clear, flowerlike skin that went so often with brown hair and eyes, and she was still so young a woman for all of the little boy and, Ben had said, a baby some four months old when Edward Cabot had left them. Her mouth was sweetly curving, gentle in its tentative smile. Cass groaned inwardly. Ben's letter had gone astray, it was plain, and she would have no time to accept her loss, compose herself, before seeing a stranger who would bring her the last of her husband's possessions.

Awkwardly Cass fumbled with his hat and shifted the bundle of books. "No, ma'am. I expect . . . I think I have business with you, ma'am — if you are Edward Cabot's wife."

"I am." Her eyes lit suddenly with a quick, happy look. "Thee is from Kentucky? Thee brings word of Edward?"

Cass gathered himself together with an effort. "May I come in, ma'am?"

"Oh, I forget my manners, sir. Do come in. Please." She swept happily out of his way and held the door wider, her face glowing with expectancy. "In this room, sir."

He looked about him at the room into which she led him. It was so clean that one had difficulty imagining that it was ever used. The chairs were uncompromisingly straight and there were but three of them. The floor was bare of rugs, but like the stone steps outside, it was white with scrubbing. There was a plain table in the center of the room, on which lay a very large Bible, a candle in its holder, and nothing else. The windows were curtained with plain white curtains, their folds, he would guess, never disarranged.

When he had taken in the room, its most surprising feature remained the shelves of books in the fireplace corner. So the woman's people, like her husband, were educated people. They read. But did a stern conscience demand that they read in such discomfort? There was not a cushion, not a throw, not even a footstool. There were only the three, hard, uncomfortable straight chairs. He tried to imagine the chairs occupied, Edward Cabot's wife in one, her mother and father in the others, gathered about the candle, each with a book. Their reading must surely be as coldly stark as the room.

He chose a chair and the young woman slipped onto the edge of one across the room from him, remaining sitting forward as if impatient to hear what he had to say. He laid the bundle of books on the floor beside him and placed his hat on top of them. Something directed him to cover them for the time being. "You *are* Mrs. Edward Cabot, ma'am?"

"I am Rachel Cabot, yes. Thee *is* from Kentucky, isn't thee?"

"Yes, ma'am. I am from Kentucky."

"I knew by thy voice. It is like that of the man who talked with Edward when he was preparing to leave. And does thee know my husband? Is the land which he has taken up near thee?"

"Yes, ma'am. Well, not exactly near, but not very far away. About fifty miles, maybe."

"But that is very far!"

"Not in Kentucky, ma'am. That's almost neighbors, you might say."

"Is it, indeed? I am so ignorant of that country. The maps are so poor, we could not tell . . . but I hope to make amends when Edward comes for us. I had word from him that he had bought land near a village called St. Asaph's."

"Well, it's not exactly a village, ma'am. There is a . . . a stockade, and a gristmill . . ."

"Edward spoke of an ordinary which he found very hospitable."

"Yes. Mr. Nathaniel Logan keeps the ordinary. There are several dwellings."

It would be impossible for her to understand what St. Asaph's was really like, he knew. There was no way she could envision the small cluster of cabins, Ben Logan's house being the only frame structure among them, or the walls of the stockade, or Nathaniel Logan's two-room log tavern. A village to her meant streets and meetinghouses and some tenderness of life carefully nourished. The raw newness, the ribald toughness, the brutal, animal lustiness of the frontier, would be as foreign to her as Rome. It had been just as foreign to Edward Cabot, which was why he had shrunk from its company, preferring to stay alone at his clearing.

"Why did your husband decide to go to Kentucky, ma'am?" he asked.

"But hasn't he told thee? He is a teacher, sir." Her head went up proudly. "He had a great desire to go to that country and to set up a school. He said it was new and needed teachers, and he felt he could do a great service there."

"Yes, ma'am." Cass lowered his eyes against the flame of love and pride in her face. "But he was physically a frail . . ."

The woman interrupted him. "Edward is not a frail man, sir. His body is not large, and he is slight of figure, but he has great endurance — and his spirit is unconquerable, sir."

"Yes, ma'am. Of course, you're right." His stock felt uncomfortably tight and he eased it with one finger. Blistering damn, how could he go about telling her that Edward had been dead and buried, his scalp hanging at the belt of a raiding Cherokee, all this time?

"But, tell me, sir. He is well? He has sent a message by thee? Has he finished building the house? It has been so long since I heard. There has been no letter since the fall. He warned me that ways to send his letters were few and that the times between might be long, but it has been more than eight months since I heard. The last letter came by the courtesy of a merchant of Louisville . . . a Mr. Brodhead. But I presume Louisville is too far from St. Asaph's for Edward to go there often." She leaned forward, her small white hands held cupped, like curved seashells, in her lap, only their restless fingers telling of her strong effort to control her eagerness. "What message has thee for me, Mr. — " she stopped and stared amazedly at him, one hand lifting suddenly in embarrassment. "Good gracious, I have failed to ask thy name!"

"It is Cartwright, ma'am. Major Cassius Cartwright."

"Oh, Major Cartwright, thee must excuse me. I am not usually so distraught. It is the knowledge that thee has seen Edward. I ask thy pardon."

"It is nothing, ma'am." He cleared his throat.

She settled herself more comfortably in the chair. "Now, tell me, tell me everything thee knows about my husband."

"I'm afraid, ma'am . . ." He sought for words. It was so brutal a thing he was under the necessity of doing that even the simplest words would not come to him. He could not even look at her, but stared instead at the floor. He heard her make a slight, choked sound, and swiftly lifted his eyes. Her face had gone so white that the fichu at her neck scarcely looked whiter. Her eyes, naturally large, had grown enormous and they implored him to set her fears at rest. "He is ill?" she said, her hands fluttering up to her throat. "Something has happened to him? Is my husband hurt, sir?"

He thought it was the cruelest thing he had ever had to do, far more cruel than having to take Willie Floyd's body home to his wife, or having to tell Sarah Comfort that her boy had fallen in the Battle of the Blue Licks last summer. They at least were there; they knew what the danger was, what the chances were. They could hope that their own men would be safe, but they knew, for they saw it happen on every side, that they might not be. They had at least the preparation that the country demanded of every man and woman who dared to invade it. This woman, Rachel Cabot, was so gently reared that she had no conception of what it was like. Her very religion, for her speech had told him she was a Quaker, shielded her from thoughts of violence, and in all probability Edward had even kept from her any idea of danger there, any knowledge of harshness. To all too many people in the east the Indian danger had abated when the war was over. He recalled that Ben Logan had said of Edward Cabot, "He has no true conception of the danger. He is skeptical of it, even though we have warned him."

And he himself had replied, "Well, one good scare will teach him."

But Edward Cabot had not been granted even one good scare. One shot was all that was allowed him, and he had not lived to be afraid. It remained for his widow to know all of his fear.

Slowly Cass brought forth the words, summoned by the necessity, "Your husband, ma'am, is dead."

"No," she whispered, her enormous eyes fixed relentlessly on his face. "I do not believe it."

Helplessly he looked at her.

"I would have known it. Something would have warned me.

Edward could not be dead without me knowing. It would have traveled all that long way and stabbed like a dagger in my heart. I would have felt his heart stop beating. My own heart would have paused . . . I could not have gone about my work all these months, teaching my son, nourishing my daughter, writing those long letters every month . . . I would have known, Major Cartwright. There is some error."

He felt such pity for her that it knotted his chest, and he cursed Edward Cabot for taking his frail body into the wilderness and getting it shot by the Cherokees — leaving her here alone, chasing a dream like a child chasing fireflies. The things men did, in the name of virtue. He wanted to be of service! Why, in God's name, hadn't he been content to be of service where his dreamer's mind would not expose his soft, untoughened body to the harsh dangers of the frontier? "I am afraid, Mrs. Cabot," he said, as gently as he could, "there is no error. I helped to bury him myself."

She accepted it — he saw by the wound in her eyes that she accepted it, and he saw by the queer, puzzled contortion of her mouth that the wound was not yet so much for his death as for her failure to know it. The instinct of love had failed her, that instinct which every woman who deeply loves believes to be infallible, and its failure shook her, for the moment, more than the fact she must accept.

He waited, averting his eyes. He did not want to see the full realization sweep over her face. His glance fell on the books on the floor, under his hat, and upon impulse he bent to pick them up. "These were his books, ma'am. Colonel Logan sent them to you." He crossed the room and placed them in her lap, for her hands did not reach for them.

Dully she stared at them. "His books? But he had a chest full of them."

"The rest were destroyed, I'm afraid."

She whimpered a little, then, and bit at the knuckles of her hand. Almost immediately, however, she straightened in her chair, held herself erect, not allowing herself the comfort of even the touch of the chair back against her spine. Her hands took the books. "Will thee excuse me a moment, Major Cartwright. I must see about my children."

Relieved, Cass stood. "Of course, ma'am. And I must be going."

"Not yet!" She threw out a hand. "Please stay a little longer. It's only — Thee must tell me . . . I shall be back."

Her skirt swept in a wide whirl and as she turned, hurriedly, it rustled softly against the door frame, then vanished through the door. He sat again, miserably. He was going to be spared nothing, then.

When she returned, in perhaps five minutes, he knew she had been weeping. There were no actual tears in the eyes she turned on him, but they looked liquid and softened and there were the beginning bruises of dark circles under them. She held herself sternly in check and presented a white, controlled face to him. "I should like," she said calmly, only the timbre of her voice giving any evidence of an inner disturbance, "to know what occurred, Major. I should like thee to leave out nothing. Do not attempt to spare me, sir. What my husband endured, I can also endure, and it is my wish to endure."

Mutely Cass looked at her.

"Please . . . sir?" A small tremor lifted the words into a question, and left it hanging between them. The room was very quiet. Outside, a bird, a night-homing bird, was crying over and over a small, monotonous song, which like Rachel Cabot's voice, ended on a question. The bird's query would never be answered, but the woman's, trying to recover her faith in her instinct, trying to bridge the chasm that had suddenly opened before her feet, required him to answer. In the chilly room, he shivered.

"It was very sudden, ma'am. Edward had built a small house, of logs — what we call a half-shelter in that country. It was built up on three sides and covered over with a blanket in front. It was meant only for his own convenience, for he meant to build a home during the winter."

"During the winter? Did he not live . . . ?"

"He was killed by Indians in October of last year, ma'am," Cass said swiftly, to tell her immediately, to let her know quickly, the worst she had to know.

"October . . ." she said, bending her head. "In October we were gathering the corn and the pumpkins. Deborah was cutting her first tooth. Young Edward began going to Mr. Lyons for his lessons." She looked up, the tormenting knowledge of her not-knowing filling her eyes, "and in October Edward was killed. Major Cartwright, how could I *not* know?" There was desperation in her cry, and helplessly he shook his head. "I had his letter in November."

"It takes so long for a letter to reach Philadelphia."

"Oh, I know . . . I know." She bent her head again and he saw the way the brown hair curled softly about her ears and how its wealth could not be hidden under the starched white cap. "He wrote that the land was beautiful, that the people were hospitable and friendly," her voice was measured, even gentle. "He said that new people were coming into the country every day and that soon there would be a great population. He told of his trip down the river, and he mentioned some of the amusing things that occurred. He liked to make me laugh." The brown eyes were tender, as she remembered. "He said that the town at the Falls was a very busy place, but that he had been able to secure a horse without difficulty and at not too dear a price." The voice went on, as if hypnotized by its own sound. Cass wanted to tell her to stop. It did no good to recall that letter; she was only torturing herself. "He said there had been no danger from the Indians for some time . . ." here the level, calm voice faltered, "he said that he believed it was greatly exaggerated." She had reached the flaw herself and she paused, taking it in. "He was not careful enough. Was that it, Major Cartwright?"

"In a way, ma'am. We warned him, of course, as we warn all new people. The country may be quiet at the time, may be quiet for six months at a time, but the danger is always present. There is never a time when the Indians can't suddenly and without warning appear. Your husband was lulled into the thought of peace by the wish for peace, I think."

"Yes. He would not even have hated the savages. Thee must tell me now," she said, gently as if to spare him, "how it happened."

"He was living on his clearing, ma'am, alone. Early one morning he got up, as usual I suppose, and he stepped outside."

"How does thee know?"

"He was found on the doorstep."

"Of course. I forgot thee must have sharp eyes in that country." She paused a moment, then steeled herself for the next question. "Had he suffered, sir?"

"Of that I can assure you, ma'am. He was killed instantly, by one shot that took him in the temple."

"Yes."

She lowered her eyes and Cass thought she must be remembering how her own hands had touched and caressed Edward Cabot's temple, must be seeing it as she had last seen it, the hair brushed back, the small vein pulsing with life. She looked at him again. "Was he . . . was he badly mutilated? I have heard stories . . ."

Deliberately, Cass lied. "No, ma'am. They burned the shelter, burned most of his books, took his cow and horse, and left him where he had fallen."

"Ah . . ." Her breath expired slowly on the dying word. "I am glad. Was it long before he was found?"

"Not long, no. He had told Colonel Logan that he would be coming to St. Asaph's to have some corn ground at the mill, and when he did not come when he had said he would, the colonel was fearful of some accident and rode out to see about him."

"Thee — thee was with him?"

"No. I was not with him. But I was in St. Asaph's when Colonel Logan returned with his body that evening."

The white-capped head went up so sharply that the curls in front of the small ears shook. "He brought him to St. Asaph's?"

"Yes, ma'am. The cemetery is in St. Asaph's. Colonel Logan read the service over him and he was buried beside Mrs. Logan's brothers and her father and her small sister."

The terrible composure broke, then, and Rachel Cabot covered her face with her hands. She made no sound with her weeping, but Cass saw the hands press convulsively against her eyes and saw the stream of tears that escaped them and ran in a slow, anguished river down her face. He let her cry, hoping that the terrible inquisition was over. "I feared to ask it," she said, at length, taking a handkerchief from her dress pocket and wiping her eyes. "I feared that he was buried alone, someplace in that awful, wild land."

"We recover them all, if we can, ma'am."

"All? Are there so many, then?"

He could have bitten his tongue. "Over the years there have been a goodly number."

Slowly her will asserted itself and she regained her control. "It was good of thee to come, Major Cartwright. It is so much better to be told, with the sympathy of a friendly nature, than to have the word come so coldly, in a letter. To talk with thee, to know thee was there — I cannot tell thee how grateful I am."

"Colonel Logan did write, ma'am. The letter went astray apparently."

"I am glad. And I thank thee for his books." She swallowed before continuing. "Will thee tell Colonel Logan that I thank him also, and will thee give a message to his wife?"

"I shall be glad to, Mrs. Cabot."

"Tell her — tell her that since my husband could not be buried in our own churchyard, I am grateful he lies beside her own people. And that I am certain he lies among brave men and women . . . and children. Tell her that I . . . that I grieve for her loss as well as my own."

"I shall tell her, ma'am."

A silence grew between them. The late sun, finding a hole in the clouds, threw long shafts through the two white-curtained windows and lay, hazy with dust motes, across the white-scrubbed floor. It touched the gray skirt of Rachel Cabot's dress and warmed it slightly. Cass was thinking he must go, wondering how to take his leave, when the silence was broken by the wailing of a child. Rachel Cabot rose, but as she went to the door the little boy appeared, dragging his small sister by the hand, faster than her uncertain feet could go, and she collapsed with a smart thump on the floor at her mother's feet. The wail increased in volume and Rachel stooped to lift the baby from the floor. "Edward, I asked thee to take care of Debbie."

"I am tired of taking care of Debbie," the boy said, slowly, articulating each word distinctly. "Besides, she's hungry."

"Get your small chair and sit down, Edward, and make no sound until I tell thee. Thee has been rude to thy sister, and disobedient to thy mother." Her voice was firm, but it remained gentle.

The boy brought his chair and placed it against the wall. He took his place on it and folded his hands in his lap. He looked up at Cass, then, and smiled. Cass thought he did not mind the punishment at all, for it brought him into the room where his mother was, and if he might not speak, he could still listen. "There is the land, Mrs. Cabot," he said. "Colonel Logan had a crop planted on it this spring and we will see that the title is cleared for you."

"That is thoughtful of thee. But of what use will the land in Kentucky be to me now?"

"Your children . . . it might be sold, ma'am."

"Of course. My head is not working right, sir. Would thee advertise it for sale, then, sir?"

"It can't be done until the title is cleared, ma'am. But if you like I will be glad to see to it."

"I shall be grateful."

Cass stood, then, and took up his hat. The baby had left off her crying as soon as she felt her mother's arms about her and as Rachel Cabot rose also, the child was curled comfortably against her shoulder, her soft, curly head laid sleepily against her mother's neck. Gently Rachel Cabot smoothed down the dress which had caught and rumpled on her arm. Impulsively Cass blurted out, "Will your circumstances be comfortable, ma'am? What will you do?"

The too-big eyes lifted. "I do not know, Major. I have not yet had time to think about it."

"Your parents . . . ?"

"My parents will make us welcome for as long as we need the shelter of their roof."

Her shoulders drooped a little, as if even the baby, fat, heavy, solid, were too much of a load for her just then.

"If there is anything we can do, ma'am . . ."

"Thee has done much already, sir. And if thee will see to the land when it is time — "

"I will see to it."

"I would ask thee to supper, Major, but my parents are away, and . . ."

Cass interrupted her. "My supper is waiting for me at Azariah Bates's tavern, Mrs. Cabot. I would not think of troubling you, under the circumstances."

"Thee understands," she said, softly.

"I will write you about the land."

"Yes."

"I will do the best I can for you — get as much profit as I can."

"Thee is good."

The room was growing dark, now, with the early dusk, its stark, uncomfortable outlines softened, but her face, as she stood near him, was still distinct. It was white and composed and the enormous eyes were steady before his look.

He bowed, and the child, suddenly seized with mischief or a vague interest, grabbed at his bent head and grasped a handful of hair, tugging at it strongly. In an awkward position, Cass peered up at her, laughing. "Debbie!" her mother scolded, at the same time trying to release the baby's hand.

The little girl laughed gleefully and continued to tug with a not inconsiderable strength. "Good gracious, sir, she will have thee bald!"

Cass, still laughing, reached for the baby's hand himself. Instead he encountered Rachel Cabot's hand, brushing it slightly before, in confusion, he dropped his own. It had been very warm and soft to touch. He felt her fingers grasp his hair and firmly detach it from the child's hold. "There," she said, "thee is free, Major. Debbie, thee is a bad girl. Did she hurt thee, sir?"

"Of course not," Cass said. "She is too small to have much strength. I hope you will not scold her. 'Twas but a natural thing she did."

The woman set her small daughter down and gave her a little spank which sent her wobbling and wavering down the hall. "She has a very strong will. Both she and Edward do have, and their father . . ." She stopped, remembering that their father would not now be of assistance in coping with those two young, strong wills.

In the awkward silence, Cass moved to the door. "I leave for Kentucky in the morning, Mrs. Cabot. I will write you as soon as there is news."

"If thee will be so good. A pleasant journey, Major."

"Thank you." His eyes lingered on her face and he found himself wishing that there was something more he could do, or say. But by the quality of withdrawal and remoteness in her voice as she had wished him a pleasant journey, he knew that she wished him gone, wished to be left alone with the stark realities she must face and to the beginning of the new life she must make for herself. "Goodnight, ma'am."

"Goodnight, sir, and I thank thee again."

As he reached the steps he heard the door close firmly behind him. There was nothing, now, to require her to keep command of herself and he imagined her leaning there, restraints gone, her terrible grief shaking her. The fool, he thought, of her husband. The reckless, feckless, selfish fool.

CHAPTER 4

Cass sat across the table from Benjamin Logan in the new frame house Ben had built for his wife outside the stockade at St. Asaph's. All evening he had been talking, reporting to Ben on his trip to Philadelphia. Ben had listened, saying little, asking a question now and then.

The soft, earth-scented August night was still about the house, save for the sound of katydids, crickets and other insects, and the boom of the frogs in the creek at the foot of the hill. A slow-moving current of air, lifted from the warm earth and stirring vagrantly, blew the candle flame and Cass watched the light move, shadowingly, across the face of the man on the other side of the table.

Benjamin Logan was another big man. He filled the chair in which he sat, amply. He was of Scotch-Irish descent and ordinarily, except with those with whom he was intimate, had little to say. He had been in Kentucky a long time, as time was counted there. He had come by way of the Gap in 1775, among the first to cross over from the Holston country. He had built a stockade, known both as Logan's Fort and as St. Asaph's, and had brought his family out in 1776, so early in the settlement of the country that his son, William, had been the second child born in the country; had brought his mother and sisters, his brothers, his wife's people, and had yet had time to give aid to any who called on him. He had known what it meant to be besieged behind the walls of his stockade; had captained the first militia, when every man in the country was on call; had been colonel and was now county lieutenant. He was a man strong, esteemed, trusted, followed — perhaps the strongest man of all those early men.

Cass liked him more than any man he had ever known, and he took it as an honor that he was accepted as a friend. Benjamin Logan had the militiaman's innate distrust of a regular, but where Cass was concerned he had overcome it, for Cass had resigned his commission in the line, had taken up land in Lincoln County, had improved it, built a house on it and lived on it when he could. He had served, and was ready to serve again, in the militia under Benjamin Logan. Ben respected the superior education of Cass, trusted him with important missions, and discussed with him problems he would have hesitated to discuss with his well-liked but more illiterate neighbors.

"That's the way it is, Ben," Cass said. "They want us to go easy until they've had time to treat with the Indians, see if they can't sway them away from the British and open the country up. It will take time, they say."

"And while they're taking time," Ben growled, "more of our people will be killed, more of our stock stolen and more of our homes burned."

The Kentuckians knew there was a ring of Indians around them. They had good reason to know — the hard fact of the swift, punitive strikes, at isolated cabins, small settlements, travelers. They knew that to their north were the strong tribes based in the lower Lakes region — the Shawnees, Wyandots, Miamis, Wabash and Delawares. Still supplied with arms and gunpowder by the British, they were formidable. To the south were the Chickasaws, the Cherokees, the Chickamaugas and the Creeks. Armed and supplied by the Spanish they were proving increasingly bold and dangerous. And yet the Kentuckians were told to be patient.

Ben shifted his big body in the slat-backed chair. "Well, you did your best. Can't any man do more. We'll just have to make out. You got your cargo, did you?"

Cass nodded. "A full boat. Enoch Fleming is taking it on to New Orleans for me."

Ben Logan stroked the grain of the table with the heel of his hand. "Have you ever thought, Cass, what would happen to our trade here if the Spanish close New Orleans?"

"There would be none," Cass said succinctly.

"You think there's any danger of it?"

"I *hadn't* thought so — not after hearing what the terms of the peace were. They are supposed to honor the old British rights. But I talked with a man in Philadelphia who set me thinking. Ever hear of General James Wilkinson, Ben?"

"I've heard of him, yes. Not lately, though."

"No. He's been retired from the army several years. Been raising horses on his place near Philadelphia. He seemed to know a right smart about the situation. He's a pretty big man in the east — at least he has influential connections."

"What's that got to do with us?"

"He's coming to Kentucky."

"Tied up with one of those land companies?"

"No. He's going on his own hook."

Ben sighed. "There's a lot of new ones these days. In the old times we knew every man and knew who we could count on." He chuckled. "In fact, you could count them on the fingers of your hands. But there's a lot of new people in the country nowadays — not drifters or movers, either. Men of means and influence. The new district court brought some of them — Judge Innes and Judge Muter . . . and the commission to settle the accounts of the military district has brought some others, Judge McDowell, Caleb Wallace, Thomas Marshall. You hear their names every way you turn these days. And some of them are fine men, I have no doubt — better men, maybe, than the older ones — smarter, better educated, more experienced in politics. But their names don't sit easy on the tongue yet."

He sounded, Cass thought, like an old man thinking of better days. "Well," he said, "they'll either prove themselves or they won't."

"Yes. But as long as you don't know, Cass — it sort of goes against the grain for them to be taking over the country. We settled it. We held it."

Cass grinned, remembering what General Wilkinson had said. "It's the age of the politician, Ben. You heroes have got to move over and give 'em room."

"Well, this hero ain't. I'll be there to be counted every time there's a political move made. What about this general, Cass?"

"He married into the Biddle family and they're backing him in his venture. He'll be coming sometime before the turn of the year. He aims to take up as much land as he can, and he's going to open a general store. Sounded as if he liked Lexington."

"We can use one there. What did he say that made you start speculating about New Orleans?"

"Nothing special. But he knows we've got to trade through there. He had a map, Ben — the prettiest map I ever saw. He'd made it himself and he knows how to make one. He don't miss much, the general. I figure he's got every move worked out. He's going to speculate in land, he's going to get the mercantile trade of everybody in the interior, and he's going to trade through New Orleans. He's a military man with experience and he'll be a help in the militia."

"What kind of a fellow is he? Did you take to him?"

"He's a little man, and like every little man I ever saw he's got his share of brag and boast, but he's shrewd and clever. He likes luxury, enjoys easy living. I think he's at the end of his tether, though, and he didn't make any bones about being ambitious to make his fortune here in the country. He's got backing, but not quite enough. He asked me to go in partners in the store with him. He needs what I'd put in it."

"Sort of a risk, ain't it?"

"I figure I'm as good a gambler as he is, Ben."

Ben moved a finger slowly down the edge of the table. He looked up with a wry grin. "You getting ambitious for fame and glory, too, Cass?"

Cass hitched his big shoulders. "Don't we all want to do the best we can for ourselves? What are we here for? What did you come to Kentucky for? What are all these other folks coming for? Every man jack of 'em hopes to better himself, or else he'd be sitting on his rear back east. I'm no different from the rest."

"Nor me," Ben said, straightening. "How much did he want you to put in?"

"He mentioned five hundred pounds. I think three hundred will be enough."

"Have you got it?"

"I will have — by the time he comes. That cargo of flour will make a better profit than that."

"Cass, you're doing good already. What do you want to go in partners with this fellow for? You'll just have to split your profits."

"Just in the store. I'll tell you, Ben. If there's going to be trouble with the Spanish, I think General Wilkinson's connections may be a help. I'm not going in business with him for love of the man, nor to be of help to him. I'm going in business with him because I aim for Cass Cartwright to keep on trading through New Orleans and I think General Wilkinson may be the man who can take care of that. He thinks to use me, and sure as God I aim to use him. That's the way of it, Ben."

"You got it figured out pretty good, I'd say. If you can't swing it, Cass, let me know." He stood. "Let's step outside and take a look at the weather."

They stood, then, the fat cushion of the grass plushy under their feet, relieving themselves silently. Overhead the sky was white with stars, but a dark bank hung blackly in the west. "It's breeding weather," Ben said softly.

"Yes. It'll rain by tomorrow, likely."

They lapsed into silence again, which was broken, finally, by the small, plaintive sound of a whippoorwill across the creek. "I never hear a whippoorwill," Ben said, "that it don't remind me of the first time we stood siege here in the fort. 'Twas a whippoorwill's call gave the Shawnees away. David Cooper caught the difference and gave the warning."

"It was a bad time, was it?"

"As bad as could be. Only a hundred and fifty guns in the country. We come pretty near not making it that summer."

"The country can be thankful you hung on."

The two men arranged their clothing and stood a moment

looking at the stars. Cass picked out the Big Bear and the Little Bear, Orion, the Seven Sisters, and the red, blinking light of the pole star. "Ben," he said suddenly, "was Edward Cabot a Quaker?"

Surprised, Ben thought a moment before answering. "Not that I know of. He didn't say. But he didn't talk like one."

"His widow is."

"You saw her, then."

"Yes, and don't ever send me on another such errand. She didn't get your letter and I had to break it to her."

"I reckon she took it hard."

"She took it the bravest I ever saw. It would have been easier if she hadn't. Hardest thing I believe I ever had to do. Worst of it was, you could tell she almost worshiped the man."

"He oughtn't ever to have come out here. He wasn't cut right to make a go of it. Not the way he went at it. If he'd stayed at the Falls, or gone to Lexington, or even gone into the fort and stayed around here, he might have made it. But for a man like him to go off alone . . . he was bound to get into trouble he couldn't handle. I tried to tell him."

"I know you did — and several others, too."

"Is she fixed all right there at her folks?"

"Well, they didn't look to be in too good circumstances, but she said they'd give her shelter. I told her she might sell the land here and make a little profit on it — which would help. She seemed anxious to try, so I told her I'd take care of it for her. How good a piece is it, Ben?"

"Pretty good. It's down on Russell Creek, I reckon you know. Down close to William Casey's land. Lays level to rolling. Could be made a nice property in time, but it's pretty far from the settlements."

"Might have a little trouble selling it, then?"

"Might. But you can't tell. William might be interested."

"I'll ride out that way and talk to him."

They moved slowly toward the house. "Wind's rising a little, ain't it?" Ben asked, turning his head into it.

Cass raised his own nose to sniff. "Believe it is. It'll rain, sure."

"Yes."

From near the zenith of the sky a star cast loose its moorings and fell, trailing a spray of silvery light behind it. "My old grandmother," Ben said, taking notice, "used to say that a falling star meant some old soul had died."

"Mine," Cass laughed, "said it meant a new one had been born."

"Come from different parts of the country, I reckon."

"Yes."

CHAPTER 5

When he had scraped the last bite from his plate and swigged the last of his tea at breakfast the next morning, Ben Logan wiped his mouth with the heel of his hand and tilted his chair back on its legs. "Cass," he said, "you still want to get some people settled down on your place?"

Cass tossed a rind of bacon out the door to Ben's dog. "The right kind of people, yes."

"This might be a good chance."

"Why?"

"Was a bunch of folks come into the stockade last night. Lost the title to their land and seem kind of at loose ends. They're talking some of going back over the mountains, but they might be persuaded to stay on and make a new start. There's several families of 'em."

"Where were they located?"

"Up on Jessamine Creek. They had Henderson grants, bought off somebody back east. Fellow by the name of Presley come along with a bounty warrant and threw 'em off. Court upheld him."

Cass always felt sorry for these people who had been duped, but he always felt impatient with them, too. "Why in the hell do the fools keep buying land they haven't seen — take somebody's word about a title! They wouldn't do that kind of thing back home. They'd go look at the land, make sure the title was good. But they come trailing in here by the hundreds without any idea what they've bought or whether they've got a title or not. They ought to find out before they pack up and leave — drag their women and children over the mountains. They could have learned easily enough that a Henderson grant isn't worth the paper it's written on."

"These folks are all from the upper end of the Shenandoah valley, Cass," Ben said. "It would have been as far to Richmond, almost, as it was to here. Besides, when folks take a notion to come to Kentucky nothing's going to sway 'em. This is the Garden of Eden — the Promised Land. And all they can think of when the fever hits 'em is to get here as quick as they can."

"And they soon find out," Cass snorted, "that instead of the Garden of Eden it's a damned bloody wilderness, full of plundering redskins and plundering land speculators and the only way they can turn it into the Promised Land is by hard work and the sweat of their brows. How many families in this bunch? What kind of people are they?"

"I didn't ask how many families there are. The leader appears to be a fellow named Cameron. Seemed sort of quiet and honest spoke. I kind of took to him. They're all related one way or another."

Cass swiveled his chair around on one leg. "I expect he heard a lot of talk about the country — heard there was land and plenty of game, and wealth just waiting for the taking. Bought some worthless claims and packed up and left out, on nothing but hearsay."

Ben grinned. "That's what most of us did."

"At least you had the good sense not to throw in with Henderson."

"The land law was different then. A man could pre-empt his four hundred and buy his thousand adjoining without much trouble. But I come into the country on hearsay."

"Pretty good hearsay, though. Your neighbor, James Knox, had been hunting over here for three years or more. There's a difference."

"Well, yes, in a way. Whyn't you go over and talk to this Cameron, anyway, Cass? They're not shiftless folks, I can tell you that. They'd make good settlers, in my opinion."

"It wouldn't hurt, I suppose."

"Not if you mean it about getting a settlement started down your way. It's going to be a time and a time before anyone heads in that direction on their own. It's too far from everywhere else."

Cass was indignant. "There's already three settlements close by. There's Glover's Station, and Pitman's, and William Casey's."

"And they did just what you've got to do — gathered a bunch of folks about 'em and sold the land to 'em and took the responsibility for getting 'em located."

Cass laughed. "All right. I'll go talk to Cameron. Where did you put him?"

"He's in our old cabin. The others are in the same row."

The stockade gate was open and he walked through it and on up the street, dusty, bare of grass, and hot to his feet even through his moccasins. He never came through that stockade gate without thinking of all that had happened here — how Ben Logan and Billy Whitley and Dave Cooper and the others had toiled all one winter to build the fort, keeping their womenfolks and children safely at Harrod's Fort during the time; how they had brought them, finally, at night and in snow, to the fresh new cabins, and how they had lived here, safe no place else, for four long years; how they had stood siege here, and lost men here, and buried them inside the walls to keep the Indians from knowing how many dead there were; how their children had sickened and died here one hot summer of the bloody flux; how they had ventured forth gradually, slowly, finally, to work their land and build their homes, and how many had lost their lives before the first crop was made or the homes finished. They had made a lot of history in this fort and he didn't doubt there was still a lot to be made. Those first Kentuckians had been a stout breed of men.

He came up to the cabin in which Ben and Ann Logan had lived in those days. Two little boys were playing in the shade of a walnut tree. They looked up at him, curiously, as he passed, but neither of them spoke and when he had gone by they turned again to their game. Cameron's children, Cass thought. He stopped before the door of the cabin and called, "Hello, the house!"

A man came to the door and stood there quietly, eying Cass. "Howdy," he said. "You want something, mister?"

Cass looked him over judgingly. He was a sandy-haired man of medium height and spare build, with big ears that stood out from his head and knobby lumps at his jaws. He had pale, almost faded blue eyes which met Cass's directly, and his face was strong-boned and lean. He had a prominent Adam's apple and a stringy neck. It was impossible to tell his age, but there was no gray in his hair yet and Cass guessed him to be in his middle thirties or maybe a little younger. "I'm looking for John Cameron," he said.

"That's me. Come in, stranger."

Two women sat by the hearth. One was slight and fair, with a very young baby in her arms. The other, who was husking corn, was larger, browner and older, with a wide mouth pinched over not very good teeth. Her hair was amazingly frizzed into a mass of corkscrew curls which stood out springily in every direction from under her cap. She blushed violently as Cass glanced at her and turned quickly back to her task.

The man made no mention of the women, made no move to present them to a stranger, so Cass hooked a toe under the rung of a stool and dragged it toward him, sat down and turned to the man. "My name is Cartwright," he said. "Ben Logan has told me that you've lost your land and are trying to decide what to do next."

"He's told you right," the man said, moving a stool near the door for himself. "We've lost ever'thing we had — land, houses, crops and all. We've got nothing left but a little plunder and a few head of stock. I reckon if he could of took that he would of, but the law didn't give him no right to them."

"You're thinking of going back over the mountains?" Cass asked.

"Some," the man admitted. "There don't seem to be nothing to stay here for — but then there ain't nothing to go back there for, either. We sold out ever'thing when we come here, and we'd have to commence over did we go back. God's name, sir," he burst out, "I don't know how it could be that a man could be so cheated! We bought the land with a honest purpose and paid good money for it. The man we bought from vowed the titles was good. He said it had all been surveyed and the claims filed and cleared. I don't know how the court could uphold that Presley feller's claim, but they did so, and there wasn't nothing we could do but get off and give it all over to him. It goes hard to lose all you've got — to work as hard as we did — clearing the land, raising our cabins, putting in a good crop, and come up with nothing. It don't seem right."

"You held a Henderson grant, I understand."

"We never knowed that. Mitchell, the feller we bought from, he never said so. What he said was he'd pre-empted the land and proved on it, and then his health broke on him and he had to leave out. He never said a word about a Henderson grant, nor no other kind. I reckon, though," he added honestly, "we wouldn't of knowed the difference. I never heard of Henderson till all this trouble come up. He had some papers that looked to be all right, and he seemed a honest kind of man."

It was an old story to Cass. By the thousands people were coming to Kentucky, having bought grants or warrants here, there and everywhere, from private individuals, from land companies, from anyone at all who had ever got hold of a title and wanted to sell it at a profit. There were men who did nothing but buy up claims and go back over the mountains with them, sell them there, usually at a very high price, swearing to the validity of the titles and moving on before trouble could catch up with them. "Did you know the man you bought from?"

"Mitchell? No. He come to the village — on his way to Pennsylvany, he said. Stayed there about a month, I'd say. He got a lot of folks interested in Kentucky land."

"I wouldn't be surprised. And probably all of them will run into the same trouble you've had. There are sharpsters in every part of the world, sir, and Kentucky is no exception. In fact, we've been plagued with them ever since the war ended. You got sold some worthless claims and I have no doubt the man knew they were worthless when he sold them to you. I'm sorry, but I expect the court had no alternative except to find for the man who held the legal title. I know it doesn't sound right, but the law is the law and if it doesn't stand on its own statutes it's not worth much here or anywhere else. It's your friend when you've got a good title—your enemy when you haven't. You have no plans, now?"

John Cameron lifted his pale eyes and looked directly at Cass. "We've got no money, mister. We'd built our cabins and planted our corn and a little hemp and flax. All our money was gone by then. We'd have got the corn in this fall and we counted on selling a bit for enough to see us through the winter. I reckon all we can do is go back where we come from. We've got friends there, anyway, and maybe us men can hire out to work until we get a new start."

"How many families are there of you? Ben said you had some relations with you."

"Yes. We all come together—all, that is, save one. My wife's youngest sister, Betsey, has got married since we come out here. But the rest of us come together. There's four families of us, all kin one way or another. Two of 'em is my wife's sisters, and the other one is my stepbrother, Jacob Bearden."

"You all come from the valley?"

The man nodded. "Lived neighbors all our lives. Born and raised in the upper Shenandoah. All in the same boat, now."

Cass made up his mind. John Cameron was unlettered, but that did not matter. His women were clean and he himself was tidy. He was not a raw, rambunctious kind of man, cursing his luck, drinking out his misfortune, storming and swaggering about. He was dazed and bewildered and he had a fair share of resentment, but he was already beginning to square up and think pretty straight. He looked to be a decent man, if not too sharp, and better men than he had been duped on land trades. Daniel Boone was having trouble right now with his titles, having never bothered to prove up his old Henderson grants. Many a good man who would have made a good citizen, better than some who were luckier or sharper, had been forced to leave the country. He determined to give John Cameron and his people a chance to stay if they wanted to. "I have some land," he said, "over on Green River, about forty-five or fifty miles from here. I'm willing for it to be settled. The title to my land is unquestionably clear. I hold some of it on a bounty warrant and I bought the rest from men who held it on the same kind of title or preemption. I personally know the men, also. There will never be any question about the titles. You don't know me, but you do know Ben Logan, and Ben Logan will vouch for me. If you and your people would be interested in staying on in the country I'll sell you a hundred acres each and help you get settled."

John Cameron weighed the matter quietly. "I've heared of the Green River. It's a mite out of the way, ain't it?"

"Yes. I'm not going to mislead you. There are only three settlements down that way right now. My settlement, and I don't want to mislead you there either, for I intend it to remain my settlement, would be the fourth. The land is fertile and good. It lies level in a valley, but the valley is rimmed in by hills. There's timber aplenty, and besides the river there are several smaller streams to make it well watered — and there are more good, everlasting springs than I've ever seen in any other part of the country. There's plenty of water to power a mill and there's a salt lick nearby. Those are its advantages. Its disadvantages are that it lies pretty far from the nearest fort or village. We've had no Indian trouble to amount to anything, but that's not saying we couldn't have any day. I expect it's because we're not very thickly settled yet. I expect you know also, though, that there's no safe place in the entire country right now."

The man nodded. A lank strand of sandy hair slipped down over his forehead and he pushed it back. "We taken the risks when we come here, Mister Cartwright."

He fell to studying the floor, and Cass gave him time. The two women were very quiet, their backs turned discreetly. Cass knew they were listening, though, not missing a word that was being said. Even, he thought with amusement, their back hair was raised with intensity of listening. Finally John Cameron lifted his eyes from his scrutiny of the floor and cleared his throat. "I couldn't be the one to say outright, sir. Would you want to talk with the others about it?"

"I'd be glad to."

"Melie," the man turned toward the women, "send Charlie and tell Jacob and Wirt and Nathaniel to come over here, will you?"

Silently the younger of the two women handed the baby to the older one and slipped past Cass out the door. Cass heard her talking quietly to the children outside. "That's my woman," John Cameron said, "and this here is her sister Nellie Smallwood that lives with us."

Nellie's mouth pinched at the mention of her name and the hundreds of Medusa-like little curls hanging from her cap shook as she jerked her head quickly around, bobbed it briefly, and rolled her eyes. She blushed again as Cass bowed and he thought, amusedly, that she was a nitwit. What was there about a man to set a woman her age to blushing? She was a thin broomstalk of a woman and must be all of thirty years old. He wondered if she was widowed and needing a man again or if she'd never been able to snare one. The latter, more than likely. Either way, though, she needn't wait long in this womanless country, if a man was what she wanted. "What interested you in coming to Kentucky?" he asked, turning to John Cameron again.

"Why, we was having title trouble in the valley. Looks like they ain't ever going to make up their minds who that upper valley belongs to, Virginny or Pennsylvany, so when this Mitchell feller come along we got together and decided we'd just sell out and try it here. Looks like we come from the frying pan into the fire, though."

"Maybe not. Maybe it will work out to your good after all."

There was a scuffing of feet in the thick dust of the road outside and a murmuring of voices. Cass stood to meet the three men who filed into the room. "This here," John said, standing also, "is Wirt Powell. He's married to my wife's sister, Sarah."

"Your service, sir," Cass said, bowing slightly to a young, chunky, powerfully built man with a head of rough, unruly red hair.

"And this here is Nathaniel McKittridge. He's been here in the country several years. He's the one married Betsey, like I was telling you."

Nathaniel McKittridge was still a boy, still slim and wiry and tall and bendy like a sapling. He was as dark-skinned as Cass himself and looked at him out of eyes as black as lumps of coal, wide yet with a youth's curiosity. He muttered shyly to Cass and moved awkwardly out of the way for the last man.

"And this here," John Cameron went on with the introductions, "is my stepbrother, Jacob Bearden."

He was an older man, nearing forty, Cass guessed, the only bearded one of the men, as tall as young Nathaniel, both his beard and his hair grizzled and his face weather-lined and lean. He looked at Cass out of level gray eyes and bent his head slightly. Cass liked him on sight. He reminded him of old Tice Fowler up on the Hanging Fork, and if he was anything at all like him he would be a tireless, honest worker, a good shot, a good hunter and a good family man. He was the same kind of man who had come early into the country and had settled it alone and on his own hook. Cass knew what a tower of strength such a man was. "My name," he said, noticing that Cameron hadn't mentioned it, "is Cassius Cartwright. I have a proposition to make to you and Mr. Cameron wanted you all to hear it together."

The men seated themselves on the long bench which was used for eating at the table and gave him their attention quietly, Jacob Bearden nearest him, then young Nathaniel, farthest away Wirt Powell. "First," Cass told them, "you should know something about me. I came into the country eight years ago, in the Virginia line with General Clark. I served as a major until two years ago when I resigned my commission and took up land on the Green River. I don't ask you to take my word for it. You've already been cheated by a man you trusted too quickly. Ben Logan, or any other man in the country you want to talk to, will vouch for me, and you can check the court records about the land I'm willing to sell you. I have told your friend about my land and I have offered to sell to you and help you get located on it." He went on to describe the land and its location, much as he had done to John Cameron.

When he had finished, Jacob Bearden asked him, "What's your terms, Major?"

"I will sell each of you one hundred acres. I don't want to part with more than that right now. And my price would be forty dollars a hundred, which is a fair price and usual in the country. The fact is, that's what I paid for it myself, so I'm not making any profit. Once again, you can check the court records for the proof of what I'm saying. I want to get a settlement started and that's why I'm willing to sell to you."

Jacob seemed to be the spokesman for the lot. "How'd we pay you, Major? I reckon if you've already talked to John he's told you we've got nothing left."

"You can pay a little each year, as you can. I can furnish you seed and tools for planting next spring. I'll help feed you this winter. There's time to get cabins raised before cold weather and you can help my Negroes with my crops this fall to help pay for your food this year and for your seed next spring. I don't mean to drive a hard bargain, but I think . . ."

John Cameron raised his hand. "We ain't asking for charity, Major. If we settle on your land with you helping us that much, we'd wish to work for what we got till we could do for ourselves."

Wirt Powell spoke up. "Where did you say yore land was at?"

"On Green River — about fifty miles from here. I've already told Mr. Cameron that its greatest disadvantage lies in its being so far from the fort. But it's thinly settled as yet and we've had very little Indian trouble."

"Reckon we could build us a fort ourselves, did we need one," Jacob said slowly. "I don't see as that would be no disadvantage."

"No, I reckon not," Powell agreed. "Ain't it pretty hilly down that way, Major? Seems I've heared it's in the knobs country."

"It is. But my land all lies along the river, most of it in bottoms. It's a wide valley with the hills to the back. Some of it runs up into the hills. All the timber is on the hills except for a narrow strip along the river."

"How much of the hundred would be timbered?"

Cass tried to make a rough estimate. "I'd say about twenty acres — thirty at the most."

John Cameron put in, "A body has got to have some timber — for building and for wood to burn in the winter. The major has said," he turned to Wirt, "that it's well watered and there's a salt lick handy."

"Where they's a salt lick the ground ain't good, I've heared. It's soured."

"The salt lick," Cass said firmly, "is across the river. But don't take my word for it. Ask Ben Logan."

Jacob pulled at his beard. "It sounds pretty good to me. I don't know as we could of expected to have such luck, after being cheated the way we've been by that Mitchell feller."

"I don't want you to decide immediately," Cass said. "Think about it and talk to Ben Logan. You know you can depend on his word. Ask him about the land, ask him anything you like about me. If you want to see the land first, that's all right too. I'll be staying until tomorrow and you'll have the night to think it over."

"You heading back down that way?" Jacob asked.

"Yes."

"Could be some of us mought just go along then. We'd need help finding it, likely, by ourselves."

"I'd be glad to have you along. How large are your families, by the way?"

Jacob spoke first. "I've got five younguns myself, oldest one, Abram, is going on eighteen. Then I got two more boys, Noah, that's fifteen and Thomas, nearly twelve. The two least ones is girls."

"There's six in my family," Wirt Powell said, "four kids and Sarah and me."

Nathaniel shuffled his feet. "There's just Betsey and me, yet," he gulped, "but I reckon there'll be more 'fore long."

The older men smiled and Wirt nudged the boy slyly. "Never wasted no time, did you, boy?"

The boy slid his eyes to the floor and the red rose in his face. "It just happened that way," he muttered.

"How many are in your family, Mr. Cameron?" Cass asked, drawing attention away from the abashed boy.

"The two boys you seen outside, and the least one that's just a month old. There's Nellie that lives with us, too."

Cass figured quickly. "Twenty-one, all told." He grinned at the men. "We'd have a pretty nice settlement to begin with, wouldn't we?" He stood, then, and shook hands all around. "Let me know what you decide. I'll be glad to have you, and I'll do all I can to help you until you've got a good start."

He thought they would decide to go with him. It was better than anything else they could do, though of course they would be paying twice for land in Kentucky. They were going to have to pay twice somewhere, however, and it might as well be here. He bowed to the women, watched Nellie bridle and blush again, and made his way outside.

The sky was overcast now, pinning the heat down with a thick, gray blanket. He gave it a brief, encompassing glance, judged the rain was still a long way off, and strode quickly down the road, his heels lifting small wheels of dust behind him. He liked all of the men of the party, with only a small reservation about Wirt Powell. That ragged head of red hair boded a temper. But temper, if controlled, wasn't a bad thing for a man to have. General Clark had had plenty of it and not always too well controlled at that. If it meant this man was a troublemaker, he believed he could handle him. If he was simply blustery and rough, he could be ignored or led or quelled. Jacob Bearden and John Cameron were the sort any man would like to have by his side, strong to work, sharp-eyed to keep watch, steady to count on. The boy, Nathaniel, would grow according to his temperament, and it was too soon to tell which way the twig had been bent; but he had liked his quiet, dark eyes and felt the long, clean-limbed young body might have the kind of steel in it that the frontier needed. He felt happy about these people, glad Ben had told him about them. They were a lucky choice, he thought, and he didn't know that he could ever have chosen better.

He began to think about the settlement. There ought to be a mill, he thought, in the cove where the Spout Spring was — built of rock which lay outcropping all over the hills. It would be a cool, dim place with a big wheel creaking in the shade. They'd build a saltworks across the river at the lick. He'd have kettles sent out from Richmond and they'd make bricks for the furnaces.

He would settle these folks, he thought, in the upper end of the valley where it narrowed, and their hundred acres each would reach from the river into the hills. He'd like Jacob and his big family at the farthest end, in the neck of the valley, where he and his boys would be a stout bulwark to the north. There was a sweet meadowy place there which ought to please him, and a boundary of blue ash for his cabin. Wirt and Nathaniel, he thought, should come next, with John Cameron at the nearest end.

It would change the valley to have houses dotted about, raised and chinked and with their chimneys smoking. There would be fences snaking across it, and cattle and sheep and horses feeding behind them. There would be more plowed land, with maize growing and round, fat pumpkins, more tobacco, and turnip patches green under the sun. There would be children playing around in the dooryards, and washings hanging on the fences and women's skirts blowing in the south wind, and already he could hear their voices calling back and forth. He felt torn between the necessity for it, even the wish for it, and the great wish to keep it as it was, beautiful, lonely, solitary. Men destroyed so much of what they sought. But, he had committed himself. He shrugged off his momentary sense of loss. Sheba and Molly, the wives of his Negro men, would be glad to have people nearby again. They had complained of the loneliness of his place. "Doan see nobody fum one yeah's end to de nex'," fat Sheba had bawled at him one day. "Hit ain't no proper way to lib, Mist' Cashus. I wish I wuz back in Virginny."

As he neared the big gate he was startled out of his reflections by a sudden and earth-shaking uproar, an avalanche of squalls and yells and squeals and shouts that brought him to a full stop and made him ready his gun. Almost immediately he thought, Somebody has sighted an Indian, and his gun at the charge he broke into a run. As he passed the blockhouse on the corner another man came tearing out, gun ready. "What the hell's going on around here?"

"Don't know," Cass shouted, "Indians, likely."

The man fell in step beside him and they had almost reached

the gate when a huge, fat black sow with a litter of young ones racing along beside her tore through the breach and headed in their direction. The two men stopped abruptly and stood, open-mouthed, watching. Hanging desperately on to a rope tied around the sow's neck, being dragged along at a tremendous pace, stumbling and nearly falling at every step, was a fat old woman. The sow and pigs were squealing shrilly, raising the almightiest noise and clamor, and the old woman was adding to it with yells and curses. "Hold up, you ornery critter! Git yerself outen this stockade an' down to the grazin' pen. God's britches!" she shrieked, "whut you think you'll find in this bare-sodded, hell an' brimstone, bloody fort! Ain't a sprig of grass inside the fence. Head her off, mister! Head her off, 'fore I have to turn loose of the rope!"

Her voice came joltingly out of the old woman as she was dragged along, each word separated from the next by a puff and a pant and the heavy clomp of her cowhide shoes in the dust. Her skirts were up to her knees and her fat legs, wrapped in red-striped cotton stockings, churned up and down vigorously. Her cap had slid down over one ear and her hair had fallen about her face. Her round, three-chinned face was as red as the flames of a fire and the sweat was pouring off all her chins in rivers. "That's telling her, mother," the man beside Cass yelled, doubling up with laughter, "go on, blister the hide offen the critter. Give her a lashing with yer tongue!"

"Shet yer damfool mouth, Lijah Brown," the old woman shrilled at the man, sailing past him, "an' git out an' head this god-damned hawg off fer me. I cain't hold on no longer. God's name, mister," she yelled at Cass, "be ye nothin' but a clod! Head her off!"

Coming to life Cass swept his hat off and, running, swung it lustily in front of the sow but, startled, she only squealed louder and swerved, picking up speed. The old woman could hold on no longer. The rope slid from her grasp and she brought up, colliding with Cass, nearly knocking him down. He took her elbows and steadied her. A swarm of men and children raced from the cabins out into the road and took out after the pig, yelling and screeching, and the animal, bewildered, ran on ahead of them, dodging from one side of the road to the other. The old woman yanked loose from Cass and picked up a stick, slinging it uselessly at the crowd. "Ye'll drive her into the fence, ye numskulls! Leave her be! Head her this way, I tell ye!"

The hog and the men and children, wild with the chase, disappeared around the corner of a cabin in a cloud of noise and dust. The old woman snorted and puffed and fanned her face with her apron. "Glory be! Now, if they ain't went an' done it. She'll hide out under one of them cabins an' I'll have to crawl under an' git her out. Passel of damfool idjuts is all they air."

Cass, eying her bulk and laughing, said, "You'd best let someone else crawl under the floor after the pig, ma'am."

She turned on him, her hands on her hips. "Who air you to talk? If you'd had the sense God give a goose you could of turned her fer me. But no, you jist stood there like a pillar of salt an' let her git by!"

"I was taken by surprise, ma'am."

"I'd think it."

The scowl on her face disappeared and she started laughing, a high, cackling laugh that shook her huge bosom and belly. She slapped her thighs with both hands and laughed so hard the tears joined the sweat on her face. "So was I," she confessed finally, "warn't nobody more surprised than me. I was takin' her down to graze an' she taken a notion to turn around on me. Got away like she'd been greased. Damfool thing to do — hanging on to her rope thataway. Mought of killed myself. Reckon I thought I was as light on foot as I used to be, which I mortally did find out I ain't." She wiped her eyes with the tail of her apron. "Well, no use cryin' over spilt milk, is they? She'll hide out an' quieten down when them idjuts leave off clamorin' at her. Reckon Tench c'n git her out 'fore night. Who are you, young man?"

"Cassius Cartwright, at your service, ma'am."

"Not so much as I'd of liked, sir," the old woman sniffed. "Yore wits must of been plumb addled."

"I confess it, ma'am. There was a considerable amount of noise. I thought it must have been Indians at the least."

The fat, good-natured old face crinkled again. "We did stir up a right smart fuss, didn't we? My name's Mag Johnson. My man is Tench Johnson, though I reckon you ain't ever had reason to hear of us."

"I haven't had the pleasure, ma'am. You've come to the stockade lately?"

"Been here the hull damn summer, youngun. Gittin' all-fired tard of it, too. If my old man don't make up his mind soon where he's aimin' to light, *I* am aimin' to make it up fer him. Don't know whut in blisterin' damnation the old fool thought they'd need of a blacksmith in this here country. Ain't a man here cain't shoe his own beasts as good as Tench. Had him a good shop up close to Fort Pitt, too. But he taken the Kentucky fever an' nothin' to do but pack up an' come down the river. An' here we be, no land, no shop, no nothin' — an' nothin' but ragtag an' bobtail in this here fort. I'd like to draw up to my own hearthplace an' smoke me one more pipe in peace 'fore I take my last breath — not that I'm aimin' on doin' that fer some time, I hope. Well, that's as may be." She shook out her skirts and made some effort at settling her cap. "I better see if they've run the legs offen that sow."

She went mumbling up the road and Cass watched her, chuckling a little at the stout, valiant old figure sagging under its own weight, the fat, creased ankles with their red stripes winding about them like a barber pole showing under the lifted skirts. She walked heavily, her shoulders swaying from one side to the other and slightly thrust forward as if they meant to get there ahead of the rest of her. Cass laughed aloud as he watched her big bottom bounce like a bowl of jelly as she stumped doggedly along. Mag Johnson, he thought. She was one that would be hard to down. He went his way still laughing, remembering how grimly she had held on to the sow's rope. Given an even chance, he thought, she'd have halted that pig right in her tracks.

CHAPTER 6

The quill scratched rapidly across the clean, white sheet of paper, the only noise in the room. He had filled one page and this was the second and final one. He was hot. At eight in the morning the heat in the room under the sloping roof was as steamy as the underside of a kettle lid. Sweat formed constantly in beads on his forehead and from time to time, feeling them near the dripping point, Cass raked them off with the forefinger of his left hand. His handkerchief was wrapped around his right hand to keep the sweat from spoiling the page. Finishing, he signed his name with a flourish, sanded the page carefully, then laid it flat on Ben Logan's table-desk to finish drying. The letter was to General Wilkinson, offering to place three hundred pounds at his disposal, and offering also to meet him at the Falls when he arrived there.

Reading it over, Cass thought, It will do. It says enough and no more. It was as brief as possible, within the bounds of courtesy. It said plainly what he could and would do. The rest was up to the general. He folded the letter and sealed it, laid it aside.

Then he stirred restlessly in his chair and eyed a fresh sheet of paper. Should he, he wondered, write to her too? He pulled the paper toward him, fiddled with it, nibbled at the point of the quill, pottered with the sand jar and the ink bottle. There was nothing of importance to say yet. He had not even been to look at Edward Cabot's land, but the temptation was very strong to put pen to paper and send her at least a brief note. He told himself she might be expecting to hear of his progress and that time had a way of stretching itself lengthily when life had dealt so severe a blow as it had to her. Perhaps news of any kind would be welcome to her.

Muttering to himself he shoved the paper aside. He was equivocating and he knew it. He stood, overturning the chair in the abruptness of his movement, and went to the window. It overlooked the small valley which lay at the foot of the hill on which Ben Logan's house was built. In front of the stockade a knot of people was gathering. He watched for a moment as men, women and children went about busily loading the horses tethered there. It was John Cameron and his party. They had sought him out the night before to say that after talking with Colonel Logan they had decided to buy his land, to go with him today. It was almost time to start, now.

"God's britches," Cass muttered, "but it's hot."

Turning quickly he strode to the desk, set the chair upright, straightened the paper and dipped the quill in the ink.

My dear Madame [*he wrote rapidly before he could change his mind*]. *I have talked with Colonel Logan about your husband's land and while I have not yet seen it, he tells me it is a pretty piece which lies well & there should be no difficulty in selling it when the title is proved. I aim to ride over that way within the next few weeks & see it for myself.*

I have your message to Mistress Logan & she asked me to send you her deepest sympathies & her gratitude for your own thoughtfulness to her. You would like Ann Logan, should you ever know her. I am at present a guest in their home & just before leaving with a group of people who go with me to the Green to take up land on my property there. This is a design of long standing with me & affords me much pleasure that it has come about.

With your permission, I shall write again when I have more news to give you about your land here. May I hope that all is well with you & your children & that I shall soon have good news to send you. I remain,

Y[r] *Hmble & Ob*[t] *Sv*[t]
CASSIUS CARTWRIGHT

The two letters in hand, Cass sought out Ben Logan and gave them to him. "If you'll see they go off with that man who's headed for the Falls, Ben, I'll appreciate it. I've got to see to Cameron's party now."

"I'll take care of the letters," Ben said. "You've done a good thing, Cass, taking these people on. I don't think you'll be sorry. In my opinion they'll make good settlers for you."

"I hope so. Come over and see for yourself when there's time. You get the men on the muster roll?"

"Yes, I got 'em. You take care, now, Cass. Let me hear from you."

Cass bent his head. "See you next muster day."

He went among the men of the party then, lending a hand with the loading of the pack animals. Each family had a pile of belongings, bedding, pots and pans, sacks of provisions, bars of lead, pouches of powder, extra guns, bundles of clothing, and a few pieces of small furniture such as Betsey's rocking chair, Mercy Bearden's spinning wheel, Melie Cameron's spool bedstead. There were also a few plowshares, scythe blades, axes and hoes.

Penned in the enclosure by the spring Cass counted, also, fifteen head of cows, six with calves beside them, and forty head of sheep. There was even a crate of hens with one big dominecker rooster clucking worriedly at his nervous harem. "Who do the chickens belong to?" Cass asked, laughing.

"They belong to me, that's who!" The scratchy, harsh voice came from behind a string of tethered pack horses. Cass wound his way among them. Seated solidly on a tussock of grass, a rope around the neck of the same big black sow that had got away from her yesterday, a pack horse already loaded with household plunder and two horses saddled grazing nearby, was Mag Johnson. Her gatepost legs still wore the red-striped stockings and her cap was still cocked to one side, her grizzled, stringy hair fringing out from under it in a frill. "Where do you think you're going?" Cass asked, looking down at her.

"I'm a goin' where you're a goin'," she said, peering up at him with one eye squinted against the sun. "These," she said, waving a hamlike arm, "is aimin' to buy yore land an' settle on it, so I jist told Tench if you'd sell to them you'd likely sell to us an' I was aimin' to give it a try. You'll have need of a good smith, won't ye? Tench is the best ye'll ever find, if I do say so myself. An' I'm a master hand at grannyin'. From whut I c'n tell, there'll be need of me amongst these folks 'fore long, an' doubtless all along. They look to be a breedin' kind of folks. You ain't put out, air ye, youngun?"

Cass pinched his chin. "Where's your man?"

"Over thar. That's him standin' by Jacob. Won't do no good to talk to him, mister. Hit's me that's made up my mind. Tench'd set here till doomsday if it was left up to him. But I'm sayin' farewell to this here fort."

"You know the terms I'm selling the land to these people on?"

Mag nodded her frowsy head. "Know 'em an' like 'em. An' we got the hard money to pay fer our'n straight off. Which is more than any of the rest of 'em has got. We c'n pull our weight, youngun, an' no fear about it."

Cass laughed. "I don't doubt it at all, Mag. Well, since you've made up your mind that seems to settle it. How are you going to get that sow and her pigs fifty miles over the trail?"

"Ain't aimin' to take the pigs. Done sold 'em. The sow, I'll lead."

"Seems to me you would have had enough of hanging on to that rope, after what happened yesterday."

Mag sniffed. "That was yesterday. I got a tight rope on her, now, an' if she don't lead she c'n choke to death. She'll lead."

A sturdy old man, in hunting shirt and leggins, left the group gathered around the pack horses and approached Cass and the old woman. Watching him, Cass studied his face. It was broad, heavy-featured, patient and good-humored. He wore an old buffalo hat square on his head, which flopped about his ears and over his forehead. There was no stoop or give in the powerful old shoulders. They looked as square and uncompromising as Cass's own, and by the swelling of the sleeves of the ancient, worn old hunting shirt it was evident that the muscles developed over the years of swinging a hammer were still tough and able. He had faded blue eyes and his beard was whiter than his hair. His eyes twinkled as he came up. "My name's Tench Johnson," he said, holding out his hand. "My woman has made up her mind fer us to go with you."

The calloused, horny old palm closed firmly about Cass's hand. "Glad to have you," Cass said, smiling. He liked the looks of Tench Johnson.

"I aimed to look ye out this mornin', talk with ye," the old man went on, "but Ben said you was writin' letters, so I misliked to pester ye. If it's suitable to you, we'd like to buy offen ye an' settle on yore land. We thought we'd best be ready, in any case, so's not to be left behind."

"Humph," old Mag sniffed. "You'd be settin' yet, palaverin' with Ben Logan, if it hadn't been fer me."

The old man smiled at his wife and bent down to scratch the sow's ears. "Would ye want the money fer the land now, Mister Cartwright? I've got it handy."

"You'd better wait till you see the land. You might not like it. Might change your mind."

"No fear of that," Mag said, heaving herself ponderously up off the grass. "Jist so it ain't penned in, it'll suit. Bring that mare 'round, Tench, an' let me git on."

"I got to git them hens of yore'n settled now, Mag," the old man said. "There's plenty of time to git you loaded."

"Well, I aim to be all set to go," she yapped at him, hauling up on the sow, which squealed protestingly.

"We'll be leaving soon," Cass told them, and he went through the milling animals and people to the front where he mounted a little shelf of rock. He called to get John's attention and waited until the people had grouped themselves in a wide circle about him. They clustered in small family groups. He looked at them thoughtfully. These, then, were his people, who had chosen him and whom he had chosen. For better or for worse their fates were to be thrown together. They would be his neighbors and his followers in the valley to which he was taking them. The die was cast and they must all prosper or fail with him. He felt a tide of responsibility for them roll over him, and already a kind of loving regard for them. They were his, now, and he must do the best he could for them. They, themselves, were good people, linked by the common tie of blood to begin with, to be linked further by their continuing proximity. They would do their part. It remained for him, Cass Cartwright, to do his.

Seeing the children grow restless, he began to speak. "There is not much danger of Indians," he said, "for we have seen no sign down our way this year. But there is always enough danger that we must take care. Try to keep the stock from straying off the trail. Try to keep the pack horse from rubbing against trees and such. We'll head for the headwaters of the Green and camp there tonight. I'm going to keep moving, so do your best to stay up. I'll lead and I'm going to ask Jacob Bearden to ride trail. That's all I've got to say, except I'm pleased you've decided to throw in with me and I'll do the best I can for you. Any questions?"

Wirt Powell flipped his hat brim up. "How long will we be on the road?"

"Depends," Cass said. "If we make good time and have no trouble we should get there in four days, even with stock. That's what I count on, anyhow."

"Just wanted to know."

"All right. Everybody set?"

The men turned to lift their wives and smaller children into the saddles. Jacob loosed the animals from the pasture and his boys herded them out before them.

Cass mounted Judah and let him prance a moment before reining him in, turning him so he could face the party. Quickly he ran his eyes over the people, then he lifted his hand, wheeled his horse, brought his arm down in a flashing motion and called out over his shoulder, "String out!"

Without confusion the families took places, making, as he saw when he glanced around, a considerable length of line. With a flash of humor he thought this must be the way Ben had felt when he brought his own people over the mountains, himself at the head of the line, carrying the responsibility, feeling as big as the side of the mountain. He did not deny it gave him pleasure to be leading these people out.

CHAPTER 7

By the time the first snow blew, light, scudding, and feathery over the northern shoulder of the hills early in November, there were three cabins finished and occupied, Jacob Bearden's, John Cameron's and Wirt Powell's. Betsey McKittridge had a fine son, but she and Nathaniel were living in Cass's big house because of the baby.

During that first snow a passing traveler brought Cass a letter from General Wilkinson. Sitting before a great fire, the snow hissing against the window, Cass read it.

Philadelphia
8th October, 1783

My dear Maj. Cartwright:

I trust that this Missive will be Received by you in time for you to Meet me at the Falls sometime during the First Week in Decbr. I know not the Exact date, but I shall leave Phila. early in Nov. The sale of my Property has been consummated, though I cannot Say to my great Pleasure. I have been Disappointed in the amount Received for so fine a property. I was Determined to sell, however, & the Matter has been done.

I have laid in a Stock of Mchdse. which should move Handsomely & it will follow me upon order as soon as we are Located. I have thought a supply of Calicoes, French goods, Shoes, ribbons, Beads & Gaudies, & a few of the Necessities, such as Needles, Buttons, crockery & Queensware, would stock us amply in the

Beginning. I have also provided a snug little assortment of Medicines; Blistering Plaisters, a plenty of Salts, Tan-bark, Laudinum & liniments. You see here the Evidences of my early Medical training. Did you not know that I once was Licensed to practice Medicine? I do not, however, intend to hang out my Shingle *in Kentucky!*

Mrs. Wilkinson & our sons will not Accompany me on this trip. They will remain with her parents in Phila.

Join me in wishing us both Fame & Fortune in our adventure! It will be a pleasure to see you again in Decbr. I beg to remain,

Yr Hble & Obt Svt
JAMES WILKINSON

Cass studied the letter thoughtfully. So he was to meet him at the Falls in December. He folded the letter abruptly and snapped it against the heel of his hand. Good. Good. He was growing a little weary of being a country squire. He was tired of the harvest season and of the raising of cabins. He needed a change. For once he was going to be glad to get back to the Falls, to talk with people of wider interests than John Cameron's relations, to sit around a table with the officers at Fort Nelson again, and to listen to the gossip of taverns and river boats.

He also felt a bladey excitement at the thought of meeting the general again. The man was exciting himself, and the challenge he offered of dueling wits and propositions girded him up. It would be good to think of something besides fodder and hay and corn, the weather, and the winter ailments of the settlement. A man's wits grew dull on such fare.

So, on the last day of November, Cass nursed his aching leg (a souvenir of the Battle of Blue Licks) and a rum toddy before the tavern fire at the Falls, grateful for the heat of the fire on his leg, and the toddy in his stomach. A cold, slow rain had been falling steadily for three days. The skies were so sullen, so heavy with rain-sogged clouds that even at noon a candle was necessary in the dark log huts, and the rain which fell so endlessly seemed but a part of the sky, lowered and thickened. To stand on the bank of the Ohio and look across to the other side was to see the same opaqueness everywhere, rain and water and land all alike, gray, curtainy with water, the shore lines lost in a fluid mixture. On such days it was hard to believe the sun would ever shine again, and the old wound in his thigh ached with a slow pain which seeped into the bone itself.

He had been at the Falls a week now, and he had exhausted most of its attractions. At best they were few. The village built on the banks of the Ohio at the Falls was not much of a town. There were several log huts huddled on the paths, a courthouse, a jail, a tavern and a store. And there was the fort. That was all. After a few riotous nights with the officers at the fort, when immoderate amounts of the new corn whisky made locally had been drunk, and rattle and snap had been played until the possessions of all the officers had changed hands until none knew what he now owned, Cass had wearied of the walls and of the company of the men. It was no different than it had ever been. There was the same dull confinement and monotony, broken only by the wild winds of rumors and an occasional scout around the country, or by an infrequent case of discipline in the stockade. After a few days of catching up on the gossip its bleakness had settled down over him again, as it had always done at Fort Nelson. He did not blame the militia for hating garrison duty. A man might as well be in prison. It was enough to drive him mad.

He had removed to the tavern, had walked the river front when the few boats arriving at this time of year had tied up, had eaten foul food and drunk raw whisky until his head ached and had tried to contain his impatience as best he could. He wished, now, he had not been in such a hurry to get to the Falls. The general's boat might be delayed for weeks.

Watching the rain streak down the one glassed window of the tavern he wondered how people stood the desolation of winter in a village. The paths which wound around and between the houses were a quagmire, mushed by the passing of men, animals and vehicles; and hogs and dogs rooted in the slops at the doors of the dark-slicked huts. Carts mired to their hubs in the pothole in front of the tavern and to walk out in any direction meant to risk going in over your boot tops.

Inside it was little better. The fires were smoky and sulky with wet wood burning slowly, and the rooms were like damp caverns, dripping with their leaks, their rough floors packed with the loads of mud tramped in on heavy boots. There was mud at home, of course, but it was a different kind of mud, cleaner somehow and subject to a little control. His black Sheba kept his boot tracks mopped up, and his fires always burned high and steady. His wood was kept dry in a good, stout woodshed.

Impatiently he hitched his leg around to bake the other side of it, sipped at his toddy and listened to the gabble of voices from the other end of the room. "Well, all I know," a man with a meaching face and a high, nasal voice was saying, "is they'll have to take my land away from me at the point of a gun. I ain't lettin' nobody tell me my title ain't good and just move me out."

"Who's trying to tell you yore title ain't good?" he was asked.

"They was a feller," the twanging voice went on, "come by the other day said he heared they wasn't no Virginny titles going to be ary bit of good. He telled it that Virginny had done give all the country this side the mountains to the Congress and they was letting the land companies have their pick. Said we'd all have to buy our land back from these here land companies. This is one coon that ain't. They can just be damned and blasted."

"You ain't from Virginny, Thomas. Don't you know them damned Tuckahoes has took up all the best land for theirselves?"

"Maybe they have, but what I've took up I like purty good, and I'm aiming to hang on to it."

"Likely he was a land company man hisself, trying to skeer you off," someone volunteered.

"I don't skeer easy."

"Me neither. But they was a feller come down the river during the summer — said he'd heared 'em talking in Philadelphy that some feller writ a piece, a pamphlet he called it, about Virginny land titles. Said his name was Paine — Thomas Paine, as I recollect — and he taken the stand that Virginny never had no title to the land in the first place."

"What! Ever'body knows Virginny got the title from the crown — it was a crown grant, plumb to the western sea. They ain't *no* doubts about that."

"Well, that's what this feller said. But he said he *had* heared that the land companies had give this Paine feller several thousand acres of good land to write the piece for 'em. Reckon he writ it to suit them, so's he could get the land."

"That must of been the way of it. If Virginny ain't got title, don't look to me like nobody would have it."

A level, resonant voice was lifted above the others. "Don't you men realize that the land companies stir up these rumors purposely, to keep you unsettled and dissatisfied? If enough of you become fearful of your titles, it is their hope you'll sell to them, cheap. They flood the country with these rumors, create a disturbance and unease among you, then pick off your lands to sell at a profit. Hold on to your titles. Prove them in court. Don't be fools."

The knot of men surged apart, growling, and Cass saw a small wispy man seated on the far side of the table. His hair was scant and his shoulders were wet, but his face was lean and intelligent. He spoke like a man of some education, and his voice had none of the drawl and twang of the rest of the men. "How do ye know, Jeremy?" he was asked.

"Where do you hear all these things?" he said, reasonably. "From strangers — men who come down the river and mix with you, mingle among you, drop their words like pebbles in a pond, leave them to ripple out over the country. Company agents, every last one of them. Sent here to cause dissatisfaction and to arouse your fears. This fellow you mentioned, Thomas. Did he offer to buy your land?"

The man called Thomas nodded. "Said he'd take it off my hands if I wanted. Said I'd best get shut of it afore I couldn't get nothing for it."

The lean-faced man ran a thin hand through his hair. "You see. And if you'd sold to him, you would have lost your land cheap. The man would have turned the title over to the company and it would have been resold at a profit."

"Why, the dirty sonsabitches! If a body didn't know, they could just plunder him outen ever' acre he's got! I wish I'd of knowed it when that feller was talking to me, Jeremy. I'd of gouged his eyes out for him."

"Pay no attention to rumor or to the counsel of strangers," the man advised the group. "If your title is threatened get yourself a lawyer and take it to court. Fight where it will do you some good."

The men filled in the opening around the table, nodding and lifting their mugs. "That's right. They's a plenty of lawyers in the country now. They're doing a landslide business, too."

There was laughter at the unintended pun, and then a question. "Whyn't you go in for lawing, Jeremy? Smart as you be, you could make a pile of money. You ain't ever going to get you a piece of land mulling in them books of yore'n."

There was wry humor in the reply. "I'm afraid my education did not include any training in the law. I wish, now, it had."

There was silence and one of the men — Cass was surprised to see it was Tate Beecham, whom he had not noticed before — walked to the door. Beecham was a man who had scouted for the army often during the time when Cass had been stationed at Fort Nelson. He was a hunter, a woodsman, and a sort of lone wolf, coming and going to please himself, undependable except in the woods, where he was unexcelled. He opened the door a crack, observed the sluicing rain, closed the door and joined the group again. "By grannies, I wish that damn boat would get in."

The men guffawed and one of them poked a finger in Tate's ribs. "You getting warm, Tate? Already crawling into bed with one of them gels?"

"No warmer'n you be. You put up yore tobaccer same as me," Beecham said spiritedly.

"You reckon Ezry can actually get ten to come?"

"If he don't, I'm loading that tobaccer on a sled and taking it home with me straight off. He *said* he could. Said he could take the pick of anyhow fifty gels that would be anxious to come out and marry up with us."

"Saying and doing is two different things."

A big, burly man, black-whiskered to the ears, licked his chops. "God's britches, I can hardly wait. It's been a time and a time since I had me a woman. I don't even know if I *can* or not, it's been such a time."

Whoops and howls and yells went up from the other men. "That's the Gawd's truth!"

Tate Beecham, thin-shanked, ginger-haired, said a little wistfully, "A man shore gets lonesome out on a stand all by hisself. I don't know but what I want mostly is just somebody to talk to."

The men jeered at him. "Talk! Talk to a woman!"

"Talk when you've just married up to her!"

"I ain't aiming to talk," the big, whiskered man boasted, "not till I'm so tard I can't do nothing else." Tobacco juice ran down his beard at the corners of his mouth and he wiped it with the back of a hairy hand and threw the spittle off on the floor. He swaggered his big shoulders. "The one I get is going to know she's got hold of a man, I can tell you."

"What I'm afeared of," a very young man, face barely needing to be shaved, said, the red mounting to his cheeks, "is that Ezra'll just pick the scum of Philadelphia. Don't hardly stand to reason a lady would come, not knowing none of us or nothing."

"Well, now," the big man scoffed, "wouldn't that just be too bad? Lady? Hell, no, you fool — they'll not be no ladies. A lady can get her a man 'thout coming to Kentucky for him. What would ye want with a lady anyhow? I wouldn't have no truck with one. What I want," he spraddled his legs and hooked his thumbs in his belt, "is a gel that's good for a quick tumble and that can hold up to do a day's work. That's what I want a gel for."

The boy subsided, hitching his shoulders up around his flaming, embarrassed neck.

"Come on," someone shouted, "let's go down and see if we can see anything coming down the river. Ain't no use setting here on our backsides the rest of the day."

Like sheep following a leader the knot of men surged out the door, whooping and yelling, stumbling over each other in their eagerness. The room was left empty save for Cass and the man they had called Jeremy, who still sat on the far side of the table, his eyes on the door that had just been closed with a thud that shook the rafters. A small smile lingered at the corners of his mouth. The room was very quiet after the noisy exit.

Now that he could see the man plain, Cass saw that he was not only thin and wispy, with sparse mouse-brown hair on a balding, domed head, but he was a hunchback, one shoulder lifted higher than the other, the neck crowded down in his collar, from which his chin lifted peakingly. But the eyes he turned on Cass, as he made his way toward him, were humorous and friendly, deep-set and intelligent.

"Your pardon, sir," Cass said, "my name is Cassius Cartwright. I overheard a little of the preceding conversation."

"Jeremy Yardley," the man said quietly, "your service. If you didn't hear it all," he added dryly, "your ears are at fault. They," nodding his head at the door, "aren't given to soft speech."

"I was beginning to wonder," Cass said, drawing out a chair, "if my ears weren't playing tricks on me."

The man's wide mouth split into a grin. "About the girls? Oh, no. You heard aright. The fools have bargained with Ezra Dutton to bring on ten Philadelphia girls — for wives."

Cass had heard of Ezra Dutton. He was a sly, weaselly man who carried cargo on the river. Cass had never employed him to carry his shipments because he had heard that the man was given to sharp dealings. It was said of him that if you didn't tally your goods before turning them over to Ezra, get his signature on the tally sheet, you'd come up short every time. Cass would have no dealings with that kind of riverman.

"What," Cass asked, grinning himself, "is the going price in girls these days?"

"One hundredweight of prime tobacco," Jeremy said, drawing out a long-stemmed clay pipe and fiddling it between his long, thin fingers. He raised a bleached eyebrow quizzically. "Are you interested, sir?"

"Oh, no. I was merely curious. I'm afraid," he continued, "that the youngster who voiced some fear as to the ladies' gentility will be correct."

Jeremy lifted his drooped shoulder. "I am certain of it. But a man's appetite grows in solitude as his sense of selectivity dwindles. If she wears skirts and will spread her legs, those men will not care if she has warts on her chin and is missing her teeth."

Cass chuckled. "Ezra is overdue, I take it."

Jeremy nodded. "By several days. Their fever rises."

Abandoning the banter Cass altered his tone. "I also heard the advice you gave the gentlemen, sir. It was excellent advice — sound and sensible. May I ask what your business is, sir?"

The man fingered the clay pipe, turning it, polishing its smooth bowl with his thumb, his eyes following the movements of his hands. "Business?" Unhurriedly he filled the pipe and stuck the stem in his mouth. "I fear I have none. I am something of a wanderer, a vagabond, if you like. A drifter, a rover." He pulled himself awkwardly out of his chair with the help of his hands on the table's edge and limped to the fire where he took up a coal to light his pipe. He continued to stand, parting his coat tails to warm his back. "In my time I have been a teacher, a preacher, a printer, a scrivener, a drunkard, a fool, and an occupant of debtor's prison. But I have no trade, nor any home, nor any family. I travel. Shall we say *that* is my business, to travel and observe the follies of my fellow man."

Cass flushed, feeling rebuked. "I did not mean to be impertinent, sir."

"I take no offense, young man." The wispy little man puffed on his pipe.

"There was some mention of your interest in land . . ."

"Oh, that. I have the temerity to hope that I may find cheap a little parcel of land someplace in this broad country and, it may be, if I find it suits me, end my travels. So far," he added wryly, "I have not been successful. The cheapest parcels are beyond my means." He spread his hands. "I am, sir, fresh from gaol."

"For what?" Cass asked bluntly.

"For my debts. I had a small printing shop. I learned printing under Benjamin Franklin, and I had the doubtful honor of doing some printing for the Congress. When I was not paid, I could not pay my own bills. My press was seized and I myself imprisoned."

Cass stared at the man, so obviously unembittered by his experience. "I'm afraid I should not have taken that so kindly."

"Oh, I didn't take it kindly. But there was nothing I could do until Mr. Franklin, in due time, persuaded the Congress to settle their accounts."

Cass drummed on the tabletop, thinking. "You have some education, sir . . . and some experience of keeping a school?"

"Some of both, though I cannot lay claim to more than a speaking acquaintance with either. The school was a small one, for the children of General Washington's staff." The smoke wreathed around the man's large, domed head, hardly more wispy nor much paler than the scant, light hair. "I can cypher to the double rule of three, I have some knowledge of grammar and geography, I write a fair hand and I am familiar with the Eclogues of Virgil." Through the screen of smoke he peered, the palish eyes twinkling. "You have need of a schoolmaster, sir?"

Cass laughed. "I have just commenced a settlement on my lands in Lincoln County. I have been counting on my fingers the number of children who are going to grow up in ignorance there if we do not provide for them. At present there are a round dozen of them, some too young yet for school, but there is a nice little clutch of them the proper age, and the Lord only knows, since my settlers are mostly young, how many more will eventually make an appearance. I can provide you with comfortable quarters, a building in which to hold your school, my own books and any others you may need to order; and if you are interested in a parcel of land I can make that available to you on terms you might find persuasive." He stood. "We need a schoolmaster, Mr. Yardley, but we also need sensible men in the country. You are a sensible man."

The hump on Jeremy Yardley's back was so formed that it did not cause him to stoop. He stood straight enough, the deformity merely bulking his shoulders and dwarfing his height. With his large, balding head, his thin, beaked nose, his wide slit mouth, he had a gnomish look. But that he was a humorous, friendly, intelligent gnome Cass was certain. By the frayed ends of his cuffs, the battered toes of his shoes, the lean cavity of his stomach, Cass was also certain that he was a hungry and penniless one.

At Cass's words, he took the pipe from his mouth, grinned infectiously, and shot out his hand. "Done, sir. I'll make you a schoolmaster. By the Lord Harry, sir, I'd trade my soul for the books you offer. A man can forget bodily hunger, sir, but he starves his spirit when he loses his books."

"Yours?" Cass asked.

The long, slender hands lifted helplessly. "They went the same way as my press — taken for debts, all but a few of my most treasured ones."

"There'll be no more of that," Cass said abruptly. "Come, sit with me. Let's have some of the taverner's stew and talk about your new situation."

The little man talked volubly all through the meal, but he tucked away three portions of stew, a loaf of bread, and he downed two pints of ale. Cass wondered when he had eaten last. He explained that he was waiting for General Wilkinson's boat and suggested that Jeremy wait also, at least until he knew how long he would be kept with his business with the general; and then some arrangement could be made for Jeremy's journey to Lincoln County. Jeremy turned empty pockets out, eloquently indicating the state of his purse.

"I'll take care of it," Cass said.

Jeremy's head ducked to one side. "How do you know I'll repay you?"

Refusing to joke about it, Cass said, "I don't expect you to. Besides, it's part of your wages."

Underlying the other reasons he had given the man for wanting him in his settlement, Cass vaguely knew that he probably needed him himself. There were times, when he had time to think about it, when he missed having someone to talk to — wanted someone who knew, as he did, what lay within the bindings of those shelved books in his study, someone who knew, as he did, that the world was larger than the valley on the Green, or the cluster of cabins at St. Asaph's, or even the jumble of buildings which made up the village at the Falls. More greedily than he suspected he looked forward to evenings around the fire, with books and good whisky and a literate man to talk to. He felt he had made a good bargain.

They had finished their meal and were enjoying their pipes when they were interrupted. The door flew open and Tate Beecham erupted into the room. "Where's Thomas? Where's Big Jim and the rest of 'em? The boat's in!"

Jeremy answered. "I don't know, Tate. They haven't been here since you all left together."

"Well, by Gawd, they've give me the slip. I stopped in at the store and they said they was coming back to the tavern. They ain't been here?"

"No."

"I got to find 'em. Ezra's boat is in, and he's brung the gels. I seen 'em." He whirled and ran out, slamming the door behind him.

Immediately there was a whooping and howling outside, a few shots fired off, and the sound of someone beating on a piece of iron. Cass looked at Jeremy and grinned. "He found them, I reckon. This might be right interesting, Jeremy. Let's go down to the dock and see."

They followed the yelling, noisy band of men, squashing through the mud down to the river. Others of the townspeople, curious, formed a crowd behind them. Still others, hearing the noise but refusing to venture out in the weather, stuck their heads out doors and windows. "What's up? What's going on? Boat in?"

"Wimmin! Wimmin! Ezra's boat has brung the gels!"

All the men were wobbly with drink and they slipped and slithered down the muddy bank, propping each other up, falling together, recovering and splashing on. By the time they reached the wharf and the small log warehouse most of them were smeared from forehead to boot toe with slime and mud. Seeing the flatboat tied up, some of them made an effort to clean themselves, using their buckskin sleeves or their old buffalo hats and skin caps. The general effect was simply a wider smear, out of which their noses bulked and their eyes gleamed. They were a filthy, drunken crew, Cass thought, and he felt a little sorry for the women who had to pair with them.

Cass limped along beside Jeremy, thinking wryly that both

were crocks, he with his aching leg, Jeremy with his hump. By picking their way carefully they avoided falling, but their boots were heavy with the clay mud by the time they reached the dock. They took shelter under the eaves of the warehouse.

The men crowded together at the end of the short pier and fixed their eyes on the cabin built amidships of the flatboat. They jostled and nudged each other, whistled, engaged in catcalling and lusty whoops, slapped each other on the backs, laughed bawdily at their own crude jokes. Only one man, Tate Beecham, stood apart from the rest, his shoulders hunched against the rain, his feet uncertainly shifting in the mud. Jeremy nudged Cass. "Tate has got buck fever," he whispered. Cass nodded.

Suddenly the men were silent. The first woman had emerged, stooping, from the cabin. She straightened and looked boldly at the crowd of men. She was a lean hank of a woman, easily forty years old, with a battered, worn face. Her nose looked as if it had been casually pushed askew and her mouth, grinning, revealed blackened stumps of teeth. Her short gown was a gaudy red, and the petticoat under it was gray with age and dirt, its hem frayed and raveled. A groan rose from the men, so spontaneous and concerted that it seemed to come, vastly, from one man. "He's gypped us," one of them moaned, "he's brung on a boatload of old witches."

Hearing, the woman flung up her head and bawled at the men. "Witches! Listen to the critter! Look who's doin' the talkin'! I don't see as you're the fine lords we wuz promised, neither. Look at ye," she screeched, advancing on them, "drunk an' filthy an' bearded as old man time hisself. Who are ye to talk? We're as good as the best of ye. What wuz ye expectin'? Silks an' satins an' pearls, mebbe? Come on, gels," she called back over her shoulder, "an' take a good look at these apes ye've done promised yerselves to." She had reached the end of the pier and shouldered her way among the men. "Git outen my way! Ezry said fer us to go to the warehouse an' wait thar. Don't be switchin' at my dress-tail, neither." She twitched it loose from a grasping hand. "Ain't but one of ye gonna hev a right to do that an' I ain't knowin' which'un that is yet. Git!" She raised her hand and took a swing at the big, black-bearded fellow who was slyly trying to untie her petticoat string.

He ducked and pretended to be frightened. "Lord, ye old bitch, ye've got a tongue in yer head, ain't ye?"

"I've got more'n that. I've got a good right hand that kin raise a whelp on yer skull, ye big baboon. Git outen my way."

The big man rolled his eyes and let out a long breath. "I'll do without," he vowed, raising his right hand, "afore I take that 'un."

Slowly the other women filed off the boat. Some of them were younger than the first woman, some of them about her age. Some of them were timid and seemed bewildered and fearful. Others were bold and even coquettish. Cass could not see them too well, for the men who had put up their tobacco crowded around the warehouse door and shut off his view, but there seemed no doubt Ezra Dutton had scraped the gutters, maybe the prison, to find them. All of them, young and old, had a drab, worn look about them, the look of having been driven and starved and beaten, and of having had to scrounge and steal and hook for themselves all their lives.

All of them were poorly dressed, some more tattered than others, but there wasn't a decent garment among the ten of them. Some had made a pitiable effort at cleaning themselves. Others had tied some poor bit of finery about their necks or waists, a ragged, limp fichu, a colored ribbon, a shawl to keep off the weather. None of the rest of the women spoke to the men. According to their temperaments they either slunk through the crowd, shrinking from the men's punching, poking fingers, their sly jabs and jokes, their lewd motions, or they giggled and rolled their eyes, tossed their heads, rubbed against the men temptingly. It made Cass feel a little sick at his stomach, as he had felt the first time he had watched a slave auction. It was an unabashed traffic in human flesh and he was ashamed to be watching it — the women driven by an ultimate need to barter their one remaining commodity for shelter and food and warmth — the men, driven by loneliness and the surge of their own appetites, to buy it. The sale of slaves, he thought, had more dignity.

"Let's go," he said abruptly.

Jeremy hesitated. "Let's wait a minute. I'd like to see which one Tate gets. He's a right good sort."

"We'd have to go inside."

"We'll just stay until Tate takes his pick."

They slid through the crowd and wedged themselves against the wall inside the warehouse, just in time. Ezra Dutton, a fat, oily little man, appeared and waved the curious crowd back. "Ain't room in here for no more," he said importantly. "Just the one's got their tobacco up for the gels can come in. Close that door, somebody."

The last man in closed the door and the dark little hut, smelling of tobacco, animal hides, tallow, hemp, and the rancid odor of damp and mold, seemed packed with sweating, odorous, milling humanity. Ezra lit another candle and stuck it in its own grease in the center of a table. "Now, boys," he said, rubbing his fat hands together, "these is the gels I promised to bring ye. These gels have come of their own free will, to marry up with ye. I ain't lied to 'em. They knowed that wuz what they wuz coming fer and that's what they're expecting. Not ary one of 'em has been brung against her will. They all signed the papers. Now, how do ye want to pick 'em?"

"Line 'em up against the wall," someone shouted, "so's we can see 'em."

"Yeah, we ain't hardly got a good look at 'em yet."

"All right," Ezra said, and he went among the women pushing at them, shoving, pulling them into line. "Come on, now, ladies. Get yourselves lined up here so's the gents can see you. Now, there's no hurry, boys," he said, over his shoulder, "take your time. Look 'em over good."

The women lined up he turned back to the men. "Now, boys, make up yer minds. How'll you pick 'em?"

"Draw lots, I reckon."

"How'll we do it?"

"There's some chips over there in a pile. Pick out ten of 'em, all sizes. One that draws the biggest from the hat gets first pick, and on down the line."

The women stood against the wall, the candlelight dim on their faces, flickering across their scared or grim or interested or indifferent expressions, picking out a dark-skinned woman here, a fair one there, a tall one, a plump one, a thin one. All of them looked huddled and weary, damp from the rain and dirty from the long boat trip. Some of them kept their eyes on the floor; others looked on boldly, listened to the men, eyed them curiously. The men, in turn, watched them, some of them going over to take a closer look, others holding back but fascinated by the women to the point of not being able to look away. There was a whispering among them as Ezra and the big black-bearded man sorted the chips and made a pile of them. "Now, I ain't aiming to be cheated," someone spoke up. "Somebody that ain't put up no tobaccer has got to hold the hat."

"Who'll it be?"

The man looked around. "Jeremy's standing over there. He can do it. He wouldn't cheat nobody."

"Come on, Jeremy. You shuffle the chips and hold the hat."

Jeremy went forward and took the buffalo hat that had been contributed for the purpose. He turned his back to the men, riffled the chips around and turned back. "Now, you men line up. I'll start at the head of the line and go down. Don't finger the chips. Just reach in and take the first one you touch."

Sheepishly, laughing and snorting and scuffling the men did as he told them. Almost fearfully, then, they reached into the hat. Some even closed their eyes, childishly, as if afraid to see what they had drawn. Tate was trembling so, as his hand reached into the hat, that he almost dropped the chip he drew. It was a pretty big one, Cass saw, but the big, burly man drew the largest one. "Whoops!" he yelped, "I get the first pick!"

He flung the chip over his shoulder, spat on his hands and hitched up his pants. "Come on, ladies, I'm aiming to take my pick. I'm a rip-snorting, fire-eating sonuvagun. I'm half alligator and half horse. I can lick my weight in bobcats and ain't nobody on the river don't turn tail and run when Big Jim Bollivar gets started. I breathe smoke out my ears and pick my teeth with chicken bones! The gel Big Jim Bollivar picks is a lucky gel.

Gimme that candle, Ezry. I'm aiming to get me a good luck at 'em afore I pick."

He grabbed a candle and went slowly down the line of women, holding it high to peer into each face. Some of the women met his look brassily, giggling a little, bridling, flirting their eyes. Others would not look up, shrank away from him, tried to draw back under their shawls and hoods, winced their hips away from his feeling hands. Big Jim took his time. "Come on, Jim," the other men began yelling, "don't take all day. We got our pick coming."

"Take one, Jim, and get it over with."

"Jesus, Jim, don't be so hard to please!"

Jim moved down the line unhurriedly. "Don't rush me. I'm a-picking a woman, not a hawg."

When he came to the end of the line and held the candle over the girl standing there, Cass saw her face plainly illuminated for the first time. It was white and peaked, heart-shaped, with big eyes staring grimly at the big man. Her hair was heavy, dark and tangled, falling tumblingly down her shoulders. Startled, Cass moved impulsively. Jeremy put out a warning hand. "I know that girl," Cass whispered urgently. "There's been some mistake."

She looked as ragged and as forsaken as she had the night she had pilfered the sailor's pay, as white and as hungry, but she held herself up proudly and looked straight at Big Jim, the small red mouth scornful. What, Cass wondered, had made her throw in her lot with this bunch of ragtag and bobtail wenches? Things must have worked out very ill for her.

Jim stood with the upheld candle over her a long time, his eyes sweeping from the undisciplined hair down the peaked white face, over the slim, narrow shoulders, down the small, childishly unformed body. "This 'un," he said finally, "ain't nothing but a pullet, but I always did like 'em young and tender." He leered at the girl. "I'll take this 'un, Ezry."

Like an auctioneer, Ezra Dutton banged his fist on the table, even starting to cry, "Sold!" — but catching himself in time he said instead, "Big Jim's picked! Next."

Big Jim's hand went out to draw the girl away with him. Cass moved forward into the light. He had no idea what he meant to do, nothing was formulated in his mind. Some compulsion made him move protectingly toward the girl. When Big Jim laid his hand on her shoulders, moved it lecherously down across her forearm and across her bosom, she flung her head up, looked around wildly and suddenly seeing Cass her eyes widened in recognition and she broke away and fled, running like a scared rabbit toward him. "Ketch her," Jim yelled, "by Gawd, I'll learn her a thing or two when I get her home with me. Trying to run off when I'm paying a hundredweight of prime tobaccer for her. Head her off there, mister."

Cass flung out his arm and the girl seized it, swung around behind him, huddled behind his back. He retreated slowly until he had the wall at his back. Out of the corner of his eye he saw Jeremy lay the hatful of chips down and move quietly to his side. Big Jim floundered up and reached for the girl. "Thankee, mister. Come on, ye little bitch. I'll frail the hide offen ye, ye try any more tricks like that."

Behind him, Cass could feel the girl's body shaking. She cowered against his back, her head pushed between his shoulders. "Just a minute, sir," he said to Big Jim.

"Eh?"

"There's an error here. This girl is not to be bartered. She is my ward. How this misunderstanding came about, I don't know, but she is not to be included in this affair."

Ezra bustled up. "She come of her own free will. She signed the paper, saying so. I picked her up on the street and she'd just been turned out of gaol . . ."

"I can't help where you found her, or what she signed," Cass said impatiently. "The girl is my ward. I know her well." He lied badly. "I left her in Philadelphia in good hands. What happened after I left is inexplicable to me, but naturally I cannot have her involved in proceedings such as these."

"He's a-lying," Big Jim snorted. "He's just trying to get her for hisself, Ezry. He can't get by with it, and I ain't aiming to be cheated out of my rights."

Cass stared at him coldly. "The girl's name is Tattie Drake. She had made her home with her uncle on Broad Street. The man is a cobbler. These facts can be verified."

Ezra consulted a list. "That's her name, all right. She never said where she lived." He seemed unhappy about the mix-up. "You're Major Cartwright, ain't ye, sir?"

"I am Major Cartwright, yes. This girl is not to be considered in this arrangement. I'm sorry, but it's impossible."

Behind him Tattie's trembling was quieting, but she still held tightly to Cass's arm. He hoped she would have the good sense to keep still. He pressed the wrist he was holding to reassure her and felt her head burrow more closely into the back of his coat.

Ezra turned to Big Jim. "I wouldn't want to dispute the major's word, Jim. He ain't a man to hassle with. He was with General Clark in Illinois and he fit at the Blue Licks. He wouldn't be needing to get him a woman this way. I don't reckon he's aiming to cheat ye."

Big Jim wasn't to be pacified so easily. "Well, she come with the rest and I picked her and I ain't aiming to give her up to him. If she's his ward, why'd she get on the boat? What'd she come for?"

"I've told you," Cass said, "I don't know . . . yet. Something has occurred since I left her in Philadelphia — but I intend to find out. You'd better pick another of these women, for my ward is *not* to be included."

"Mister," the big man said blusteringly, peering squintily into Cass's face and blowing his foul breath over him, "I can gouge a man's eyes out without half trying. You value yer eyesight, don't ye? Well, it's Big Jim Bollivar ye're trying to cheat, and that won't have none of it."

Cass turned loose of Tattie's wrist and without warning shot a fist into the big man's stomach. The air belched forth in a windy gust and the man bent over, clutching his belly. Cass threw his knee up and caught the point of the bent-over chin, thrust and kicked at the same time, and Big Jim fell backward onto the muddy floor, groaned and lay still, as big and as heavy as a felled ox and as unconscious as whisky and the toe of Cass's boot could make him. The other men stared at him. One of them finally shrugged. "Well," he said philosophically, "I reckon that takes keer of Jim. Let's get on with the picking."

"We'll be short one woman, Ezry," Thomas said. "Somebody'll have to do without."

Tate, who was standing near Jeremy shivered a little and threw his chip down. "Hit'll be me, then. I ain't got no taste for this, noway. Druther to get my woman by myself, do I ever get one."

Jeremy chuckled. "Glad to be shut of the business, Tate?"

Shamefacedly Tate hung his head. "Ortent to ever got mixed up in it. My old ma would of knuckled me good for it. A man gets so lonesome, though. Gets mixed up in his head. I just mostly wanted me somebody to talk to, and to make a little noise around. Seems like sometimes I can't stand that empty cabin no longer. I get to talking to myself, just to hear something besides the quiet."

Cass only halfway heard him. He was looking at Tattie, whom he had drawn around into the light again and beginning to wonder what he was going to do with her. Take her home with him, obviously, and let Sheba clean her up. Thank God, he thought, there are other women there now. Maybe Mercy Bearden . . . Ezra Dutton was pulling at his arm. "Who's going to pay fer the gel's passage down the river, Major?" He spoke querulously. "I stand to lose a right smart on her."

"I'll pay," Cass said, shortly. "How much?"

"Well, the boys here was paying a hundred pound . . ."

"Not in tobacco. How much hard money?"

Ezra figured, biting unhappily at his long thumb nail. "Twenty shillings, I reckon, would be about . . ."

"Ten shillings," Cass said, tossing him the money, "and not another farthing. You're making money at that. You've half starved these women coming down river. Come on, Jeremy—Tattie. Let's get out of here."

Later, over her fright, her stomach full, Tattie forgot to be grateful and eyed him sulkily and distrustfully. "Ye never come," she accused him.

Jeremy watched them curiously, silently, having never opened his mouth about the entire affair, his eyes calmly studying them both. Cass had not taken time yet to explain. He had not forgotten, however, how quickly, quietly and loyally Jeremy had lined up beside him when the trouble threatened.

"I couldn't," he told the girl. "My horse went lame and I had to have him shod. I saw every woman I knew in Philadelphia about a situation for you . . ."

"Like hell ye did," she muttered.

"I did, Tattie, believe me. I went the next morning and saw every one of them."

"Yah!" she mocked, her mouth curling. "Ye never give me another thought . . . jist got rid of me."

"There's no way I can prove it," Cass said, patiently, "but I saw Mrs. Ainsley, Mrs. Morris, Mrs. Rush . . ." He ticked them off on his fingers.

"Why didn't ye come?"

"I've told you. My horse cast a shoe. I had to have him shod. I wrote a note to Azariah, however, explaining that I hadn't been able to get you a situation, and I enclosed some money for you."

"Ye're lyin'."

"Why would I lie? I could just as easily tell you I *had* forgotten about you. It would make no difference now. But I don't do things that way. I made you a promise and I kept it, to the best of my ability."

Sullenly Tattie fingered her shawl. "Who'd ye send the note by?"

"A scrivener across the road from the blacksmith shop."

"Him!" She was scornful. "Ye was a fool, then. He taken the money an' tore up the letter, likely. Ye'd have done better to got the blacksmith's boy to fetch it. He's honest, leastways."

"I suppose that's what happened. It never occurred to me . . ."

"It's plain ye're not very smart, mister. The least imp of the streets knows better'n to put faith in that scrivener. He'll do ye fer yer last farthing an' turn ye over to the watch fer good measure." It was evident she was beginning to believe him.

"Now," Cass said, settling himself more comfortably, "how

came you mixed up in this sordid mess? What possessed you to sign up with Ezra Dutton?"

The girl retreated into sulkiness again. "None of yer business."

Jeremy leaned forward. "My girl, it is quite a deal of his business. He has just put up ten shillings for your freedom and apparently guarantees your future. He has . . ."

Cass waved him down. "Never mind, Jeremy. Listen to me, Tattie Drake. You can tell me or not, just as you like, but you can put aside your sulky airs and behave more generously or I'll take you right back to Ezra."

Contemptuously Tattie stared at him. "Ye wouldn't. Ye're too soft."

Cass stared back at her unbelievingly, his mouth dropping open. Then he began to laugh, hearing Jeremy's soft chuckle joining him. "Out of the mouths of babes," he said. "All right, Tattie. I wouldn't return you to Ezra Dutton. But I would like mightily to know why you signed up with him."

Tattie's mouth quivered uncertainly, then stretched into a small smile. It was the first time Cass had ever seen her face lightened from its usual sober, drawn, burdened look. Why, she's right pretty, he thought, surprised. When she gets a little flesh on her and learns not to scowl so much she's going to be a handsome child. He leaned forward and put a hand on her wrist. Quickly she flipped it off. "Keep yer hands to yerself, mister."

Flushing, Cass brought his hand back. "Very well. I'm sorry. Go ahead with your story."

She knotted the fringe of her shawl and bit her lower lip, finally lifting her eyes. They were a very light gray, with small dots of brown turning them almost green. They looked, Cass thought, like a small stone he had unearthed from the bed of the river once, agatey and round and smooth. She fidgeted under his look, then began talking, hurrying, the words tumbling out as if now that she had made up her mind to tell her story she wanted to get it over and done with. "My uncle beat me when I got home that night an' my aunt made me pack my bundle an' git out. I done all right fer a time, fer I had that sailor's money, but it run out an' I didn't have nowheres to go, so I took to beggin' an' sleepin' in the barns an' stables. An' one night old man Custer found me in his stable an' called the watch. They locked me up."

"In the gaol?"

"Where do you think?"

"How long were you kept there?"

"I never kept no count. It was a long time, though."

"Were you mistreated?"

"How do you mean?"

"Were you starved, or beaten?"

"Not beat, no. But we never had much to eat, an' the place was hot an' steamy an' damp. Seemed like all of us got the ague from the damp."

"All of you? How many were in there with you?"

"I never figured it up. A sight of 'em, though. Warn't room to sleep good. It was a awful filthy place, too."

"When did they release you?"

"Turn me out? Well, I don't rightly know what day it was. The weather was cold, though."

Cass did some figuring. "You must have been kept in gaol all summer!"

Jeremy, who had lit his pipe, blew a soft blue cloud over the table. "The poor, Cass," he said quietly, "get no justice. I know that gaol in Philadelphia, remember."

Cass gazed soberly at him. These two, he thought . . . these two, both crippled in their way, had a knowledge he could only guess at. No Cartwright had ever seen the inside of a gaol, or was ever likely to. By virtue of his birth, by virtue of his father's wealth, by virtue of his training, he had advantages they could only dream of, none of which told much of the inner man. For all he knew either Tattie or Jeremy was a better man than he was. "Go on," he said to Tattie. "When you got out what happened?"

"It was two or three days after I'd been turned out, I'd guess, an' I was hungry an' tryin' to scrounge a place to sleep, an' I run up on that Mr. Dutton at the tavern. He takened me inside an' bought me a dinner an' told me if I'd sign up with him I wouldn't never have to go hungry again an' I'd have me a good home."

"Did he tell you what you were signing up for?"

Tattie raised her eyes wearily. "Oh, sure. He told me. I didn't see as it would be any worse than the way things was." She laughed suddenly. "I've not ever been with a man yet, Major Cartwright, but I was goin' to. That's why I was hangin' around the tavern. It's the only way somebody like me kin git along, when she gits old enough to. I've knowed I had that to count on since the day I was born. Long as I could manage without, I put it off, but I knowed I couldn't put it off no longer. Men that stays in the tavern pays purty good, an' if ye're lucky sometimes ye kin even pick one up that'll keep ye for several weeks. Mary Jenkins had her a officer that she stayed with a year, one time. Ye kin stay warm an' eat good. Name of God, I'd of gone with any man that promised me enough to eat an' a bed to sleep in out of the weather. 'Twouldn't of made no difference to me if he was in it with me. They're all like a boar pig anyways."

Cass met Jeremy's eyes across the table. They were soft and liquid with pity and mercy and kindness and a sort of pleading which Cass did not understand. He turned back to the girl. "How old are you, Tattie?"

"Fourteen, near as I kin make out. I don't rightly know. Old enough," she said, a tight little smile marking her mouth knowingly, "if that's what you'd want of me."

"My God!" Cass exploded, standing abruptly, "shut your foul little mouth. I don't want anything of you. I'm going to take you home with me and you're going to have a room of your own, and my black woman, Sheba, will feed you and wash you and take care of you, and you're going to Jeremy's school and get a little learning inside that befuddled head of yours! You're going to learn there's some decency in people, because you're going to live among them, and I hope you're going to turn into a decent person yourself. Now, get yourself up to that room Billy's made up for you and go to bed. Sleep the rest of the day, if you want. I'm going to the store and buy you some clothes that haven't been torn to tatters and aren't full of filth and vermin. Sweet Jesus, the notions you've got stuffed inside that thick skull of yours!"

The girl leaned back in her chair, pulling her skirts down over her knees. "Well, you needn't shout at me. You'd have notions, too, if ye'd been cuffed around like I've been. What notions I've got I've had to learn, so's I could eat an' keep my nakedness covered up. What you want to be so high an' mighty fer?"

Jeremy intervened. "Do as Major Cartwright says, Tattie. He means well. Your hard days are over. You needn't fight any longer."

Tattie's green eyes swung around on him. "Who're you?"

"He's the schoolmaster in my settlement," Cass said. "You can trust us both, Tattie."

She looked from one to the other, running her eyes over Jeremy's patched clothing, running them over Cass's good black. Then she sighed. "I mought as well." She stood and marched with a straight back to the foot of the stairs which wound upward in the chimney corner. On the third step she turned and glowered at them. "Jist keep in mind," she warned, "I never ast to be beholden to ye."

Jeremy and Cass watched her out of sight, her thin, broomstick legs carrying her sturdily up the curving stairway. Then Jeremy looked at Cass and smiled. "My friend," he said, "you've taken on yourself considerable of a burden in that one, but I think it's very noble of you."

"Noble, hell," Cass mumbled disgustedly, "I'm a noble fool if you want to know. Come on and let's see what they've got at the store she can wear."

CHAPTER 8

Four days later General Wilkinson arrived.

The low sea cloud of rain and mist and fog had cleared away, blown east in rags and shreds, and with no nonsense, by a brisk west wind which unveiled the sun, ruffled the swollen water of the river and tangled the black limbs of the willows on Beargrass Creek.

Tate Beecham brought the news, out of breath from his run up the riverbank. "She's come, Major. She's just tying up. Bound to be yore party, sir, for it's a powerful loaded boat."

Tate, Cass thought, eying the greasy bearskin cap which many Kentuckians wore during cold weather and the equally greasy hunting shirt and pants, seemed always to be announcing things. It was he who had first discovered the arrival of the boatload of girls. Now he had peered out the general's boat. He must do nothing but hang around the warehouse. When, he hastily amended, he wasn't hanging around Jeremy in the taproom. For some reason Jeremy liked this tall, ginger-haired, thin-shanked splinter of a man and put up with his odorous company. During the three days of continued waiting, Cass had often found the two together, talking quietly, Tate apparently perfectly at ease with Jeremy. He always shut up like a clam when Cass appeared, squirming uncomfortably, making an excuse before long to be on his way. It was a holdover, Cass knew, from the days when a strict line had been drawn between officers and men, between regulars and militia, when Cass had been Major Cartwright, who could and did give orders to Tate Beecham, scout.

"Where does he live now?" Cass had asked Jeremy once.

"He's never said."

Cass lifted an eyebrow. "I should have thought you would have asked."

"It is none of my affair, is it, my friend?"

"Probably not. But we are mostly curious in this country about the affairs of others."

"I have not yet acquired that trait," Jeremy said quietly.

"You will," Cass told him, laughing. "What do you see in the man?"

"Loneliness — the wish to talk — the desire for the company of his fellow man, even that of a stranger, for a little while."

"Do you think he is a good man?"

Jeremy smiled. "I do not know. Does it matter?"

"No."

Cass gazed at the hunchback. He wondered where Jeremy's fund of lovingkindness came from; if it had been stored up through the years of being made fun of because of his deformity — and that must have been all his life; if it had come because of his having roamed about, like a rolling stone, seeing all manner of men, piercing their weaknesses and pretenses, seeing the cracks in their armors, observing, as he had said, the follies of their natures — and he must have seen more of its evil than its good; if, perhaps, it had come because he had lost so much. He had neither family, home nor belongings. He had been imprisoned and mistreated. It would have made a lesser man, Cass thought, bitter — the things life had done to Jeremy Yardley. But so far as he could tell it had shaped and formed Jeremy only into the mellow mold of good humor, patience, concern, interest, loyalty and that special quality of love for his fellow men which can only be termed lovingkindness. How would it have been with him, he could not help wondering, and with humility he thought he could never have done so well.

When Tate burst in to announce the arrival of the boat, Cass dressed carefully to meet the general, settling Sheba's fine-stitched ruffles about his wrist, making certain his stock was folded precisely, adding his father's silver buckles at his knees. He wanted to do honor to James Wilkinson's elegance.

To his amazement, however, he found the general on the dock dressed in a butternut hunting shirt with brightly dyed red thrums down the sleeves and with a bearskin cap on his head. The two men stared at each other, the general's eyes running up and down Cass's black suit, Cass trying to take in the skin cap and hunting shirt; then they broke into simultaneous laughter. "My friend," the general said, advancing and holding out his hand, "we seem to have reversed our roles. I thought I was dressing properly for the occasion. I seem to have erred. Give me a moment in which to take off this masquerade and I shall be ready to accompany you." He disappeared hurriedly into the cabin of the flatboat.

While he waited for him, Cass arranged for his boxes and trunks to be carried to the tavern. There seemed to be an immoderate number of them and Cass reflected that the general certainly did not travel lightly. But then, he was moving into the country, not merely traveling through it, and that must make a difference.

Up the bank Jeremy and Tate were standing, watching, and Cass saw them laughing together. Lord, he thought, what had possessed the man to rig himself out in such an outfit! He would have made himself the laughingstock of the country if he had walked up the streets and into the tavern so rigged out. It was lucky Cass had caught him first.

When the general rejoined Cass he was as sashed, collared and buckled as he had been in his own home. He had also regained his pompous dignity. Privately, Cass chuckled. The frontiersman's garb was not the most becoming garment the general might wear. He was not properly built for it. His rotund body required the framework of his gentleman's coat and his short legs needed the reinforcement of the buckled trousers and hose.

"It was good of you to meet me, Cass," he said as they walked toward the tavern.

"It is my pleasure, sir," Cass replied. "Was the voyage down the river tedious?"

"Tedious? No. It was in fact quite interesting. And I was comfortably situated." He smiled broadly at Cass. "I do not believe in indulging myself in inconvenience when convenience will serve me better. I required the captain to fit my quarters up rather well and I laid in a good supply of foodstuffs so that I need not be under the necessity of partaking of what passes for meals on a boat. The time required by the voyage is long, but I brought a box of books and the passing scenery was intriguing. There were also some moments of excitement, these last few days, with the river so swollen. We got turned stern foremost more than once in the swift currents."

"I would think it. It was a matter of some concern to me, sir. I hoped you would have no difficulty."

The general waved a soft, white hand. "None at all. None at all." He was looking about him, now that they had reached the top of the riverbank, with curiosity, taking in the sordid little cluster of houses, the muddy paths and roads, the bulking, gloomy fortifications. If he was disappointed in the village his face did not show it. It reflected only an eager interest. "So this is the Falls," he said.

"This," Cass echoed, "is the Falls. Not much of a place, is it?"

"About what I expected," the general said pleasantly. "All frontiers are rough until they are civilized a little. The western frontier in New York State is quite similar to this. I recognize the log huts, the fort, the tavern and gaol and courthouse. It takes time, sir, to bring the refinements of life to a new country. A sensible man does not expect to find them waiting for him. The place is a little," he continued, cocking his head and smiling, "on the damp side, perhaps. But I recall you said it was a very moist place."

"That's putting it mildly, sir," Cass said, steering him away from a mudhole. "You'll lose your slippers, sir. Some of these holes appear to be bottomless."

The general peered down over his stomach unperturbed. "I shall have to purchase boots, Cass, immediately."

"Yes, sir. It would be wise."

As they went along Cass pointed out John Sanders' trading boat. "He takes tobacco, skins, anything people want to barter, gives them a receipt for it, then when he sells the stuff down the river he redeems the receipts."

The general's hand caressed his chin. "Runs it like a bank, doesn't he?"

"You might say that. The receipts pass for money and it is very seldom that the original owner redeems them."

"I see. Is there a shortage of money in the country, then? Is the medium of exchange the produce?"

"Mostly. Tobacco, hemp, flax, salt, tallow, skins . . . whatever comes handiest for a man to deal in. But we get some hard money, too, through the trade down the river with New Orleans." Cass laughed. "You'll see an astonishing number of different kinds of coins here, sir. Spanish dollars and piasters, French louis and ecus, duccatoons and rix dollars from Holland, goulds and ducats from Austria, frederics and florins from Prussia, crusadores and moidores from Portugal, lire and pistoles from Italy—even the sequins and tomonds of Arabia and the maces and rupees of India are circulated here."

"My word! How is their value determined?"

"By weighing them in balances. With all the variety we get, though, the amount is still pretty small, and with paper money as valueless as it is, we fall back on barter a lot. We pay our officials in tobacco and hemp, we pay our taxes in skins and tobacco, and about the only paper you'll see floating around is John Sanders' receipts and the land warrants. People endorse them and use them as cash."

"Interesting. Interesting." The general sidestepped another mudhole. "I have picked up, as you know, a considerable number of those land warrants. And my first item of business must be to look about the country and lay out my claims. How are the roads, Cass? Can I hire an equipage here?"

Cass stared at him. "Roads, sir? We have no roads. We have trails and paths . . ."

"No post roads?"

"No, sir. Not yet, though we often hear rumors that Virginia intends to legislate in our favor for several."

"How do carriages get about?"

Carefully Cass replied. "I don't believe, sir, there is a carriage in the whole of Kentucky."

"You mean there is no wheeled traffic?" The general was so amazed that he stopped dead still to stare at Cass.

"Oh, yes. Wagons get about, for short distances — where the going isn't too rough. There are too many streams, sir, and we have only one ferry licensed for operation."

"Where is it?"

"At Boonesborough — across the Kentucky River."

The general stroked his chin again and resumed walking. "Thirty thousand people," he mused, "and they all travel by horseback. There must be quite a network of these trails, however."

"Well, yes. They're the old buffalo trails, some of them quite wide and well packed. The main road into the country is the Wilderness Trail, of course — through the Gap and up from the south. It will be a long time before wheels go over it, however. It's been widened since Daniel Boone blazed it out, but it's still just a trail. With more river traffic using Limestone as a disembarkation point there's a trail from that place, on the north, through Lexington to Crow's Station — and there's a trail from the Falls to Crow's Station also. Danville is its new name, and that's where they all meet — the Wilderness Trail, the Limestone-Louisville road, the Limestone-Nashville road."

"Hmmmh." The general was thoughtful. "Is it much of a village?"

"Not a village at all yet. Just a crossroads, with a tavern and a courthouse and a few cabins."

"Do these roads go through Lexington?"

"Yes, sir — by way of Danville."

The general's face became alert. "Cass, I must have a horse at once and if you will secure me, also, a trustworthy man to guide me about the country, I will lose no time in becoming acquainted with it."

"I shall be glad to . . ."

"No, no." The general waved him away. "There's no need taking up your time. You have your own affairs to see to. Provide me with a good horse and man and I shall be perfectly at ease."

"The country isn't entirely safe, sir."

"I am aware of that. I shall expect my guide to know the proper precautions."

The man had nerve, and courage, Cass thought. You had to credit him with that. Not many, new to the country, would start out over it in the face of Indian scares and troubles.

At the tavern, preoccupied, the general took a chair by the fire, stuck his muddy shoes onto the hearth. He did not even notice how bogged they were. He sank his chin into his collar and gazed at the flames and Cass had the feeling he had forgotten his presence. "If you're hungry, sir . . ."

"Eh? Oh, food. Yes. Something hot, Cass, and some good whisky."

At the mention of whisky Cass winced. "I fear our whisky is only a Kentucky product, General. The taverner can give you ale or rum . . ."

The general waved his hand. "No. The whisky, please. I am chilled from this long, wet day on the river."

"I don't wonder." Cass went to the bar and brought him back a small tumblerful.

The general took it and sipped curiously. "You say this is made locally?"

"Yes. Largely from corn."

Once more the general sipped. "It's raw, of course, but do you know, Cass, it has a good aroma and flavor. With aging, it wouldn't be at all bad."

Cass laughed. "There isn't time to age it, sir. The men are too eager for it."

"When it's made in larger quantities, perhaps someone will think of aging it. They'll come up with a good Kentucky whisky, when they do."

Over their food the two men talked, or rather the general talked and Cass listened. Occasionally he asked a question, waited courteously for a reply, then resumed the eloquent flow of words in the deep, resonant voice which could make even a comment about the weather sound profound. "I am going," he said finally, "to take a quick look around . . . largely in the interior near Lexington, for I am convinced there must be our location, and I shall take up some of these land warrants near there also. I shall also examine the land available near here. When I have filed my claims, I shall then be ready to determine the site for our store. Until then, my friend," he smiled engagingly, "I shall not have to trouble you. Perhaps a month, two months, then I can send word to you and you can meet me in Lexington. We can agree upon a location and lay the foundations of our venture together."

"Make certain," Cass cautioned him, "that your claims don't overlap someone else. There's a great deal of trouble these days with titles. Your warrants will be good, probably, but you'll save yourself a lot of difficulty if you choose land that is not already pre-empted."

"I shall take care. My God, Cass, I am excited! I have burned all my bridges behind me and I look to the future, now, in Kentucky! I am exhilarated by this entire adventure and I mean we shall both make our fortunes here."

"I hope you are right," Cass said, dryly, eying the short, plump little man whose face was beginning to flush from the whisky and warmth.

Unnoticing, the general continued expansively. "This is a land with an unlimited future. A man of shrewdness, which I flatter myself I am, sir, can make both his name and his fortune here. This may well be the glory road for me — for us," he corrected himself. "A man needs only to know how to seize the moment, to have the courage to dare new and bold things — this country," he said, leaning forward and looking directly at Cass, "must be recognized by the government, must be given assistance and must be heard. I mean to force the attention of my friends in the government, sir. I have their ear, and I intend they shall listen."

"That will be fine, General."

"A man of influence, sir, is needed here. The government has turned away its eyes from these western waters too long. They have listened to John Adams and John Jay and Robert Morris and have become timid. The time requires boldness and, sir, I am a bold man."

Cass dropped his eyes. Here in a log tavern, on the western water itself, the little man's brag and boast sounded oddly out of place. Perhaps too many men had already bragged and boasted here. Cass thought of the quiet wisdom of some of the men who had latterly come into the country, men such as Thomas Marshall and Judge McDowell. He thought of their conservative ways, their dignity, their air of breeding and learning. Beside them James Wilkinson was like a small rooster, crowing shrilly, ruffling his short wing span, making a lot of noise and stir in the barnyard. It was the opinion of such men as they that the men in the east instead of growing timid had grown ever bolder, determined to gain for themselves and their businesses in the east every advantage, to keep turned the stone wall of inattention to the west, for fear some of their advantages would drain off into it. But it was true that the general did know many men of influence. Perhaps the little rooster making a stir in the barnyard was just what the country needed to rouse it up a little, and perhaps the shrill crowing *could* be heard back east and attract the attention Kentucky was presently denied. "You may be right, sir," he said.

"Now," the general took out his pipe, "what arrangements have you made for me?"

"I have engaged a room for you here, General, and I trust you will not be too uncomfortable. I fear you will have to share it with me for this night, but if you have no need of me at the moment, I shall be returning to my place immediately and you can perhaps persuade Billy to put no one else in with you."

"A little hard money, I presume," the general said, laughing, "being the best persuader."

"You are correct, sir. I shall attend to purchasing a good horse for you and will attempt to provide you with a man to accompany you on your travels."

"Splendid. Splendid, Cass. Give me the names of the leading men in the interior. I shall expect to call on them and make their acquaintance."

"I would immediately seek out Judge Innes, sir, at Danville, and Judge McDowell, Caleb Wallace, George Nicholas . . ." Cass ran down the list for him, "and if you want to meet some of the earliest men in the country you couldn't do better than to look up Ben Logan at St. Asaph's, Isaac Shelby at the Knob Lick, James Harrod at Harrodstown. Shall I make a list of them for you?"

"It won't be necessary. I shall remember their names. I have an excellent memory."

Jeremy and Tate had come in, but seeing Cass and the general at the table they had passed it by and taken seats by the fire. Cass called them over. "General, I should like you to meet the new schoolmaster of my settlement, Jeremy Yardley, and a genuine frontiersman, Tate Beecham."

As graciously as if they had been congressmen the general rose and advanced to meet them. "Your service, Mr. Yardley. Cass, you didn't tell me you had begun your settlement. Mr. Beecham." He did not flinch from Tate's big, horny hand, nor from the strong odor that emanated from him. He ran his eyes over Tate's worn, shapeless buckskins and began laughing. "You should have seen me in *my* Kentucky clothing this morning, sir. I was a vision to behold! I see, now, how they should properly be worn."

"We seen you, sir," Tate muttered, uncomfortable, but honest. "We was on the dock."

"Cass rescued me from making an utter fool of myself. Be seated, gentlemen, and may I offer you something to drink?"

"You may, sir," Jeremy said, "I'll have a hot rum toddy and I expect Tate will want plain whisky."

James Wilkinson was a man of many parts. With a felicitous manner, accompanied by his pleasant voice and friendly speech, his intelligent interest and apparent candor, he soon had Tate Beecham so at ease with him that the awkward, shy backwoodsman talked without hesitation about his experiences in the country, answered willingly any questions put to him, and ventured his opinions frankly. The man could charm a snake, Cass thought. He noticed, however, that Jeremy sipped his toddy and kept his silence. Humorously he wondered what Jeremy thought of the man.

"I must take care of your needs, sir," he interrupted finally. "The general," he added for the benefit of the others, "wants a good horse and a guide to accompany him on a journey through the interior."

"John Teale would have the best horse," Jeremy volunteered, "and Tate here is the best scout in the country."

Cass looked at Beecham questioningly. "Have you got the time for it, Tate?"

"Nothing *but* time, this season of the year."

"Well, there's your man, General. Make your own terms with him."

"Excellent. We'll have no difficulty over the terms."

"Mind if I come along with you, Cass?" Jeremy asked.

"Wish you would," Cass told him.

They left Tate and the general by the fire. As soon as the door was closed behind them Cass asked, "What do you think of him?"

"The general?" Jeremy pulled his old hat down over his meager locks and limped carefully along. "He a friend of yours?"

"Not exactly." Cass told him how he had met the general and of the proposed plan to go into business with him.

Jeremy eyed him quizzically. "You know what you're doing, I reckon. I'd say to keep your eyes open. I've heard tales about Jim Wilkinson, plenty. He's a big hand to play both ends against the middle and to see that Jimmy Wilkinson comes out on top. They tell that when he was in the army he was everybody's friend, till he got what he wanted, then the song changed its tune. He was thicker than thieves with Granny Gates for a time. Gates treated him like a son. But when Wilkinson found someone with more influence than Gates he turned on him and helped ruin him. Even fought a duel with him — said Gates slandered him. He's real touchy about his honor, you'll learn, but there's plenty that think he's not got much to be touchy about. He was mixed up in that Conway cabal against Washington, when part of the Congress wanted to get rid of the general. It never did come out which side Wilkinson was on, but he found out about it — going through Gates's papers, I guess, and dropped a few words to one of Washington's aides. It got back to Washington in time for him to make a fuss about it and save himself, but whether little Jimmy was trying to discredit Washington, or trying to save him, nobody knows. He was Washington's clothier general the last two years of the war, though, so evidently the general thought he did him a service. Didn't make much of a clothier, however. Washington finally had to recommend he be dismissed, but Jimmy saved his face by resigning."

"How do you know all this, Jeremy?"

"Common talk around Philadelphia during the time, boy."

"How does he keep his influence? He's a friend of Thomas Jefferson's."

"Sure. He's a friend of a lot of men of influence. Don't misunderstand me, Cass. He's as clever a man as you'll ever know, and he's able. He's not all bluff and bluster, by a long shot. He thinks well of James Wilkinson, it's true, but when he puts his mind to it he's got something to think well of. He's a good soldier, when he wants to be; he thinks in a big way, and just often enough he can pull off something big to make it stick. He's bold and he's got courage, and what's more important he's patient and he studies people and knows how best to get on their good side. He knows how to appeal to men. The flaw in him is that he don't know James Wilkinson too well. He believes every word he says about James Wilkinson. Just don't you start believing him, and you'll be all right."

"Do you think he can be of any service to this country?" Cass asked the question thoughtfully. He put a lot of credence, somehow, in Jeremy's opinion.

"If he's so minded," the little man replied, shrugging. "If his own interests coincide with those of the country, he could, and probably would, do it a world of good. If they don't, don't look for much."

Cass grimaced wryly. "Got an ox by the tail, haven't we?"

"He never fooled you, did he, Cass?"

"No. I knew he intended to make use of me. I figured I could make just as good use of him, since he was coming to the country anyway. If he can make his own fortune here, I might as well let him help make mine." Cass grinned down at the small, slight man crippling along beside him, one arm thrown wide with every step in the need for keeping his balance.

Jeremy's pale blue eyes twinkled and he nodded. "Figured your head was screwed on right."

"What I'm really alarmed about, Jeremy, is that the Spanish will close the Mississippi to our trade now. If they do, it has occurred to me that if the general is engaged in downriver trade himself he might use his influence with the men in the government to help open it again."

"That makes sense."

"That's what I thought, and it's why I wanted in business with him. We've got to keep that river open. I'm obliged to you, Jeremy, for speaking out frankly, though. You've told me some things I needed to know."

The hunchback grinned. "Paid a little on my debt, maybe."

"Paid a lot on it."

They had reached the tavern stable and were standing outside. Cass hooked down his saddle and bridle. "We'll be leaving for my place in the morning, since the general won't be needing me. That suit you?"

"Suits me fine. I'm getting weary of the Falls."

"Don't take long, far as I'm concerned. Have you seen Tattie today?"

Jeremy nodded. "She came down early and ate her breakfast with me. Went to the kitchen, then. Said she was going to help if they'd let her, just to pass the time. Said she wasn't used to being idle."

Cass slid the bit into his horse's mouth and led him outside. "She's got a lot of energy bundled up in that skinny little body of hers, hasn't she? But I'm wondering what her mind is like."

"When we put her to the books you'll know. My opinion is she'll make a good scholar. She's curious about everything. Asks a lot of questions. Anybody that's curious usually learns," he chuckled, "though not always what one expects."

Cass cinched the saddle on the big stallion. "Tell her, will you, that we'll be leaving early tomorrow, just in case I'm held up and don't see her." Putting a foot in the stirrup he swung up into the saddle. "If that girl ever gets over her tempery and wild ways, she might come to a good end."

Jeremy grinned up at him. "Depends on what you call a good end. I'll tell her, Cass. John's got a little chestnut mare out at his place that would make the general a good horse, if he's willing to sell her."

Cass stared down at the hunchback. "How long have you been around the Falls, Jeremy?"

Impudently Jeremy returned his look. "A month, my friend . . . but I've got eyes in my head."

"I believe it."

He swung the stallion around and trotted him across the barn lot. "Put up the gate for me?"

"I'll do it," Jeremy yelled. "Don't pay more than thirty dollars for that mare. She's a mite sway-backed."

Cass laughed and sent the stallion sloshing down the muddy road. He didn't know when he had been so drawn to a man as he was to Jeremy Yardley. He was a little, wispy, sawed-off runt with no illusions about his fellow man, but as Ben Logan would say, he was a good man to tie to.

CHAPTER 9

Late that night, having bought the mare Jeremy recommended, having completed arrangements with Tate to serve as the general's guide, having also completed arrangements for the storage of the general's effects during his travels, Cass led James Wilkinson up the narrow, twisting corner stairs to the chilly loft room that was all the space Billy Tibbles could offer to overnight guests at the tavern. A thin board partition ran down the middle of the room, and on the other side of it Tattie Drake lay, already asleep. Cass set the candle on the window sill and motioned to the straw pallet on the floor. "I regret, sir," he said, "I can't offer you the comfort you made available to me when I was a guest in your home. If your wanderings bring you near my place, however, I shall try to make amends."

"I've slept in worse places than this, Cass," the general laughed, making light of the cold room, the bare rafters, the wide open spaces in the mud chinking, "and I've slept with far worse bed companions. I'm grateful it isn't worse."

"There are no bugs at any rate," Cass told him. "Billy's wife is as clean as possible under the circumstances."

"I wonder," Wilkinson said, looking about, "where my small portmanteau is. My immediate necessities are packed in it."

"By the flue, I think, sir."

The general retrieved it, then clapped his hand to his brow. "My word and honor, Cass, I had completely forgotten. I bring you a letter, sir." He dug it out of the satchel and handed it over, slightly crumpled from being packed among his shirts and small clothes. "I trust a few hours' delay won't make any material difference. It was given me by Azariah Bates."

Cass took the letter over to the candle. The handwriting was unfamiliar. "Will you excuse me while I read it?" he asked perfunctorily, breaking the seal.

"Of course. Which side of this munificent bed of ours are you accustomed to sleeping on?"

Cass grinned at him. "Both, I'm afraid. Take whichever you prefer and hang on like death or I'll roll you off on the floor."

"I'll remember that."

Glancing quickly at the signature of the letter, Rachel Cabot, Cass took a quick breath. He pulled up a stool and held the sheet close to the dim, yellow light. She wrote a free, open hand, easy to read, almost elegant in its fine strokes, unadorned with flourishes, and spaced widely enough that the letters did not overlap. She did not abbreviate, he noticed, as men, writing, so frequently did.

20th, October, 1783
Philadelphia

My dear Major Cartwright:

Your thoughtful Letter has come to hand, by Courtesy of Timothy Martin, and I beg to express my Gratitude for your Consideration. Also I am moved by the Expressions of Sympathy from Mistress Logan. I have a great feeling of kinship with Mistress Logan because my dear Edward lies at rest beside her own dear ones in the Cemetery at St. Asaph's. How I should love to Visit his Grave, Major. I know that I never shall, of course, but I sometimes feel that if I could only place a few small Flowers on the mound that covers the Mortal frame of the Dearest Man who ever lived, I could better cope with my feelings of grief and Solitude.

I rest comfortably, Major Cartwright, in the Knowledge that you will attend to my Affairs in your Country to my best Advantage, and at your Discretion. I do not wish to hurry you in the Matter, of course. I am sure that in your Wisdom you will arrange it as Expeditiously as possible. If, however, that has al-

ready been done, I can make good use of any Funds you may be holding for me. My small Edward's tuition must be Paid at Mr. Lyon's School, and my Father has suffered a recent setback in his Health which has prevented his Attendance upon Business. I should be Grateful, therefore, if you have been able to make any Progress in the matter and can Report to me.

I trust that your personal Affairs proceed to your Liking, and I beg to remain, sir,

Yours most sincerely,
RACHEL CABOT

At the bottom of the page there was a brief, more hastily scribbled footnote, less formal in tone. "I do thank you, Major Cartwright, for advising me so promptly. Deborah is learning to talk. She now has a vocabulary of six words, which I shall not burden you with repeating, but they delight a mother's heart, as you may suspect."

Smilingly, Cass folded the letter. He wished she *had* repeated Deborah's six words. In his mind's eye he could see the mother and child, Rachel bent tenderly over the chubby little girl, softly, clearly saying a word, waiting for the child's voice to make the effort to say it after her. Again he recalled the baby's swift snatch at his hair when he had bowed to her mother, and Rachel's quiet, but firm, admonition. It was an eloquent small picture Rachel had given him in that short footnote. The letter, correct and formal, told him that she had been properly instructed; the footnote was her own warm heart speaking.

He opened the letter again and read it through once more, frowning. Her father was ill — how badly, she did not say, but he could no longer work, so it must be a matter of long standing. She was in need of funds, for Edward's tuition — for food, perhaps? For wood for fires? For warm clothing for herself and the children? There was a stricture in his chest as he thought of Rachel Cabot being in tight circumstances, saving and scrimping on food and fuel, on whatever she might need, and his conscience smote him. He had never been to see William Casey about buying her land. The settlement of John Cameron's party, the pressure of the fall harvest, the buildings needed for the new residents, all the work of the autumn had distracted him so that he had never found the time — but he should have, he thought. He should have made the time. Now, when she needed it, he still had nothing further to report, and worse, no funds to send her.

Lightly he paced the floor, from the window to the flue and back again. The general was already in bed, near the wall, his back turned to the light. He moved. "Something troubling you, Cass? The letter brought bad news?"

"No. But it requires immediate reply. I am going downstairs, sir. I'll try not to disturb you when I return."

"You couldn't," the general told him succinctly. "When I get to sleep it would take an army to waken me."

Borrowing Billy's writing materials Cass composed his reply to the letter. An idea had slowly formed in his mind. He told Rachel Cabot that he had proven the title on her land, that he had found a buyer for it, and that he was sending her the amount the buyer had paid to hold the claim. He told her that he would send the balance by reliable hand as soon as it was collected. He did not lie, except about the title, for he had determined to buy the land himself. She must have funds and have them immediately. He sent her all he had with him, and promised himself he would send a goodly amount when he had in hand the returns from his shipment of goods to New Orleans.

In closing he asked Mistress Cabot to kiss the small Deborah's hand for him, "the very one," he wrote, "which tugged at my hair so mightily," and he said that he would like to hear the six-word vocabulary for himself.

As he finished writing those words he stopped, stared into the low-burning fire, chewed on the end of the quill and thought, why not? Why not go to Philadelphia with the balance of the money? In, say, six weeks or two months the general would be located. He could make up another shipment for New Orleans, perhaps it would be provident to check the general's order for the store. There were many good reasons why a trip to Philadelphia would be profitable. And he could see, he told himself, what her circumstances were truly like.

He said nothing of that in his letter, however. He begged to remain her humble and obedient servant and he thought, as he signed his name, how literally he meant those common words which ended all letters and which so rarely had any meaning whatever.

CHAPTER 10

The big house was crowded now. Looking down the long table at meals, Cass remembered how spacious the house had used to seem, so big that he sometimes felt that he rattled around in it, lonesomely, and how large the big, square table had been with his solitary plate at one end. It was no longer so. Gathered for each meal, now, were Betsey and Nathaniel, who still occupied the spare room, Jeremy, who had bunked temporarily with Mag and Tench, Tattie, to whom Cass had given his own room, moving his effects downstairs into the office, and himself. Sometimes when he looked about him he thought, humorously, that he had fathered a family mighty quickly, and like most fathers he often felt beset by the daily problems and ill prepared for them.

Sheba was very happy these days. She had always been a cheerful woman, given to song and laughter, but she went about nowadays with one of her Methodist rejoicing hymns on her lips most of the time, and with a chuckle for every occurrence. She especially adored Betsey's baby and young James, as the child had been named, was most often to be found tucked into his cradle in a corner of the kitchen, where Sheba entertained him with a tireless monologue in a language only he could understand as she went about her work. There were no more lonely times for her. All day there were people about and things going on.

The men came and went. On bad days they gathered in one end of the storeroom, along with Mag's sow, Queenie, who Jeremy vowed slept under his bed, where they mended harness or boots, made bullets, dressed skins, or worked on the chests Nathaniel and Jeremy were making for their homes.

Jeremy used the dining room for a schoolroom four hours of the day. Cass thought he would never forget the shining look on Melie Cameron's face when he had announced that Jeremy would hold school, and that eventually there would be a regular schoolhouse. If he never did another good thing in his life, he thought, he had made one woman happy. Her children would not be raised up in ignorance. They might grow up on the frontier, and they might have need to be rough and tough along with the times, but they would learn their letters, be able to sign their names, learn a little something of the grace that had been hers in the old home. She and John Cameron came to him one night, John saying, "I don't know what arrangements you have made to pay Master Yardley, Cass, but count us in when the time comes."

Touched by the dignity and generosity of the offer, as yet unable to be met but sincere in its promise, Cass told them, "Master Yardley is to be paid this year with a plot of ground and a house. When the time comes, however, each family with children can contribute to his salary."

The women stayed busy with the housework. There was a lot of mopping up to be done after a bunch of men that brought mud and slush and snow in every time they stepped out, and there was weaving and knitting and cooking and washing and ironing. Cass often saw Tattie in Sheba's kitchen at the ironing board. She was fleshening up a little, he thought, but not much. Her face had lost some of its pointed, peaked look and her cheeks were not quite as pale as they had been. But she was still a tiny thing, unformed, and looking like a child with her narrow shoulders and hips, her flat, unshaped bosom.

Sheba had looked askance at her when Cass brought her in. The whites of her eyes had rolled up and she had muttered to him, "Whut you bringin' po' white trash home wid you fur, Mist' Cashus? Dat 'un is a minx, an' no good'll eber come ob her. Whar you find sich as her, anyways? Whut bizness you got wid a young chile like dat?"

"That one," Cass told her calmly, "is my ward. She is my responsibility, now. She comes from Philadelphia and I knew her there, Sheba. She's come upon hard times lately, but she is *not* poor white trash and I don't want to hear of you mistreating her. Understand," he grew stern, knowing the snobbishness among Negroes about their white people, "she is to be treated as my sister or any other member of the family."

Sheba mumbled.

"What did you say?" Cass was sharp with her.

"I say she doan look lak it."

"I told you she has been caught in hard circumstances. She's been hungry, Sheba, and without proper clothing. She needs feeding up, and see that she has some good, warm clothes to wear."

Because there wasn't a lazy bone in Tattie's body, however, Sheba had come to accept her, though she did not immediately grow fond of her. No one could, Cass had to admit. The girl remained sulky and stubborn, silent around the older women, silent even with Cass. When she did talk, it was to storm out at him over something, as she had done the day they arrived.

Cass had determined that her story should be known only to himself and, of course, to Jeremy. He knew that Jeremy would never breathe a word of it. He wanted her to have a chance, so to the entire settlement she was introduced as his ward, a girl he had known in Philadelphia and whom he had now brought to live in his house. He had debated asking Mercy Bearden or Melie Cameron to make a place for her, but oddly he felt reluctant about placing her with them. He told himself that they already had their homes full, Mercy with her large family of children, Melie with her sister, Nellie, in addition to her own household.

His story was accepted, and if there were whispers about it, as he guessed there were, for Tattie was not too prepossessing either in her thin, broomstick looks or in her makeshift clothing, he did not hear them, for no one, of course, dared mention the matter in his presence. There was a new law in the district for binding out indigent and orphaned children, but he also shrank from making her a bound girl. Let them talk, he told himself. Sheba and

Jeremy and I will make something of her and they can talk out the other sides of their mouths then.

It was Tattie who scoffed at the story. "What you settin' me up better'n I am fur? I ain't ashamed of myself. I ain't never done nothin' to be ashamed of — or not much, anyway — no more'n I had to do to git somethin' to eat an' wear. Ain't no use lyin' about me."

"It isn't lying," he told her. "If you aren't my ward I don't know what you are, and I did know you in Philadelphia. There's no use everyone knowing you've been in prison, and there's no use their knowing how you came into the country. It is no one's business but yours. People will talk, in spite of everything, and some day you might be glad not to have your entire story known."

She had snorted, scornfully. "What you aimin' to try to make outen me? A lady?"

"Yes," he had snapped, his patience gone thin, "if you're going to live in my home that's precisely what I intend to make of you."

"Ain't you never heared," she said, sulkily, "that you can't make a silk purse outen a sow's ear?"

"I can try."

"Anyways," she added, "I never ast to live in yer blasted home."

"Why did you run away from Big Jim and hide behind me, then?"

She had refused to meet his eyes and had been slow to reply. "Well," she said finally, "I never wanted to go with *him*, but," she flung up her head, "there was several I wouldn't of minded goin' with."

"You're free to go when you please," he had told her coldly, a little ashamed of himself but weary of her defiance.

"Mebbe I will," she said, "when I git ready."

He had walked off and left her, afraid that he would end by shaking her until her teeth chattered. She was as provoking a wench as he had ever come across.

From the store at the Falls he had bought goods, muslins and calicoes and even a few silks, and she and Sheba had made several changes of dress for her. Clean, fresh looking in a blue short gown and a striped petticoat, she looked even younger than her years. Her hair, washed and brushed, had turned out to be a pretty, dark brown with enough natural curl in it to make it hang appealingly around her face. Her skin was very fair, slightly freckled across the nose, with tiny blue veins showing at the temples. Her teeth were good and the daily brushing with saleratus and salt which Sheba had imposed on her was gradually whitening them. If only her eyes weren't so everlastingly cloudy and mutinous and her mouth so stubborn and defiant she would have been a nice-looking child, Cass thought. It took considerable faith on his part to hang on to the belief that kindness and time and gentleness would relax the mouth and bring merriness and happiness to the eyes. But he gripped that faith hard and acted upon it as best he could.

She had accepted his room without comment, barely looking at the big walnut bed and chest, the large braided rug which Sheba had made for the floor, the white linen curtains at the windows. He could not tell that it had impressed her in the least. She said nothing, but Sheba told him later that she kept it nice. "She smart, I got to say. She keep her baid straight an' de floor swep' up, an' her things laid away. Doan let no muss or dust collect. She clean wid herself, too. But, I 'clare, Mist' Cashus, she de silentes' chile eber I seed. Doan hardly open her mouf."

"She's had a hard time, Sheba."

He could only guess at the emotions of a fifteen-year-old girl who had scrabbled most of her life for enough to eat and wear, who had gone hungry too often, cold and ragged most of the time. He could imagine how distrustful she might feel that any kindness would last. He knew nothing of a child's pride, hurt, anger, hope or fear. He could not interpret her sullenness in such terms. He could only caution Sheba again and again to treat her kindly and set patience as his own goal.

It was sorely tried again the morning he told her she had to go to school. She boiled over stormily. "I won't!"

"You will. You talk like a guttersnipe."

"An' that's jist what I am. It's good enough fer the likes of me."

"It's not what I intend you to remain."

"Oh, you an' yer intentions. You make me sick. I ain't goin' an' that's the last of it. I got things to do better'n goin' to yer old school. I got to do the ironin' fer Sheba an' help with . . ."

"You've got nothing to do that will keep you from going to school. Sheba can get someone else to do the ironing, or you can do it in the afternoons. You're going," he said firmly, "and *that's* the end of it."

"You'll see," she flung out at him, "you can't make me go!"

"I can and I will — if I have to take a limb to you." Inevitably she had made his own temper rise.

Her chin went up and she clasped her hands behind her back, her green eyes narrowing stubbornly at him. "You wouldn't dast."

"See if I wouldn't. You go to the dining room at eight o'clock in the morning or I'll march you there myself, and that will be a shame before all the other children."

"I ain't no child."

"What are you? A woman grown? Look at you!"

Jeremy had come in in time to hear the last of the quarrel. He eyed them both quietly, poked up the fire a little, then said, "Tattie, I'm cold from being outside so long. Will you make me a cup of tea? Perhaps Mister Cass would like one, too."

Cass flung himself into a chair. "If she's going to make it, she may as well make a pot."

When the girl had left the room Jeremy spoke gently. "Don't you understand why she doesn't want to go to school, Cass?"

"Just more of her stubbornness, I guess. She's the most provoking girl I ever saw."

"It isn't that at all. The child is proud, and whatever she may say, she *is* ashamed of her background. In school she will be the oldest in the group. I doubt if she's ever had a lesson in her life. All the other children, even the least ones, have had some teaching. She suspects that, even if she doesn't know it, and she's afraid they will make fun of her. I strongly suspect they will, too. Put yourself in her place. How would you feel to be starting out to learn your letters, to do the simplest sums, with a group of children much younger than you?"

"Jacob's Noah is her age."

"Yes, and Jacob's Noah can read fairly well, figure a little, and write pretty good."

Cass felt sulky himself. "Well, why didn't she say so? The girl drives me distracted."

"Would you have said so? Ten thousand hot pokers wouldn't make her admit her real reason for not wanting to go to school."

"What do you suggest, then? How is she ever going to learn?"

"Let me work privately with her for a little while. I think if she sees she can learn quickly, and I believe she can — and if she thinks she has caught up with the older ones, she will be happy to go."

"When will you have time to work with her?"

"I'll make the time. In the afternoons, maybe."

"Over the ironing board, no doubt," Cass scoffed.

"That's the one thing she does well, Cass — the ironing. That's why she has taken it over for Sheba. It's the one thing she can do to redeem her feeling of uselessness. And if I have to teach her over the ironing board, I can. It might even be the best way. If her hands are busy at something she feels earns her a little respect, perhaps she can find a little pleasure in busying her mind."

Cass was a little put out that Jeremy understood her so much better than he and he still felt irritated, but he pushed the feeling down determinedly. He was as bad as Tattie if he couldn't control himself.

When she brought the tea, laid out nicely on a tray with a clean cloth, her face flushed from the fire, her lower lip caught between her teeth in her effort to keep from spilling the liquid, he made himself say quietly to her, "Master Yardley will talk to you about the school, Tattie."

She shot a quick glance at Jeremy, who smiled at her, set the tray down and waited, her hands once more clasped behind her back. "Not now, Tattie," Jeremy told her. "If you'll pour the tea, I'll talk with you tonight."

She drew a quick breath at his suggestion that she pour the tea and moved awkwardly. "Can't you pour it, sir?"

"A lady always pours tea for gentlemen, Tattie. Sit down behind the table there, pour Mister Cass a cup, one for me, and then pour one for yourself."

"There ain't but two cups . . . I ain't got the time . . ."

"You can get another cup, and there is plenty of time. I'll take one spoon of sugar and a little cream, please."

Uneasily she drew up a chair behind the small table, looked helplessly at the pot, the cups, the plates, the thin, sliced cake Sheba had provided. Jeremy began to talk to Cass and left her with her dilemma. Amused, Cass watched her from the corner of his eye. Evidently she realized she must perform this unfamiliar task, so she set about it grimly. She arranged the plates, carefully poured the tea, added the cream and sugar, placed a slice of cake on the plate and handed it, with awkwardness but without disaster, to Jeremy. When Jeremy had accepted it, Cass said, "I take sugar, but no cream, Tattie."

With more assurance she prepared his plate and handed it to him. Then she went for another cup. Jeremy glanced humorously at Cass when she piled several spoonfuls of sugar into her cup and diluted the tea with a generous serving of cream. Probably, Cass thought, she has never in her life had enough sweets. Her tea was going to be thick and syrupy, but if she wanted six spoons of sugar, let her have it.

"I'd better have a spoon, Tattie," Jeremy reminded her.

The hot color at her oversight ran up her neck and she hurriedly gave him a spoon, bowl foremost. Without comment Jeremy reached for the handle and Cass saw the simple deed of handing a spoon to a guest become a lesson in good manners for Tattie. He saw it register with her that silver must be handed with the handle toward the guest, saw her reverse the spoon quickly, saw her eyes meet Jeremy's in recognition. He felt as if he himself were receiving a lesson in how to teach. He stirred his tea ruminatingly. "Tattie, I think it would be a nice thing if you could have our tea for us every afternoon — during the cold weather, that is. It warms a person quicker than anything else."

She was not entirely at ease, but she relaxed a little against the stiff chair back. "If you say so."

The two men talked quietly together. Cass noticed that the girl watched them carefully as they handled their cups and the food and that she managed her own in imitation. Each made a point of asking for another cup, and without hesitation she took another cup herself. When neither of them took more cake she looked longingly at the four slices left, but took none either. Cass looked imploringly at Jeremy to suggest she help herself, but Jeremy shook his head. She must learn to control greed, too.

Sheba stuck her head around the door once, her eyes popping, but Cass put up a warning finger and she withdrew silently.

They did not try to draw her into conversation. Instead they talked easily about the work they had been doing that day, things that must be done tomorrow, about the weather and its effects on their plans, about the progress being made and still to be made. She sat quietly, sipping at her tea, listening, and Cass thought that for the first time she was probably beginning to understand something of the life of the settlement, of his plans for it, of what was going on all around her but which might not have made much sense to her. He felt grateful to Jeremy for this thought and wished, a little wistfully, he had had the foresight to think of it himself. It was such a little thing, but it had been a very happy one.

When they stood, finally, Tattie rose uncertainly. It was Cass who told her, "Tea's over," smilingly. "You can take the tray to the kitchen, now, Tattie."

She ducked her head at him and went out with the tray, and Jeremy silently applauded.

From that day, the tea at four o'clock became an institution. Tattie became adept at managing the tray and the first time she made the cake for it Sheba drew Cass aside to whisper it to him. "You brag on that cake, Mist' Cashus. She done made it all by herself." The fat, black face glowed delightedly. "Say she had to hab somethin' extry today — you'all wukkin' hard down in de bottoms an' done all wore out. Tain't nothin' but my ole yaller cake receipt, but she do it by herself."

After the first few afternoons it also became evident that Tattie freshened herself proudly for this new duty of hers. She came to the dining room with her hair brushed and shining, tied in a clean, unrumpled ribbon, a fresh apron over her short gown. How quickly she learned, Cass thought, and felt his own kind of pride in her.

Slowly they drew her into their talk. At first they managed it with occasional questions, which she answered but made no attempt to enlarge upon. Gradually she grew more easy with them, especially with Jeremy, and would volunteer a remark of her own once in awhile. Because they so often came directly from her lessons, she and Jeremy sometimes related to Cass what they had been studying together, and occasionally Jeremy caused her to repeat a lesson entirely for him.

Then as the winter set in in earnest, with the cold creaking the black limbs of the trees about the house, with rain streaking the windows, or snow falling silently and whitely about it, they often listened as Jeremy read to them. Tattie had a way of propping her chin in her hand at such times, her heels hooked on the chair round, her eyes fixed on Jeremy, her whole pose one of complete attention. Once when he was reading from *The Narrative of Captain John Smith* she had let out a gusty breath at a pause in the reading. "Did that there truly happen, Mister Jeremy?"

"Did *that* truly happen, Tattie. 'There' isn't needed."

"Did that truly happen," she obediently repeated.

"Yes, or very nearly the way Captain Smith tells it. There *was* a settlement in Virginia at that time, and while no doubt the good captain embroidered his story to make it more interesting, the basic facts are true."

"Lord," she breathed dreamily, "jist fancy, now — a real Injun princess savin' his life fer 'im."

Helplessly Jeremy laughed and she looked at him, startled, then more self-consciously. "I never said it right, did I? God's name," she burst out, "it's jist like bein' in irons, tryin' to think ever' time you open yer mouth what's proper to say! Ye'd best jist give me over as a bad job, Mister Jeremy."

"You're doing fine, Tattie," he reassured her. "Rome wasn't built in a day."

"What's Rome?"

"A city — a big city in Italy."

"How long did it take to build it?"

Cass laughed, and spoke up. "Longer than it's going to take you to learn to speak the King's English, Tattie."

Surprisingly she laughed with him and it was a joyous thing to hear, a sweet, high, childlike laugh that was full of glee at the idea. "I dunno. My head is awful thick."

Cass reached out an indulgent hand and tugged at a curl. Not until he felt her stiffen did he remember that she did not like to be touched. Hastily he withdrew his hand. "Your head is all right," he said, hurrying a little to cover his error. "Not a thing wrong with it, is there, Jeremy?"

"Not a thing," Jeremy agreed, sucking on his long old clay-bowled pipe. "Not a thing."

When she had gone Cass asked him when he would be putting her in the schoolroom with the other children. "I think not yet for awhile, Cass."

"Why? Isn't she doing well?"

"Extremely well, and that's my principal reason for wishing not to put her in the schoolroom. She is learning better this way. Oddly enough, now, the others would hold her back. She needs a different kind of teaching."

Cass shrugged. "As long as you are willing to take the time."

Toward the middle of January a warm spell of weather set in. Suddenly, with the whole valley frozen, the hard granite skies cleared and a golden, warming sun came out. The ground thawed and became spongy with moisture and the eaves of the house dripped all day. The ice on the river turned rubbery and slushy and the meadows stood in boggy pools of water, the canes swaying greenly above them. In the bright sun the white parchment trunks of the sycamores fringing the river were brassy and gleaming, and all the little streams in the hollows became roaring freshets. The people of the settlement went about in their shirt sleeves, turning their faces gladly to the sun, exclaiming over and over how good it felt, how fine it was to get out of the house without being bundled up, how nice it was to walk on earth that didn't feel like iron under a body's feet. Cass saw Tattie laying her pillows to air on the fence, the wind blowing her skirts about her, her hair lifted and streaming. She waved to him and called, "It's just like spring, ain't it?"

"Don't be deceived," he told her, "this can shift overnight."

"I know, but ain't it fine while it lasts?"

Jeremy let the children have a recess in their studies in the middle of the morning so they could run and play in the sun and he, himself, took to standing sleepily against the side of the house, baking, watching them. Cass grinned seeing the little deformed man standing so one morning, his face tilted, his eyes slitted, his wispy hair tangling in the wind. "Don't catch your death," he warned.

Too lazy to move Jeremy opened one eye wider. "This little angel breeze wouldn't give a baby a chill." He motioned down the valley with his chin. "Company's coming."

"I saw him awhile back." Cass leaned his own long frame against the wall. "Don't recognize him yet."

"Tate."

"Likely. How'd you know?"

"Knew that old mule-faced horse of his."

Cass chuckled. "He rides loose, don't he?"

"Loose as a sack of meal."

Silently then they watched the lone horseman make his way down the road. He rode a winter-shaggy gray horse with an ugly, long face and an ungainly, ambling gait. The man himself sat slouched in the saddle, easy, loose and sloppy. The horse, muddy to his belly, poked along and the man appeared to be asleep. As he neared the gate Cass went to meet him. "You picked good traveling weather, Tate."

"A mite wet," the man admitted, "but it's better'n freezin'."

"Just leave your horse here," Cass told him. "One of the Negroes will see to him. Come inside."

As they went in, Jeremy rang the handbell that called the children back to their books.

Over a tumbler of whisky Tate Beecham told his news to Cass. "The general's seed a mort of the country, an' he's took up more land than you'd expect. Around twelve thousand acres on the Kentucky — 'bout midway betwixt the Falls and Lexington. That was on the sixteenth day of last month. A week after, he taken up eight thousand more nearby. Gives him twenty thousand in that neck of the woods. Then he come on over to the Falls an' done some sashayin' around an' taken up ten thousand close by thar. He made three entries thar. Never made but the two on the Kentucky."

The ginger beard was bristly and luxuriant. The man had a habit of gathering it in his hands and squeezing it, then letting go and brushing it with the back of his hand. As he talked he alternately squeezed and brushed. Above the beard soot and grease were baked into his face and forehead, only a little streaked by the dampness of the last few days.

"Did he go to see any of the men at Danville and Lexington?"

"Seed 'em all, I'd think. Visited a heap with Judge Innes. Seemed to take more to him than the others. But he dressed hisself up real fine an' called on 'em all. I don't recollect that he missed e'er one. Sweet Jesus, Cass, but that man's a popinjay fer clothes, ain't he? Had to git him a pack animal jist to tote his things. He shore admires that uniform of his'n, too. He'd allus put it on when he was aimin' to call on somebody — sword an' all."

Cass laughed. The man had shrewdly staged his show. General James Wilkinson, late of the United States Army, rank, sword and sash, had graciously presented himself to the most influential men in the country. Cass had no doubt that he had charmed most of them. He knew exactly the genial voice, the affable manner, the urbane presence the man would present. It would be difficult to resist him.

"He said to tell you," Tate continued, swigging down the last of his drink, "to meet him in Lexington the twentieth, if you could make it. If not, he said he'd stay on an' wait for ye, an' to come on when ye could."

"He liked Lexington for the store, then?"

"Oh, shore. Ever' man he talked to advised him. He said it would be goin' ag'in the will of the people to situate anywheres else."

"How'd you get along with him?"

Tate grunted. "Got along with him good. Kept my mouth shut an' done what I was hired to do."

"What did you think of him?"

Tate slewed a slant-wise look at him. "Want to know? Or you want me to make you a purty speech about him?"

"I want to know."

"He's nobody's fool, but he's bitin' off considerable of a chaw. He's give his note fer some of that land an' he's mounted up more of a debt than appears to be smart to me. He's a military man, an' no slight intended to *you,* but I don't take to 'em. He's overbearin' an' vain an' in my opinion he's mostly breath an' britches."

"Well," Cass chuckled, "we'll see. You supposed to go back with me?"

"Nope. I'm paid off. Be all right with you if I visit around with Jeremy a spell?"

"You didn't have to ask, did you?"

"No — reckon not. But I don't like to misput nobody."

"Stay on as long as you like. I'll have to leave in the morning, I expect. This is the sixteenth, isn't it?"

"Accordin' to my figgers it is."

"Yes. Well, many thanks, Tate. I'll have to make ready. Go on back to the kitchen and tell Sheba to feed you."

He watched the thin, spindle-shanked man amble down the hall, chuckling. Breath and britches, eh? The general wouldn't think much of Tate's description of him.

CHAPTER 11

Six weeks later, nearing Philadelphia, Cass rode shiveringly through a frozen world and wondered at the compulsion that had made him make another winter crossing of the mountains. Last year he had vowed he never would again, but here he was, with less excuse — a trumped up business trip to disguise his constraint — enduring the discomforts of weather, bad taverns, poor food, and saddle weariness.

There were times, at his most miserable, when he wondered if he was entirely sane. Surely only a madman would have begun this journey on so vague and obscure an impulse. More than once, tempted to turn back, he had told himself that Rachel Cabot was not his responsibility; that she was a grown woman, capable, in all probability, of carrying whatever load fell to her lot; that it was officious of him to worry and that any assistance he might offer, granting she needed it, might very likely be unwelcome. But, in spite of all he told himself, and perhaps because of it, he continued eastward, drawn by the pride in her letter and by the memory of her frail strength. She would endure, he felt certain, any hardship rather than appeal for help, and when he thought of what might befall her he found it intolerable.

Riding in thin sunlight which glittered off the snow and lanced unwarmly through the black limbs of the trees, he thought with satisfaction that he had at least left everything in good shape at home. Abram, eager to go, had been sent to survey Edward Cabot's land on Russell Creek. Jeremy was in the big house to see that things there ran smoothly and the many hands in the settlement would get the spring plowing and planting done when the time came.

Remembering that Tattie had not wanted him to come, he smiled. She had made something of a scene, only a small one, serving their tea on the day before he left. "I don't see why you have to go."

"I've told you, Tattie," he'd said, "a part of my business is the trade with New Orleans. I can only purchase what I need in Philadelphia."

"You've got the tobacco to ship down."

"Tobacco is only a small part of what I trade in."

She had slipped back into her guttersnipe speech. "Ye'll freeze the marrer in yer bones, ridin' all that piece in the winter."

"I'll get cold, certainly. But I'm a seasoned traveler, Tattie. I know how to take care of myself."

She was not happy about the trip, however, and nothing would convince her it was wise. "I jist wish ye wouldn't go. Somethin'll happen . . . jist wait an' see."

"Now, what could happen?" An idea occurring to him he asked her, thoughtfully, "Are you homesick for the place yourself, Tattie?"

"God's britches, no!" she exploded. "I don't ever want to see the damned place again. I don't see why anybody would want to go there."

"Well, I must," he said sensibly. "What shall I bring you? A new bonnet? Some silk for a new dress?"

"Jist bring yerself back," she snapped at him, "all in one piece."

He had laughed cheerfully. "I intend to do that, my dear."

When she had left the room Jeremy had looked at him smilingly. "You know why she is so reluctant to have you go, don't you?"

"Haven't the vaguest idea. Some more of her crankiness, I guess."

"No. She's going to miss you. She's very fond of you, Cass."

"I hope so. She's grateful, I suppose, though I sometimes wonder — she can be so sulky."

"You don't really want her to be grateful do you, Cass?"

"Well, no. What I want is for her to be happy, I suppose."

"I think she is. And everything she does, you know, is done to win your approval."

"Nonsense. She tries much harder to win yours."

Jeremy drew slowly on his pipe. "You're very obtuse, Cass."

But Cass had turned to his papers frowningly. "Jeremy, when Tate returns from surveying Edward Cabot's land I wish you would send him to St. Asaph's and have him file the claim in my name."

"You're going to buy it without seeing it yourself?"

"Yes." Conscious of evasion he had added, "I know that country pretty well." Changing the subject he continued, "If the weather fairs, have Caesar and Leck plow the bottom lands early. See that they put hemp and flax where the corn was grown last year. During the winter, have them work on the bricks for the new house, and help Tench with the mill as much as they can."

"When do you expect to be back?"

"It's hard to tell. By the middle of April, maybe — anyway by the first of May I should think. But I leave everything in your hands, Jeremy. Your judgment is good."

Jeremy had looked at him tenderly. "Your acquaintance with me is very brief to have so much confidence. I assure you, however, it is not misplaced."

"I know it," Cass had laughed, "or I shouldn't be resting it in you, my friend. Not even good companionship would make me risk my affairs with a man I did not trust. I am a close businessman, Jeremy."

"Which is a good thing for all of us who depend on you," Jeremy had replied, hoisting himself awkwardly out of his chair. "A good journey to you, Cass. Keep well."

Lexington was a village so small yet that the stumps of the felled trees still cluttered the main street, and cows and pigs fed upon its grass. Cass found the general enthusiastic and garrulous. A site had been found for the store and a log building begun. A site had also been selected for his home nearby, and he had ordered the building of a good frame house. In the short while he had been in the country he had met and visited every man of importance, had gained the confidence of most of them, had retained the services of Judge Innes as his lawyer, had acquired over twenty thousand acres of land and talked vastly of the future.

The two men spent hours going over the manifest of the cargo of goods for the store. "We had better get some grindstones, a few more kegs of oil, some molasses, some soda and sulphur," Cass had suggested.

With an expansive gesture the general had agreed. "Get what you think we need, my boy."

Cass had grinned. It was sometimes difficult to remember that the general was only two years older than himself. He spoke so often as if he had lived half a hundred years, encompassing most of the experiences of mankind in them; and he looked so much older than he actually was. He had a way of speaking broadly and benevolently, as from the peaks of eminence. Cass did not mind. His first military awe of him had slowly diminished, but he thoroughly enjoyed the man. He was an excellent companion, sociable, genial, affable, with a ready wit and a gift for satire which Cass found delightful. He may be a rogue, he often thought, but he's a damned interesting one.

"When can we open the store?" Wilkinson asked.

"Better ship the goods down on the spring tides," Cass said. "Land them at Limestone and haul overland to the store." He ruminated on dates. "Sometime in May, I should think."

"Good. Good. We shall be ready for the summer season. I shall occupy myself in the meantime with overseeing the building of my house and there are some further travels I wish to make."

Cass nibbled at the end of his quill. "Would it be inconvenient for you, in your travels, to visit the salt furnaces on the Licking?"

"I can make it convenient, Cass."

"I'd like to have several barrels of salt. There's a shortage in New Orleans and I could get a good price for it. Load it on at the Falls with the flour I'll be sending down from Fort Pitt."

"Salt? A shortage in New Orleans?"

"My agent, who has returned from there, informs me we can get at least double the present price. There's plenty of it in this country. It only needs to be shipped down. Ben Logan holds some warrants of mine. Draw on him for funds."

"I'll see to it."

Cass had then been entrusted with letters for the general's wife, his financial backers, friends and associates in Philadelphia. "Tell my dear Ann," he said, "that I am well and in good spirits. Tell her also that I shall certainly come for her by fall."

Thinking of the kind of home Ann Wilkinson had been accustomed to all her life, Cass said, "Will she like this raw, new country do you think?"

The general was not a foolish man. "At first, no, probably. But I flatter myself that where I am, my wife will be happy."

Knowing, having seen the love between them, Cass did not doubt it, though it amused him Jimmy should be so certain.

Arriving in midafternoon of a cold, windy day in the first week of March, Cass went directly to Azariah Bates's tavern. It was always his headquarters when he was in the city. Azariah made him welcome with a good hot rum toddy and an excellent meal and made available to him the room in which he liked to stay.

From its small window under the sloping eave Cass could look out over the adjoining roofs across the town in the direction of Rachel Cabot's home. Down the street to the west the roofs stretched and overlapped, giving way finally to fields and woods. Beyond the sparse, winter-thin trees were the hills, the nearer ones a dark indentation upon the sides of the farther ones, which were paler, lighter blue in color, more gently formed and rounded. He stood and looked for a long time.

Now that he had arrived he felt a strange, discomforting reluctance to see her. Only a short distance away, there at the beginning of the fields, was the home of her parents. As he stood at this window she was going about in those austere rooms, preparing the evening meal perhaps, answering her children who would be somewhere near her, serving her father, it might be, if he was still abed. The late, thin sun would be shining through the windows, on the soft brown hair, perhaps, and on the fair, tranquil face with its tender look for her children. Her slight, slender form would be bending to them, the gentle voice reproving or commending, the warm, small hands touching, caressing. It gave him a turn to realize that he was here finally, within the limits of the same town, the same wind blowing against her window as against his, the same watery sun shining on her roof.

Trying to assess his feeling of reluctance, for the first time he looked squarely at his true purpose in coming, and it jolted him. Even to himself he had made much of bringing her the money for her land. It was in a pouch, waiting to be carried to her. It was hard money, which he had had difficulty in securing because of its scarcity; but he had known only hard money would be of assistance to her. An unfamiliar tightness in his throat, a heat on his skin, told him more than his head did. Feeling shy about even mentioning her name to Jeremy or anyone else he knew, he had trumped up the business trip. But what he had not known until this minute, until these beating, rushing emotions betrayed him, was that he had also trumped up the necessity for bringing her the money. He had told himself that he would see for himself if she was in need. He would see for himself, and do what he could for her, because she was a brave, lonely woman, dealt a cruel blow and left unprotected. Until now, when he stood, his knees weak and his stomach feeling twisted, he had not accepted that necessity underlying a deeper one — simply the unabating need to see her again under whatever circumstances, because he loved her.

Love, he thought despairingly. I love her. It brought him no joy, and shuddering slightly he turned away from the window. No sensible man could hope for her love in return. He had let himself in for a very heavy heart. She was too new a widow. She had loved her husband too devotedly. He ought never to have come. He should have mistrusted the impulse which had compelled him. He should have seen where he was being led and withstood it. But it was done, now.

Putting away the clothing he had brought with him, hanging the coat on a peg in the wall, laying his smallclothes in the chest, he determined he would call, pay his respects, leave the money with her, and take his departure. He would put Rachel Cabot out of his mind, then, forever. The anguished wrench he felt at even the thought told him how difficult it was going to be. He muttered to himself that it would be better to do it and suffer the worst immediately than to prolong it over a period of time, perhaps years. She was the kind of woman, he thought, who might serve her husband's memory for the rest of her life, devoted to the worship of a dead love, happy, in whatever happiness she might feel, in the enshrinement of his youthful image. She would never marry again, he thought, for having been the witness of her devotion, he did not think another man could ever win even its shadow.

Where, he wondered, had his usual practical mind and sensible control of his emotions been? Why had they deserted him? Remembering, he could see all the warnings, which somehow, for some reason, he had misinterpreted. Did a man always, he wondered, fool himself so blindly? Could his reliance upon himself thus be so easily undermined? What was different, for instance, about Rachel Cabot's form or face or speech that he was so drawn to her? Dozens of girls he had known were more attractive. He had danced with them here in this city. He had hunted and breakfasted and dined with them at home, in Albemarle County. He had seen at least twenty that were more beautiful, perhaps more gently reared, more suitable as wives. Why had there been no answering passion in him for a single one of them? Always he had been untouched, enjoying briefly their gaiety, their humor, their beauty, but, with no difficulty, leaving them behind. What was there about this one woman who, he now knew, had lived constantly with him, never leaving his memory, accompanying him in everything he did, since the day he had brought her the news of her husband's death? How was she different?

He could not say. He wondered if any man, actually disinterestedly trying to probe his feelings could ever say. He only knew it was true, and for him, he thought, tragically true.

Deliberately then he put it aside, went down to the taproom and drank until all sensible thoughts fled his mind, until he could retire at midnight, weaving on his feet, barely able to accomplish the stairs, but in a haze of mind which admitted neither sorrow nor grief. He fell, fully clothed, across his bed and slept soddenly.

Dully the next morning he set about his intentions. With great effort of will he dressed and went about his affairs, determinedly putting Rachel Cabot out of his mind. He would, he decided, call on her just before he left the city. He would see to everything else first. Then he would have no recent memories to torment him and he could achieve his purposes in some semblance of peace.

He spent two weeks delivering James Wilkinson's letters, calling on his wife, dining with her in her parents' home, purchasing the additional goods for the store, arranging for their transportation to Fort Pitt, purchasing again a cargo of flour for New Orleans. He kept very busy each day, leaving himself little time for thought, and he renewed his acquaintance with the people who had been kind to him the year before. Still kind, they kept his evenings full of social engagements, so that eventually, when he had finished everything he had been charged with, the time had passed rather more rapidly than he had expected. But there was finally nothing more to be done.

He dressed himself one afternoon, took up the pouch of money, and set out, heavily, for the narrow stone house in the edge of the city.

He saw at once that she was thinner, the rounded face now slimmed until the cheekbones looked high and prominent, the fair skin so pale that it looked almost transparent. There were dark shadows under the eyes which were neither serene nor tranquil, as he remembered first seeing them, being now merely enormous and troubled as he had left them. "Major Cartwright!" she exclaimed, opening the door to him. "What brings thee to Philadelphia?"

She swung the door back and admitted him. The hall was bare of the bench and desk which had occupied it before, and the austere room in which he had sat was cluttered with boxes, the bookshelves empty of their contents, the white curtains no longer hanging, only the table and chairs left as he remembered them. "I must apologize for the disorder in the house," she said. "I have just this morning been packing my father's books."

Confused, Cass looked about, then took, as before, a seat on one of the uncomfortable chairs. "It looks," he said, "as if you were moving, bag and baggage."

"Thee would not have known, of course. My father died two months ago. My mother determined to sell this house and to remove to her brother's . . . to my uncle's . . . to make her home."

"You?" he said quickly.

"I go with her, of course."

The white fichu was just as white and just as fresh, but it sagged a little over the bosom which had been full enough for a child's needs before, and the gray dress which had rounded so sweetly over her hips hung too long and loosely about them now. Cass's heart smote him. "Where does your uncle live?"

"He lives near Fort Pitt. He has a land holding there. He is without a wife, his own having died last year. He offers us a home with him."

"It will be very rough for you there. I know Fort Pitt."

The slim shoulders lifted. "It does not matter. Except for my children . . ." She looked at him, all the sadness of her situation, the worry about her children, the new grief for her father, the old grief for her husband, in the wide, shadowed eyes. "I wish they might be educated, as their father would have wanted . . . would have seen to, had he lived. I grieve to think they cannot have their natural advantages . . ."

"Must you go? Is there no other solution?"

"Sir, my father's debts — it was necessary to sell this house to pay them. There is nothing left . . . or not enough. We are fortunate to be offered a home."

She was very tired, he could see. The weariness sat like a heavy weight on her whole body. There was no sound in the house and he wondered if she were alone here, if she had been doing all the necessary work of packing. He brought out the pouch of money. "It is fortunate that I came before you left," he said, stressing the words a little. "Your land has been sold, as I wrote you, and having to come to Philadelphia on other business I took the liberty of bringing the remainder of the purchase price to you myself."

He handed over the pouch. "I wish it were enough that you need not go to Fort Pitt. It may alleviate your immediate distress, however."

She took the pouch, weighing it in her hand. There was a light of relief in her eyes. "It will mean at least," she said, "that I need not be dependent upon my uncle's generosity for more than shelter and food. My children may have a few books. As best I can, I will teach them. I am grateful to thee, Major, for thy kindness and trouble."

He could not bear to be thanked by her. "Then let me help further," he said, jumping to his feet, waving his hand at the boxes. "Let me help you finish your packing."

She hesitated, then confessed, "The boxes do prove very heavy, sir. Perhaps if thee can help with the . . ."

"Of course they're heavy. Much too heavy for you." He peeled off his coat and laid it across the table.

Hastily she took it up. "I fear the table is dusty, Major. Thy coat will be ruined." She hung it on a peg. "Let me dispose of this pouch." She stood a moment, thinking, biting childishly on her thumb. Cass waited, watching her. She glanced up, then, laughing. "My trunk, of course. It will be safe there."

She hurried from the room and Cass heard her going upstairs. When she returned she set him the task of clearing out the kitchen cupboards, arranging their contents in the barrels and boxes provided for them. He was clumsy and she laughed at him, as she helped, but it was good to hear her laugh. He thought it may have been a long time since there had been much humor in her life.

Late in the afternoon, as the light was beginning to go, she fed them cheese and bread and hot tea on the bare kitchen table. As she laid it out, Cass asked, "Are you here alone? Has your mother gone ahead with the children?"

Slicing the bread, she answered, "My mother has gone. My uncle came when my father died and she returned with him. She was ill. The children are at a neighbor's across the road—where we have been staying since my mother left." Sending him a smile she added, "I could not bear to be parted from them for so long a time."

"Of course not. How do you propose to travel to Fort Pitt?"

"It is arranged. My uncle is sending a wagon for the boxes. We shall go with the wagon." There was a moment of hesitation, then she added, "The furniture is to be sold except for a few pieces my mother wished to keep."

Some intonation of her voice, its hesitancy, perhaps a slight wistfulness, made Cass wonder. "Are there things of your own you wish to keep?"

The hand slicing the bread trembled a little. "There is Edward's desk . . . but my uncle says there will be room for only . . ." She swung around, laying the knife on the cupboard, throwing her head up and shaking it quickly as if willing herself to put this, too, aside, refuse it room to hurt.

Cass felt a dart of anger. Her uncle must be a very unfeeling man to deny her this one small comfort. His fears about her future in such a home, with such a man at the head of it, increased. "Surely there must be room for one small desk."

"He says not. And truly it is not important, Major Cartwright. I need nothing of Edward's to remind me of him. How could I, when I have his children?" She smiled waveringly at him, but he knew the desk meant much to her. Edward Cabot must have sat often at it, reading, studying, planning their future together. She should have it, he decided. "The desk," he said, abruptly, "shall go in one of my wagons. I have a shipment of goods going downriver from Fort Pitt."

The radiance of her face rewarded him. She closed her eyes a moment, then blinked them open, the lashes stuck in small wet triangles. "Thee is a kind man, Major. I tried very hard to tell myself that Edward's desk was not important. But one becomes attached . . . and he had it as a child from his father. It meant much to him."

He kept silent, unable to reply. When she sat and they began to eat, he asked, "When are you expecting your uncle's wagon?"

"It should be here any time. It could arrive tomorrow . . . and most certainly before the week is out."

Cass thought of the rough journey over the mountains, the poor inns and taverns, the cold and wet that was almost certain to be a part of the trip. Slowly a plan began to form in his mind. She and her children should not make that journey in the discomfort of a loaded wagon. "Ma'am," he said, hesitating because he did not know how far her pride would let her go in accepting his help, "I shall be going to Fort Pitt myself next week. My wagons will be leaving Monday. I wish you would consent, for your children's sake, to ride with me more comfortably. I shall be taking a light wagon, covered, and with spring seats, through, for shipment to my home. We shall be traveling in a train so that the proprieties would be observed . . ." he finished a little lamely, thinking it might sound preposterous to her.

She met his look directly, the clear, deep eyes pensive and grave. "Major," she said quietly, "I think thee must be my good guardian. I had a great dread of this journey — not for my own sake, for I am hardy — but for the sake of my children. Deborah suffers easily from a catarrh of the throat and I feared for her on such a journey. I cannot thank thee enough." She added simply, "And I am certain that in thy kindness the proprieties will be strictly observed."

Fiercely he wished he might offer his guardianship permanently. Almost he blurted out that she need not go to this uncle's if she did not wish it. She could, instead, continue down the river with him. But he caught the impulsive words back, with effort, and spooned sugar into the cup of tea she poured for him. "I think you will be comfortable," he said, "as comfortable as is possible on such a journey, at any rate."

"I am certain of it."

He had had no intention, of course, of taking a spring wagon home with him. As always he would have ridden to Fort Pitt on Judah, waiting in comfort here in the city until the wagon train had got over the mountains, knowing that as rapidly as he could travel on horseback he could overtake them in plenty of time to oversee the loading onto the boats. But he could use it, he thought, on the place. A little wryly he knew that even if he had had to abandon it, sell it at a loss, it would have not troubled him. His usual good business sense counted for nothing against the privilege of helping Rachel Cabot.

He felt, also, a lightening of heart, a sense of gladness that he would be with her on the journey. It would take several weeks at best. Each day he would be with her, see her, talk with her, hear her voice. At the moment he did not ask for more.

CHAPTER 12

Each day until her uncle's wagon arrived at the end of the week, Cass rode out to see her and to see if the wagon had come. He felt an untroubled patience during those days, knowing the time of the journey yet lay ahead of them. The days were warm and fine and sunny and he usually took a carriage so that she and the children might enjoy a drive in the country.

When the wagon finally arrived, however, it was a day of miserable rain and wind, and he refused to allow Rachel out of the house. He oversaw its loading and sent the driver to a stable to wait out the storm as well as to wait for his own wagons.

Three days later, with a vagary making sense only to itself, the weather changed and they left Philadelphia on a day so spring-like as to make the senses rise like the sap in the trees. The sky was an enormous blue height over them, the air brisk but warmed by a brilliant sun, and the black trees, making a palisade along the lines of the streams, gleamed like dull metal in the shimmering, intense light.

Cass drove the light wagon himself and the six goods wagons, heavily loaded, followed. With the sun warm on the canvas covering, young Edward and Deborah beside themselves with excitement, tumbling about in the deep straw in the floor of the wagon, with Rachel on the seat beside him, Cass felt his heart swollen inside him with contentment. He had an illusion of being the head of a family which he well knew would end soon, but he set himself to enjoy every hour of the journey.

He was himself so gay, so happy, that Rachel, however she must have felt at leaving her old home, was soon laughing with him, lifting her face to the sun, watching with a pleased look her children playing in the straw. Cass thought she looked less tired, less troubled and worn than she had been. The fairness of her skin was less transparent and there was a fragile trace of coloring in her lips and on her cheeks. He meant, if it were possible, for her to remember this journey with pleasure. For that reason, partly, he had persuaded, with a handsome sum of money, one of the drivers to bring along his wife. She could take the care of the children off Rachel at times, and sluttish though she was, she was at least another female and she provided the strict propriety required.

Knowing the state of the inns along the road he had also provided a supply of food and bedding, intending to make use of the taverns only in foul weather. Rachel and the children could make a comfortable bed in the straw of the wagon, with Hildy, the driver's wife, nearby. At least there was no vermin in the straw.

It was nearly three hundred miles from Philadelphia to Fort Pitt. It took them four weeks to accomplish the distance, and they were subjected to every kind of weather, but for the most part they could count themselves fortunate. March and April being the changeable months they are, they had their due share of rain and wind, but they also had a goodly proportion of fair days when the sun was increasingly warming and bright and the long miles unrolled a pleasant scene and enjoyable hours.

Between Rachel and Cass there slowly grew an easy, trustful companionship, and gradually Cass came to understand that much of the virtue of possessing a wife lay not in the romantic attachment, with its surging emotions and white-hot passions, but in the unspoken certainty of one woman by your side, quiet, calm, steady, unceasingly loyal. That it would be an everlasting comfort and strength he began to discern, as Rachel unhesitatingly sided with him in the small crises which beset them occasionally — such as the time her own driver became quarrelsome under the influence of too much drink; such as the time one of Cass's wagons mired in the deep mud of the mountain road and there was a difference of opinion as to how best to pull it out; such as the time all the drivers wanted to stay over a Sabbath near a tavern and Cass felt they should keep moving along, Sabbath or no. At such times, with her quiet voice and her grave, poised manner, upholding him, she was invaluable, and as his love for her grew, his admiration and appreciation also increased. Her physical strength was slight — she often showed signs of weariness at the end of the day — but her spirit — like Edward's she had maintained — was indomitable. She never complained, either of the roughness of the roads, and they were terrible, of the filth of the taverns when they were compelled to endure them, of the bad weather, of the profanity and uncouthness of the drivers, or of her children's occasional tempers and ructions. She managed a grotesque relationship with Hildy with grace and serenity, and she furnished Cass with a self-esteem he could hardly have done without under the circumstances.

Cass also grew fond of the children. He had that rare ability to get along well with children of any age, largely a simple matter of accepting them rather carelessly as young savages, with few expectations of either good behavior or understanding, and of leaving them as free as possible to pursue their own ends. He made no effort to attract the boy and little girl to him, but because of that perhaps, and because of his easy undemanding friendliness they liked him, pursued him constantly and had recourse to him when they wanted something their mother refused them. He made it an unexceptionable rule to uphold her decision, but seeing the twinkle in his eye occasionally, they never failed to try again.

So they came at last to the final day of the journey. Almost within sight of the grim old fort and both silent, they rode through the woods along the road which General Braddock's redcoats had stained so deeply with their blood in the old war between the French and the English. The scene was somber and, for his part, Cass's feelings were somber, too. Tomorrow he would take Rachel to her uncle's home and in every likelihood he would never see her again. There was so much unreality in it to him that it was like pondering one's own death. It was certain, but yet it would never occur.

As if to emphasize the finality of the day, the sun was overcast with leaden clouds, the dark gray of pigeon wings, the dark woods close beside the road making the heavy atmosphere even more brooding, and Rachel had not spoken since they had eaten their lunch. She sat beside him, her hands folded in the neat, precise way she so often placed them in her lap.

When he glanced at her, however, he saw that she was not looking at the trees, or even at the slow-moving, muscle-rippled backs of the horses. She was staring at her hands, her face, in repose, grave and a little drawn. As certainly as if she had told him he knew that she was afraid of this new situation into which she was going, that she feared and dreaded it and that its nearness was almost overpowering her. To go into the home, even of the dearest, kindest relative required great courage, but increasingly, from a small word here and a tiny, dropped, unconscious hint there, Cass had become certain that Rachel's uncle was a mean, miserly man who begrudged the shelter of his home. Inwardly he raged against the fate which had required it of her, at the same time wryly acknowledging that without it, without Edward Cabot's foolhardiness and all its subsequent results, he would never have known her. Reasonably, he could assure himself that it would have been better had he never known her. Emotionally, he could not imagine his life having been complete without it.

As if they, too, felt the uneasiness of the air, the brooding stillness of the dark woods, the sunk spirits of their masters, the horses plodded slowly along, barely moving the wagons. Edward and Deborah were asleep in the back of the wagon, and for some reason none of the drivers was yelling at his team or cursing the animals or quarreling with his neighbor. There was an almost tangible quality in the silence.

Breathing deeply, lifting his shoulders to rest the tired muscles, Cass turned to Rachel, meaning to say something humorous to relieve the quality of darkness that lay all about them. A small tear had formed in the corner of her eye and as he watched it, it rolled free and ran, without losing its perfect globule shape, down her cheek. In a second he had stopped the team and secured the reins. His hands freed he took hers. "Rachel . . . there is no need of this at all. You are sad because you must live with that old man, here in this wilderness. You need not. I hadn't meant to say it . . . I didn't think there was any use in saying it, but I wish you would come with me to Kentucky . . . you and the children. Let me take care of you. I love you, and as my wife your life need not be hard. Don't go into your uncle's house and waste the rest of it. Please — for your children's sake as well as your own. It will never work out right. You'll only be miserable there, and the children will grow up in despair and unhappiness."

In his urgency the words spilled out and he had no feeling of self-consciousness. Imagining, once, that some day he might be able to tell her he loved her, he had wondered how he could bring himself to utter the words. He had thought he would feel too shy to say them. Caught, now, by concern for her unhappiness he forgot himself entirely and the words tumbled out, sincere, bold, free and simple.

In her misery Rachel stared at him, the tears flooding her face now. She freed one hand to fumble for her handkerchief, and finding it she held it over her eyes, her slim shoulders shaking in long shudders that wracked her whole body. She gripped Cass's hand hard with the other hand. Feeling angry and sore and beset, but not at all helpless, feeling instead fully determined, Cass put his arm about the shaking shoulders. "Cry, if you like, my darling . . . but I am not going to allow you to go into that old man's home. We can be married at the fort, and I shall take you down the river with me."

She shook her head hopelessly from side to side. "No . . . no."

"I will not have you say no," he told her. "It is the only solution. You cannot, if you love young Edward and Deborah, expose them to such a life as they would have there."

Glancing around the canvas cover he saw that the other wagons had drawn up and were patiently waiting for him to go on. He motioned for them to go around him and with curious eyes the drivers slowly pulled their teams up beside, then on past the halted wagon. Hearing them, Rachel straightened, dabbed at her eyes, held her head erect to present a dignified front.

When they had all passed, Cass then resumed his argument.

"You can say, if you like, that Kentucky is a wilderness, too, and I must confess that it is. But at least you would be mistress of your own home, and I am not, whatever else I am, a mean, penny-pinching old man."

"My mother . . ." Rachel faltered.

"Your mother can also come with us."

"No," she was shaking her head, "it won't do, Cass. I cannot have thee burdened with so many of us."

Cass laughed. "My darling, if you only knew how many people I already have under my wing! Neither one nor a dozen more can make the least possible difference. I have told you about my settlement. In addition there are in my house," and he counted them off for her. "You see? Except for a little more crowding until the new house is finished, there can be no inconvenience."

"Thee is building a new home?"

"The bricks are being made at this moment. Ah, Rachel, it can be anything you like. How fortunate that it hasn't been begun. Build it to please yourself. Make it as large or as small as you like. Only say you'll let it be your home."

In spite of herself, Rachel's face had lost some of its look of despair. She caught her lower lip between her small, extremely white teeth. She met Cass's look, listened to his pleading, and he felt she was considering his words. But even as he watched, the face saddened again and she shook her head. "I cannot, Cass. Marry thee? Thee is dear to ask it. I have the greatest affection for thee, but I do not . . . Cass, you must know . . ."

"You do not love me?"

The tears brimmed her eyes again and she dashed them away, her breath catching in her throat. "How can I? When Edward . . ."

He took both of the small hands between his big ones, clasped them tightly. "Rachel, believe me, I do not expect it. I know your feeling for Edward and I don't expect you to love me. If I am not repugnant to you . . . if you can live in the same house with me without . . ."

He did not know what he meant to say. He wanted somehow to reassure her, and yet he did love her, he did want and mean to be her husband. Primarily, though, he wanted now to save her from the humiliation of her uncle's home. He bent his head and kissed her hands. "That will work out, I'm certain. I love you, that is enough. All I own and all I am are at your disposal. I ask you to accept it and let me protect and guard you. I promise you, Rachel, that you will not regret it."

Gently she freed her hands and with one of them touched his head. "Thee is more than kind, Cass. Let me think upon it, will thee?"

"How long?"

"When shall we reach Fort Pitt?"

"Within two hours."

"I shall tell thee when we arrive." She turned, clutched her skirts and clambered over the seat into the straw in the back. "Now, drive on, Cass, and let me think alone."

"Is there any problem because I am not a Quaker?" he asked.

Her laugh was small, but comforting. "Does thee not know that I was read out of Friend's Meeting when I married Edward Cabot? He was not a Quaker, either."

"I see."

"The speech, the dress," she continued, "are but habits, Cass. There is no problem."

He watched her arrange herself on the straw between the two children, settle an arm across young Edward, and his heart sank. She would spend these two hours, he thought, with her arm around the child-image of the man, remembering her husband. She would be beset by those cherished memories, and she would end by refusing to allow another man to enter them. He turned back and picked up the reins, clucked to the team, and did not look back again.

As he drove into the village which constituted the town outside the fort, he wondered that she made no sound and did not join him. Over his shoulder, however, he saw that she had gone to sleep. Even in her sleep, though, she had not released her hold upon her son. His small curly head lay peacefully against her shoulder, and her arm still lay across his body, which was curled against her. Her face looked young and defenseless, smudged under the eyes, the mouth slightly open, her light breath stirring young Edward's hair. It occurred to Cass that he had no idea what her age was. It also occurred to him that nothing mattered less.

The other wagons had waited for him in the edge of the village and he drew up beside them. "Drive to the wharf," he told the men. "I'll join you there later."

Motioning Rachel's wagon to follow him, he drove on to the tavern.

He had turned the team over to a hostler and was thinking he must waken Rachel and the children, when a small man, with a thin, meaching face, bowed shoulders and a concave stomach, walked over to the driver of Rachel's wagon, which had pulled up behind him. "Well, you got here, I see. Took you long enough. Where is my niece and her children?"

The driver motioned to Cass. The man wheeled around, his small, deep-set eyes raking Cass from head to foot. "Who are you, sir?"

Cass told him. "Mrs. Cabot is asleep, as are the children. I shall waken her . . ."

"What is she doing riding with you? I sent a wagon for her."

Cass tightened his lips. Until he knew what Rachel intended doing he could not afford to make this man angry. "I was coming to Fort Pitt myself, and I offered her a place in my wagon. Your own was rather heavily loaded and looked to be uncomfortable for a woman and children."

"It was none of your business . . . far as I can see."

"I made it my business, sir," Cass said, coolly.

"I see you did. Well, wake her up. I've no time to waste."

But Rachel herself, wakened by their voices apparently, appeared. As modestly as possible she crawled over the seat and Cass gave her a hand over the wheel. "Your uncle . . ." he started to say.

Rachel, making no move to join her uncle, stood beside Cass and looked at the man. "How is my mother, sir?" she asked, quietly.

"As well as usual," the man said, shrugging his shoulders. "She still complains of her side. Get your children, Rachel, and let's be off. I have been waiting in the village three days for your arrival. Most inconsiderate of you to waste my time."

There was the sound of crying from the wagon and Rachel whirled around. It was Deborah. She often wailed a few minutes when waking. Cass put out a hand. "I'll get her."

Edward was awake also, lying with his eyes open, one finger stretched up counting the bows under the wagon sheet as Cass had taught him to do. "Four . . . five . . . six . . ." he was saying, not attending to, nor disconcerted by, Debbie's crying. "She's wet," he said, seeing Cass. "When is she going to be big enough to stop wettin' herself? I'm all wet, too."

"She's just a baby, Edward. Come along, now. We're at Fort Pitt."

He brought both children out with him, and seeing her mother Deborah wailed louder and leaned toward her. Rachel took her, but the ignominy of having wet herself again, which Rachel was trying to break her of, had upset her too much to be immediately comforted and she threw back her head and stiffened herself and only wailed the louder. "Sh, sh," Rachel was saying, trying to soothe her, "there, now, Debbie. Cease thy crying."

The old man was looking on, his mouth pinched and disapproving. "Needs a good whacking, I'd think. You've probably spoiled her. She'll have to learn not to cry. I don't like crying children."

Rachel flushed scarlet. "Sir, she is tired . . ."

"Well, tired or not, make her hush. Children at best are a nuisance. When they yell and cry, I can't abide them."

Rachel stiffened and her head came up suddenly. "Sir," she said, her voice gone cold, "our circumstances have considerably altered since we last had conversation. There is no longer any need to burden thee. Major Cartwright has taken us under his protection and we are going with him to his home in Kentucky . . ."

The old man, who had started off, wheeled around. "And none too soon, I expect. Riding with a man clear across Pennsylvania. Likely he's had his fill of you, when it pleased him. You've disgraced yourself, madame."

At the preposterous and contemptuous words, anger swelled so hugely and hotly through Cass that without thinking he strode forward, gathered up the old man's coat front and dangled him at arm's length, shaking him. "You will apologize to your niece for that, sir. And if you were a younger man I should thrash you within an inch of your life!"

"Put me down!" the old man screeched, his scrawny old neck twisting, "put me down! I'll have the law on you!"

Rachel touched Cass's arm. "Cass," she admonished gently, "he cannot harm us now. Let him go."

Disgusted, Cass let the old man drop, watched him shakily arrange his clothing. "What about your mother?" he asked Rachel, testily.

Cass answered for her. "Mrs. Cabot's mother will go with us. I shall have the pleasure of driving out for her as soon as I have her daughter comfortably settled."

"Well, I wash my hands of the whole mess of you. That's what I get for trying to be charitable." The old man marched off stiffly, his bandy legs carrying him quickly, in a scurrying sort of motion, down the street.

"Well!" Cass said, explosively.

Weakly, Rachel began to laugh. "Oh, my dear, my dear. Thee should have seen thy face."

"I could have killed him!"

"I know . . . I know." She leaned her forehead against his arm. "It was the way he spoke of Debbie . . . the children. I couldn't abide having them under his influence. I am so grateful to thee, Cass."

Cass drew her within the circle of his arm and bent his head to touch her cheek. He wished, a little wistfully, that it had not been wholly her deep-rooted mother love which had decided her, but he was too glad she had decided to quarrel with it. Time, he thought, would work in his favor. In time, given his devotion and his entire love, she would forget Edward, or if not forget him, remove him far enough from her life that he, Cass, would have his own place. He caressed the soft hair against his cheek. "We shall be married tomorrow. We shall go for your mother, and then, if the weather is fine, the next day we shall start down the river."

CHAPTER 13

Never had a homecoming been more vexatious.

The difficulties, small frustrations, exasperations, all began even before they embarked from Pittsburgh, when Cass could not obtain a barge for the voyage. He tried as far as Redstone Old Fort, but the season was growing late and they had all been engaged, so he had, apologetically, to make do with a flatboat. Flatboats, as yet, were not being built for comfort. In later river traffic one was to see commodious cabins luxuriously furnished, but in this earlier time the cabins were always makeshift affairs, small, usually leaky, mere shelters thrown up for use in bad weather. The crew of a flatboat usually slept, ate and lived on the open deck.

Rachel's mother, Mary Hewett, was a tiny, frail woman, not at all well. Seeing her, Cass was dubious about the wisdom of her undertaking the voyage at all, but since there seemed to be no alternative, he did what he could to make the flatboat's cabin more comfortable. He had a lean-to hastily thrown up alongside of it, to shelter Mrs. Hewett's big bed. He brought on board several comfortable chairs, new, straw-filled mattresses for the bunk beds, a store of foodstuffs, and a box of books to beguile the tedium of the hours.

Seeing how crowded the women and children were in the tiny cabin, he had proposed that he bunk with the pilot and crew in the half-shelter at the other end of the boat. It added nothing to his sense of esteem that Rachel agreed rather too hastily and, it was impossible not to observe, with something of relief. Since the wedding she had seemed to withdraw into a quiet, almost frightened reserve which, he could not help feeling, had something of regret in it. She had grown more formal, reverting to Major Cartwright when addressing him, and when he returned to the tavern at night during the days he was busy arranging for the journey, she had worn an anxious look as if fearing his attentions to her.

Scrupulously he had avoided making any demands on her, wanting to give her time to become accustomed to the idea of him as her husband, desiring very much that she should learn he had no intentions of forcing himself on her, that he was willing to wait until she herself was ready. But it was impossible not to notice the small wincing movements she made if he impulsively caught her hand, laid his arm about her shoulder, made any intimate or caressing gesture. And it was impossible, he found, not to be a little impatient of it. Her efforts to overcome her reluctance were even more painful to witness. It was as if she told herself, This man is now my husband and though I do not love him I must suffer, for duty's sake, whatever he demands.

Rather gloomily, therefore, and feeling sore-pressed, Cass dumped his effects on the bare boards of the deck alongside the crew's. It was not, he thought, a very adventitious beginning for a wedding journey. It was easy for him to forget that he had persuaded Rachel and that she had made no pretense of returning his love. She might, he thought irritably, at least have allowed him the comfort of sleeping in one of the bunks, instead of agreeing immediately that the cabin was too small and they were too crowded in it.

There were three flatboats in their small flotilla. One was loaded with goods for the general's store in Lexington; one was loaded with goods that Cass was shipping to New Orleans, and they were traveling on the last one. It carried, besides themselves and the crew, Cass's horse, Judah, the new light wagon, and Rachel's slim store of household things.

The general's goods were to be unloaded at the small village of Limestone and carted from there to Lexington. An added exasperation to all the other small, minor irritations of the voyage was that the general was not there when they reached the village and it depended upon Cass to arrange for the overland haul.

It was there that he learned, also, through gossip, that the general had bought up nearly all the salt in the country, was hoarding it and selling it at triple the usual price. More than a little aghast at what his suggestion had set loose in the man, Cass could not help chuckling over his shrewdness. He wondered why he had never thought of it himself and decided that he had yet too much of the neighborliness of the early days in him, when no one had had too much of anything, when it was share and share alike in all things. That was a quality the general lacked, apparently. He thought it a quality many newcomers to the district were going to lack and that the early inhabitants, naïve under necessity, must learn to change their ways in order to meet the changed conditions.

Leaving Limestone, drifting on down the river to the Falls, there had been an Indian scare. Not amounting to much — simply some hideous yelling and firing off of guns which Cass knew meant only a handful of redskins unable to attack but perfectly willing to frighten — it had, however, scared Rachel's mother into a fit of such heart palpitations as to cause her to swoon. Listening to Cass's explanation of the Indians Rachel had not been too badly frightened, but when her mother fainted she had gone white and trembly and Cass realized that Mrs. Hewett was even more seriously ill than he had guessed. Thoughtfully he watched her summon her self-control. Rachel, he decided, would probably face Indians undaunted herself, but where one of her dear ones was concerned her fears turned in on her, and her resolution could be undermined. It made him think anxiously of the future for her in a land where doctors were few. What if one of the children fell ill? What if her mother died?

He was greatly relieved when they finally reached the Falls and he could settle his family in Billy's tavern, the voyage behind them and an approximation of civilization reached. It was raw and crude, but the damp, the constant motion of the flatboat, the hazards of the journey downriver were over. Seeing them as comfortable as possible, already recovering in spirits from the long river trip, he set about completing his shipment for New Orleans. The general had provided him with ten barrels of salt, over which

Cass grinned, wondering how he had spared it; and in a matter of a few hours it was loaded and the flatboat was headed downstream. There was next the business of engaging a wagon and team to haul Rachel's furnishings. That done, having given the women and children a day and night in which to rest, they could leave by the Nashville trace, the family loaded into the light wagon, the heavier one following, for home.

Cass would have liked to see Caesar's old black face waiting for him at the Falls. He felt unreasonably nostalgic for his own people; but there had been no way to let them know, so the homecoming was going to be a complete surprise to all of them.

Rachel tried to be interested in the country they drove through, but she was too concerned for her mother — riding the last weary miles on the straw in the back of the wagon — so that Cass finally gave up pointing out to her any of the well-known landmarks, or any of the, to him, beautiful features of the land. It was all meaningless to her. She was too weary herself, too obsessed now with reaching their destination and making her mother comfortable. In all fairness he realized it had been a difficult journey for her and she could not be expected to share his enthusiasm.

What happened when they arrived was not calculated to contribute either to comfort or to easiness of mind.

Spying him at some distance from the house, Jeremy's sharp eyes evidently identifying him, there had come spilling out from the fenced enclosure a herd of galloping horses and yelling men. Every man in the settlement, Cass thought, grinning, must have saddled a horse immediately and joined the cavalcade. They came at a dead run across the valley, whooping and whipping their horses' flanks with their hats, long hair and beards flying in the wind, buckskins greasy and worn, looking more like savages than civilized men.

Forgetting everything for the moment — Rachel, her mother, the children — feeling a deep, thrilling yearning for them as they came headlong across the valley to meet him, Cass stood suddenly himself, let out a long, echoing yell, beat up the team and sent the wagon flying across the ground. He was not conscious of Rachel clinging, terrified, to the wagon seat, nor of the children's frightened cries, nor of her mother's moan from her bed in the back. It did not occur to him that any, or all of them, might be thinking this yelling mob of wildmen were enemies, or that he was whipping up the team to escape from them; that Rachel, seizing Deborah, had even begun praying. Full of joy at being home again, full of the warm love for his people, free at last of the thousand and one pestiferous demands on him the past few months, full of relief and feeling a wild, fine, surging of pure animal spirits, he reacted automatically and naturally, giving rein to his jubilance and delight. "Yay, Tate!" he yelled, as the ginger beard went flying past, "you still here?"

"Wait till you hear!" Wirt Powell shouted, riding perilously near the off wheel. "Tate's a married man! Settled down!" The last words floated in thin air, for Wirt had passed, whacking his whip enthusiastically against the side of the wagon.

Eagerly Cass identified them as, in his excitement, he continued to stand and beat the horses. There was John Cameron, his sober face lit with a wide grin. There was Nathaniel, black head bent over his horse's mane. There was Jacob Bearden, and old Jeremy. The sight of Jeremy hunched in a saddle, his elbows flapping, made Cass roar with laughter. There was even Tattie, dark hair flying, skirts streaming. They were all shouting at him simultaneously and he yelled his greetings. "Jeremy, you old son-of-a-gun! Hold him, Jere, you'll go ass over teakettle! John! Jacob! Nathaniel, how's the boy? Tattie, who told you you could ride that horse?"

Tattie's happy, high voice came floating toward him. "I can ride her, though, can't I?"

So happy he thought he would burst, Cass shouted at her. "You sure can, honey! You ride fine!"

Flying past the wagon they turned their horses and went thundering by again. Cass flayed the horses, racing them to the fence, whooping and yelling, gone entirely wild in the excitement.

It was only when they drew up at the gate and he turned to Rachel that he saw what he had done and, sobered, knew with a sinking feeling that there was absolutely no way in which he could explain it. There was no doubt she thought they were all barbarians. He stared at her white face, at the big, shadowed eyes, at her arms clutching Deborah so tightly and painfully. Belatedly he thought of Mary Hewett and turned to look at her. She had not swooned again, thank goodness, but she was holding one hand over her heart as if she might, any minute. What a fool he had been, he thought bitterly. What a blind, unthinking, unfeeling, reckless, damned fool he had been. Rachel would never forgive him.

He made no comment, however, save to say, quietly, "We are here."

She had no time to reply, for the women of the house came flocking out, Sheba leading the way, laughing and crying at the same time. "You is back, Mist' Cashus! You is back! We done commence to think you got yo'self kilt up thar in them mountains someplace. Done wonderin' is we ever gonna see you ag'in."

Cass threw himself over the wheel and ran to meet her, grabbed her fat bulk off the ground and hugged and kissed her. "Sure, I'm back. Nothing ever happens to me. Just got delayed a little. Mag, you old witch, you! What have you been doing while I've been gone?"

Mag, her cap as usual over her ear, her dresstail pinned up and her red-striped stockings showing to her knees, clapped him heartily on his back nearly knocking the wind out of him. "Been havin' us a hellacious time, boy! Been breedin' that sow of mine. Had to cover her 'bout six times 'fore she took, but by Gawd when she took, she took! Farrowed last week and we got six of the purtiest pigs you ever laid eyes on. Come on, take a look."

Conscious of Rachel's ears, Cass winced. Lord, Mag had the saltiest tongue!

The men came circling around. "Know what she named 'em, Cass? Tell him, Mag."

"Aw," she hung back, " 'twas Jeremy's notion to name 'em. Me, I'd of just called 'em pigs."

"Go on. Tell him."

Jeremy stood to one side, his eyes twinkling. "You tell him, Jere," Mag said.

"No. They're your pigs, even if they do sleep under my bed."

"They don't neither — well, not ever' night. Just when Queenie takes a notion to come in outen the weather."

Tattie had joined the group, her cheeks flushed, her eyes sparkling, her mouth spread in a wide, happy grin. Cass was delighted to see how much she had grown and filled out. She looked healthy and sturdy, now, with a good color in her face. Even her broomstick arms and legs were beginning to have shape. She giggled. "Jeremy says he's going to move to the stables. Says they won't stink half as bad as Mag's room."

"Ye're just jealous, is all," Mag said flatly, "the hull damn bunch of ye. Just wishin' she wuz yore hawg. Come next winter when them pigs is ready to kill and eat ye'll wish they'd of slept under yore beds. Ain't none of ye that's poked fun goin' to git a bite, neither."

"Gwan," they jeered at her, "tell him their names, Mag."

Reddening a little she named off on her fingers, "Isaiah, Hosea, Jeremiah, Elijah and Ezekiel. Them's the boars, and the last 'un, she's a little runty shoat, he said we ort to call her Jezebel."

The men roared with bawdy laughter, and in spite of his uneasiness — what must Rachel be thinking? — Cass joined them. Jeremy, off to himself, was chuckling quietly. Cass looked at him lovingly, thought how like his dry sense of humor to suggest the prophets of Israel as names for a litter of pigs.

Tate slouched up lazily. "What's this about you getting married?" Cass asked him.

The men laughed bawdily. Tate flushed, but grinned manfully. "I reckon hit's so."

"Who?"

"Well, who's they to marry 'round here," Mag said. "Ever'body else is done stalled 'cept Nellie, ain't they?"

"Well, I'll be damned," Cass said. "You didn't waste any time, did you, Tate?"

"Warn't no profit in wastin' time, way I saw it," Tate confessed, still blushing, still grinning.

Wirt guffawed leeringly. "Done got her bigged, Cass."

Reminded again of Rachel's ears, Cass turned to the wagon. To his amazement, he felt a little shy of telling his people of his own nuptials. He guessed they had been thinking he had brought another family of settlers with him. He could find no way to tell them differently except in blunt plainness. "I have brought a wife home with me, too, and it's time you met her. Rachel, my dear . . ."

But she was not on the wagon seat. Evidently she had got into the back to see to her mother.

A silence so heavy it could be felt, like a burden, settled down over the people. "God's britches," Mag shrieked, then, pulling at her skirts, "whyn't ye tell us, boy?"

Hastily they all arranged themselves politely, the men removing their hats, the women making hurried, sketchy movements toward their skirts and caps.

Cass mounted the wheel. Rachel looked up at him as he stuck his head under the canvas. "Can we get my mother into bed immediately, Major? Her heart is palpitating again."

"Yes, of course." He withdrew. "John — Jacob, take down the tailgate, will you? Mrs. Cartwright's mother is in the back. She is ill and needs to be taken into the house at once. Sheba, get a room ready."

Gravely, but quickly, the two men went to the back of the wagon and the group of people made way for them as they lifted out the mattress of straw and quilts on which the small, fragile woman lay. Sheba, scuttling toward the house, called back, "Which room, Mist' Cashus?"

"My room, Sheba." He completely forgot it had been Tattie's room for some time. "It will be more comfortable for her."

When her mother had been carried in, Rachel collected young Edward and Deborah and Cass handed them down. They waited solemnly, eying the strange people circled around them, until their mother joined them, taking a hand of each. Cass took Rachel's arm. "This is my wife, and these are her children, Edward and Deborah. I know you will make them welcome."

With dignity Rachel looked at them, her enormous eyes taking them in, bending her head slightly as she acknowledged the name of each person presented. She was very tired, Cass could tell, but she was drawing on her last reserve to be gracious, kindly, courteous. She went to each woman and extended her hand. "Mag, I want to see those pigs. Betsey, Major Cartwright has told me of thy young James. I know he is a fine baby. Tattie, I hope we shall be good friends."

Tattie stared at the hand held out to her. She was like something turned to stone, Cass saw, her face, all color gone, set and expressionless, her mouth and nose suddenly looking pinched, her freckles standing out against the pallor of her skin. Unnoticing, Rachel continued to hold out her hand, smiling politely.

Jeremy moved nearer Tattie, but before he could reach her, she abruptly jerked her shoulders up, flung her head back, spat angrily at the small white hand and, whirling and lifting her skirts, fled into the house.

"What the hell . . . ?" Angry and amazed, Cass took a step to follow, compel her to return and apologize. Jeremy took his elbow, held it firmly. He bowed to Rachel.

"Ma'am, we are delighted that Cass has brought a wife home with him. We make you welcome, though it is his home, not ours. In his generosity he has opened it to us. It should be our aim to be equally generous to you and yours."

Cass understood that Jeremy was tiding over the rude episode, by ignoring it lessening its shock; that he was reminding the people of their duty, telling them thus that in spite of their surprise, in spite of what they might think of their leader bringing home a wife with an invalid mother and two small children, he was still their leader — their host, actually, his home theirs only on his sufferance.

Rachel was touched by the sweet courtliness. "Thee is . . . ?"

"He is Jeremy Yardley, Rachel, the schoolmaster here."

"Oh, of course. Major Cartwright has talked much of thee. I shall be so happy to have my small Edward study under thee."

"And I shall be happy to have him. Cass," turning to him, "I think some rearrangement of the house may be necessary. Betsey and Nathaniel have fortunately removed to their own cabin. . . ."

In the end, and because Rachel would not be separated from her children, it was decided that the big room downstairs, in which Cass had been sleeping, would become theirs. With something of satisfaction Cass watched the men move another double bed into the room, their thinking naturally being that Rachel would share Cass's bed and this one would serve for both the children. He saw Rachel turn her eyes from the beds, quickly. He guessed that she would have liked better private quarters for herself and the children. But the house was crowded and he made no move to suggest it. For one thing, he would not shame himself before his people, and for another he decided that Rachel must acknowledge now, publicly if not privately, that he was her husband.

Tattie's clothing was moved across the hall from Mrs. Hewett. No one had seen her since she had fled from the yard, but Sheba reported that she had gone racing through the house like something was after her. "Come thu' de front doah, swished thu' de house lak dey wuz a debbil after her, went runnin' out thu' de back doah. Doan know whut ail de chile. Cryin' lak her heart done broke. Wouldn't tell me nuthin'. Jes' keep on runnin'."

She did not appear for supper, either. "Eatin' wid Mag an' Tench, prob'ly," Sheba said. "She lak to do dat, times."

Her absence was passed off lightly. Cass thought it just as well. He was still angry with the child and he meant to give her a good talking to. It was clear they had all spoiled her and she was getting out of hand. She would have to be brought to the mark. What could possibly have got into the little vixen to make her behave so rudely toward Rachel? The guttersnipe in her was a long way from being rooted out.

The table was almost as full, but the faces were a little different. Betsey and Nathaniel were gone, and in their stead were Rachel, young Edward, and Debbie, with pillows piled on a chair for her.

Sheba, honoring her new mistress, had put on a linen cloth and she had got out the blue willow plates and the heavy, slightly tarnished silver, the lovely luster bowls, all of which Cass's mother had insisted he bring back with him when he had first built his home. In the candlelight the table was very pretty, and Cass saw Rachel's eyes going over it, saw her face reflect her pleasure and her relief. He supposed she must have thought, after such a welcome, that they lived like savages. With some pride he thought that the Hewett household had not held the gracious, beautiful linens and tableware he possessed. From what he had seen of it, he doubted they had leaned much even to the luxury of beauty. He was delighted that Sheba had thought of setting the table so, and it pleased him also that Jeremy put on a fresh shirt and tied a stock about his neck, held Rachel's chair for her elegantly and made small, graceful conversation with her as easily as if they had been at dinner in Philadelphia.

Young Edward and Deborah were nodding before the meal was fairly finished and Rachel excused herself to put them to bed. "I think I shall retire also, Major," she told Cass. She laughed awkwardly. "I feel very weary."

Cass and Jeremy stood. "Of course, my dear. I shall talk a while with Jeremy, if you will excuse me."

She nodded pleasantly but her face went red and, her eyes averted, she told Jeremy goodnight and left the room.

Jeremy watched her straight, slight figure disappear, then seating himself again he turned to face Cass. "Well — you took us all by surprise. You kept this possibility very well hidden from us."

Cass felt ill at ease. "Jere, I took myself by surprise." He related then, how it had come about, confessing at the last, "I don't know how it will work out. I don't know whether she can be happy here in this country or not. She has been gently reared, of course, and it must seem very rude to her."

Jeremy chuckled. "Especially that 'hellacious' welcome today." He lit his pipe. "But, love conquers all, my friend. She will be happy here because she loves you."

Uncomfortably Cass agreed. He had not told Jeremy, naturally, that Rachel did not love him. "Now," he said, turning to other things, "tell me what's been happening."

Jeremy talked and Cass listened. The mill was finished and Mag and Tench would move into it soon. "Next week, probably," Jeremy said. "It's a stout building, Cass, and pretty. Tench knows stonework, there's no doubt about it. It will stand for a century, and the wheel, though big, is so lightly balanced that a trickle of water will turn it."

"Good. Good. Has he ground any corn yet?"

"Been waiting for you. Mag said the first turn should be for you."

Moved, Cass grinned crookedly. "We'll grind tomorrow, then."

Jeremy talked on. Several thousand bricks had been fired and were stacked, ready to begin the building of the new house. Cass nodded. "We'll wait until Rachel decides what kind of house she wants."

The Cherokees had been raiding all spring. Benjamin Logan had begun holding regular muster days again and he had had to call out the militia four times. "Any sign around here?" Cass asked quickly.

"No. But as close as William Casey's. They lost a lot of their stock last month — and one man killed."

Cass shook his head. "They're likely to hit us any time."

"We've kept a good watch — been careful. I was mightily relieved to have Tate here, though, I can tell you."

"I can imagine. I was surprised to find him still here, though."

"Since he's married Nellie he wants to stay on. Wants to buy some land of you."

"I'll be glad to sell to him. He's a good man. What does he intend to do with his other place?"

"Sell it."

"When did they get married?"

Jeremy hunched his bulky shoulder. In the candlelight his eyes were full of humor. "They aren't, actually. I went through a form of ceremony with them, which isn't legal at all I suspect, since I'm not a justice, but I thought it necessary under the circumstances. I had the justification, further, of having once been a quasi-minister of the gospel. Tate didn't, as Wirt is so fond of reminding him, waste any time."

Cass felt a thrust of emotion, an upwelling of love for this gentle, friendly, compassionate man. He laughed. "It's probably as legal as half the other marriages in the country."

"Yes."

Cass stretched his long legs. It was good to be at home, before his own fire, talking with Jeremy again. Given his choice of the whole world he thought, he would pick this place and this man for the best. And now he had added Rachel. No man in his senses, he thought, could ask for more than he now possessed. A home, friends, a wife and, he added wryly, a family already well started.

Sheba stuck her head in the door. "Mist' Cashus, that chile ain't come back yet. Reckon you bettah git out an' hunt? Reckon she done plumb run off?"

Cass was on his feet instantly. "Good Lord! Hasn't she been in the kitchen with you?"

"No, suh, she ain't. I ain't seed her since she come runnin' thu de house. It's gittin' late, too."

More irritated than alarmed, Cass turned to Jeremy. "What's come over the girl? She was in fine spirits when we first got here. Looked so well and happy . . . then she took that sudden dislike of Rachel . . ."

Jeremy gazed at him reflectively, smiled gently and shook his head. The man really did not know, he thought. "Well, I expect she's rather bowled over. Tattie's sort of been the darling of us all, and Rachel is a . . . well, a rival, in a way."

"Humph," Cass snorted, impatiently knocking out his pipe, "she'll have to get over that. There was no excuse for her rudeness to Rachel and I mean to tell her — we'll have to search her out I suppose. You know her better than I. Where would she be likely to go?"

"The stables, I expect. Somewhere near her horse. I didn't think you would mind, so I've been letting her ride that new mare."

"No, of course not." Cass's eyes lit up. "By grannies, the youngster can ride her, too, can't she? She's got a good seat. If she likes to ride, she can have the mare."

"Perhaps if you tell her that, it will make her less unhappy. Cass, be gentle with her. This thing — it hit her pretty hard."

"Jere, you're daft about the girl. Why should it hit her hard? She's got to grow up. Learn such things as manners and behavior."

"She went a long way toward growing up today."

"Well, she didn't go far toward showing any knowledge of manners. There's still a lot of the guttersnipe in Tattie, and that's the end on't. If she behaves herself her home will be no different. Rachel is a gentle woman. She would be thoughtful of Tattie, given an opportunity, and Tattie can be very useful to Rachel."

"You're a blind fool, Cass Cartwright," Jeremy said, but he said it softly, his smile tender and loving.

Cass grunted. "Come on. Let's get started."

They found her where Jeremy had expected her to be, rolled up in a ball in the straw of the stable where the mare was penned. She was asleep, her face still swollen from weeping, one hand curled into a fist against her mouth as if, forcibly, she had tried to hold back her tears. She looked so small and young and defenseless that Cass's anger and impatience drained away. He felt only a deep pity for her. What did he know, after all, of a young girl's feelings? He picked her up gently, shaking his head and saying softly, "You're a very foolish little girl, Tattie. You've given us a bad time."

She wakened a little, snubbed back a hiccup, laid her head trustfully on his shoulder and allowed him to carry her to the house where Sheba took her in charge, clucking scoldingly over her.

Jeremy said goodnight and, feeling his weariness finally creeping over him like an ague, Cass left Tattie to Sheba's care and went to his own room.

His own big bed was empty. Between the two children Rachel lay asleep in the other bed. The prickle of anger was like an irritating rash on his neck. He would not have this! By God, he had been more patient than any man he knew would have been. As dear as she was, as good as she was, Rachel was being too highhanded. She had married him, hadn't she? She certainly knew what being married to a man meant. She could not plead ignorance of the facts of life. She had two children to prove that knowledge. He should have asserted himself in the beginning. He had been too soft, too easy with her.

He strode to the bed, then stopped short. The dark hair was spread over the pillow, her head turned slightly toward the baby. There were dark, shadowed circles under her eyes, and as he watched, she took a deep, sighing breath, moved slightly, but did not waken. He sighed himself and thought, wryly, that this was the second time within an hour that he had approached a sleeping woman in anger, and the second time the anger had drained away in pity. Tattie had looked too young and vulnerable. Rachel looked too weary and worn. He turned away. Let her sleep and rest if she could. It had been a long, hard trip for her. There had been no love to sustain her; she had left the only home she had ever known with all its familiar, cherished ways, and had come, with a stranger, into a strange country. Wait, he told himself, until she has recovered. Wait, and let her become accustomed to the new home. Wait, and maybe she would turn to him.

The next morning he learned that Tattie had refused to move into the room waiting for her, had insisted that Jeremy take it, and had slept in his bed in the lean-to with Mag and Tench. She took her breakfast with them, also, and Sheba said she vowed she would move to the mill with them when they went. Rubbed the wrong way already by Rachel's action the night before, sore from facing the reality of his situation, Cass went, angry again, to find her. "You will *not*," he told her, harshly, when he found her washing up Mag's breakfast dishes, "move in here with Mag and Tench. I will not have it!"

She flung around, the dishrag dripping in her hands. "*You* will not have it? You have nothing to say about it. I will do what I please, Major Cartwright, and if I choose to live with Mag and Tench I will do it. If they are good enough to offer me a home and I choose to accept it, it is none of your business!"

Cass went white. He could have struck her. "It is wholly my business. Have you forgotten that I made myself responsible for you? Have you forgotten — ?"

"I have forgotten nothing," she lashed out at him, drawing herself up proudly. It would have been comical if he had not been so angry. "I know I owe you ten shillings for my passage, and I owe you for my bed and board. I shall pay it back, every penny of it. But I will not be beholding to you for anything further, and I will *not* stay in this house with that mealy-mouthed, white-faced rag of a woman you've brought home as your wife. I will *not*, do you hear me?" She was in such a passion that she was trembling all over.

"By God," Cass said, grabbing her arm suddenly, "you will do as I say, and I won't have you talking about my wife that way! You were impossibly rude to her yesterday. You showed your true colors. You're nothing but a little vixen, a guttersnipe, and you've got too big for your station. If I have to beat you, you're going to behave yourself!"

Before he knew what she was about, she drew back her free arm and slashed him across the face with the wet dishrag. It nearly blinded him. He tried to hold her, but she became a wild thing in his hands, screaming at him, biting, kicking, storming at him in all the vile language she had known all her life, until, awed by her strength and her temper, his own anger cooled and he set himself only the task of keeping her from hurting him or herself. Finally, seeing her quieted a little, he turned her loose. "Very well, Tattie. I don't know what has come over you to make you act this way, but you can do as you please."

She fled from him to the corner of the room and cowered there, her face bent in her hands, her shoulders shaking. Suddenly he felt only affection for her. He followed her, touched her head. "Don't cry so, child. I'm sorry. I was angry. I did not mean to hurt you."

In grief now, rather than anger, she swayed in the corner, her hands wet with her tears. "Why'd you do it? Why? Why'd you wed her?"

He sighed. "Why does any man marry? I love her, Tattie."

The face she lifted to him then was so twisted with anguish, so torn with grief, so wrenched with blind and hurt love that it was impossible to mistake its meaning. With a sinking heart Cass knew what Jeremy had been trying to tell him. It was true, the child did love him. He could have wept for her pain, and he thought there was no way he could tell her that she would outgrow what she felt now; that some time there would be someone for her who would banish every thought of him, and he would be no more than a memory. Tenderly he took her face between his hands. "Tattie, Tattie . . ."

"Don't," she wrenched away, "don't . . ."

"All right. Now stop your tears. If you don't want to stay in the house with us, you need not. If you will be happy with Mag and Tench, of course you may go with them. Perhaps it will be best."

He thought wearily how nothing was turning out as he had planned. First Rachel, now Tattie — a man could sure get himself skewered on the horns of women's feelings. They were unpredictable and full of passions and fears and tears and tempers no man could understand. He had cooked up for himself a fine kettle of fish. "Do what you please, Tattie."

She went with Mag and Tench to the stone mill in the Spout Spring hollow the next week.

CHAPTER 14

Cass opened the letter Tate Beecham had brought him from Benjamin Logan and read it hurriedly. It was to tell him that the trustees of Transylvania Seminary would meet in Danville on November 6 while general court was in session, for the convenience of those members who had business with the court. It urged him to be present. "There is other maters of business to the importince of the country which I wish to take up with the citizens," Ben said, "and I hope for your presense and council." He smiled over Ben's spelling, but he took in his meaning.

Cass was a newly appointed trustee of the school which had had its beginning when the Virginia Assembly, in May of 1780, had set aside eight thousand acres of land in Kentucky County for the purpose of establishing a public school. He had not, of course, attended a meeting of the trustees yet, but he determined immediately to go. When he had accepted the office, he had accepted the duty.

Much had happened, both in the district and in his own settlement, during the summer and early fall. The whole southern section of the country had been constantly harried by the Cherokee and Chickamauga Indians. Though a treaty had been effected with them, it seemed not to make the least bit of difference. Walker Daniel, the promising young attorney general and the proprietor of the village of Danville, had been ambushed and killed in July. A little later a family of nine on the Wilderness Road had been wiped out, and a party of twenty-one badly hurt. Every settlement, including Cass's own, had felt the hand of small, marauding bands. Stealthily, in the night, without any warning, they crept into barn lots, stole horses, killed cattle, set fire to barns and cribs. At Cartwright's Mill, which Cass's settlement was becoming known as, no fire was set and no horses were taken from the stables. Some stock in the outer pastures was lost, but the threat of the next time hung over them constantly. Tate Beecham, with Wirt Powell accompanying him, rode scout through the hills all summer long.

The whispering rumors of separation from Virginia were growing, too, being spoken aloud now. They were encouraged by the efforts the Watauga settlement to the south was making. John Sevier was leading his people to separation from North Carolina. With or without the state's consent, it was said, they were going to separate, set themselves up with their own government. They even had a name chosen. They would become the state of Franklin and once established they would petition for admission to the union. Kentuckians were saying if Watauga can do it, why can't we?

At home there had also been changes during the months. Jeremy had finished his large, one-room cabin and moved into it. He closed the school during the hot months and proposed that it be held in his house when it re-opened; that it be held there until the school building could be erected.

Cass missed his presence at meals and about the house, but Jeremy's big, clean, cool cabin was always open to him and he visited there often. There were times when he did not know what he would have done without the sane, reasonable, objective counsel of the little hunchbacked man. He could go striding in, hot under the collar, vexed almost to the point of apoplexy by the various, and often petty, details of his problems as leader of the settlement, and after an hour's talk, a cool glass of ale, come away rested, eased of his burdens, in a good humor again. Jeremy was exactly the balance he needed, for in his own hotheadedness he might sometimes have made a hasty and ill-considered decision. He occasionally felt that every man in the settlement was a fool and he the biggest one of them all for bringing them there. Jeremy restored his temper.

Tate Beecham had bought a hundred acres at the far end of

the valley, near its broad mouth. With little fuss and bother he had quietly built a double log house, moved Nellie into it in time for her baby, a tiny, dark-haired boy, to be born. Tate was another tower of strength to Cass, in a quite different way from Jeremy. Where Jeremy talked and Cass listened, Tate acted, always wisely, always knowledgeably. The settlement was safer for Tate's presence.

Mag and Tench were gone, of course, from the big house, and with them, Tattie. That was still a sore point with Cass, but he stood by his word. He hadn't the heart to compel the girl to live unhappily and he was convinced, belatedly, that she would have been miserable in Rachel's presence. He saw her only when he had business at the mill or at Tench's blacksmith shop which adjoined it. She had never been near the big house since leaving it. She looked well enough, though Mag said she was off riding the mare Cass had given her too often. "It ain't safe," Mag said, worried, "with all them Injuns raidin' around. I've told her, but it don't do no good."

Cass sought her out then. "Tattie, when you ride, be certain you don't leave the valley. Don't go back into the hills."

Her mouth had been sulky and, as in the early days, a scowl quickly creased her forehead. "I'll ride where I please," she had said, shortly.

"Then I'll take the mare away from you."

She had shot him an angry look. "It would be just like you. You have to have everything your own way, don't you?"

"It's for you own good, Tattie. You've got sense enough to know the hills aren't safe."

"What difference does it make, what happens to me? I'd be good riddance off your hands if the Indians did catch me!"

"Tattie, do you think I am not at all fond of you? Do you really think it does not matter to me what happens to you?"

"I don't think you give a good Goddamn about anyone, except that soft, thee-thou woman you're married to." She had laughed, without humor. "You sure took your ducks to the wrong market, there, Cass."

"That's my own affair."

She had shrugged. "Certainly it is. And it's my own affair where I ride."

She had walked away from him then and his eyes had followed her, distressed. She knew very well he would not take the mare away from her. He had not the heart. He felt too guilty to take the one thing she loved now from her. But what to do with so stubborn a girl?

She was becoming quite a woman, he noticed. Her hips, which had been as straight as a boy's, were rounding, and her waist, more emphasized by the rounded hips, was a very slim, very neat waist. Her hair, a dark, dark chestnut in color, was loose and glossy about her shoulders, and when she turned to take the path to the mill he saw that her breasts were pushing pointedly at the goods of her bodice. That, also, he thought, would be a problem one of these days. Soon she would not be a child and it was inevitable that it would be noticed. He supposed all the single men in the country would be flocking around her before long. It surprised him how much he disliked the idea.

Rachel had asked about Tattie's move to the mill and Cass had turned it off lightly. "She seems to have adopted Mag and Tench as parents."

"But did she not live here before?"

"Of course. But so did Mag and Tench. So did Betsey and Nathaniel."

Rachel had laughed lightly. "Thy family has dwindled since we came, Major. There is left only my mother, the children and me."

"They were all only temporarily under my shelter, Rachel. And my family exactly suits me the way it is."

She had never asked for, and Cass had never ventured, an explanation for Tattie's behavior on the day they had arrived. It was as if a door had been closed, not to be opened again. Cass sometimes thought Rachel must have been so tired, so concerned about her mother, that she had not even noticed it. He was glad enough to let the matter rest there.

His own relationship with Rachel was not the least of his troubles. For a while after their arrival he had allowed her the privacy of her bed with the children to which she had managed to slip away each evening long before his retiring time, so that there was never even the embarrassment of undressing in the same room with him. Then quite calmly one night he had followed her and said, as casually as he could, "I think you should share your husband's bed now, my dear."

She had flushed, bent her head and replied so softly that he could barely hear her, "Yes, of course."

Then with that lift of her head which he had come to know meant she was summoning her courage, she had unhurriedly slipped her dress from her shoulders, undone her cap and hair, braided the dark coils without haste and with, he was sure, clenched teeth, slid into the bed. "Is thee coming now? It is very early."

It was not exactly a plea, but it had sounded wistful and hopeful. Cass had hardened his heart. Having gone this far he could not now retreat. "I'm coming now," he had said.

He had refused to extinguish the candle, but he need not have given it any thought for she had turned on her side so that her back was to him as he undressed. She did not move when he came into the bed — but her flesh was cold when he touched her.

He was certain that she wept, quietly, afterward, and he cursed the ghost of Edward Cabot which haunted even, perhaps especially, his bed.

It kept him from very often making any demands upon her. She was never again reluctant, as if, having determined he was entitled to her body, she would give it as graciously as possible; but it remained a dutiful gift, rather than a joyful one, and too often Cass turned to her in grim determination rather than in any deep, overflowing love and need. It was no way for a husband and wife to live, he knew. It kept him strung up and edgy, but he clung to the hope that in time their life, by its very regularity, its sharing of common problems and burdens, its inevitable intimacy, would become normal, natural, and that slowly the shadowing memory of Edward Cabot would fade. Love, Cass knew, could grow — out of the soil of daily life. He placed all his hope on that knowledge.

During the day, as she went about her work and duties, Rachel was tranquil and placid, calm, serene. Gradually she took over the management of the house and the Negro women. Both Sheba and Molly soon adored her and without lifting her voice she controlled them. The house was beautifully, efficiently and smoothly run and if there were ever any problems Cass was not aware of them. She was a perfect mother, a perfect daughter, a perfect housekeeper. With acid humor Cass reflected that her perfection stopped short only in wifehood.

The other women of the settlement appeared to like her also. At first they had been a little stand-offish. She had queer, Quaker ways; she was from the city; she was educated; she was a lady. They were shy with her for a time, but she was so soft-spoken, so gentle, so helpful, so lacking in proud ways and arrogance that slowly they came to trust her and out of their trust came their genuine liking for her. It was true they never called her Rachel. Miz Cartwright she always was, but they came to her with everything — Betsey, when young James had the summer flux; Nellie Smallwood, with swollen ankles just before her baby was born; Melie Cameron, who could not break her youngest from bed-wetting at night; Sarah Powell, pregnant again, with morning sickness so violent she could not stir until the middle of the day. Rachel drew on her own experiences, her slender store of medical knowledge, her calm good sense, to advise and counsel them all.

She, herself, became pregnant almost immediately. Cass felt like a fool when she told him. Quietly, sensibly, as she did everything else, she told him one night when they were alone, preparing for bed. Shortly after Cass had required her to share his bed she had moved the children to the spare room upstairs. He knew it was because she would not have them in the same room with them, now that they had begun to live together. Wryly, he guessed that in the temple of her own thoughts she probably called it carnal knowledge they had of each other. Whatever it was, she had had Caesar move the other bed and the children now slept across the hall from her mother, safe, Cass thought with sour humor, from the sound of a creaking bed, or the quickened breathing of a man.

The words she used in which to tell him were also sensible and unexcited. "I am going to have a baby, Major. I thought thee would wish to know."

Feeling foolish, feeling guilty — it seemed impossible that a child could have been conceived under the circumstances, sinful somehow — Cass's anger flared up at the formality of her address. "Goddammit," he burst out, "can't you even call me Cass when you tell me you're going to have a baby!"

His profanity must have shocked her, but she gave no sign of it. She was brushing her long, shining hair, her shoulders round, white, bare, beneath it. She turned on the chair. "Why, of course. I did not know thee wished it. My mother always . . ."

"You always said Edward, I notice. It was never Mr. Cabot."

Her chin had lifted. "I shall call thee by thy name henceforth, Cass."

"Not unless you want to," he had said, shortly. "When do you expect the baby?"

"In April."

The brush went stroking through the heavy hair, lifting, lingering, her arm arching roundly to bring it again, at the end of its stroke, to the part at the center of her head. Cass felt a sudden sweeping, almost overwhelming, desire to kneel beside her, bury his head in the soft, gleaming hair. She would suffer it, he knew. She would even, probably, hold his head to her, as if he were young Edward or Deborah needing consolation. She would be gentle, soft and quiet. But he was also certain that would be the only response she would make. Never would she turn to him with the strength and strangling tightness of passion aroused, and that was what he wanted from her — not gentleness or tenderness or even goodness. He wanted her to turn hotly, gladly, with flesh aquiver from wanting him. With an effort of will he put the thought aside. "Do you want this child?"

"A baby is always a sweet thing, Cass."

"That is not what I asked you," he said brusquely. "Do you *want* it?"

"Why does thee ask? What difference can it make? Thee surely knew it might happen . . ." It was as near as she had ever come to accusing him.

He was asking, he realized, only because if she welcomed the child's coming it would make him feel less guilty. And, of course, she was right — what difference could it make? The child was begun, and only death was more inevitable than the birth of a child, once conceived. He shrugged. "You are right — it makes no difference. I should be a little happier about it myself, though, if I thought *you* anticipated it with some happiness."

She had turned around to face him, smiling at him. He knew, by now, all her smiles, her gracious one, her well-mannered one, her public one, and he knew that the sweetness of the smile she turned on him was genuine. She would not allow herself to be unforgiving. "Of course I am happy about it. It is not my nature to be very demonstrative. I cannot go into extravagant fits over anything. But it would be monstrous of me not to love my own child . . ."

"Even if it is mine?" The bitterness still lingered.

"Thee is my husband, of whom I am very fond. Thee seems to think I have no affection for thee . . ."

"I don't know what to think of you, Rachel. I don't even know whether you are happy."

She lifted her brows, questioningly. "But of course I am happy. As happy as it is possible for me to be . . ."

"Without Edward. Isn't that what you mean?"

She returned his look steadily. "Thee knew my feelings, Cass."

He felt ashamed. "All right, my dear. Let's never discuss it again. I had hoped you might come to love me. Perhaps you will. Perhaps you won't. There is no excuse for me. You did warn me. I suppose I ask for the impossible." He hesitated. "I love you so very much, though."

She had come to him quietly, placed her arms about his neck as he had known she would do if at any time he appealed to her. "I could not be more fond of thee, Cass. And I do try, thee knows that. Give me time. Be patient with me."

He accepted it as the best she could do, as enough for the time being, and he did his best to put away from him the greatly different thing he desired of her. For all he knew, he told himself when she had gone to sleep and he lay awake beside her, this was as much as Edward had ever had of her. Perhaps the reason she so cherished him was because he, like her, had been gentle and tender, asking little, demanding nothing. Patience, he told himself — patience.

The board of trustees met, as called, on the sixth day of November. The next evening, taking advantage of the presence of many of the leading citizens at general court and at the meeting of the trustees, Ben Logan asked for a meeting to discuss the situation of the country. Not all these men were citizens of Danville, though some were. Not all were militia men, though many were. They were the leading citizens of the district, from all parts of it, gathered together, by the circumstances, in one place.

In a very parliamentary manner the group elected a chairman who called upon Ben Logan to explain the purpose of the meeting. Ben spoke calmly, clearly, judiciously, to the point. He had learned, he told them, that the southern Indians were joining forces and that they were planning a serious and punishing invasion of the country. He reviewed what all present already knew, that the Cherokees and Chickamaugas were harassing the inhabitants unbearably, and that the citizens had no recourse to retaliation.

Full discussion followed. Cass took little part in the discussion, but he listened interestedly. Nothing new was brought out in it, for the entire country knew what pressed them all. There was only the bitter recognition that they were helpless; that as long as Virginia refused them retaliation they could only defend and suffer. There seemed little alternative. As it grew late and the discussion appeared to be getting nowhere, the meeting was adjourned to meet again the next day. "What do you hope to accomplish, Ben?" Cass asked him, as they sat over a final glass of toddy.

"I don't know that I expect to accomplish anything. Don't know that anything *can* be accomplished. But it seemed to me the people ought to know their perils, ought to face them and decide something. Official action ought somehow to be taken, if nothing more than another petition to Virginia. Not," he added bitterly, "that we haven't already sent them enough." He banged his big fist on the table. "*Something* must be done, Cass. We can't go on losing people and stock. They have got to be made to realize what we are suffering."

"Then if a petition comes out of this meeting, it will be as much as you hope for?"

Ben nodded gravely. "Don't see as much else *can* be done."

But Cass saw the small knots of men huddled in corners of the tavern, talking heatedly together. Some, he knew, were arguing for an immediate expedition against the Indians, and hang Virginia. Even, hang the Continental Congress. They *had* to protect themselves. Isaac Shelby, from Knob Lick, Christopher Greenup, a lawyer right here in Danville, Ebeneezer Brooks, all favored an immediate expedition. In another corner more conservative men were shaking their heads. It could not be done. It would be illegal. It would be rebellion.

"What *about* taking things in our own hands?" Cass asked Ben. "What about mounting an expedition ourselves?"

Ben shook his head. "If it is passed, I will lead it. But it would be against the law."

Cass pondered the question himself. What would they accomplish by an immediate expedition? They would burn a few Indian towns. They would take a few prisoners. For a few months they would scare the Indians into leaving off their raids. The effect would not last long. You had to be ready to do it again and again. But, he thought, more important than that, they would bring down on their heads the wrath of the government. It seemed to him that the time had come to consider realistically the probability of separating from Virginia; but he found he could not go along with the idea of rebellion. It should be done, if it could be done at all, legally, in an orderly fashion, and with the good will of Virginia. Perhaps, he told himself, it was because he was a Virginian that he felt this reluctance to go in the face of law and order. But he felt it, and he thought if it came to a vote the next day he must vote with the more conservative elements in the group.

When they reconvened, Ben had new information for them. The southern Indians had been persuaded to give up the idea of an immediate invasion, but they all knew this meant only a temporary reprieve. The vital question of their own responsibilities remained unchanged. They determined to face it now.

Ebeneezer Brooks, tutor in the home of the official surveyor, Thomas Marshall, seemed to do most of the speaking for those who wanted immediate action. Again and again he was on his feet, impassioned by zeal. More quietly, more deliberately, Caleb Wallace pointed out that no person had the right to call out the militia, or to borrow for public use such things as money, arms, ammunition, food.

Brooks, on his feet again, shouted, "Then let them volunteer! If we cannot call out the militia, we can enlist volunteers who can raise their own funds, direct their own operations, and, when the time comes, submit their own reasons for proceeding against the Indians to the government. We can organize an expedition without calling out the militia."

The voices of caution answered patiently. Any expedition would be irregular and contrary to law . . . to Virginia law.

"In that case, gentlemen," Brooks proposed, "I question whether the time has not come for us to demand a separate government. I submit that this convention of citizens should take steps to consider it."

A buzz of conversation rose and Isaac Shelby had to bang upon the table to restore order. When the room was quiet again, Ben Logan rose to his feet and moved that a petition giving the true state of affairs be offered to the Virginia assembly.

There was now a feeling of confusion and it was proposed that this convention, not being duly elected, had no right either to petition or to consider. Not being official, it could only discuss. Firebrand to the end, Brooks shouted, "Then let us elect a convention with authority."

And it was so decided.

"Now see what you've done," Cass told Ben Logan when the meeting was adjourned, grinning at him.

Ben scratched his head. "Lord, I never thought to commence something that would end in separation." He peered at Cass. "How do you feel about it?"

"I'm for it," Cass said shortly. "If it's done legally and in order. I think the time is ripe."

"Maybe so. Maybe so. I'd hate to see us go off half-cocked, though."

"That's what we'll have to guard against."

Ben walked off, shaking his head and watching him Cass thought how strange it would be if the instrument of fate should be this honorable, unpretentious, almost illiterate man.

Delegates to be elected by militia companies were to convene on December 27, empowered to consider the steps to be taken "to devise, if possible, some means of preserving the country from that immediate destruction which seemed then impending."

Though delegates to the next convention were to be elected by militia companies, this did not mean that only members of the militia could vote or that only members were eligible for election. The country was organized by militia companies. They were not only the military organization but the civil organization covering definite geographical areas. Taxes were collected by militia companies as units; minor civil officials, like constables, were appointed by the same units. It was the simplest, indeed about the only way, that delegates could be elected.

From Danville, Cass went to Lexington. James Wilkinson had gone east during the summer to bring back his family and they had arrived a short time before. Cass felt it only the decent thing to do to pay his respects.

He found them not quite settled yet in the new dwelling, Ann Wilkinson still overcome by the bleakness of her surroundings. "It is so raw and ugly, Major Cartwright. If only the pigs did not run loose in the street. If the people were only a little more gentle . . ."

"My dear," James interrupted, "our home will be a gathering place for those of gentle rearing in time. You will see. Bear with the village for a time. We shall make our own gentleness around us."

Ann Wilkinson laughed. "Of course, Jimmy. But you are always gone, you know. Shall I make it alone? Look at my feet, Major! Never did I expect to see such clods of shoes on them.

But the mud is so deep . . ." She threw up her hands and left the room, one of the small boys calling for her.

"Is she going to be happy here, Jim?"

The general lifted his shoulders. "When this first shock at the rudeness wears off, I think so." He shifted the conversation abruptly. "How did that meeting go, in Danville? I wish I had been notified."

"It was a hasty thing, called by Ben. No one was notified. He merely asked those in Danville at the time to come together and talk a few things over. But an elected convention, with power to act, is to convene in December."

"What did you discuss?"

The general paced the floor. "So the group was divided in their thinking? What do you think of the chances of separation?"

"I think it has to come. It isn't only the matter of protecting ourselves. This is a big area of land west of the mountains, and it is rapidly becoming populated. We are too far from Richmond for them to be aware of any of our needs, civil as well as military. As we grow those needs increase and we ought to become a separate government and a member of the federal union in our own right. I was not for mounting an immediate expedition because I would like to see us separate from Virginia legally and in good order. It is the only way we can be admitted into the union. Look at the Watauga settlements. Congress is never going to recognize the state of Franklin, because they have illegally separated. We must use care, for we do not want that to happen to us."

James Wilkinson poured a glass of Madeira, handed it to Cass, poured himself a glass and thoughtfully sipped at it. "Cass, I have just come from Philadelphia. The Spanish are going to close the river. It's the talk of the whole east. It's only a matter of *when* they decide to do it. And the fools in Congress will sit idly there and allow it to be closed, allow it to remain closed. Indeed, it is to their interests to have it closed. In that way they will accomplish, simply by their neglect, what the Indians have failed to accomplish. With the river closed, emigration will dwindle away, for people will not be attracted to a country with no market . . ."

Cass laughed. "Oh, now, James. There aren't six men in the country who trade downriver."

The general leaned forward. "But there *will* be. If the river can be kept open men of means and prominence will be attracted to the country."

"And," Cass countered good-naturedly, "you can sell them parcels of all that land you've been buying up."

"Certainly," the general snapped, shortly. "Why else does a man speculate? Another consideration is that manufactures will be established here in time. They will *not* be established if the river is closed. What I'm wondering, Cass, is if this country should become a member of the union. With the east begrudging us the emigration, afraid we shall become a power that will oppose their interests, concerned as they are only in shipping and trade on the coast, why shouldn't this country take its fate in its own hands? If, as an independent government, we treated with Spain ourselves, we might gain the day."

Cass reflected on what Wilkinson had said. There was much to be said for it. No man, taking serious consideration of the state of affairs, could help having a growing feeling that the east was alarmed by the phenomenal and rapid growth of this western country; that they saw it as a deadly competition of their own welfare; that willingly they would have kept it swaddled and helpless. And yet . . . he saw the lean, intelligent face of Thomas Jefferson, heard the mild, unimpassioned voice — "You *are* a drain on the union, and it is a struggling union." There was the other side. "That would be rebellion, James," he said.

The general's eyes blazed. "Did not the colonies rebel against George III?"

It was, Cass thought, always a matter of self-interest, among nations as among men. Dig deep enough and the same motive was always there. We, he thought, on the western waters, because our fortunes are involved here must always be hammering away for our own good and interest. They in the east, because their fortunes are involved there, must look askance at us and ask themselves, how much trade will that country drain away from the seaboard? But only two years before they had been united in a common effort — the rebellion against Britain. "I do not think we want rebellion, James. We must be patient a little longer."

"Do you intend to sit here and do nothing if the river is closed?"

"I intend to vote for separation from Virginia in a legal and orderly fashion, and I intend, if that happens, to use all the influence I have to petition Congress for admission to the union. If the river closes, I intend likewise to petition Congress for its opening. We are Americans, James. We cannot afford to go off, as Ben Logan says, half-cocked."

The general muttered, "It might be better if we did." He gazed at his hands, peaked into a steeple, and continued thoughtfully. "Have you forgotten the geography of this land, Cass? It is an empire unto itself. The mountains are the perfect dividing line, and the river is the perfect opening. There are many natural reasons why it could exist separate and independent of the east. The empire of the west," he murmured softly.

"Are you thinking of becoming the Washington of the west, James?" Cass asked, chuckling.

The general laughed also. "There have been many less worthy aspirations, my friend."

"There have been many more worthy, too. It proved to be the road to glory for General Washington, but it might prove to be the road to ruin for you. Now, tell me, how is the business?"

"Going along splendidly, Cass. We have had a good business all summer, though it is largely, I must own, due to my connections in the country. I have ridden far and wide to bring in trade and stimulate it. We can't," he added cautiously, "pay you anything on your investment yet, but you have nothing to fear."

"I did not think it. I asked only out of interest."

"I know. Are you realizing any profits from your settlement yet?"

Ruefully Cass owned that they were slow. "But I have good men on the land and we are making a start."

"You need a town, Cass. Township lots would make you more, and make it faster."

"Oh, we have a town mapped, but in that part of the country a town will grow very slowly. I don't expect it to pick up until that section is partitioned into a county. Perhaps we can get the county seat, then, and we'll be well situated."

"You are too far from the center of population, Cass. I always thought so. I am interested in a township myself, but you may be sure that when I select a location it will be more conveniently located."

"You're going to get a lot of irons in the fire, James."

The general laughed. "Well, my boy, the more irons the better. If you can't turn a profit one way you can always turn it another then." He changed the subject. "Is your wife well?"

"Reasonably. She is expecting and has some discomfort."

James Wilkinson's eyes twinkled as they met Cass's. "Fruitful so soon! Good man, Cass." He quenched the twinkle immediately, seeing no response from Cass. "A man needs a family, my boy. You will see. A son or two adds luster to a man's life."

"I expect so."

He had time, riding home, to think over many things. The store was doing well, it was true. There was no lack of trade, but talking with Hugh Shiell, the easterner whom James had recently persuaded to invest heavily with him, Cass had learned that all the profits were immediately needed for other projects in which Wilkinson was interested. "What is he doing with so much money?" Cass asked.

"Paying notes — buying more land." Shiell spread his hands deprecatingly. "I sometimes think the man has gone land mad. He is talking now of land in the Floridas, of land in Louisiana. He thinks he can build an empire with enough land."

"He lives well, Hugh."

"Aye, he will never pull in his belt where his living is concerned. The best is none too good for the Wilkinsons; and he says it is necessary for him to make a good appearance. He robs Peter to pay Paul, but a little of it always sticks to Jimmy's pockets. The trade in the store is good, Major, but it will never realize you a penny of profit because James is always in the fire and must have the cash. I have paid, personally, for the last two shipments of goods, and I have advanced him a considerable sum to pay on his debts. I cannot long continue to do that, sir, without some return."

"Then don't. Tell James to hand over the cash from the store."

"I wish it were that easy," Hugh Shiell sighed.

"You will have to protect yourself some way, man. Why don't you cut your losses and get out?"

"What do you intend to do?"

"Oh, I'll string along a bit longer. I am not at hand for the general to get at, you see."

"We have both, Major, been caught with our trousers down."

Cass laughed. "Well, we were grown men, sir. It was our privilege."

Wilkinson, Cass thought, was an imponderable. He was shrewd enough to dream of empire, and feckless enough to spend himself into bankruptcy. If the river closed, he thought, James might become dangerous.

If the river closed? The river *was* closed. Cass found his agent waiting for him when he got home. "They seized your shipment, Major. Impounded it. Said they were closing navigation to all Americans until the United States made a new treaty with the crown. Said the old treaty with Britain wasn't good. Threw me in the calaboose for a week. I didn't bring you back a farthing for that cargo, Major — not even a receipt."

Thoughtfully, Cass took stock of his losses. He had always depended upon his shipments downriver for the bulk of his money. This heavy loss on one cargo hurt him, but not irretrievably. He was not, thank goodness, overextended. It meant less hard money in hand, but it did not threaten any of his real security.

Now that the blow had fallen he found that he had been expecting it for so long that what he felt was more a sense of relief than anything else. And a sense of excitement. Now, he thought, surely *now* the Congress would immediately begin proceedings with Spain. Now they could all, he, James Wilkinson, the others, bring to bear the pressure of an accomplished fact instead of a threatening possibility and surely they would get action. He must, he thought, see that James wrote every man of influence he knew, hammer consistently away, chip at all the edges of Congress, for even if it meant war with Spain, surely the Congress would not tamely submit to the closing of the river.

CHAPTER 15

But it did.

For two years the Congress did nothing but talk while the river remained closed. John Jay, Secretary of Foreign Affairs, said it was impossible under the Articles of Confederation for major treaties with foreign powers to be made and he became vehement in his urging of a new federal constitution.

Kentuckians, however, could see nothing but the inaction of the Congress.

They had moved, through two more conventions, toward separate statehood, and if that movement had begun in indignation because they could not defend themselves against marauding Indians, it had proceeded in even greater indignation against the closing of the river. So inflamed had the country become that navigation of the Mississippi had now become the primary issue, and men who had counseled patience, who had tried with reasonable, cool heads to steer the country's way through the troubled waters, were now divided in their judgments and uncertain in their own minds. Cass himself felt torn in two. It was one thing to have patience; it was another thing to stand still and watch the country's prospects dwindle.

A clique of men, known largely as the "Danville Club" had rallied behind the cry of "separation immediately," whether legal or illegal. They talked of the stifling of manufacturing prospects; of the loss of emigration; of the loss of trade profits down the river. They were all men of prominence and most of them men of means and large land holdings. James Wilkinson was one of the most vocal of the group. Others were John Brown, who had come to the country in 1783, who owned much land, was a graduate of Princeton and had a brilliant legal mind; Harry Innes, the attorney general for Kentucky district; Caleb Wallace, whose patience had worn thin; Judge George Muter, Isaac Shelby, Christopher Greenup, Benjamin Sebastian, Richard Anderson, Alexander Bullitt and others. It was a powerful group. Among them were many men Cass liked and trusted. If he was troubled occasionally by the knowledge that these men represented powerful and personal interests more truly than they did the country at large, he also recognized that leaders must usually come from such interests. They were men of fine intellect for the most part; men with an understanding of politics and diplomacy. It was very difficult, Cass felt, for any honorable man, and he felt himself and most of the others to be that, to determine what was right to do.

He stood at the window of his room in the tavern at Danville and looked out on the hard-frozen snow. It was a bright, cold day, the sun brilliant on the white-covered ground, the smoke of the adjacent chimneys climbing, cold-thinned, in a slow spiral. It was December again, and two years, almost exactly, since that first called convention of 1784 had met in this same village.

Cass watched a small, slate-colored bird with a thin breast pick nervously at the crusted surface of the snow and wondered, idly, why any bird should remain in this frozen land during the winter. He himself was full of aches and chills and the sight of the thin-feathered bird, the snow, the icicles hanging from the eaves and fences, the smoky breath of people in the square, made his nerves tighten and a shudder creep from one cold vertebra to another down his spine. In addition he felt uneasy and sore-pressed. He was waiting for James Wilkinson.

Cass was not any longer an active partner in the store at Lexington. A year before when Hugh Shiell had got wet crossing a flooded stream, had subsequently been taken with lung fever and died, James had turned to Cass for help. Shiell had not terminated his partnership with the general as he had threatened, but had continued to loan him money, to carry the burden of the store, and though the two men quarreled often, he had never closed in on James to collect. Now he was dead. James owed vast sums of money to his estate, and to many others if the truth was known, and he asked Cass to advance him two thousand pounds. Cass could not. "James, with tobacco in storage for two years, with the river closed to trade, where do you think I would get that much money?"

"Can't you raise it on your lands, Cass? I am desperate. If you don't help me I'll have to go to the money lenders."

Cass had thought wearily that it was the most futile thing in the world to help James Wilkinson. To advance him money was like throwing corn to geese. He gobbled it up and only asked for more. He had absolutely no head for finances. He bought land wildly on speculation, then had to sell to pay off his debts. He was constantly in financial difficulties.

Strangely enough, however, the precariousness of his financial situation had never hurt him in public opinion. Cass thought probably very few people knew of it. Garrulous usually, the general was a man who could be very reticent about some things. He lived like a man of great wealth. He maintained a gracious home, he spent lavishly, entertained constantly, was ingratiatingly charming to influential men, and in the brief three years of his residence had easily become the most popular man in the country. Everyone liked him, with the possible exception of Humphrey Marshall whom he had defeated last year as a delegate to the convention; everyone thought him brilliant and clever; everyone trusted his political judgments.

"Can't Ann's people help?" Cass had asked.

The general had shrugged. "A drop in the bucket."

"I'm afraid then, James, you'll have to sell some more of your own lands. I simply haven't the money, nor can I raise it."

They did not quarrel, however. Feeling he should protect himself Cass wrote off his investment in the store and notified James he would not be responsible for any debts incurred in its name. The two men remained friends, and in some ways good friends. There was no one Cass enjoyed more than James Wilkinson. He had wit, humor, a gay and easy conversation, and one could always count on a lively evening spent with him. There was the troubling undercurrent of vague distrust; but more often than not Cass put it aside. James's ideas too often coincided with those held by every other man in the district. Give the man credit, he told himself, for what is due him. And due him was a good deal of respect for shrewd reasoning. If he was looking out for James Wilkinson it was no more than he, Cass Cartwright, was doing, or than John Brown, Harry Innes, Benjamin Sebastian, Alexander Bullitt and all the others were doing. Always one had to come back to the motive of self-interest, and no man was absolved of its guilt.

He turned from the window and picked up the letter from Wilkinson. It was written under date of December 12, 1786.

Clark [it began without preamble] is playing Hell. He is raising a Regiment of his own, and has 140 men stationed at Opost, already now under the command of Dalton. Seized on a Spanish boat with 20,000 Dollars, or rather seized three stores at Opost worth this sum, and the Boat which brought them up. J. R. Jones, Commissary General, gets a large share of the plunder, and has his family at Opost. Platt comes in for snacks. He brought the Baggage and a thousand pounds of small furs to the Falls the day I left. Plunder-all (here a word was illegible) means to go to Congress to get the Regiment put upon the establishment. He is the 3rd Captain. The taxes, he tells his associates, are necessary to bear his expenses; but he don't return. I laid a plan to get the whole seized and secured for the owners. Bullitt and Anderson will execute it. Clark is eternally drunk, and yet full of design. I told him he would be hanged. He laughed and said he could take refuge among the Indians. A stroke is meditated against St. Louis and Natchez.

It was a troubling letter. Harry Innes had handed it to him when he arrived in Danville, without saying to whom it had been addressed. It did not greatly matter. Cass felt an affection for General Clark, which was natural, since he had served under him a long time. But the whole country knew he had become intemperate. He was just returned from the expedition to Vincennes, the Opost of the letter. Evidently Wilkinson had run upon some treasonable machinations. If George Rogers Clark had actually seized Spanish property in Vincennes, if he was actually raising an expedition against St. Louis and Natchez, it was serious and the country could not ignore it. He hoped, devoutly, that it was not so. "What do you make of it, Harry?" he had asked Innes.

Innes had shrugged. "It looks bad to me. James asks us to meet with him when he returns."

The delegates to the fourth convention had been daily meeting in Danville since September, three months now. They met only to keep the convention alive, because no business could be transacted without a quorum, and no quorum could be obtained because most of the delegates were off fighting Indians. They were beginning, like Cass, to straggle in now and it was hoped the convention could obtain the quorum soon.

After two conventions in which the matter of separation from Virginia and statehood had been considered, weighed carefully, the third convention, meeting in August of the year before, with full authority to act, had finally resolved to send a petition to the Virginia assembly requesting separation. No one, Cass thought, could call them hasty or ill advised. Patiently they had taken their time.

The petition had been duly presented and it had been accepted in a spirit of good will and gracious assent by Virginia. An enabling act had been subsequently passed. Certain conditions, however, were imposed. "Kentucky," the assembly said, "must become a member of the Confederation at the same time that she becomes a separate state." Furthermore, the assembly instructed Kentucky to call another convention to consider the terms of Virginia's proposals. If the convention adopted the terms, it was then empowered to name a day after September 1, 1787, on which Virginia's authority over Kentucky should come to an end. There was the additional stipulation that before June 1, 1787, Congress must have agreed to the separation and must have consented to the admission of the new state to the union. Remembering Thomas Jefferson's quiet statement that Virginia must take care that Kentucky came into the union, Cass felt the assembly had been wise.

Everyone felt relieved and felt, further, that it was only a matter of procedure now. Delegates were elected that summer and the date for the convention set for September. No one could foresee that it would be one of the worst summers in all the history of Kentucky for Indian incursions; nor that the situation, finally becoming insupportable, would demand that expeditions be mounted and that practically every fighting man in the country would be away when the time of the convention came.

In desperation, the few delegates not on the expeditions sent off a message asking the assembly for more time and stayed hopefully on in Danville, helpless, watching time run out. Matters had taken a most unexpected turn and the convention which had been expected merely to set the date for Virginia's authority to end, had deteriorated into a daily meeting for roll call and a weary querying of every traveler, "Have the troops returned?"

It was early in the summer that the decision had been taken to mount the expeditions. Kentucky had reached the boiling point over the continued Indian forays and over their inability to retaliate. It was finally agreed by even the most conservative leaders that volunteers must be raised and an invasion of the Indian towns planned. The people were breaking out into small but vicious raids on their own responsibility, and there was too much possibility that Indians innocent of injurious intent would be the victims. To people fired by indignation, angry beyond control, any Indian was a bad Indian. They shot first, then looked to see if he was one of a tribe at peace with them. It did not much matter to them in the long run. If a tribe was keeping the peace this month, it would be breaking it next. There was no keeping a permanent peace with them; they were as slippery as eels and they signed any kind of treaty in order to get the gifts the government gave them, not caring or knowing what the treaty meant, with no intention, in the event, of keeping it. That's what Kentuckians thought of the redskins, and many of them said, and said it often, that the only good Indian was a dead Indian.

In the spring and summer of this year the Indian situation grew steadily worse. Most of the raids seemed to come from the Wabash region and the area around the Falls was very hard hit. General Clark estimated there were fifteen hundred warriors in the Wabash tribes and he believed they were being encouraged by the British traders still in possession of the northern forts. Enough, however, came from the Shawnee towns to convince the Kentuckians that the last treaty, concluded only the year before by the Commission of Indian Affairs, George Rogers Clark, Richard Parsons and Samuel Butler members, was being ignored. "They'll never keep a treaty," the people said, "the government is just wasting time and money. The only way to treat with Indians is with gunfire. Call out the militia."

But both Virginia and Congress steadfastly refused, as they had been doing, to allow the militia to be called out. The assembly was then bombarded by letters, almost every responsible man in the country writing, petitioning it to take action. "The settlements are being abandoned," they said.

"The Chickamaugas have moved onto Paint Creek, to join with the Shawnees," they warned. "We are being encircled."

Still the assembly refused, so in desperation the leaders gathered and determined to mount an expedition composed of volunteers. They would pay their own way, call on Virginia for nothing, neither arms, ammunition nor supplies. It would have nothing to do with the Virginia-paid militia. And Cass, like the other leaders of the country, saw no alternative.

There was one answer, finally, to their pleas. It came from Patrick Henry, the governor of Virginia at the time. Touched perhaps more personally than the members of the assembly, for his brother-in-law had been one of those killed near the Falls, he wrote that he would do what he could in behalf of the country. In a private letter to Ben Logan he also told him that he could call his county lieutenants together "to adopt the best measures for defense."

Kentucky had never been denied the privilege of defending itself within its own borders, so the governor's letter to Ben Logan was interpreted as permission to call out the militia. It was taken to mean that an expedition now had the approval of the governor.

Jubilantly the expedition was ordered and mounted and in late

September got under way. Under George Rogers Clark one arm was to ride against the Wabash Indians, near the old town of Vincennes. Under Ben Logan the other arm was to invade the Shawnee towns. Being on the muster of the Lincoln County militia, Cass had served with Logan; had witnessed, participated in, the burning of the seven principal towns. Without difficulty, for Logan was an admirable leader and implicitly trusted by the militia, the towns of Mackacheck, Wappatomica, New Piqua, Will's Town, McKee's Town, Blue Jacket's Town, and Moluntha's Town had been subdued and many Indians had been taken prisoner. The expedition under Logan was a complete success.

Returning to Kentucky, according to plan Ben Logan sent the men who had served under him on the Shawnee expedition to General Clark, who had been delayed in starting. Cass had been relieved of this duty because of illness. His bad leg had troubled him all during the Shawnee expedition and eventually he had come down with ague and fever. Being released from further military duty, being a delegate to the convention then stagnating in Danville, he had hastened there to nurse his chills as best he could. He did not know what had happened at Vincennes.

There was a knock at the door. "Cass?" It was Harry Innes.

"Yes?"

"James is here. We are gathering downstairs."

"I'll be down immediately."

The taproom had been closed off to the public, Cass saw, and a group of men were gathered about a table near the fire. He recognized Thomas Marshall, surveyor for the Kentucky district, John Brown, Judge Muter, James Garrard, Christopher Greenup, Edmund Lyne, among others. James Wilkinson was the center of attention, on the floor in front of the fireplace, and with him was a man Cass did not know.

"Be seated, Cass," Wilkinson said, waving him to a chair. "Gentlemen, I have called you together to bring before you news of a most serious and disturbing character. This gentleman with me is Mr. William Wells. He has in his care several documents which I felt this council of men should peruse and which, confidentially, I believe to demand its attention and action. Mr. Wells, may I have first the letter."

Wells was a stringy man, dressed in outdoor clothing, obviously a little drunk, a little ill at ease, but obviously also enjoying his sudden elevation to prominence in such a gathering. He took from a packet a lengthy letter which he handed to the general. James did not immediately open it. "First," he said, "I propose to give you something of the background which requires us to investigate this matter. As you know, gentlemen, the state of Georgia recently erected a new county in the Louisiana province on the banks of the Mississippi River. This county, called Bourbon, embraces the Spanish fort at Natchez. Some of you may recall we heard rumors that it was done for the purpose of colonizing that portion of the country; and that four commissioners were duly appointed to go to Natchez and organize the county government. They were instructed not to commit any act of hostility against Spain. In defiance of their instructions, however, they demanded the surrender of the district by the Spanish commander and they threatened him with violence when he refused. It has been persistently rumored, as you know, that some of our own frontiersmen had planned to settle in that district and that when expelled by Spain they became enraged, threatening to return in sufficient numbers to take the country by force. One of those commissioners, gentlemen, and one of the leaders in the plot to invade the Spanish territory, was Thomas Green. This letter which I hold in my hand was written by Thomas Green, who at the time of its writing, was at the Falls, in close touch with General George Rogers Clark. I shall read those parts of the letter which appertain to some plans the two men were apparently making. I might add that the letter was written three days ago — on December 12. I quote now from the letter which is addressed to the governor of Georgia:

"Honored and Respected Sir:

. . . Matters here seem to wear a threatening aspect. The troops stationed at Post Vincennes by orders of General George Rogers Clark have seized upon what Spanish property there was at the place, all at the Illinois, in retaliation for their many offenses. General Clark, who has fought so gloriously for his country, and whose name strikes all the western savages with terror, together

with many other gentlemen of merit, engages to raise troops sufficient, and go with me to the Natchez to take possession, and settle the lands agreeable to the lines of that state, at their own risk and expense; provided you in your infinite goodness, will countenance them and give us land to settle it agreeably to the laws of your state. Hundreds are now waiting to join us with their families, seeking asylum for liberty and religion. Not hearing that the lines are settled between you and the Spaniards, we therefore wish for your directions concerning them, and the advice of your superior wisdom.

. . . General Clark, together with a number of other gentlemen will be ready to proceed down the river with me, on the shortest notice; . . . As to the further particulars, I refer you to the bearer, Mr. William Wells, a gentleman of merit, who will be able to inform you more minutely than I possibly can of the sentiments of the people of this western country.

THOMAS GREEN"

Wilkinson's voice stopped and for approximately one very long minute there was not a sound in the room. The faces of the men around the table and along the wall looked stunned, unbelieving. Then someone back of Cass raised his voice. "By God, if that letter is true, Clark has got us in a pretty pickle! If he has really seized Spanish property at Vincennes there'll be the devil to pay. Virginia will raise holy hell and the Congress will probably have to go to war with Spain!"

"Blast!" someone else said, "the assembly will never hear our petition now!"

"What's got into Clark?" another voice asked. "He is usually a sensible man. This sounds like the action of someone gone mad!"

"Or drunk!"

The talk buzzed on. James Wilkinson stood with the letter in his hand, listening, smiling a little, taking no part in it, letting it simmer, flare, blaze, as it would. Cass himself felt a great sadness. General Clark had his own dreams of empire, of greatness, of military prowess, of fame and fortune; but he had taken a risky and poor way to achieve it. Nothing, he thought, could stop the man's ruin now.

The discussion waxed furiously until Mr. Marshall, who could always be depended on to remain cool-headed, said, "Gentlemen, we have no proof that these things Mr. Green writes about are true. We must first, before any action is taken, ascertain the truth."

Wilkinson turned to William Wells who had seated himself, but who was still weaving a little, even though seated. "May I have the other document, Mr. Wells?"

Wells hunted around in his packet a moment, came up with another paper.

"This, gentlemen," Wilkinson said, "is a document executed on December 4, at the Falls. It should have great bearing on the veracity of Mr. Green's letter."

He read:

"Whereas, William Wells is now employed by Colonel Thomas Green and others to go to Augusta, in the state of Georgia, on public business, and it being uncertain whether he will be paid for his journey out of the public treasury: should he not be, on his return, we, the subscribers do jointly and severally, for value received, promise to pay him, on demand, the several sums that are affixed to our names, as witness our hands:

Thomas Green	*Lb* 10.00
John Williams	1.00
George R. Clark	10.00
Lawrence Muse	3.00
Richard Brashears	5.00
James Patton	3.00
James Huling	1.00
David Morgan	1.00
John Montgomery	1.00
Ebeneezer Platt	1.00
Robert Elliott	.10
Thomas Stribling	1.00"

Flourishing the paper, Wilkinson said, "I shall pass this document around for you all to see. Some of you know General Clark's handwriting. You can determine for yourselves if his signature is genuine."

In silence the document was examined. Cass had no doubt, having seen the signature many times on official orders, that it was the general's. The poor fool, he thought, the poor deluded fool.

Several other men present had seen the general's signature on letters, in correspondence they had had with him. They vouched for its authenticity.

Mr. Marshall's mouth grew thin when he had examined the document and heard the verifications. "Gentlemen, there seems to be no doubt that General Clark has acted without reflection and authority. What would you deem it proper for this body to do?"

No one spoke. Each man looked at his neighbor. It occurred to Cass that Mr. William Wells had not proved so much a man of merit as Mr. Green and the general had supposed, and he wondered how James had got hold of him. No matter. If William Wells had been induced by, say, a larger sum of money than guaranteed to trade his loyalties, he still bore evidence of a greatly damaging character. James had probably heard rumors, run him to ground, offered him money, given him a few drinks to assuage his conscience. It did not alter the facts in hand.

"Before we determine our action, gentlemen," James was saying, "there is another kind of evidence we need to pursue. One of the men who served at Post Vincennes under General Clark, one Neeves, a private soldier, has returned. We can question him . . . I have him waiting in another room, and we can thus have an eyewitness account of the proceedings at the post. Do you agree?"

There was a murmuring assent and the soldier was sent for. He was a shabby sort, but Cass knew too well the danger of judging any militiaman by his dirt, his generally unkempt look, or by his purposely blank look. Most of them from the back country had a way of hiding every emotion, and even intelligence, by a stolid, expressionless face.

After a few preliminary questions, establishing the man's identity and his company, Wilkinson asked him, "Are you willing to tell this assemblage, in your own words, what happened on the expedition to Post Vincennes?"

"Yes, sir. I don't figger the truth ever hurt nobody."

"Proceed, then."

"Well, we was with Ben Logan at the Shawnee towns first, but when we come back from burnin' them towns, Colonel Logan sent us to General Clark. We didn't none of us like the idee much, for we thought we'd done our part and we wanted to get on home. But Colonel Logan said he'd promised and we went along because Colonel Logan is a fine man and we never wanted him to get in no trouble on account of us.

"Well, the general, he decided to send the provisions and some of our equipment down the Ohio and up the Wabash by boat and to take us over the land to the Post. It was a damned long march, sir, and nothing much to eat. We come to French Lick finally and that was when the general did a thing we didn't none of us like. He taken one of the horses belonging to one of our men for his adjutant — just taken him, high-handed like. We asked Colonel Barnett, our commander, to try to get the horse back for the feller, but the general wouldn't even give him the satisfaction of talking with him."

"Just a minute, Neeves," James Wilkinson interrupted. "What condition was General Clark in at the time?"

The man puzzled his brows. "Well, he was tired, and I reckon he was some worried . . ."

"No, no. I mean, was he under the influence of spirituous liquor? Was he entirely sober?"

"Oh, that. Well, sir, General Clark ain't to say cold sober much of the time no more. Don't reckon you could rightly say he is drunk, either, but he tipples all the time. Everybody knows that."

Mr. Marshall intervened. "Do you know that for a fact, Neeves, or is it merely rumor?"

"I know it for a fact, sir. I've seen him drinking. He carries it on his person all the time and takes a drink when he pleases, any time."

"Even when in command of an expedition?"

Neeves grinned. "Well, sir, I'd say he needed it worse then than any other time."

"I see." Mr. Marshall's voice was cold. He did not approve of intemperance, Cass knew. "Continue, please."

"Well, when Colonel Barnett couldn't get no satisfaction from the general the hull damn company gathered together and we fired off our guns."

"For what reason?" It was Mr. Marshall again.

"We aimed to let the general know we didn't approve of him taking a man's horse away from him."

"Go ahead, Neeves," Wilkinson said.

"Well, we went on, and when we got to Post Vincents, the boats hadn't got there yet and we didn't have nothing much left to eat. We didn't want to go no farther. The general, he said the Indians was farther on up the river, but we thought it foolish to go walking into a fight without nothing to eat. I reckon it was to please us he waited a few days and the boats come up. But most of the stuff had got wet and wasn't hardly fit to eat. We made out, though, and the next day the general talked us into going on."

"How far did you go?" Cass asked.

"We went on to the mouth of the Vermilion River. There wasn't no Indians there and we didn't have nothing to eat at all, now, so we just flat out told the general we didn't aim to go another step — that we aimed to turn around right there and come home."

Wilkinson chuckled. "Any military man, gentlemen, knows that when he has outrun his line of supply he must retreat." He turned briskly to the soldier. "Now, Neeves, I want you to be very careful in your recollection of what occurred next. These gentlemen must hear only the truth."

"Yes, sir." The man wrinkled his brow trying to choose his words. "The general, he give in to us and we come on back to the Post. When we got back to the Post he decided to garrison the place and he commenced enlisting men and officers to fill out the garrison. That's what he *said* the enlistment was for. There was a boat had just come up from New Orleans with goods for three of the merchants in the town . . ."

"Just a minute," Wilkinson interrupted. "Were they Spanish merchants?"

"Yes, sir, they was Spanish. Everything on the river is Spanish, now."

"Continue."

"The general, he said the boat had come up the river without a pass and that when Americans went down the river without passes they had their cargoes seized by the Spanish, and what was sauce for the goose was sauce for the gander. He said he would seize the cargo of the boat, on account of they had seized so many American cargoes. Said it wasn't nothing but just. And said the cargo would help provision the garrison."

"And did he seize the cargo?" Mr. Marshall asked, leaning forward a little in his chair.

"Yes, sir, he did."

"Did you," Wilkinson asked then, "at any time hear anything concerning a proposed expedition down the Mississippi to seize the Spanish fort at Natchez?"

"Oh, yes, sir. Everybody in the army heard it. 'Twas common talk that the general was aiming to provision the expedition with the cargo he seized. And mostly everybody believed it, though he claimed it was to provision the garrison."

Mr. Marshall had another question immediately. "But that is merely rumor, is it not? You do not know, of your own experience, that an expedition was planned?"

"No, sir. I don't know it for a fact. The general wouldn't be likely to take me into his confidence."

There was a ripple of amusement around the room, which soon subsided into the serious attitude the situation demanded. "Are there any more questions?" Wilkinson asked.

"Yes," Cass said. "What did your company do, Neeves, when you got back to Vincennes?"

"Well, sir, we just taken our foot in our hands and stumped it on back home. Only sensible thing *to* do, looked to us."

There was another burst of laughter, then Wilkinson told the soldier he could go. "Don't leave the village, however, Neeves. We may need you again."

"Yes, sir. I mean, no sir. I'll be close by."

"Mr. Wells," Wilkinson said, "I think you may be excused now, sir, too."

Mr. Marshall spoke. "Mr. Wilkinson, just a minute. Shouldn't we have those documents?"

"We have no right to interfere with their delivery, sir — but I have made copies of them. I have them here with me."

When William Wells had left the room, Wilkinson turned to the uneasy group of men. "I think I owe it to you, gentlemen, to tell you that when I was at the Falls earlier this month I heard so many rumors of these things that I determined to run them down if possible. Of course it is common knowledge that the men of Colonel Barnett's company mutinied, since they have already arrived home. They brought with them many of these stories of General Clark's defection. I gathered what information I could at the Falls, concerning Mr. Green and the general, and I learned that Mr. Wells would be the carrier of their documents to Augusta. Without authority, but with a deep sense of what is due this country, I intercepted Mr. Wells and was able to persuade him of his duty." He turned winsomely to Thomas Marshall then. "Sir, we are all delegates to this convention. I believe it would meet with the approval of everyone present if you should now take the chair and let us decide upon a course of action."

Thus appealed to, Mr. Marshall took the chair, and after much discussion it was decided to send a committee to wait upon General Clark and question him concerning the matter. The men appointed to the committee were, James Wilkinson chairman, John Brown, Harry Innes, James Garrard, Christopher Greenup and Edmund Lyne. They were instructed "to wait on General Clark and receive from him such information as he may think proper to make respecting the establishment of the corps at Post St. Vincents, of the Seizure of Spanish property made at that place, and such other matters as they may consider necessary to give satisfaction to the members of this committee."

The meeting was then adjourned.

CHAPTER 16

Several of the men continued to sit about the table by the fire, unable to leave off the discussion of the affair. A few, those who lived in Danville, dispersed to their homes; but Cass, deeply troubled, took his aching bones to his room, built up a roaring fire and sat before it trying to bake some of the ague and pain out of himself. His thoughts were on General Clark and the situation he had got himself into.

Some thirty minutes had passed when the door opened a crack and James Wilkinson thrust his head in. "Cass? May I come in?"

"Of course," Cass told him. "Do."

"I noticed downstairs," Wilkinson said, closing the door, "that you looked ill. I thought you might have a fever."

It was part of the charm of the man that he was genuinely thoughtful of others' comfort.

"I have, plague it," Cass admitted, "chills every other day and fever with them." He grinned crookedly. "That's one reason I wasn't mixed up in General Clark's little affair at Vincennes."

"You can be grateful for the chills and fever, then. Every officer with him is suspect. Cass, I always have my medical bag with me, as you know. Never travel without it. Why don't you let me bleed you for that fever?"

Cass warded him off. "No, thank you. The last time you bled me I nearly bled to death."

"Will you submit to tart bark, then, and a blistering plaster?"

Cass nodded. "That, I allow, won't kill me."

James brought his bag and Cass swallowed the bitter dose, bared his chest to allow the plaster to be applied. "There," James said then, "I'll give you another dose of the bark before you retire. And that plaster should draw off the fever before long."

Cass buttoned his shirt. "I'm grateful, James. I was feeling pretty ragged. There's some whisky on that chest and hot water in the kettle on the hearth. Will you mix us a toddy?"

"I will. It will do you good."

The drinks mixed, James Wilkinson pulled another chair to the fire for himself. "You were foolish to go on that expedition with Logan, Cass."

Cass shrugged. "I am a militiaman."

"There are hundreds of militiamen in the country. There aren't too many men of intelligence."

"I don't take that point of view, James. I owe just as much to the country, perhaps more, than that man Neeves you had downstairs. Where did you pick him up?"

"Oh, he lives not far from here. I heard him talking in the tavern the other day."

A little wistfully Cass said, "I could almost wish you had never got on the trail of all this about General Clark, James. It will ruin the man."

Wilkinson's eyes blazed. "I intend it to. It was a shameful affair, Cass, a shameful affair. The management of the entire expedition to Vincennes was slack and stupid and I am convinced that Clark should be exposed. No man as intemperate as he has become, as reckless as he is evidently willing to be, should be trusted with leadership. I, for one, firmly believe he intended the Spanish goods to provision an expedition to march on Natchez. He cannot abrogate such authority to himself. He acted arrogantly and he has involved the government in an embroilment with the Spanish crown. At this point in our negotiations with Virginia, and with our hope to be admitted to the union it is folly not to repudiate him."

"I know. I know all of that, James. But you never served under him. You don't know . . ."

"I served under General Gates when he was an intelligent officer, Cass, but I did not hesitate to expose him when he became a fluttering, weak, foolish old woman. Men who lead cannot afford to be weak. General Clark is not the leader he once was — his judgment is impaired and the sooner the people learn that, the better off the country will be."

It was true, Cass knew. The entire Vincennes expedition showed evidence of a weakening judgment, a vacillating hand. No man would have dared mutiny under the General Clark Cass had served under. He would have had that company of mutineers over the barrel and under the lash before a man of them could have blinked an eye. The General Clark he had served under would never have got himself mixed up with a small and sordid villain like Thomas Green. He would have turned the man out with a roar of anger he would not ever forget. The General Clark he had served under might easily have commandeered the Spanish property to provision his men, but he would have requisitioned it properly, giving his own personal receipts for it.

It did not make Cass feel any better, however, to realize the truth. Having known the general in his better days, having respected him wholly, there was a deep pain in the knowledge that he had come to this bad end — for there was no doubt it would be the end of his leadership and his influence. Cass sighed and changed the subject. "What's this I hear about you founding a town? I came through Lexington and Ann told me you had laid one out at Frank's Ford on the Kentucky."

Wilkinson replied enthusiastically. "Yes. Finally, I've found a good location. Humphrey Marshall owned some four hundred acres there at the ford — on the north side of the river, in the bottoms, and I bought it from him. Paid him a hundred and thirty pounds sterling for it, and I figure I got a bargain. I have petitioned the assembly for the right to establish a town there, and to operate a ferry across the river."

Cass nodded. "It should do well. It lies midway between Lexington and the Falls and both the town and the ferry will be usefully located. For once, James, I think you've used your head. What are you going to call the town?"

"Everyone calls it Frankfort, so I think we'll just leave the old familiar name. How did it come to be called Frank's Ford, do you know?"

"Yes. Fellow named Frank was ambushed and killed by Indians as he was crossing the river there. People got in the habit of identifying the place by the incident."

Wilkinson chuckled. "Rather gruesome, isn't it? But I thought it would be best to leave the familiar name. Might help the sale of lots. I am building my own wharfage there and intend to build a warehouse, operate the ferry, build a home. In fact a double log house is already going up. Would you like to see the plat of the town, Cass? I have it in my small trunk."

"I'd like very much to see it."

When Wilkinson returned he laid out before Cass a large map of the proposed town. It was, as his maps always were, beautifully drawn. The town was systematically laid out, the streets lined in exquisitely, and named. "This is the principal street, as you can see," he said, pointing.

Cass laughed. "I see you have named it Wilkinson, after yourself."

"Why not?" Wilkinson was unperturbed. "I may as well go down in history as the next man. And it's my town. The next street is Washington, for General Washington, of course; the next one for General St. Clair, the next one for my wife, Ann."

"What is that street by the river . . . Wapping?"

"That one was suggested by an Englishman, John Instone . . . for the Wapping Stairs on the Thames. Here is the public square between Market and Clinton; and on the east, Lewis Street, for General Andrew Lewis; on the west, Madison, for our good friend James Madison. Here," he pointed, "I propose to build my own home and I shall reserve the entire river front from St. Clair to the bend of the river for my wharfage."

"How are you going to dispose of the lots?"

"At public auction. We intend to require that each purchaser build a dwelling house at least sixteen feet square, with a brick or stone chimney, to be finished fit for habitation within two years from date of sale."

The general turned away to fill his pipe and light it. Cass took up the plat of the town, pleased with its craftsmanship, admiring it. With maps, James Wilkinson was a perfectionist and he turned out drawings that were works of art. Every street on the plat was precisely drawn, the pen strokes as fine as engraving. Except one. Cass frowned, turning the map to read. A street on the north edge of the town was drawn in with less care, as if it had been added hurriedly. Miró Street, he read. Miró? He knew of only one Miró — Don Esteban, the Intendant of Spanish New Orleans. Cass puzzled over the name, still frowning. Seeing the frown, James Wilkinson said, "What is it?"

Cass pointed to the street. "Is this street named for Don Esteban Miró?"

"Yes."

"I didn't know you knew him. Didn't know you had ever taken a shipment downriver."

"I haven't. And I don't know the man. But I propose to take a shipment down the river, and very soon, Cass. That is one thing I wanted to talk with you about. I thought it might help to get a shipment through to have a street in a Kentucky town named for him." He grinned infectiously.

Cass snorted. "Not unless Don Esteban has suffered from softening of the brain."

"Well, I'm just trying to lay a little groundwork. I have heard the man is subject to flattery."

"Don't count on his being flattered by *that,* James. It takes something more substantial."

The general lifted his eyebrows. "Perhaps I can provide that, too."

Cass rolled up the map and handed it to him. "Do you propose to make this trip downriver any time soon, James?"

"As early in the spring as possible. Just as soon as I can get a sizable cargo together. By the way, you'll let me have your tobacco on consignment, won't you?"

"God's britches!" Cass stared at him. "You're serious, aren't you? You're likely to end up in the calaboose, my friend."

"I don't think so — and I was never more serious in my life.

We have accepted the closing of the river like mice, not men, Cass, and I propose to advance boldly and see what happens. I flatter myself that if any man living can deal with the Spanish, I am that man. If enough of you with stored tobacco will trust me with it, I aim to take a cargo to the very doors of the King's warehouse in New Orleans."

"And if the cargo is seized?"

"You lose your tobacco, my boy. But remember, I shall be risking my neck."

Cass felt a tide of mounting excitement. The man is just bold enough to try it, he thought, and he may be exactly the man to bring it off. It was just possible that with his smooth affability, his polished skill at flattery, his talent for conversation and for appeasing, he could so impress Don Miró that he might turn the trick. If he pulled it off — if he really opened the river — Cass swung about the room, his imagination fired. No one had thought of so boldly risking himself and a shipment. James was right. They had written thousands of letters, to no avail. Action might serve them best, now. "By jove," he said, "I wish I could go with you. I know Don Esteban . . ."

"I thought of that," Wilkinson said, regretfully, "but I concluded, Cass, that Don Miró might not take kindly to someone who has traded downriver before. I think I had better go alone, and I think I had better pose not so much as a trader, but as a merchant — taking a shipment to Philadelphia, for instance, by way of New Orleans."

Cass nodded. "You're right, of course."

The general continued. "It will have to be handled very delicately. One man, alone, may be able to do it. Several men would probably land in the calaboose."

"Yes, I see that."

"You've been downriver, Cass. What are the places of danger?"

"The minute you leave the Ohio and get onto the Mississippi. You will have to have a pass from St. Louis to continue downstream. I don't know who is commandant there, now, but he'll stop you if you don't have a pass. The next port of inspection is at Natchez. You will have to have a pass to continue from there. *But*, if you get by Natchez, you'll get to New Orleans. St. Louis and Natchez, they can stop you. Incidentally, what do you intend to do about passes? The Spanish haven't granted one to a Kentuckian since the river was closed."

Wilkinson tilted his head and grinned up at Cass. "I shall apply, of course — probably to Richmond, first — but do you know, Cass, I think I shall just take my chances on being able to talk them into letting me through. I'll run the risk of being seized, but there is something to say for a confrontal face to face."

"In your case," Cass chuckled, "there is much to say for it. You could talk a mouse into nibbling at the cheese in a trap. It might very well be the best way to go about it. Well, James, you'll get my tobacco, certainly; and you should have no difficulty getting the lots of every other big planter in the district." He poured drinks for them again. "Let's drink to your success, General Wilkinson. With all my heart I hope you have good fortune."

The general's eyes twinkled as he lifted his glass. "I think I shall have it."

They talked on for awhile longer about the proposed trip down the river, then, fingering his township map, the general said, "Cass, I intend to reserve some of the choice lots in this town for my own friends. Would you like one?"

Cass shook his head. "You forget I have a settlement of my own."

"You will never get that little settlement incorporated, my boy. It is too far from the main roads. No one wants to situate in a town so far from the center of things."

"Maybe not," Cass said comfortably. "Maybe the town will never be a reality. But we have a nice little settlement, in one of the prettiest parts of Kentucky, and I would not trade it for your town or any other."

"I see." The general studied the fire. "Well, in that case I'll have to ask you to loan me the money then." Dryly he added, "I had hoped to sell you some lots."

Cass's laughter shook the rafters. "What do you need money for this time?"

"I'm short of cash for the trip downriver. It cleaned me out of hard money to pay for the land for my town."

Cass reflected. He had written off three hundred pounds on

James's bad management already. Any more money was likely to go the same way. But — if James succeeded in this venture, it would be well worth ten times the lost investment. "How much do you think you'll need?"

"About two hundred pounds, I'd say."

Cass grimaced. "A hundred is all I could raise, James."

"That will do. I'll find the other some way. You'll send it right away, though, won't you? I need to make arrangements for a barge, hire a crew, do some circularizing about the shipment."

"I'll do better than that. I'll give you the money before we leave Danville."

"Fine."

In the warming glow of wine and revived hopes, something of the former intimacy of the two men was resumed and the general asked about Cass's settlement. "Everything going well?"

"It was when I left."

"Tattie still running the mill?"

"Yes. She had been helping Tench, you know. When he died last year she took it over. She does a splendid job, too."

"She's made a charming girl, hasn't she? But she should not be running that mill, Cass. Why don't you send her to Ann? Let her visit and go out in society a little. She is too handsome and spirited a girl to stay buried down there."

"She would not go. She is too engrossed in the mill." He relaxed, thinking. "She made a surprisingly strong young woman. She was such a wispy little guttersnipe I never expected it. She was all legs and arms and thin little pointed face for months after she came. Suddenly she began growing and filling out. She is not tall . . . she never will be a tall girl, but she is buxom and hearty and stout. Fine color, too. You should see her, with flour all over her face and hands, hair dusty with it. She is like a Flemish peasant woman. She is earthy and lusty, with a sort of rich bloom on her. Rubens could have painted her — The Miller Girl."

His voice as he spoke of Tattie slowed, as if he tasted or savored the words he used; as if, conjuring up her image — glowing, sturdy, impudent — he savored the picture he drew of her. He frowned, then, bringing himself back. "She is still bawdy and boisterous, though. No one can handle her, though Mag tries. Mag is a poor choice to have the care of her. She gets much of her salty tongue from that source. But," he lifted his shoulders, "I don't know what else can be done."

"How old is she now — I forget."

"Eighteen, I suppose — or near it."

"I should have thought she could be of help to Rachel in the house."

"Tattie? Help Rachel? She would die cooped up in a house. Besides, she isn't needed. There are Sheba and Molly, and Molly's girls who are getting big enough to help." Cass laughed. "I shouldn't like to live in the house Tattie managed. She has no talents in that direction. Flyaway, out riding the wind on that mare of hers, worried about the millstones, grubbing in her garden patch. A house can't contain all that energy."

It was snowing again and against the dark windowpane there was a steady hissing sound. Both men were silent for a time, listening. Cass poked up the fire. "Do you know we have a minister now?"

"Was that a necessity?"

"The people thought so."

"What faith?"

"I have never been able to determine. He seems, however, to satisfy them all, good Baptists, Methodists, and Presbyterians alike. He is a saintly old soul who just drifted in, he and his wife. We gave them shelter for a few nights and they stayed on. We have a new blacksmith, too. Though actually," he added, "he is not needed. Any man in the settlement is a good enough smith to serve our needs."

"Who is he?"

"Young Frenchman. Peter Balleu. He is not married and I don't expect him to linger long."

"Why?"

"Too restless. And there is a shortage of unmarried girls in our settlement. Faith and Charity Bearden are a little young for love yet."

The general chuckled. "There is Tattie."

"By God, he'd better not . . ." Cass checked himself. "Tattie is not interested in men."

The general glanced quickly at him. "Not in a blacksmith, I hope."

"No."

The wind blew against the side of the house and a branch scraped against the window. "It's been a bitter month, hasn't it?" the general said. "Listen to that wind. Had you got very far with your new house before the cold set in?"

"We have given up the idea of building it. Rachel says she has grown accustomed to the old house, prefers it. We have boxed it in with siding, painted it, built on two rooms. It is comfortable enough, I suppose."

James Wilkinson pinched his chin. "Is this pregnancy making her as uncomfortable as the last one?"

Cass lifted his brows. "Not having been home for several months, I don't really know, but when I left she seemed to be faring much better this time."

"Perhaps," the general said, smiling, "*this* one will be a boy."

"Because you have three boys, James," Cass said, "it does not necessarily follow that all men want sons." If Cass had been disappointed that Rachel's child had been a girl, no one had ever heard him say so. "Mary is a nice baby."

"I'm sure she is. I still say, however, that a man needs sons."

"I have young Edward."

The general might have said it was not the same thing, but he did not. He kept his silence, sucking on his pipe.

Cass grew reflective, his fingers making a steeple under his chin. "Rachel finally visited Edward's grave," he said, after a time.

"That was foolish of her — most unwise."

Cass's shoulders lifted. "A determined woman is difficult to thwart." He stood, groaning a little at the ache the movement started. "James, if you will excuse me, I am going to have a hot drink and go to bed. I had better pamper this chill a little, I think."

"Do." The general stood, also, knocking out his pipe. "And sleep late in the morning. Come down for roll call when we convene, then go back to bed. I shall be on my way to the Falls, of course."

"Yes."

The general watched Cass walk across the room, favoring his bad leg, limping.

Cass's relations with his wife were entirely his own affair, he thought, and certainly Cass never discussed them; but there was something wrong with the marriage. He, himself, did not like Rachel Cabot, had never liked her. Not, he was quick to admit, that she was not a good woman, even a pretty one in a frail sort of way; but the general's taste in women ran to gaiety and wit and humor, as well as to beauty. His Ann was also a good woman, but she had never allowed goodness to make her dour. Rachel Cabot was like weak cambric tea, flavorless, bodiless, cool, and passionless — when a man's palate, at Cass's age, demanded a rich, heady, full-bodied drink. What a tragedy, he thought for the hundredth time, Cass had married Edward Cabot's widow. He did not, he felt, agree with Addison that "a perfect tragedy is the noblest production of human nature."

"Goodnight," he said, closing the door softly behind him.

CHAPTER 17

It was a few days later that the committee appointed to wait upon General Clark reported to the group which had met and constituted itself a committee at large.

James Wilkinson, as chairman, reported.

"We waited upon General Clark," he said, "who is now at the Falls, and we laid before him our knowledge of Mr. Green's letter. We asked for an explanation. The general admitted that he had seized the Spanish property but he insisted it was done to provision the garrison which he deemed necessary to maintain at Post Vincennes. He denied anything but a passing acquaintance with Mr. Green and he denied, further, any knowledge whatever of a letter written by him to the governor of Georgia. He denied having signed a document guaranteeing payment to William Wells. He insisted that he had acted throughout in the interest of the country, and that he had never had, or ever proposed to have, any intention of raising an expedition in co-operation with Mr. Green."

A question was raised. "But he did admit seizing the Spanish property."

"Oh, yes. He said he was entirely justified, his theory being that since the boat had no pass it was illegally in transit. He felt it a just retaliation for the American cargoes seized in New Orleans."

There was a snort from Mr. Marshall. "If everyone takes it upon himself to retaliate for such events we shall soon find ourselves at war with Spain."

Another question was raised. "Did he admit to enlisting officers and men?"

"He did. He insisted, however, they were to garrison the post. He felt a garrison was necessary to prevent Indian raids upon Jefferson county."

"I think he has a point there," Cass said. "A strong garrison at Post Vincennes would greatly discourage the Wabash tribes."

Several of the men nodded in agreement.

"But not," Wilkinson quickly added, "without the proper authority from Virginia."

"What," Mr. Marshall asked then, "was your opinion of the general's remarks, Mr. Wilkinson?"

James Wilkinson lowered his eyes, before raising them to look frankly and candidly at the square-faced, incorruptible older man. "Sir," he said, "in the face of incontrovertible evidence I fear I must say that in my opinion the general was not entirely truthful."

"Is that the opinion of the rest of the committee?"

"Yes, sir. I report for the entire committee. Furthermore, gentlemen, we shall be in the bad grace of the Virginia government, as well as the Congress, over this, I fear."

It was exactly what everyone present feared. John Jay was trying to treat with Spain. The Congress was moving very slowly, being very meticulous about its procedures. They were not going to feel very kindly toward Kentuckians if Spanish property was seized, if they gave the Spanish government continued grounds for rebuttal, if expeditions were rumored and threats made.

Something obviously must be done, and though Cass felt a great reluctance to see it done, he knew it must be the disavowal of General Clark's actions. Kentucky could not take the blame for his impetuousness. If it looked like treachery to the man who had done so much for them, he should have been more discreet. Had it not been for the document bearing his signature endorsing the payment of William Wells, Cass would have been inclined to believe he had done nothing more than act highhandedly, taking what he needed when he needed it. The general was very good at doing such things, and in the past he had been upheld generally.

He had gone too far this time, however, and the country could not be held accountable for him.

After discussion it was decided that the general must be censured and that a committee should be appointed to draw up a letter to the governor of Virginia. They agreed "to disavow the mode adopted for the establishment at Post St. Vincents, reprobate the Seizure of Spanish property and solicit the interference of the Executive." The committee was also instructed to "urge the absolute necessity of Supporting a Military Post at St. Vincents . . . and carry into effect the Treaty proposed by General Clarke."

Cass thought, with grim humor, how inconsistent it was of them to reprobate the man who had the penetration to see that a garrisoned post at Vincennes was a necessity, at one and the same time they petitioned for the post. Jonathan Swift's hard, gem-like words flashed into his mind. "There is nothing in this world constant, but inconstancy."

The committee appointed to draw up the letter were: James Wilkinson, chairman, Harry Innes, Judge Muter, James Garrard, Christopher Greenup, John Brown and Edmund Lyne.

When the letter they had written was read, Cass knew that James had composed it. His florid style was immediately recognizable, and Cass instantly deplored it. He thought a clear statement of the facts, with the enclosures of the copied documents, would have been sufficient; but James could never resist the opportunity for eloquence. Cass did not personally care for the use of the word "outrage" in connection with the affair at Vincennes; he did not know of any reason to believe, as James said they did, that "property had been plundered to a very considerable amount and that it has been generally appropriated to private purpose." Nor did he like a paragraph which alleged that "daily attempts are practised to augment the banditti at Saint Vincennes, by delusive promises of lands, bounty and clothing, from the officers appointed by General Clarke."

During discussion of the letter he objected; his objections were discussed and voted down. It was clear, now, that the entire group of men had come to believe that General Clark was guilty of every outrage, and was determined he should be punished.

Not until he went to sign the letter did Cass know that he could not. He waited until everyone else had signed, then with the quill in his hand, he looked at the long list of signatures. It came over him that not a man present had ever served with George Rogers Clark but himself; not a one of them even knew him well; not a one of them had been in the country during the years when Clark and Ben Logan and James Harrod and Daniel Boone and John Todd and David Cooper and Cassius Cartwright had been settling the land and fighting Indians. Some of them, it was true, had fought in the Continental army, had splendid records; but they had not fought in Kentucky. And just as they had come into the country after the first hard years were over, so they were sitting in Danville now. It was still the George Rogers Clarks, the David Coopers, the Ben Logans, the Cass Cartwrights, who were fighting Indians. Not John Brown and James Wilkinson and Harry Innes. They had not gone on the expeditions. Cass laid the quill down. "Gentlemen," he said, "I cannot sign this letter."

Mr. Marshall gave him a stern look. "Why, sir?"

"I believe I have the right to refuse. This convention cannot properly do business without a quorum. No quorum has been present at our meetings. Therefore, although we have proceeded in an orderly fashion, this group is not a constituted committee of the convention. It remains a committee of interested private citizens. As an elected delegate to the convention I should feel it my duty to add my signature if this letter represented the will of the convention. As a private citizen, and as a former officer under General Clark's command, I feel no such obligation. As you know, I object to some of the wording of the letter, but beyond that I cannot help ruin the man who has done so much for this country."

"Even," Harry Innes said heatedly, "if he has been proven in treachery?"

But Cass did not have to reply. Smoothly James Wilkinson intervened. "I think I understand Major Cartwright's hesitancy. Had any of us served under the general we might feel, as he does, a very natural reluctance to see him censured. And the major is correct, of course. We do not constitute a committee of the convention. It is purely a matter of sentiment, is it not, Cass?"

Before Cass could reply, Mr. Marshall spoke again. "You do, do you not, concur with the general decision of this committee?"

Cass hesitated. "Yes, sir — in the main. I see that some action must be taken. I feel that the general has been unwise and that the course of his actions is embarrassing. I know that sentiment cannot warm the cold facts — but I wish they could. If any of you had ever known him in his prime . . ." He left off, helplessly. They had not, and he had voiced the truth. Sentiment could not warm the cold facts. But he could not sign the letter. "If you will excuse me, gentlemen."

He bowed slightly, felt a feverish shiver overtake him, and went to his own room.

CHAPTER 18

A quorum was finally obtained, but not until the year had turned and 1787 had been ushered in. Meeting, then, in January, the convention very quickly passed a resolution in favor of separation from Virginia on the terms of the enabling act. Everyone, it appeared, was pleased.

The pleasure lasted only twenty-four hours. A messenger reached them then with astounding news. Their own message, asking for more time, dispatched when they had grown panicky when the expeditions had stayed away so long, had reached Richmond quickly. The assembly had acted immediately. And now there was a new enabling act extending the time to January 1, 1789. The new act also provided that the Congress must grant admission six months prior to that date, July 4, 1788. Kentucky must call a new election in August and meet in convention again in September to consider the new enabling act.

Every member of the convention was disgusted. All those weeks of sitting idly in Danville, meeting daily to do nothing but call the roll, unable to obtain a quorum, had been wasted. The whole thing was now to do over again. Almost a year would have to pass before they could get down to business. Wearily they moved to adjourn and submitted to the Virginia proposals. There was nothing else to do. They had, they realized, brought the delay upon themselves in their panic.

Cass took his ague and fever home where Rachel put him to bed and at his request called in Jeremy to nurse him. "The affairs of this district," he told the little hunchback, "can run along without me for a time. My bones ache, Jeremy, and my head is fevered, and I think these chills will loosen my teeth in their roots. To no good end. I cannot see that we have accomplished a thing, either by the expeditions or by the convention. Kentucky, Jere, is plagued with too many individualists."

The pale, intelligent eyes in the lean face twinkled. "Every frontier is settled by the individualists, Cass. The conformists stay at home. Kentucky will weather through. It will howl like a scalded cat at every turn of affairs. It will hesitate, delay, protest, quarrel, fight within its own borders, but it will eventually unite. Individualists though they are, there are men of uncommon good sense here . . . you, yourself, among them. Men of unselfish devotion and good will. You will prevail."

Cass chuckled. "Not so unselfish, Jeremy." He then related to Jeremy the tale of George Rogers Clark, and of James Wilkinson's proposed trip down the river, and of what he himself had decided to do.

Jeremy listened, rubbed his chin with his slender fingers at the end. "Why shouldn't you profit from his adventure?"

"Just don't call it unselfishness."

"If the time ever comes when you must decide between self-interest and the interest of the country, Cass," Jeremy said, "I would be willing to wager a good, round sum that you will forget what benefits Cassius Cartwright. You have consistently stood with the conservative elements in the conventions, yet your tobacco has stood in the warehouse at the Falls and was a dead loss to you."

"Common sense, Jere. Better to lose several tobacco crops than my whole investment in the country, which separation and sovereignty might well do." Broodingly, he added, "George Rogers Clark will be ruined."

"You did what you could."

"You never knew him, Jeremy. In his day he was magnificent . . ."

"In his day," Jeremy reminded him soberly.

Cass flounced on the bed. "Oh, I know. One of the first things James Wilkinson ever said to me was that the day of the hero was over, and the day of the politician had arrived. It is a sorry day, in my opinion."

"Nevertheless, it is true — and the country had better develop some good politicians."

"Government, it seems to me," Cass continued, "is all a mass of intrigue. Here is John Jay, willing to barter the navigation rights of the Mississippi away for twenty years — for the trade with certain islands which can only benefit men on the east coast."

"Congress will never pass that treaty."

"If they do, they are insane." He grinned ruefully. "They could do nothing better calculated to lose the west. We are still demanding to be heard, however."

"And you are still a drain on the easterners, a threat to their security, a thorn in their flesh."

Cass spread his hands. "You see? Section against section." He clenched his open fist. "But by God we've got as good a man as they can ever come up with! If James Wilkinson opens the river they'll have to sit up and take notice. It may break their damned hearts to do it, but we'll be much more than a thorn in their flesh then. We'll be men, standing on our own feet, doing what they can't do for us."

"I see."

"Wilkinson's own good is always at the center of everything he does, Jere, but he's got a practical head on his shoulders. He gets things done. He goes straight at the realities. Whether he means to or not, he may do this country its greatest good. He may force the Congress to take notice of us."

Jeremy laughed softly. " 'Who are a little wise, the best fools be.' "

"Don't quote John Donne to me!"

"Don't be a little wise, then." Jeremy leaned forward suddenly. "Have you thought of any connection at all between this affair concerning General Clark and James Wilkinson's sudden decision to go downriver?"

Cass stared at him. "No. Of course not. What connection could there be? Except they both have to do with the Spanish . . ." He broke off, unbelievingly.

"Exactly," Jeremy said tersely. "How would the Spanish react, for instance, if they were suddenly confronted with proof that an expedition had been threatened against them?"

"Well, of course, Jere, that was what the committee foresaw and was trying to prevent — their anger. Naturally they wouldn't like it."

"Have you thought how a very clever man could use those documents James Wilkinson has in his possession? How shrewdly he could make it appear there was still a threat? How smoothly he could appeal, as the man who had largely averted the disaster, as the man who discovered the plot, as the savior of Natchez, if not New Orleans, for some gracious return for his activity? Do you not believe he could thus obtain for himself almost anything he desired from the Spanish?"

Cass hitched himself up in the bed, his mind instantly grasping the implications. "Blast and damn, Jeremy, you've hit it, and I've been a blind fool. Why, of course he'll get that shipment through. They'll give him the freedom of the river! Those papers about Clark and Green . . ." he paused, thought for a moment, wrath suddenly flowing over him, "God damn his scheming hide! He engineered the whole thing against Clark! He did it purposely! It's all very plain. *He* heard the rumors. *He* stumbled on the documents. *He* brought in the evidence. *He* called the committee together. And we were all dupes! Do you suppose he forged . . . manufactured that evidence against Clark? No! I saw the man's signature myself. It was not forged, I'd take my oath on it."

"Oh, no," Jeremy said quickly. "I don't think he would do that at all. Not that he would hesitate if it served his purposes, but it wasn't necessary. I think there *was* the evidence. Clark was most foolish. Wilkinson heard the rumors, thought immediately of the use to which proofs could be put, set to work to find the proofs, then presented them. He worked with the time and circumstance, as usual, to his own advantage. He is a man of expediency. He has got rid, in a very clever way and to his own honor, of a man who has had considerable influence in Kentucky in the past. the same time he has had, almost unbelievably, the good fortune to come into possession of some documents which he can use to further his good fortune. You can almost see his mind working, can't you? My guess is those documents are already on their way to the Spanish, and that before very long they will be saying that General James Wilkinson of Kentucky is their very good friend, and of course if he wants to come down the river he may. And naturally he is going to take a shipment down the river while this good fortune of his is still hot off the coals. Strike while the iron is hot."

Cass pulled at his chin, thinking. "With the best intentions in the world, Jeremy, a man can be made a fool of by James Wilkinson."

"I think I warned you of that, some time ago."

Cass grinned. "And in my eagerness to get the river opened, I forgot it. I practically financed his trip for him."

Jeremy's shoulder lifted. "He would have found the money. I hope *all* he is aiming at is opening the river."

"What else could he have in mind?"

"Have you forgotten the 'Washington of the west'?"

"My God!"

"We are an excellent prize for the Spanish to capture. We would be a perfect buffer between them and the easterners. They cannot love this westward expansion of ours and they must suffer anxiety concerning it. Wilkinson has publicly, from time to time, voiced a desire for separation and sovereignty. It would be in character for him to see himself as a prime mover in capturing Kentucky for Spain."

"What good would that do him?"

"You don't think he would keep faith with Spain, do you?"

"Oh, Lord, of course not. But Kentuckians will never do it! We have no love for the Spanish."

"You have no great love for the union, either. Especially since John Jay is willing to barter away the navigation rights of the river. How many of the Kentucky leaders are friends of James Wilkinson?"

Ruefully Cass confessed, "Nearly all of them. All of the most influential ones, at any rate." He pulled at his chin. "How blind we've been, Jeremy."

"He is a difficult man to see through, Cass. When he returns, however, from that trip down the river, you must watch the situation very carefully. If there is anything suspicious, you must thwart him. You must see that he does no damage. Kentucky must not leave the union."

"That's a pretty large order."

"You'll have help. I have faith in the people of Kentucky."

Rachel interrupted them by appearing in the doorway with a tray. Late in her pregnancy, she was grossly distorted, and short of breath from her exertions. Watching her bend awkwardly to set the tray, with its bowl of good, thick soup, on the table beside the bed, hearing her breath puff and pant, Cass thought that pregnancy did not add luster to Rachel's appearance. With their first child he had been amazed at how large she had grown. He had rarely seen a woman so big. She must, he had thought at the time, be with twins. Mentioning it to her, a little awkwardly, she had smiled. "It is but my way. My babies are large."

And as she had said, the baby when it came had been both large and fat. She had weighed nearly ten pounds. He had not been surprised, then, when pregnant again Rachel had early begun to increase in bulk and now that the later days were upon her was so huge as to look deformed. All her usual grace was lost during a pregnancy. Not only her body but her face, hands and feet swelled, and the usual fair, pale skin became splotched with ugly brown spots. The veins at her temples beat visibly and the least effort of movement made her breath short.

In the almost three years of their marriage they had reached a kind of plateau of dull, colorless, prosaic life together. Rachel's time was entirely devoted to the home, her children, her mother (who continued an invalid), the duties required of her in the settlement. She rarely spoke with Cass about anything else; seemed, indeed, to know nothing of the affairs of the country, or to be interested in them. It was as if she lived on a small island containing only herself and the settlement; the day-to-day happenings around her, the routine of her own hours.

For the past two years Cass had been away from home much of the time. Restless when kept there too long, he had developed a deep concern for the country which took him riding about, meeting with other men, talking, arguing, counseling, attending the conventions. The slightest provocation sent him off for weeks at a time, away from the big house which irritated him with its feminine atmosphere, into a purely masculine world.

He had known, very shortly, before the first year was out, that it had been folly to marry Rachel; but he had pity enough to know that she could not help her temperament any more than he could help his own. He had simply erred on the side of hope, and though he relinquished that hope hardly, he did it finally with an inevitability which buried it forever. As it faded, dwindled, diminished, there went with it also all his feeling of yearning, passionate love. He did not cease to feel affection for Rachel. He did not cease to wish that she might be happy. But he did cease to love her. Love must feed upon something. It cannot grow, nor can it even exist, in a vacuum. Irrevocably it must die if not nourished. Rachel could not only not nourish it, but Cass came to feel that she did not want to.

They shared the same room. They discussed the problems of their common life — a small illness of one of the children; young Edward's rapid growth; Mary Hewett's latest heart pains; the new babies in the settlement as they regularly came along; Deborah's saucy little tongue; the occasional death, Tench's, the stillborn child of Nellie and Tate; the quality of the wool sheared that year from the sheep; whether or not to build the additional rooms on the house. It was the kind of talk which drove Cass wild, but which he dutifully carried on when Rachel began it. And yet he had, he knew, as pleasant a home as any man. There were no quarrels, because there was no feeling strong enough to provoke them. Everything in his home was quietly, pleasantly, smoothly handled. For that he was grateful most of the time, but he occasionally wanted to throw a poker across the room, just to make some noise, some difference, in the regular and peaceful routine.

He still turned to Rachel, but out of habit now, or out of sudden need, with no hope that there would be any response. He did it almost automatically, sleeping suddenly afterward, like, he sometimes thought, any animal relieved. He did not allow himself more than an occasional bitter thought about it. He had, he told himself, a better marriage than most men. If it lacked those things he had hoped for, he had only himself to blame for hoping. On the surface there was nothing which other men would not envy him. Only a few, Jeremy perhaps, James Wilkinson, guessed at his deep, invading, constant sense of loss. And he never discussed it with them. He had determined long before to make the best of it.

Rachel straightened from setting the tray on the table, eyed Cass reproachfully. "Thee is flushed, Cass. Thee has been talking too much. Jeremy, I trusted thee."

Cass accepted the napkin she laid across his knees. "We have been talking, yes. But I think we have talked ourselves out now, my dear."

She handed him the bowl of soup. "For today, perhaps. But thee will be at it again tomorrow. No more of it, Jeremy. I shall banish thee if thee does not obey."

"We shall be good," Jeremy promised, smiling at her. "I will read to him now, or let him sleep."

Cass dipped into the soup.

"Sleep would be better for him. Eat it all," she told Cass. "It will nourish thee. Besides, Sheba will be distraught if the bowl comes back to the kitchen with a drop left in it. She will think thee has not enjoyed it."

"It won't be difficult," he told her. "It's very good soup."

"I will return for the bowl," she said, walking heavily across the room, the floor shaking under her steps.

"Don't bother," Cass called to her. "It makes you short of breath. Jeremy?"

Jeremy quickly volunteered. "I will bring the bowl when I come to supper, Rachel."

"It will be thoughtful of thee," she agreed. "Try to sleep, now, Cass."

He nodded impatiently. He hated to be ill. He was an irritable, fractious patient, for he was almost never ill. His leg, of course, bothered him occasionally, but outside of that he rarely had an ache or pain. To be bedridden, with chills and fever, made him stew and fuss. He finished the soup and turned eagerly to Jeremy again. But Jeremy shook his head. "Go to sleep, now, Cass. We can talk later."

He was able to be up again within a fortnight, feeling a little drained of strength, his knees weak, thinned somewhat from the fever, but rid of it finally and rid of the bone-shaking ague which had accompanied it. He spent a few weeks at home until he could fully regain his strength.

He laid out the spring plowing and planting plans for the Negroes. He ordered the erection of the little log chapel the kindly, saintly old man who had come among them so desired. He counseled with Wirt Powell, who had grown restless in the confines of the settlement, about moving across the river. Wirt wanted to operate the salt furnaces and build a small distillery. Cass, since he owned all of the valley on both sides of the river, agreed to exchange the plots of land and to furnish Wirt with whatever help he needed.

He also took several days in which to ride over all his property, to see, to examine, to investigate and appraise everything he owned. He was, after all, a very careful businessman; careful with his property, careful with its administration. This valley represented his entire fortune. He could not afford to be careless with it.

He came, one morning, to the mill and to the smithy which adjoined it. He loved this particular small cove in the hills, had always loved it. It had a wide, level opening into the valley which he had never planted but had allowed to grow in the heavy grass which did so well in it. He came, therefore, into sight of the gray, stone mill and the blacksmith shop, over the velvety green of the natural pasture.

The path followed first the winding, willow-fringed creek which sprawled across the pasture, purling clearly over its white stones. There was no prettier place, he thought, in all of Kentucky. The hills rose protectingly behind the cove, looking, with their winter-bare trees along the tops, like sleeping animals with stiff, bristled roaches.

Following the creek upstream, he came to the narrow neck where, near the great, gushing spring which the entire settlement called the Spout Spring, the mill was built. Looking at the gray stone building, Cass recalled how the blacksmith shop had been built next to it for the convenience of old Tench. It was in an awkward place for daily use, and now that Tench was dead he thought he might move it nearer the big house. The whole community had to use it and it was in an out of the way spot. It was beginning to look shabby, too, he noticed.

The wheel was not turning at the mill, so Tattie was not busy. He was glad. His conscience had been bothering him since James Wilkinson had suggested Tattie visit his wife. He ought, he thought, to ask her if she would like to go to Lexington for a little while. He could not, of course, make her go. He actually had no authority over her, for obstinately she had insisted on paying her debt to him. Out of her share of the mill profits she had saved until the day when, almost arrogantly, she had come to him. Protesting, he had been compelled to accept it. "I will not," she said proudly, "be beholding to you."

"Tattie, can you not forget it? I have long since put it out of my mind. It is so small an amount."

"It wasn't a small amount to me," she had said firmly. "It took me a long time to save it up."

"Then keep it. Use it for something you need . . . some pretty or bit of finery."

"The worst need I have right now," she had insisted, "is to know I am free of your hold on me. As long as I owe you this debt you can tell me to do this, do that, like I was Sheba or Molly. I want no more of it."

There had been nothing to do but take it, and for a time he had wondered if she would now, having paid her debt, leave the settlement. But she had stayed on. He supposed she had become fond of old Mag, felt some loyalty to her. He knew, besides, she loved the little patch of land on which the mill was built, loved it almost passionately, and loved also the mill itself. She was an excellent miller, able always to grind a fine flour, a good turn of meal.

Smoke curled up from the chimney, but the living quarters, at the back of the mill, were very quiet when he dismounted and strode up to the door. Usually Mag, or Tattie, was singing. Mag had taught Tattie an unconscionable number of bawdy tunes and she had a fine, loud voice for them. He thought sometimes she sang them purposely when he was around, knowing the words occasionally made him wince. They nearly all seemed to have something to do with a bed and a boy.

She was old enough to know about both, he had to remind himself. But it always surprised him, the reluctance which he felt at the thought of Tattie marrying. Men had come around occasionally; it was inevitable. But, in her laughing, bawdy way, she had sent them packing, saying she wasn't ready to commence having younguns and as far as she could see that was all a girl got out of marrying up with some man. She was doing very well, she insisted, and she meant to stay free a while longer.

The outside door was slightly ajar, so instead of knocking Cass pushed it open. Because Tench had made it and he was an excellent workman, the door made no sound on its hinges. It swung evenly and perfectly balanced, with no noise.

The room which served Mag and Tattie for parlor, bedroom and kitchen was a big one, warm, comfortable, untidy, with a smell of the mill, of baking, of wood smoke, of leather (from the saddle which Tattie always flung down in one corner), of oil, of tobacco even, from Mag's old pipe. There was little of the womanish smell which permeated his own home. It might almost have been the quarters of two men. Cass always liked to come here. Mag would put on the kettle, brew him a cup of strong tea, give him a hoecake, cackle at his stories, and smoke as long with him as he liked. Tattie, sprawled across the bed, short gown up to her knees, would listen, laugh, tell her own tales of the mill, and often sing one of her salty songs for him — usually unrequested.

Pushing the door wide, Cass blinked in the gloom. There were only two windows, both small, and he had always to grow accustomed to the dimness of the room. "Mag?" he called, "Tattie?"

There was a scurrying sound near the bed, a movement, the sudden thud of a foot against the floor. "God's name, Cass Cartwright!" Tattie exploded, "you might knock before you come busting in!"

"I'm sorry. Were you asleep? Where's Mag? The door was ajar."

He crossed to the table in the center of the room, the objects in the rest of the room slowly coming into focus. "Are you ill, Tattie?" He peered at the big bed in the corner.

She was sitting in the middle of it, the bodice of her gown unlaced, the shoulders pushed down so that her bare flesh showed. Her hair was in disorder, and her face was flushed. He started to her, then stopped short.

Against the wall, a little huddled, staring at him in both fear and confusion, was the young Frenchman, Peter Balleu. His black hair, worn unusually long, was also disordered. He was a handsome fellow, as dark-skinned as Cass, but much younger, slimmer, leaner. Nervously he ran his fingers through his hair. He was breathing loudly, as if trying to control his fright. His eyes darted past Cass toward the door.

Cass took in the scene slowly — the tumbled bed, Tattie's unlaced bodice, her disordered hair, the young man's fear — and a quick, slashing anger flooded him. In two strides he reached the side of the bed, yanked Peter Balleu to his feet, cuffed him on both cheeks and sent him stumbling across the floor. "Get out!" he told him, controlling his voice with difficulty, keeping it low but unable to keep the venom of his anger out of it. "Get out of here! Pack your things and get out of the settlement. If you're still here within an hour, I'll kill you!"

The boy recovered his balance, looked fearfully to see if Cass was following him and scuttled crabwise through the door, clutching his burning face.

Cass did not even look to see if he had gone. He knew he had. If he had been an older man, not so much a boy, he thought he would have killed him on the spot. He jerked Tattie across the bed, flung her over his knees, turned up her skirts and began beating her with the flat of his hand. He wished, viciously, he had a horsewhip.

She struggled and screeched at him but he held her with a strength which was doubled by his anger, and continued beating her until his arm was weary and his hand ached and stung. By then Tattie was reduced to a weeping, hiccuping child. He flung her aside. "Lace up your dress," he told her. "Make yourself decent."

Sobbing, she tried to obey him. Her fingers fumbled with the laces. "Here," he said, "I'll do it." He threaded the laces through the eyelets, yanked on them tightly.

"Ow!" Tattie yelled, wincing.

"Shut up! I ought to strangle you with them. Don't say a word to me, or I'll beat you again. Now, go wash your face and comb your hair."

Strangely cowed she splashed water on her face, ran the comb through her hair.

"Now, come here," Cass told her.

She sent him a slanted look. "You aren't going to beat me again, are you?"

"I don't know. I may. But I certainly am going to tell you a few things. Dammit, come *here!*"

She approached him slowly, the way an erring child approaches an angry parent.

"Now," he said, when she finally reached him, "sit down here beside me."

Hesitantly she sat down on the edge of the bed. He had never known her to be so subdued. He must have frightened her horribly, and probably hurt her considerably as well. But his anger still urged him. "If you are wanting a man, Tattie," he told her brutally, "take one. But marry him, don't dally around with him. You've got sense enough to know it won't work. You'll end up in the family way and in shame. You're woman enough to know that. Mag has taught you that much, I'm sure."

She kept her head down, refusing to meet his eyes, but her mouth was growing sulky. "Nothing happened."

"I know that. I have eyes. The boy's clothing was secure, even if yours wasn't. But it might have. Don't you know you can't fool around with a man that way? It's stupid and silly. A man won't always stop when you tell him."

She flung her head up, angered now herself. "It's none of your business! If I want to dally, and maybe I do, I'll do it!"

She started to get up, but Cass flung out his hand, grabbed her arm. "You will not. I won't have it!"

Like a wildcat, then, she turned on him, beating his chest with her fists. Cass thought, more humorously now than angrily, how often he had had to struggle with this temper of hers. "*You* won't have it!" she was saying, pounding at him fiercely, "it's always what *you* won't have. I'm going to have what *I* want, and it doesn't matter whether it's what *you* want or not! *You* have nothing to do with me! You don't own me, do you hear? You have been paid. I don't owe you a penny. You can't tell me what to do!"

Cass rolled backward on the bed, to protect himself as much as anything else, and Tattie rolled with him, crawled over him, straddled him as a boy might have done, her fists still pummeling him, her hair falling into her eyes, her face drawn up in an angry knot, the words spitting out of her contorted mouth. Cass reached around her shoulders, pulled her down, held her against his chest where her arms, pinioned, could no longer move. She struggled and twisted, rolled and turned, but he had a good purchase on her and slowly she gave it up. Finally he felt all her weight, let go, limp, heavy against him, and he heard her gasp sobbingly.

He continued to hold her, and gradually the heavy weight of her invaded his body sweetly, drugged him, bore him down. Her head was on his shoulder, her hair across his face, the smell of it, strong with her own smell, in his nostrils. Slowly, almost blindly, he turned his face until his mouth, seeking, found hers, and through the clinging strands of her hair, he held it there. So this, he thought dazedly, is why I was so angry — why she has always made me so angry.

Dreamily, almost sleepily, he felt the tip of her tongue against his lip and a long, sweet shudder ran the length of his body. A second later she had torn her mouth away, was whispering hissingly in his ear, "Do ye want to dally with me, yerself, Cassius Cartwright?"

She sprang away from him, stood over him, hands on her hips. "Well, you will not!"

He struggled upright on the bed, confused.

At that moment they heard Mag coming up the hollow, singing lustily:

"O, waly, waly, gin love be bonnie
A little time while it is new!
But when 'tis auld it waxeth cauld
And faes awa' like morning dew."

"Oh, God." It was a half-groan dragged out of Cass. He could not bear Mag's bawdiness now. He fled, feeling as guilty as Peter Balleu must have felt, through the mill and over the hill.

The following morning he rode away to Lexington, where he astonished Ann Wilkinson by going on a spree which lasted a week, during which time he was not sober for so long as one whole hour.

All he got for his pains was an aching head to add to his aching heart.

CHAPTER 19

Calendar of events, 1787.

February. The Virginia assembly repudiated George Rogers Clark, thereby sealing his fate. A resolution was passed that Virginia's representatives in Congress should be given all the evidence pertaining to the matter of Clark's actions in Vincennes, together with a record of the assembly's action, so that the Spanish minister, Don Gardoqui, could be informed of the situation and of their disavowal of him. Congress forthwith agreed with the Virginia assembly and Secretary of War Henry Knox was ordered to take steps to remove the illegal garrison at Vincennes. Clark was stripped of his reputation and left to pay, out of his own pocket, the expenses incurred by the expedition.

February. Ben Logan went to Richmond on private business. While he was gone his brother, John Logan, colonel in the militia and in command during Ben's absence, called out volunteers in Lincoln County and led them deep into Cherokee country to the south. They were on the trail of a marauding band of Chickamaugas but when they overtook seventeen Indians they shot first and inquired later. The party happened to be friendly Cherokees. A stink and a roar went up from Virginia. The governor wrote Harry Innes, the attorney general for Kentucky, "We have reason to believe the late hostilities committed upon the Indians have roused their resentment." To John Logan he wrote, "The late Expedition against the Indians, said to have been under your command, has made an impression disadvantageous to the Character of this Commonwealth." No one in Kentucky gave a damn.

Harry Innes, pressed to take legal action, got tough with the governor. He justified John Logan's raid and warned the governor that the western country, if it could not obtain protection from the east, might "Revolt from the Union, and endeavour to erect an Independent Government."

February. Cassius Cartwright's second daughter was born. Cass was away from home and Rachel named her Sarah, for his mother.

April. James Wilkinson, with a loaded barge, left for his trip downriver to New Orleans. He departed from his own wharfage in Frankfort, where he had built a double log house, in which his wife, Ann, refused to live. She preferred, she said, the gentilities of Lexington to the backwoods of Frankfort. Wilkinson carried with him the tobacco of nearly every large land owner in the district. "I shall return with your profits," he promised grandiosely, "or else I shall perish." It impressed the country generally. It did not impress Cass.

May. The Extreme party, under the leadership of John Brown, called a convention of representative citizens to meet in Danville to consider the action of Congress with regard to the navigation of the Mississippi. John Jay's proposed treaty with Spain, ceding the navigation rights for a period of twenty years, had made him the most hated man in Kentucky. If Congress approved the treaty, Kentuckians would be in an ugly mood and separation and erection of an independent government was almost a certainty. The convention duly met, but ended in fiasco when it was learned that Virginia bitterly opposed the treaty and that Congress would not ratify.

July. The Council of the Virginia assembly sent the appointments of James Wilkinson, Harry Innes and Richard Clough Anderson as commissioners of Indian affairs. The repudiation of George Rogers Clark was complete.

July. James Wilkinson reached New Orleans.

July. The Congress of the Confederation passed the Ordinance of 1787, which set up a government in the western region north of the Ohio River, called the Northwest Territory. A territorial governor was to be appointed, a secretary and three judges. When any portion of the territory reached a population of 60,000 or more, it might apply for admission to the union as a state. There were to be not less than three states or more than five created out of the region, and they were to be admitted in every way equal to the existing states. An important provision of the Ordinance was that no man born in the Northwest Territory was to be a slave and that no law should ever be passed there that would impair the obligation of the contract. The Ohio River thus became the line between the slave states and the free.

August. The election for delegates to the fifth convention was held. Cass was re-elected, along with Benjamin and John Logan, from his district.

August. The first issue of the *Kentucke Gazette,* John Bradford proprietor, was printed in Lexington. This was the second newspaper established west of the Allegheny Mountains, there having been one in Pittsburgh for several years. In the first issue Mr. Bradford apologized for the appearance of the paper. "My customers," he said, "will excuse this my first publication, as I am much hurried to get an impression by the time appointed. A great part of the types fell into pi in the carriage of them from Limestone to this office, and my partner, which is the only assistant I have, through an indisposition of the body, has been incapacitated of rendering the smallest assistance for ten days past."

The establishment of the newspaper was the result of a movement begun as long ago as the second statehood convention, when a need for distributing the news of the conventions was felt. Henceforth the arguments of both the extreme and the conservative parties would be aired publicly and stimulatingly.

September. The fifth convention met in Danville, voted once more in favor of separation, accepted the Virginia proposals and time limits, and passed a resolution to call another convention in July of the following year to begin drafting a state constitution. The fifth convention also asked that a Kentuckian be designated as one of the Virginia delegation to Congress and named John Brown who, therefore, became Kentucky's first and only representative to the Congress of the Confederation. It was a very quiet convention, James Wilkinson not being present. He was still in New Orleans.

November. James Wilkinson arrived in Charleston, South Carolina, on his journey home from New Orleans. From there he went to Richmond where he lobbied vigorously against ratification of the new federal Constitution.

Calendar of events. It had been a year in Kentucky of yeast and ferment, of passion, heat, and debate; it had been a year of sharply drawn lines with friendships cemented through political differences. It had been a year of loyalties made firmer, and of loyalties broken. The judgment of even the best men was touched, swayed, directed, by the current of events; directed and controlled, in large part, by the economic interests of the country which, in the last analysis, meant their own interests. It had been a year which saw the emergence into power of a small corps of men; men of good intent, men for the most part incorruptible, but men swayed by their passions, hot from what they felt to be injustice, intense in their determination to right what they believed to be wrongs. It had been a boiling, seething, passionately articulate year and, torn this way and that, Cass often felt as if Kentucky were a powder keg, so explosive that the smallest spark would set it off.

In the entire twelve months he had rarely been at home more than a few weeks at a time. When his second daughter was born, he was with John Logan, shooting Cherokees. Since they were volunteers, not militia, assuming the responsibility for their own expenses, he had felt they had a right to retaliate against the Chickamaugas. Kentuckians generally considered them renegades anyhow. He was sorry they had shot friendly Indians — but the friendly Indians had some of the horses stolen in Lincoln County, seven of them his own. Perhaps they were not so friendly after all.

In April, he had seen James Wilkinson off on his trip to New Orleans, his tobacco crops for three years consigned to the shipment.

In May, he had attended the meeting called by Harry Innes, John Brown, Judge Muter and Benjamin Sebastian and while he had taken no part in the discussions he had interestedly watched the meeting bog down at the news that Congress would not ratify Jay's treaty.

In August he had been re-elected as a delegate to the fifth statehood convention, and in September he had attended the convention. Perhaps, he thought, because James Wilkinson was not present to usurp the floor with his eloquence and flowing oratory, his heat and his passions, it had been a quiet convention, moving with dignity and proper reserve through its affairs. James could certainly keep any body of men in an uproar.

But not all of his activity and preoccupation with the affairs of the country could assuage the misery which gnawed at his vitals. In his infrequent intervals at home he had sedulously and conscientiously avoided Tattie. He had no intention, he told himself, of becoming embroiled with her even, he had to add ironically, if she would allow it herself.

Home, now, for the spring planting, he could not avoid seeing her occasionally, nor could he prevent the quick, squeezing emotion which the sight of her bosomy, plump-hipped figure roused in him. A glimpse of her apple-green short gown, of a striped petticoat, of quick, flashing feet on the mill path, would set his heart to thudding; the mare racing down the valley, Tattie's skirts flying, her hair streaming, her voice shouting exultantly, would make him look long and wistfully; the sound of her laugh, high, gusty, often bawdy, would make him close his eyes, so he might not see the glowing, high-colored, animated young face.

Once when he came upon her unexpectedly, at the Spout Spring, finding her drinking from the trough which channeled the water into the millrace, the sight of her, bent, her hair tumbled around her shoulders, caught him so sharply that he felt an almost unbearable ache in his throat. He could smell her hair, as he had smelled it that day in the mill, taste it against his mouth, feel it on his face; and only by the greatest effort of will was he able to keep from sweeping her into his arms again, overpowering her resistance, taking her young vigor and lusty strength to himself.

When she straightened, the water flashed in the sunlight on her face, sparkled against her skin like jewels. Seeing him — seeing, he had no doubt, the struggle he was having with himself — she grinned mockingly at him, wiped the water from her mouth with the back of her hand. "Good morning, Major Cartwright. 'Tis a lovely day, isn't it?"

"I hadn't noticed," he said shortly.

"What? Not the sunshine, nor the new willow buds on the trees? Nor the new grass in the pastures? Nor even the birds commencing to sing? Thee must be most unnoticing then, Major." She often teased him by making mock of Rachel's Quaker pronoun.

"Stop it, Tattie."

"Thee is out of humor, perhaps, this morning?"

"I said stop it!"

"What am I to stop? Talking altogether in thy presence?"

"You know very well what you are to stop."

"But you like," she said softly, cruelly, "to hear Rachel say 'thee,' doesn't thee?"

"Rachel has said it all her life. It is the habit of her faith. You are doing it as a mockery."

"And what if I am? Is she so sacred I dare not mock?"

"Tattie, you are determined to be a hellion, aren't you?"

"Guttersnipe is a better word, isn't it?"

He groaned. "I wish I had never heard the word. You have thrown it up to me often enough."

"You used it often enough — and if the shoe fits I intend to wear it. What do you want with the guttersnipe this morning, Major? More dallying?"

"No." He exploded.

"Then begone with you," she said. "You are trespassing. This is Mag's land and you are not welcome."

In amazement he gazed at her. Did she really think Mag owned the mill? Did she not know that Tench had only run the mill for him? He sputtered, beginning to tell her, then broke off sharply. If she knew she was still beholden to him there was no telling what she might do. She might even pack her belongings and leave the settlement. It did not occur to him that such a consequence might be the best solution of his problem. He only shut his mouth tightly, turned on his heel and walked away, angry again at her, troubled by her, enchanted by her. Fine state of affairs, he told himself — married, the father of children, in love with a girl who despised him, who made mock of him, who was, it had always been clear, a child of the gutter. He would conquer this passion, he told himself, or kill himself trying.

To make it more awkward, young Edward developed a great love for the mill and the millpond that spring, and a great fondness for Tattie; and it often seemed to Cass that all he heard in his own home was Tattie, Tattie, Tattie.

All the children of the settlement liked her, for that matter, flocked around her, so the boy was not alone in his affection. Often she was to be seen with all the young children in the community gathered about her, running swiftly with them across the valley to pick wildflowers, or to the river to search for shells and pretty pebbles. They had a way of clustering about her in the late afternoon, to listen to her stories or songs.

She had a pen full of pets which they loved — a black lamb which Mag would have killed but which Tattie rescued; a raccoon; three squirrels in a cage; half a dozen dogs and cats, and even a small skunk which frequently sent the children home smelling loudly.

The first time young Edward had come home smelling so strongly, Rachel had held her nose to bathe him, thrown his clothing outside to be washed, and the entire house had to be aired for several hours. "Where did thee find a skunk, Edward?" she asked.

"At Mag's," he had said. "Tattie has got one for a pet."

Cass, who had been reading, looked up. "Do you go to the mill very often, Edward?"

The boy had nodded, smiling happily. "Yes. I like it there. Mag always has sweet cakes, and Tattie is very kind. She has so many pets and she lets all the children play with them. Except," he added, grimacing, "the skunk. She tells us not to bother him or he will make a stink."

"A smell, Edward," his mother corrected.

"Tattie says stink," he said.

"But thee must say smell. It is more refined."

"Oh, refined be damned," Cass said. "A skunk stinks, Rachel. Tattie is right."

"Very well." She never quarreled with him. Never opposed his opinions in any way.

Curious, Cass asked, "What made the skunk stink you up today, Edward?"

"I poked him." The boy's small, handsome face turned toward Cass unafraid, frankly confessing what he had done. He had, Cass thought, the virtue which had probably belonged to his father as well as to his mother — of refusing to take refuge from his actions by evasion.

Rachel was horrified. "After Tattie told thee not to? Edward, that was very wrong of thee. At the mill thee must obey Mag and Tattie."

"Well," he said, obstinately setting his chin, "I never smelled the stink and I wanted to."

Cass shouted. "Well, now you have! What do you think of it?"

The boy's nose wrinkled. "Phew! I won't ever poke him again."

"There, Rachel," Cass said. "Lesson well learned by experience."

"And by disobedience," she said succinctly. "Edward, thee cannot go to the mill again unless thee promises to obey Tattie."

He gave his promise readily. "Oh, I'll obey her. There aren't any other animals that stink, anyhow."

Cass chuckled. "Your mother is right, though, son. At the mill Tattie and Mag are to be obeyed — for your own safety. The mill can be a dangerous place for children. Tattie will take care of you, if you mind her."

"Yes, sir." The youngster hitched his braces up over his shoulders. "Some day, Tattie said, when I get bigger she will take me in the boat on the millpond."

"Only," Rachel interrupted, "be sure thee waits until thee is bigger."

"Yes, ma'am."

He scooted, fresh and shining, out of the house to play again.

Picking up the basin of water, Rachel watched him with loving eyes. He grew more and more like Edward all the time, she thought. She tried very hard to love all her children equally, but this first child, this son, this image of Edward, occupied a very dear place in her heart. She could not help it and it often troubled her. "I wish," she said, sighing a little, "he had not that spirit of disobedience. He will come to harm some day of it, I fear."

"Nonsense," Cass told her. "The boy is like all boys — curious. He has an excellent mind. He wants to know the facts about everything he sees. It is a good trait, Rachel."

She smiled, touched his shoulder briefly. "Thee comforts me, Cass."

"He is a good boy, my dear. Don't make a mollycoddle of him."

There was a wailing cry from upstairs. Rachel cocked her head, listening. "'Tis Sarah, waking from her nap . . . as hungry, likely, as if she had not been fed two hours ago."

She hurried out of the room with the basin of water, passed hastily through again on her way upstairs. Cass watched her lightly climb the stairs, calling ahead of her, "I am coming, my darling. Hush thy crying, thy mother is coming."

Her voice, speaking to any of her children, always held a fluty note of love.

Cass reflected that he had never seen his wife give nurse to either of his children. She always, modestly, retired to the privacy of another room.

He picked up his book and returned to his reading.

CHAPTER 20

General James Wilkinson was quite pleased with himself.

In a few short weeks he had accomplished what the Congress of the Confederation had been unable to do, and he had accomplished it to the very good profit of himself. The yokels in Kentucky would never have thought of the scheme which had occurred to him, and had swallowed whole cloth his improvisation upon its theme.

He had seen immediately, of course, the use to which that reckless affair of Clark's could be put. The germ of the idea had formed at once. Why not use those copies of Green's damaging documents as confirmation of a threat? Why not make them the basis of a profitable relationship with the Spanish. Why not, he was even bold enough to dream, make a personal alliance with Spain, get Spanish money behind him, draw Kentucky away from the United States. That done, he thought, any loyalty to Spain could be dispensed with. Given his own empire he could make and break treaties at will. If it proved profitable, the new country could ally itself with Spain. If it did not prove profitable, it could ally itself with Britain, who would welcome such an alliance, he felt certain, with open arms. A clever man could play each against the other; at the same time, pulling the strings on both, he could slowly build his own edifice.

Oh, it was a bold dream, he knew. He did not fool himself about that. But it was not an impossible one, and the necessity for boldness had never daunted him. The first thing to do was to set the machinery moving. Get down the river, frighten Don Miró and the Spanish into opening the river trade — but wait. He might as well make a penny on the monopoly of the river trade. He was always short of funds. If he could talk Don Miró into granting him a monopoly it would furnish him with a fortune during the time he was working out the balance of his scheme. Yes — it would have to be a monopoly.

It must look good in Kentucky. He must, he thought, be the hero of the hour. But he had laid the groundwork for that already. He thought, smilingly, of the ease with which he had influenced the principal men in the district. They could be led by the nose, any of them, and all of them. He had them in the palm of his hand.

His first clever move had been to apply for a passport to the Virginia government, knowing, naturally, that it would not be granted. It was merely for the record. He had then told everyone he would go down the river without a passport. He would take the risk. He would run the gamut of the river ports. "And if," he had said gaily, "I land in the calaboose, my friends, you must come to my rescue."

It had been swallowed exactly as intended.

At the same time he had sent, secretly, a letter to St. Louis, addressed to Francisco Cruzat, commandant of that place. He sent it by Carberry, a man who had served with him in the army and who was now a retainer of his. He knew the man's unswerving loyalty to him, and he also knew his dull, unquestioning mind. He enclosed in the letter the copied documents which, he said, revealed General Clark's duplicity.

He had composed that letter with great care. "I am actuated to begin this correspondence," he had said, "because of my sentiments on what is due to public faith and my unwillingness to see the dignity of my country exposed." He told Señor Cruzat that the "outrage" committed by General Clark and "a small number of unprincipled men" was "generally disavowed in Kentucky." He assured him that due to a memorial which "we have addressed the governor on this subject" justice would be done. Moreover, he stated, "ample reparation" could be had if the merchants so outraged would bring suit against General Clark in the Kentucky courts.

He continued. "At this very moment, a certain Colonel Green and other desperate adventurers are meditating an attack on the posts of his most Catholic Majesty at Natchez, in violation of the laws of their country, of the faith of treaties, and of the custom of nations."

He, James Wilkinson, considered this warning to be only his duty "In order to prevent this act of piracy and in order to enable you with certainty not only to forestall but also to take vengeance upon the authors of this plot." He promised, "we shall do everything in our power here to foil this band." He expressed some anxiety however that "they may elude our vigilance."

He was of the opinion, he said, that such an expedition as was proposed could not start before the middle of February "which gives you time to inform his excellency, Don Miró, of the projected plan."

Reading over the letter he thought it one of his masterpieces. His name would now be familiar, he would appear in a good light when he started down the river, and he was not likely to be stopped.

When Carberry returned he reported that Señor Cruzat had been very kind to him, that he expressed his gratitude for General Wilkinson's concern and that the information had been forwarded to New Orleans. "Good. Good," General Wilkinson said. The first step had been accomplished.

Carefully, then, he arranged for the journey. He took with him only Carberry and a Negro servant, departing in a large canoe ahead of the loaded barge which was to follow more slowly.

At the confluence of the Ohio and Mississippi rivers he again sent Carberry to St. Louis with a letter. He thanked Señor Cruzat for his civilities to Captain Carberry on his former visit, assured him that the captain would continue to render every good office within his power whenever such might be needed or requested. In return, he said that he was on his way to Philadelphia via New Orleans and wished "a passport for my Person, Servant & Baggage." He wished, he said, "to pay obedience to the Regulation of the Government of his most Catholic Majesty."

It worked. He was allowed to pass down the river and he was graciously received at Natchez. After some days of conversation and the gift of a pair of fine blooded horses to Grand-Pré, the commandant at that fort, he was given a letter to Don Miró and continued on his way.

On July 2, he arrived in New Orleans, immediately presented himself, with letter, to Don Miró, and was cordially received. Thereafter he was frequently entertained in the home of Don Esteban and within two months the business had been concluded.

He flattered himself that no other man living could have made a better deal with the Intendant. Suavely, delicately, affably, he had represented to Don Miró the situation in Kentucky. He spoke with apparent candor and frankness of their discontent with the state of affairs, hinted at their willingness to withdraw not only from Virginia but from the union, mentioned briefly, but tellingly, the interest Great Britain might have in aiding the Kentuckians, spoke wistfully of his own preference to see them allied with Spain.

On the whole, he chuckled, remembering, he had managed to scare the pants off Don Miró, who foresaw an army of Kentuckians, wrathful over the continued closure of the river, invading his country. He also thought he foresaw that if he did not deal with this young man, who looked so much older than his thirty years, who was so obviously a man of great influence in Kentucky, England would step in, ally herself with the Kentuckians, and an English army might come marching into New Orleans. Forever lost would be the Spanish glory, then.

Temporizing, however, Don Miró asked the general, whom he was now calling Don Jaime, to put his proposals in writing, in the form of a memorial which could be sent to Madrid. "It is for the records, you understand," he said, "merely for the records."

"Sir," Don Jaime had replied, "I shall be glad to memorialize the King himself, but if such a document should ever be seen by any other eyes than ours, my fame and reputation in my own country would forever be extinguished."

Assured that the paper would be kept confidential, would be seen only by official eyes, Don Jaime had turned gladly to the composition of the memorial. He was never happier than when his pen was flowing persuasively and eloquently. His gift for words was free, bounteous and endless.

The terms concluded with Don Miró were expressly set forth. Don Jaime proposed that, in return for the favor of exclusive navigation of the river to himself, "and for such consideration as my services may be deemed to merit," he would undertake to bring about the secession of Kentucky from Virginia and an alliance with Spain, either as a sovereign state or as a vassal state, whichever seemed possible and desirable.

In his elegant hand he wrote that "the Kentuckians will take up any proposition, no matter how desperate, in a cause of the utmost importance to them and their posterity."

In order, he suggested, that separation from the union might be brought about, the Spanish minister, Don Gardoqui, should "without hesitation deny absolutely to Congress the navigation of the Mississippi." His ink flowing, Wilkinson thought he must make this plain. He could not otherwise profit from a monopoly in the river trade. If the fools opened the river to all, his own pockets would be no fuller than the others'.

He continued. Should Spain grant the navigation to the United States, the westerners would be grateful to their own government and would have no zeal for withdrawing. However, if the United States continued to fail in its efforts, and if Spain, willingly and freely opened the river, at the proper time and within a few years, the westerners would owe their gratitude to the Spanish and would express it by allying themselves to the crown. "This conduct," he added, "will make them partisans of Spain . . . With these pretexts the steps of the withdrawal from the federative government to the negotiation with the Court of Spain will be natural and immediate."

He went on then to suggest a system of policy and defense which included building a Spanish fort at the juncture of the Ohio and the Mississippi. Delicately he hinted that Spain open the doors of colonization to certain leading characters in Kentucky who would be willing to come under His Majesty's protection as subjects. His tongue in his cheek he chortled over the idea of obtaining a foothold in the Spanish domain. It could be done!

The memorial was duly presented to Don Miró. On the next

day, Wilkinson wrote another paper professing his loyalty to Spain. It took the form of an oath of allegiance. At some length he detailed how his personal fortune demanded a change of allegiances. He told how he had rendered very valuable services to the colonies during the Revolution, but that the successful conclusion of "this event having rendered my services no longer needful, released me from my engagements, dissolved all the obligations, even those of nature, and left me at liberty, after having fought for her welfare, to seek my own. Since the circumstances and policy of the United States have rendered it impossible for me to attain this desired object under her government, I am resolved, without wishing them any harm, to seek it in Spain . . ."

He a little believed it as he wrote. Who else but the imbecile Congress was responsible for the pinch he was in at this moment? Every acre he possessed would be taken for debts if he didn't pull this scheme off. He hoped for a pension from Spain for his services; and he needed the monopoly of the river trade. He had no qualms whatever about expatriating himself. He would have sworn allegiance to the polar bears in the Arctic to get what he wanted, and it meant nothing since he had nothing but contempt for the Spanish and had no intention of keeping such an oath.

Before he left New Orleans, Don Jaime gave his good friend the Intendant a list of the settlements west of the Alleghenies and a map of their approximate locations. He also gave him a list of the prominent men in Kentucky who, he said, could be counted on for interest in their plan. Indiscriminately he listed nearly every man of influence in the district. It did not matter that most of them would have denounced him wrathfully had they known what he was doing. He needed a long list of men the Spanish had heard of. So down they all went; Brown, Bullitt, Shelby, Greenup, McDowell, Todd, Anderson, Sebastian, Innes, Logan, Cartwright . . . and when he had finished the page was full.

In return, he did not get *quite* all he had hoped for. Don Miró assured him that Spain would probably look with favor upon his plan, and hinted that he could count, eventually, upon being compensated for his services. The word "sole right" or "monopoly" was not included in the grant giving him the right to ship cargoes down the river, but Don Jaime told himself he could handle that. Which he promptly proceeded to do by giving the Spanish a list of merchants whom it would be dangerous for them to trade with; and he made certain that the list included every man financially able to ship down the river.

Taken altogether, he thought, surveying his achievements, he had every right to feel pleased. It now remained necessary only to walk the tightrope he had stretched — appear zealous for Kentucky to Kentuckians, zealous for Spain to the Spanish. He had no doubt at all he could do it. Who, he wondered, had said a man couldn't have his cake and eat it too.

CHAPTER 21

*Cass went to Lexington in February when the general was ex*pected to return. Ann Wilkinson had written him a note that she had heard from Jimmy in Philadelphia. "He is bringing me, he says, a new carriage, and four Negroes. Oh, but I will be glad to see my Wilkinson again! His absence has been a long, dreary time for me. He asks you to join him at your earliest convenience after his return."

Cass stood, among the rest of the gaping crowd, and watched the triumphal entry of James Wilkinson, who drove rapidly down the main street of the little town in an elegant carriage drawn by four high-stepping, matched bays. The new Negroes surrounded him as he reclined, impressively, on the quilted cushions of the new carriage, and he wore, Cass saw, a new suit of the latest cut in men's clothes.

Cass grinned, watching the parade. No conquering hero could have staged his entry better. The general casually puffed at a Havana and bowed graciously to the people who lined the streets. The man was a superb actor, Cass thought, well aware of the value of the limelight. No one, seeing his return, could doubt the success of his venture.

Cass waited until the next day to call upon him. Ann deserved a little time alone with her husband. But he found the general already busy sending out agents to buy up produce to make up another shipment. "I have gained," he told Cass pompously, "the entire confidence of Don Miró — so much so that he calls me his 'dear Don Jaime.'" He smirked a little at the memory, then resumed briskly, "But I must immediately take advantage of his good will and keep the river flowing with my cargoes."

He waved Cass, with a light movement of his small, white hand, to a chair opposite him. "The journey was a complete success, Cass — a complete success."

"Yes," Cass said, "I judged it was . . . from your new equipage. Tell me about it."

Carefully editing, the general related his adventures. He knew how to tell a story well and there was enough color, enough adventure in what he could legitimately tell that it remained interesting. He boasted of the Spanish he had met, of the dinners with Don Esteban, of his friendship with the commandant at Natchez. He chuckled as he told about the blooded horses for Grand–Pré, intimating that he had thus bribed his way down the river.

"So you have opened the river," Cass said, reflectively.

"Not yet to free and unlimited enterprise," the general confessed. With a show of modesty he continued. "I was fortunately able to arouse in Don Miró such feelings of friendship and admiration that he was willing to allow me certain advantages. But I, of course, shall extend them to my friends."

"Of course," Cass said, dryly.

"I have driven the opening wedge, Cass. To be sure, our people must trade with New Orleans through me for a time. I could not answer for the safety of shipments downriver by anyone else. However, I confidently expect that within a few years any Kentuckian wishing to take his produce down the river will find it safe and profitable."

"I see," Cass said. "In the meantime, naturally, you will make a nice, fat profit yourself."

"Naturally," the general replied calmly. He grinned at Cass. "After all, I took the risks."

"Yes. James, I can use my share of the profits of this journey of yours. I have been postponing many improvements on my place until your return when I had those profits in hand."

The general turned to his desk, searched through a litter of papers there. He handed Cass a warehouse receipt. "I regret to tell you, Cass, that I return from this trip almost as penniless as I departed. The shipment was entirely impounded in the King's warehouse, as you see by that receipt. The money for it is not to be paid out until the shipment is cleared from Madrid. But of course that receipt will be redeemed at that time."

Cass studied the receipt. "Apparently you were paid in cash for your own goods. That new carriage of yours must have cost you a pretty penny."

"Borrowed," the general said, "every farthing of it. Borrowed of course," he added, "against my profits."

"I see. Well, you have done the impossible, James. I congratulate you." He stood.

The general rose also. "I am making up another shipment immediately, Cass, which should fare better. It is my opinion that by the time it reaches New Orleans Don Miró can clear it at once. The Spanish, you know, do everything very slowly, and Don Miró is actually not a free agent. He must have permission from Madrid for every move he makes. I should like to be able to count upon your tobacco again, Cass."

"It depends," Cass said, slowly.

"Depends on what?"

"James, did you use those documents relating to General Clark in your negotiations in any way?"

Unflustered, the general returned his look.

"Certainly. How do you think I got down the river? I used them to very good advantage. I frightened the wits out of Don Miró with them."

Cass fumbled with the warehouse receipt, feeling a little sick. "You had that in mind from the beginning, didn't you? You ruined a man purposely. And you used a group of men with honorable intentions to serve your own needs. You deliberately ruined George Rogers Clark."

The general shrugged. "The man was a fool."

"You cared nothing for the welfare of the country, did you? What you saw was an opportunity to make a clever deal. And we were all dupes for your scheme. James, you have always openly spoken out for separation from Virginia and privately, to a number of us, you have intimated that we should set ourselves up independent of the union." His voice sharpened. "Have you made a deal with Spain?"

Coolly James Wilkinson faced him. "What do you think I came into this country for in the first place, Cass? To tend a village store? To speculate interminably in land? I haven't listened to Thomas Jefferson expound the course of empire for nothing!"

"Thomas Jefferson does not want to see this western country out of the union."

The general swayed forward, his small, cleft chin jutted out. "Thomas Jefferson wants to see the Spanish off this continent—just as any sensible man does! I am dealing in a dream so vast, Cass, that only men of great mind can understand it. A dream of an empire clear to the western ocean! What happens to this puny little district is immaterial beside the great sweep of that dream. But it has to begin here. I tried to tell you in Philadelphia. I thought you had the mind to perceive, as I do, what may be achieved. I even dreamed you would join me!"

Cass stared at him. "Is Thomas Jefferson behind you in this scheme?"

"Of course not. Thomas Jefferson is in France, as you very well know. But I have heard *him* dream, too, and I know that he believes as I do, that this nation must some day reach from ocean to ocean."

"I believe you are mad, James. This is folly."

"No. But you, I see, are caught in the net of your own petty concerns. I am disappointed in you, Cass."

"I am caught in the net, as you put it, James, of what happens to Kentucky. I have no idea what kind of scheme you have contrived with Don Miró, but I know it will do one thing. It will further the insane ambitions of James Wilkinson. You see yourself as the great conqueror and hero, don't you? Well, I see you as a rogue and traitor. And I am afraid history will see you in that light, also. I must denounce you, James."

James Wilkinson's eyes went so coldly black as to become almost opaque. "Who," he said, with dangerous softness, "will believe you?"

He had only contempt for Cass, now. It was evident in his cool acceptance of the challenge. Cass guessed that he had no further use for him and deemed him fit only for discard.

"I don't know yet," he said slowly, "but I shall not let that stop me. No, James, I shall not be shipping any more tobacco down the river with you. My 'petty concerns' do not include treachery."

Outside, the air was cold and crisp; the sky was light with the hard brilliance of winter stars. Cass drew in a long breath. He had set himself a difficult goal, he knew. James Wilkinson was truly the hero of the hour. He had easily been the most popular man in the district before he made the trip downriver. Now he would be set upon a pedestal. No one would believe he could do wrong. Cass had to find someone who would listen.

CHAPTER 22

*It was, of course, Jeremy who listened first. Cass told him in de-*tail of his encounter with the general, even, with conspicuous lack of humor, of the Spanish appellation, Don Jaime. Jeremy merely lifted his sparse eyebrows and continued to brood. After a time he asked, "How much do you have to fear in this next convention?"

"It is hard to tell," Cass said. "On the surface, nothing. Our petition goes to the Congress this spring. They may be acting on it this moment. John Brown was to present it immediately the session opened. If they admit us, the convention *should* simply sit for the purpose of recording the action and for resolving another convention to write a state constitution. There is no knowing, however, what objections James may raise. I expect any small requirement made of us to be an opportunity for him."

"Whom can you count on among the leaders?"

"Most of the really influential men," Cass said, "are aligned solidly with James. There is, however, Thomas Marshall, who is an avowed federalist and who, I think, would not countenance for one moment any talk of leaving the union. There is Ben Logan, of course. John Allen of Fayette County has a steady, legal mind. Joseph Crockett is another man of federalist leanings. Judge McDowell, I think, would lean our way, but as chairman of the convention he can hardly be counted on — he must remain impartial. That's about all, Jere."

"You'll have to see them, then, and talk very strongly to them.

They will have to be the core of the fight in the convention. But what I would do, also, Cass, is to get out into the country and begin to circulate rumors. Go to the people with them. See the men you have named, of course; but you'll have to fight fire with fire. Tell everyone you know what you suspect about Wilkinson. Let the rumors about him begin to whisper about the country. It is very difficult to run down rumors, and they can be very damaging. Nothing travels faster than gossip, for people love it. Set it afloat. It will worry 'Don Jaime' I guarantee you, and what will worry him most is that he cannot put his finger on it. You cannot seek out thirty thousand people and make your denial to each of them, for each may accuse you of a different thing. He is *counting* on you to make an effort to sway the leaders. I would sway the people, also."

Cass looked at the wispy little man, one shoulder hitched so much higher than the other, his lean papery face white and seamed with his years. "Jeremy," he said gravely, "your mind is like a knife blade, whetted and honed. It was a fortunate day for Kentucky when I met you in the tavern at the Falls."

Jeremy shook his lank-haired head. "I believe in the people."

Cass followed his advice and set floating about certain rumors concerning General James Wilkinson. Within two months he had the pleasure of hearing them repeated to *him*, garbled and enlarged, but that did not matter. People were talking.

"What did he do with all that money he got for the tobacco he took downriver?"

"How did he get past Natchez?"

"What did he do with those documents on General Clark?"

"How did he know about General Clark?"

"What's this about the Spanish calling him 'Don Jaime'?"

"How did he pay for that fancy carriage he brought home with him?"

"What kind of a deal did he make with the Spanish?"

"I don't know about this General Wilkinson. Looks to me like he's trying to line his own pockets."

Jeremy chuckled when Cass reported. "Good. Good. That's exactly what we want."

It was hot when the members of the sixth convention assembled in Danville on July 28. Heat waves shimmered up from the dusty village square and the delegates wiped perspiring foreheads.

There was as yet no news from the east—no word from John Brown as to any action the Congress had taken on their petition to be admitted to the union. Time had run out on July 4.

All spring there had been an occasional bitter rumor that John Brown was having difficulty; that the petition had been presented; that it had promptly been referred to a committee. Then word came that the petition was being smothered in the committee. It was said that everywhere John Brown turned he ran into a stone wall of indifference. It was said also that he felt very strongly that the Congress would not admit Kentucky until a northern state could also be admitted, say Vermont or Maine, as a balance of power.

The delegates to the convention were therefore meeting once more merely to keep a convention alive. They had no business to transact until definite word came from John Brown.

It came. In an acid letter addressed to Judge McDowell, chairman again of the convention (as he had been of all the conventions, save that first impromptu meeting Benjamin Logan had called so long before), John Brown wrote that not until July 2 had Kentucky's petition come up for a vote before the Congress. At the last moment, however, the news had arrived that New Hampshire had ratified the new federal constitution, making the ninth and required state, and a new government was in order. Bitterly, John Brown added that the Congress had immediately decided it should conduct no more business, that all business should now be referred to the new government, and they resolved that Kentucky should once more go through the long process of petitioning Virginia and a new Congress for statehood.

Solemnly Judge McDowell read the letter to the convention. And the convention promptly erupted. With horror Cass immediately saw the danger, for James Wilkinson was at once on his feet, his voice hoarse with emotion, shouting, "Gentlemen! If the Congress will not have Kentucky as a state in the union, then we are thrown on our own resources! We have patiently dealt with Virginia and the Congress. The time has come for us to act for ourselves! Gentlemen, I move you . . ."

There was so much disturbance in the room that Wilkinson's voice was lost and quickly Cass got to his feet. If he could just get Judge McDowell's eye! If he could just get a motion before the house to adjourn until tomorrow! It would give time for tempers to cool, time for clear, reasonable discussions before action could be taken, time to see all the men of conservative leaning and map out some plan of action. Ah, the judge was looking squarely at him, his fine, lean face showing his distress at this turn of events. "Mr. Chairman," Cass shouted above the furore, "I move you that this convention adjourn until twelve o'clock noon tomorrow, to give us time to digest the news contained in Mr. Brown's letter."

There was an immediate second from Thomas Marshall, and Cass called for the question without discussion. He could see James Wilkinson struggling with the group of men around him, trying to get through, trying to make himself heard before the question could be put. Cass almost held his breath. Judge McDowell was so deliberate. He kept wetting his lips, looking down at the letter he held — he had almost a dazed look. "Question, Mr. Chairman!" Cass shouted again, "Put the question!"

The judge glanced up, seemed to square his shoulders, come to a decision, and having decided, acted promptly. "Gentlemen, do you vote that this convention be adjourned until twelve o'clock tomorrow?"

A chorus of yeas went up. There was a vociferous nay from Don Jaime, but it was too late. The convention was adjourned. The sweat poured from Cass's face.

He was still sweating as he worked through the afternoon and night. He went to see Thomas Marshall, Ben Logan, John Allen, Joseph Crockett, Judge McDowell. He reminded them again, frankly, that he believed James Wilkinson was intriguing with the Spanish and that he would try to run through a motion for immediate separation and sovereignty. Each of the men Cass saw now admitted he had heard rumors. Mr. Marshall was especially concerned. "I fear we were tools in his hands in the Clark affair, Major."

"I know it, sir. He used those documents to get passed down the river. I cannot prove it, Mr. Marshall, but I believe he is scheming with the Spanish."

Ponderously the old gentleman reflected, then gave his opinion. "Even if he were not, sir, he is for separation and sovereignty and we do not want that. We believe in the federal union. We have ratified the Constitution. We must act, as we have always acted, in good faith toward our own government."

Cass expelled his breath in relief.

When he talked with Judge McDowell the judge listened gravely, then he drew from his portfolio a slip of paper. "This sliding letter," he said, "was enclosed in Mr. Brown's letter to the convention. As you see, it is addressed to me. I wish you would read it, Cass."

Cass read it, growing more and more perturbed. The Spanish minister, Mr. Brown said, had made certain advances to him in private conversations. Don Gardoqui had said "that if Kentucky will declare her independence and empower some proper person to negotiate with him that he has authority and will engage to open the navigation of the Mississippi." He added, however, that Gardoqui had stated "that this privilege can never be extended to them while part of the United States," because of certain trade obligations. John Brown concluded the private letter by saying that he had the permission of Don Gardoqui to mention these proceedings to a few friends in Kentucky.

"Are you going to present this letter to the convention, sir?" Cass asked.

"No, I am not. It is a private letter. I am going to try to ascertain, Cass, how it comes about that the Spanish minister can approach Mr. Brown on such a matter."

"Ask James Wilkinson about it," Cass said shortly. "He will know."

"You know nothing of the matter yourself?"

"Sir, I am a federalist, as you well know. No one in the extreme party would take me into his confidence. But we are going to be faced with a motion to withdraw from the federal union tomorrow unless we move quickly to prevent it."

Judge McDowell peered at him over his spectacles. "You seem very certain, Cass."

"It seems evident to me, sir, that James made some kind of a trade with Don Miró when he was in New Orleans. There has been just about time for Don Miró to be in touch with Madrid and for them to instruct their minister. It is a tempting offer, is it not?"

"Not to me. We do not want to be an independent country."

"There are some who do. Ask James about the letter, sir."

Caucuses of both parties were held that night. Report came to the conservatives that Wilkinson's men were full of glee. It was said that when he saw John Brown's sliding letter, Harry Innes had done a quickstep in the middle of the floor and chortled, "It will do — it will do."

The conservatives dug in. They were determined it would not do. "They are certain to put a motion to go ahead and frame a constitution immediately. We must rally our forces and defeat the motion." They rounded up every man not actually in the other caucus. They talked and talked and talked and in the end they believed they had enough men committed to vote nay to defeat such a motion; and committed to defend their own motion to proceed legally according to the congressional resolution.

Cass, himself, did not go to bed at all that night, and John Allen and Joseph Crockett remained by his side. They were tired men when they went into the convention at twelve o'clock noon.

Rallied around Don Jaime were his special friends, Caleb Wallace, Harry Innes, Benjamin Sebastian and others. On the other side of the room sat Cass with the conservative element. The roll was called. Immediately, then, Wilkinson was on his feet: "Mr. Chairman, it is evident that the powers of this convention so far as it depends on the acts of the Legislature of Virginia have been annulled by the Resolution of Congress. I move that these powers be so annulled, and that it shall be the duty of this convention, as the representatives of the people, to proceed to frame a constitution of government for this district, and to submit the same to their consideration with such advice relative thereto as emergency suggests."

There was, of course, an immediate second, with discussion following.

All day, and all the next day, the discussion waxed hotly; as hot as the broiling sun outside, the tempers of the men in that small log room bubbled and seethed. Wilkinson's clique spoke often and loudly, Wilkinson himself on the floor frequently, eloquent, pleading. "We have been patient long enough. We owe it to ourselves, to our children and to posterity, to take immediate action."

In rebuttal the ponderous voice of Thomas Marshall grew hoarse as he pleaded for legality. "Let us give the new Congress an opportunity! Look at the state of Franklin to our south, gentlemen. They are already in financial and organizational difficulties. The Congress will not admit them to the union. They are held in rebellion. Gentlemen, we do not want to follow the example of the state of Franklin."

Cass added his own pleas when he could. John Allen, lawyer himself, was often on the floor. And no man, of either party, could tell how the vote would turn. In between speeches Cass, John Allen, Joseph Crockett, lobbied. "Vote nay," they pleaded. "We are Americans, remember."

There was anger in some of the replies. "The Congress don't want us. They don't care about the western country!"

"We *have* to give the new government a chance. Don't vote us out of the union!"

Some men were now uncertain. "What if the new Congress won't admit us either? By God, we've been patient long enough."

They were answered with the same plea. "We'll cross that bridge when we come to it. When the new Congress turns us down is time enough to consider what we shall do then. Vote nay on this motion. Save the district for the union at least long enough to give the new Congress a chance."

But no man could tell how the vote would go. "I can't be certain of a dozen men," Cass lamented that first night to John Allen.

"Nor I," was the answer. "No one can tell until the question is put."

Late on the second day of the long, wrangling discussion, one of Wilkinson's men called for the question. Cass looked about the room, caught the eye of the men of his party. Wearily they all nodded. It might as well come now. They had done all they could. Down Cass's back ran a shiver of apprehension. This body of men were going to vote, now, and when the vote was counted, Kentucky might well be in the hands of Don Jaime and the Spanish.

The roll call began. Cass closed his eyes. He could not yet tell.

"Yea."

"Nay."

"Yea."

"Yea."

"Nay."

"Nay."

Thomas Todd, clerk, was recording the votes. No one spoke while he totaled them. The air was heavy with the silence. No sound could be heard except the heavy breathing of tired men. Watching Thomas Todd's pen move, watching his head bent over the record, Cass thought wearily that however the vote went, now, they had done their best.

He saw Todd lift his head. If he looks at James, Cass thought, it will mean he has won. But Todd looked instead at Thomas Marshall, at him, at, finally, Judge McDowell. "Sir," he said, "the nays have it."

Weakly Cass leaned back on the bench. God, he thought, how did we ever do it!

But he knew how they had done it. The little delegates, the men not committed either way, had listened to the plea for patience, for reason, for law and order. And it was victory — for the time. No constitution would be framed at this convention.

CHAPTER 23

Before the convention adjourned, however, Wilkinson, not so easily defeated, was able to engineer and put through a resolution so radical that it laid the groundwork for a terrific battle to ensue. The resolution called for a new convention to meet the following November, and to continue in power until January, 1790; to have delegated to it "full powers to take such measures for the admission of the district as a separate and independent member of the United States of America; and the navigation of the Mississippi, as may appear most conducive to those purposes: *and also to form a constitution of government for the district and to organize the same, when they shall deem necessary or to do and accomplish whatsoever on a consideration of the district may, in their judgement, promote its interest.*"

The resolution was ramrodded through. Little time was given for discussion. Everyone was worn out with the heat and the long tense discussions that had gone before and few of the delegates saw any danger in the resolution. They were tired of all these elections and tired of calling new conventions. They saw no good reason why they should not elect next time a permanent convention with full power to act; and the resolution was very cleverly worded. The dangerous clause was attached at the last, when tired delegates might not even hear it as it was read to them.

Hearing the resolution pass, Cass knew they had given the new convention absolute power. It need not even refer its actions back to the people. It would be, he saw clearly, the supreme ruler of Kentucky for the next two years.

He looked across the assembly room at James Wilkinson and James, insolent, unafraid, deliberately thumbed his nose at him. Don Jaime was, indeed, a long way from being licked.

"There is only one thing to do," Jeremy told him.

Cass was tired to the bone. Home had never looked sweeter to him. Almost apathetically he lay in a hammock made of barrel staves which Caesar had slung between two of the great elm trees. He had told Jeremy every detail of the convention discussions. He swirled the drink of cool ale he held in his hand, swung the hammock with one foot. "The people again?"

"Of course. Summon your leaders and all of you ride — ride over the entire country again and tell the people they must instruct their delegates. Tell them what to instruct. Tell them their delegates must be sent to the convention committed to vote *only* for legal separation. It is the only way you can break the absolute power given to the convention."

Cass shook his head. "I don't know, Jeremy. This action of the Congress has even the people roused now. They feel we have been bandied about long enough."

"It's your only hope, man. You must get enough committed delegates into that convention to hold hard and firm. And you must begin at once. You'll have to gird up your loins for that convention in November."

"My loins," Cass said wryly, "need rest. I was never so tired in my life."

"You can rest," Jeremy told him, "when the convention is over."

"You're right, of course," Cass said, swallowing the last of his drink, "but if I don't take a few days before then, I'm going to fall apart."

Jeremy chuckled. "Take a week, then. We can't have you falling apart. The country needs you too badly."

It was one of those things, he thought later, that seem to be decided by fate; for if he had not been so weary he would almost certainly have ridden off immediately and he would thus have been away when Rachel's mother died. As it was, he was at home, doing little but eating, sleeping, and pondering.

They were at the breakfast table. For some time Mrs. Hewett had been so much better that she had been coming downstairs for her meals; she had even been taking some part in the household chores. Just the day before she had worked for several hours at the big loom.

They waited a little while, then Rachel said, "Mother must not be feeling very well. Go ahead with thy meal, Cass . . . and the children. I will see if she wants her breakfast on a tray in her room."

She was not gone long, but when she returned she was very pale and dazed looking, as if she had suffered some shock. "What is it?" Cass asked, rising immediately and going to her.

"I cannot wake her, Cass. I think she is . . . She is quite cold."

Cass took the stairs two at a time.

Mary Hewett had died in her sleep.

When he returned to the dining room Rachel was quietly in possession of herself, entirely composed and in control of her emotions. She lifted her eyes to his. He nodded. "She is gone."

She made no reply immediately. Instead, she looked out the window at the heat-struck landscape, at the leaves, already wilting under the morning sun, at the last webby, smothering mist rising from the river. "She insisted on working at the loom yesterday," she said, then. "I should not have allowed it. The exertion, I think . . ."

"You are not to blame yourself," Cass interrupted swiftly, moved by the one tortured look that swept across her face.

"No. It was what she wanted, after all." She turned quietly to her children, and Cass never again heard her speak of her mother.

Cass stayed at home one more week and then he felt he must be about the business of the next convention. "I do not like to leave you," he told Rachel.

"Thee must see to thy affairs, Cass. I shall be all right," she replied calmly.

"If it were not that the entire country may suffer . . ."

"Thee must go, Cass. I cannot have thee neglecting thy work for me."

She was, Cass thought, like a violin string stretched taut. She could never allow herself the release of emotions freely spilled and poured out. Always, whatever she felt deeply she kept within herself, contained, controlled, held in check. He wished that were not her way, but it was, and even now she would neither ask nor accept comfort from him, or from anyone else. In the end he rode away, telling himself that perhaps she even preferred to be alone with her grief. He knew, he thought, so little about her inner feelings.

The burden of his words now was, "Instruct your delegates. This convention must not have so much power. It will vote us out of the union."

"Why ain't it right for us to set up for ourselves? They don't want us in the union!" He heard it so often he thought the whole country must have been infected with Wilkinson's plea.

"Give the new Congress a chance," he always answered. "If we leave the union we shall find ourselves at war with the United States. They will not willingly let this western country go."

"Then why don't they let us in the union?"

"When the new Congress meets, they will. Let us give the new government an opportunity. Let us be patient. Instruct your delegates to vote only for law and order. If you don't, you'll wake up some morning and find you are no longer Americans!"

Joseph Crockett rode likewise, as did John Allen, and Ebeneezer Brooks. Brooks, who had begun as a hothead, had long ago switched to the conservative side; he wanted separation, he said, but he wanted it legally.

They rode, they talked, they stumped, until their voices left them and the flesh melted away from their bones. They became gaunt, whispering men. But as the summer wore on they thought they could begin to see some effects from their strenuous work. And they had an unbelievable stroke of good luck.

It was early in September, and Cass, so worn he could hardly sit erect, was at the home of Mr. Marshall in Lexington. "I think we have covered every county, every village, and almost every man in the district, sir."

Thomas Marshall, whose son John was soon to become Chief Justice of the United States Supreme Court, looked at him over his spectacles, his face square, honest, plain. "There is a matter I would lay before you, Cass. Judge Muter had a letter from Mr. Brown, shortly after the convention adjourned, in which he made it very clear that if we would declare ourselves independent, Spain would open the Mississippi. He mentioned having had some private conversations with the Spanish minister, who assured him of this, and who told him, further, that unless Kentucky did declare itself an independent government the navigation rights would never be granted."

"Yes, sir. That same news was in the sliding letter enclosed in Judge McDowell's."

Mr. Marshall, who now believed as firmly as Cass that James Wilkinson was dealing in treachery, cleared his throat. "Yes. Well, Judge Muter has no knowledge of that letter. It was never shown to him. He has, as you know, Cass, been somewhat vacillating in his opinions. He has, at times, been greatly influenced by the extremists. But this letter is troubling him. The judge is beginning to have his eyes opened. He has showed me the letter and asked for my counsel. I have counseled him to publish Mr. Brown's letter."

Cass sat up. "If he would do that, sir, it would be the most powerful move he could make."

"I regret to say he is not willing. He insists it is a private letter and it would be a breach of trust to expose it to the public eyes. I wish very much you would see him. He is living here in Lexington, now, almost a neighbor to me. See if you can persuade him."

"Yes, sir," Cass said briskly. "I'll be happy to see him."

When he called on him that night, the judge listened carefully to everything Cass had to say. He also allowed Cass to read John Brown's letter. It said nothing more than the note to Judge McDowell had said, save in its opening paragraph Mr. Brown committed to paper his opinion that the convention would probably feel it must immediately frame a constitution, "as you have proceeded too far to think of relinquishing the measure."

"We would like you to publish this letter, sir," Cass said, handing it back to him.

"I cannot do that, Major Cartwright. It is a private letter." He peered at Cass. "I am greatly troubled. Sir, do you believe that Mr. Brown and Mr. Innes, Mr. Sebastian, the other friends of General Wilkinson, are implicated in this scheme you believe so strongly?"

"Judge Muter," Cass replied thoughtfully, "I do not impugn the names of those gentlemen at all. I believe, however, they are mistaken in their judgments, misled in their interests, misinformed in their knowledge. I do not believe them corrupt as I firmly believe General Wilkinson is. In their zeal for the country's good, I believe them to be hasty in their conclusions, and one must certainly grant that the Congress has given much ground for impatience and distrust."

"I have myself, you know, been influenced in that direction considerably. But I had no knowledge, no suspicion of intrigue."

Cass looked at the amiable, nearsighted, aging man. He was, he thought, a man who never in his life would purposely do a wrong thing. But he was a man of so little astuteness that he could easily be led to do many. The judge continued, hesitantly. "Do you think these other men are likewise as ignorant?"

"I do not know," Cass said honestly. "But, sir, I have been as close to General Wilkinson as any man in the country, and I have been told nothing of the details of his personal plans. For that reason I do not believe he has confided wholly in any man. Mr. Brown, as our representative in Congress, was approached by the Spanish minister. He was by duty bound to deliver Don Gardoqui's proposals to someone in the district. There is nothing shameful in his having heard them, and by his willingness to divulge them, he erases any stigma from his actions. General Wilkinson, sir, in my opinion, is using the legitimate concerns of his friends for his own purposes, making dupes of them all."

"Then, by God," Judge Muter exploded, "we shall stop him!"

"The great danger, sir," Cass continued, "is the power given to this convention. We may well find ourselves voted out of the union if the convention is given this power unrestricted."

"We shall take steps to hamper that power," the judge promised. "I cannot publish this letter, but over my own name I can publish a strong protest. The people must recognize their danger."

The judge committed himself almost immediately. There appeared a long letter in the *Kentucky Gazette,* over his signature. And the letter exploded a bombshell. It boldly repeated the fears Cass had expressed, roused the people to the dangers that threatened them if they elected an unhampered convention. He suggested, boldly, that there were sinister influences at work that might commit Kentucky to a course of action that the great majority of the people could not approve. Clearly, concisely, pointing out the illegality of any action setting up a new state without the consent of Virginia, the judge said, "The federal constitution also prohibits the states from entering into any treaties or alliances with each other or foreign powers. There is, therefore, no possibility of the convention legally taking the slightest action toward securing navigation of the Mississippi, but there is strong implication that illegal action of some kind is contemplated by means of an attempt to treat with Spain."

The result of Judge Muter's letter, siding so strongly with the conservatives, combined with the long, tireless rides over the country, was that many of the delegates were elected with instructions. They were told to vote only for legal action. There were still enough uncommitted, however, to promise a good, stiff fight in November.

CHAPTER 24

On a deathly still, brassy hot day in mid-September, Cass was at home again. The elections were over and he had nearly two months in which to catch up with his personal affairs.

Tobacco was being cut and he walked through the proud, yellowing fields, watching the men bend, slash, and stack the ripening stalks. It was fine tobacco. It had been a perfect growing season — rain when it was needed, once a week at least, and now this long, dry spell for ripening and cutting.

All the people took a hand in it, even the women who were able. Mercy Bearden's strong, tall body moved slowly down a row behind her husband, stacking the cut stalks as Jacob handed them to her. The Negro women were beside their men, and old Mag was stacking for Tattie who refused a woman's job and wielded a knife as capably, as economically as any of the men.

With her skirts bunched up around her knees, her legs and feet brown and bare, her dark hair as knotted as a skein of yarn, she was singing as she worked. Any sight of her now made the muscles of Cass's chest draw and bind so that to breathe was an ache and a pain; and there was always that feeling of complete emptiness, of disaster and catastrophe and anguish.

Seeing him draw near, Tattie threw back her hair, grinned at him and began singing lustily:

" 'A bed, a bed,' Clerk Saunders said,
'A bed for you and me!'

'Fye na, fye na,' said may Margaret,
'Till anes we married be!'"

Flushing, knowing she meant him to hear the words, knowing she was at her tormenting again, he walked on. But his legs felt stiff and his mouth was dry and his blood was turgid; and he wished, angrily, he might take her here in the tobacco fields, on the hot, dusty earth, between the tall rows of hanging, concealing, acridly odorous tobacco stalks. To relieve himself, the binding in his chest, the ache in his loins, he grabbed a knife from Caesar and fell to slashing at the stalks in a fury of motion. Caesar wiped his black face thankfully. "Sho' hot, Mist' Cashus. Gwine rain soon. Hope we gits dis heah tobaccer in de barns 'fore it comes, tho'."

Cass only grunted and kept on slashing.

He was grimy, dirty and sticky from the tobacco gum when the day was over. "Rachel," he called into the house from the back door, "I'm going to the river to bathe. I'm too filthy to come in. Bring my clean clothing here to the door, will you?"

Rachel clucked over his ruined clothing. "If thee meant to work in the fields, Cass, why didn't thee come to the house first and change?"

"Didn't know I was going to. Just had a notion to try my hand at it again."

He followed the path to the river, thinking as he went how long it had been since he had bathed there. Not, he thought, since Rachel had taken over the house. She saw to his bath daily, having Sheba take it to his room, and there was no need to seek the river. It would be good, he thought, breaking into a run, to swim and splash in the stream again.

The sun had already set, leaving a long crimson gash in the saffron sky behind the bold, dark face of the cliffs. The light over the valley was still golden, softly hazy as if filled with an infinitely fine dust, ambient, luminous, warm. Against the hills it was faintly tarnished with the green of grass and leaves and trees. Cass slowed in the edge of the trees, thought how he loved this place, this river, this beautiful golden valley. Here, he thought, if there was peace anywhere on the earth, it should rest here. How alien to its quietness, its beauty, were the troubles of the country. How alien to its perfect charm were his own troubled passions and disturbed heart. He stood against the bole of a great elm, stroked the gray lichen covering its bark, felt a little quietness descend upon him.

He lingered a moment longer then continued, his footsteps softened to soundlessness by the thick mat of grass under them. He came, then, to the bank of the river and behind a screen of small bushes began stripping off his clothes.

Some sound, some feeling of movement, made him glance up and around. Tattie, wholly naked, was coming slowly from behind the willows on the island. Her hair was pinned up into a hasty knot on her head, a few strands escaping childishly down her neck. Her throat, seen thus without the cloak of dark hair which usually hung about it, looked sweetly young and vulnerable. Her face, her arms and legs were the color of honey, or lightly browned bread; but the rest of her body was white — beautiful, milky, firmly fleshed. Catching sight of her without warning, Cass felt a shock of excitement followed by anguish so painful that he groaned. My love, my darling love!

She walked slowly over the gravelly beach of the island, her toes curling over the small pebbles, wincing occasionally from a sharp one. At the water's edge she stooped, picked up a shell, examined it for a moment then tossed it aside. She dipped a toe in the water, shivered, drew it back, lifted her arms to make sure her hair was secure, then plunged into the stream.

Cass watched as she swam rapidly toward the foot of the dark cliffs. She was beautiful in the water, like a young animal, strong, as easily at home as if it were her natural element. He remembered that Mag had told him Tattie swam in the millpond every day during the summer. The still waters of the pond must be almost lukewarm in this heat, he thought. She had preferred the cold, running stream today.

When she reached the foot of the cliffs she turned on her back and floated, the green water barely washing her white body. Through its translucence the paleness was heightened, was made shimmery and rippled.

Cass turned away suddenly, jerking on his clothing, striding rapidly from the place, the old emptiness taking possession of him. This, he told himself, is for the rest of my life. For the rest of my life, he repeated, the ravaging words beating their waste and loneliness in time to his steps, in time to his breathing — in time to his pulse. He stumbled across the meadow, barely conscious, aware only of his acute pain — the memory of the white, shimmery band of flesh a lash across his own flesh. "For the rest of my life," he could only mumble, and stumble toward the long, lonely years.

CHAPTER 25

This time he did not run away. He had learned there was no place to run.

Instead he divided his time between the autumn work in the settlement and a few trips for conferences with the leaders of his party. They mapped out their program of action; tried to foresee every move the extremists would make, tried to be prepared for it. They realized Wilkinson would have strong reinforcement this time in the presence of John Brown, who was out of office now because of the new federal government. He was a delegate to the convention from Mercer county.

The conservatives felt almost certain that Brown would raise the question of Don Gardoqui's conversations with him. They feared this because it was so tempting an offer to have done, finally, with the whole troublesome question of navigation of the river. They took counsel and held to their program. Stand firm for legal action.

In October, Cass was at home again. Rachel, he noticed, was growing thinner, seemed more withdrawn and quieter. He asked her one day, "Are you feeling ill, Rachel?"

She was shelling late beans from the garden, to dry for the winter's use. In surprise she looked up at him. "No. Why does thee ask?"

"You are too thin, I think."

"It is but the heat of the summer, I expect. It was very trying. I am glad the fall is come."

He guessed that she was still grieving for her mother. It was natural that she should be, and only time could heal it for her. And as she said, the heat had been very oppressive all summer, lasting later than usual, well up into September. Only the past two weeks had there been any real relief from it.

Cass went into his study.

The tobacco was in the barns; the hay was mowed; the corn was almost ready to cut. Everything was in good order. He had good people in this settlement he thought, for the hundredth time — people who did not fear honest work, who were faithful and dependable. He did not know what he would have done without them the past few years when it had been necessary for him to be away from home so much. Quietly, accepting the need for his absence, trusting his judgment, realizing perfectly how hard he was still laboring for their welfare, they had done the work of their fields and most of his. He would not, he thought fiercely, trade them for all of the people in the towns of the district. His people knew the meaning of loyalty, had dignity and pride, knew what neighborliness meant. They might never have a town here in the valley, but they had what was better, a fine, strongly rooted, healthy settlement. He had given them all he could, and they in turn were giving back to him generously.

He took up a letter from Mr. Marshall which lay on his desk. The letter suggested they meet together a week before the convention opened, to clarify a few details, to go over once more their program of action. He drew paper toward him to begin his reply, thought a moment, then pushed it aside. He would ride to Lexington himself, since a letter would have to be sent by messenger in any event. Humorously he thought that at this time of year he could be spared more easily than any man he might send.

He felt restless, however, and he moved about the room, going finally to the window which looked up the valley toward the little cove where the mill stood. He knew he looked out that window too often. He knew he should discipline himself better, for there was no denying that he never went to the window without the small hope that he might catch a glimpse of Tattie. It was strange, he told himself, watching the path that wound through the willows, how often he did catch a brief sight of her. It might be nothing more than her bent back as she stooped over the vegetable beds in her garden; or the flash of her skirt rounding the corner of the mill; or the sight of her strong young arms lifted as she hung the wash on a line. It was, he often thought, like biting down on a sore tooth, these small glimpses of her, the pain sharp and glancing but somehow relieving. He had had, he thought bitterly, all that he could ever have wanted in his own grasp and he had been too foolish to know it until it was too late. Misguided, men created so much of their own unhappiness for themselves. But what could a man trust if his instincts led him astray?

It was a soft day, with the smoky haze of fall hanging over the hills, and warm now that the chill of early morning had been baked away. Soon, he thought, his eyes traveling across the valley, the trees would begin to turn; the hills would blaze with color, the air would become crisp and fresher with cold, the meadows would brown and the high grass lean slantingly under its weight of seed. A little while yet of brightness and winy sharpness, then the snows and the deep cold would come again. He dreaded the winter this year. He wondered why. He was getting older, he thought — twenty-nine, now — no longer a very young man. But young enough, he thought, wincing from his present unhappiness, to live out twice his years yet. Fretfully he pulled at the curtains. He wished Rachel did not insist upon curtains in every room of the house. They made him feel closed in and smothered. There was no sight of Tattie this morning.

Someone, though, was coming down the path. Mag? He got a glimpse of red-striped stockings through the willows, and he grinned. Mag and her everlasting red-striped stockings. She wore nothing else, and he bought them for her by the dozen pair. For all her salty tongue she was a marvel of steadiness in the settlement. She had been exactly the leaven he had hoped she would be. No one could very long give himself airs around her, or stay angry, or hold a grudge. She could shame the proudest spirit into humility, or laugh the deepest quarrels into thin air. Earthy herself, she reduced every problem to its barest essentials, surveyed it with plain common sense and made it disappear. Cass wished she could be a delegate to the convention. She would bruise Don Jaime's pride for him! When Mag got through with him there would be little left of his elegant eloquence.

She was coming very fast he saw, running, stumbling along, slowing to a walk, then breaking into a run again. She was always so untidy that you could never tell whether she was more disheveled than usual, but she had certainly taken no time to think of her appearance this morning. Her dress was kited up about her waist, which was about normal for it, but her hair looked a little more blowsy than usual, and she kept hurrying. Suddenly Cass knew that something was terribly wrong. He should have known it instantly, he thought, flinging about and running from the room. He had never seen Mag move faster than a slight dogtrot before. The fact that she was stumbling and running down the path meant only one thing. Something had gone badly wrong at the mill. Tattie! Those heavy millstones!

His heart was tight with fear by the time he met Mag. She was out of the cove by then, cutting across the meadow. He grasped both her arms. "What is it? What's happened?"

She was bent over, clutching her side, breathing so heavily, gasping so loudly, that she could barely talk. She pointed to the mill. "Master Edward — " she gulped out, "Tattie . . . in the millpond — they're drowndin' . . . hurry!"

"My God!" Cass flung her aside and fled up the path. Over his shoulder he called back, "Get Jacob! John Cameron!"

The way seemed endless. He thought he would never get out of the willows and across the pasture. He was running so hard that the young trees were flying past him, he could hear his feet pounding on the hard dirt of the path, but it seemed to him he was almost standing still. His mind had run on ahead of him, picturing the scene, Tattie and the boy in the deep, still water, already past rescuing perhaps. He heard himself groan, felt the stitch in his own side as he reached the slow climb up the hollow.

When he reached the pond he was almost ready to collapse. He flung himself down the bank, slipping and sliding, taking no care to look where he was going, his eyes on the water, searching, hunting. They found a patch of white, floating billowingly, caught in a clump of young reeds. "God!" he cried, moaningly. He snared it with a dead limb, dragged it in. It was Tattie's dress. Standing, holding the wet, cold garment, he felt deadened. He was too late! But he kept looking, wildly, continuing to search the surface of the water.

Then he saw Tattie's head bob up, seal-brown, hair water-slicked, hanging in her face. She shook it out of her eyes, took a few gasping gulps of air and disappeared again. "Tattie!" he shouted.

But of course she could not hear. He flung off his shirt, slid out of his moccasins, and plunged in, his breath still coming painfully. Fool, he thought. What good can you do so out of breath you cannot dive? He came up, swam toward the place where Tattie had disappeared, treaded water and waited anxiously. The boat, he saw, was overturned. She must have been taking young Edward for the long promised boat ride on the pond. Somehow, in some way, probably through the boy's fault, the boat had upset.

It seemed to him a terribly long time since she had gone under. She was exhausted herself, he had no doubt. He began to flounder around, his breath coming a little easier now. She came up a few yards away and he swam toward her. It was the deepest end of the pond they were in — all of thirty feet he knew. "Tattie!" he called.

She turned her face toward him and he was horrified at its whiteness. She looked half drowned. "Tattie, don't dive again! Where is he?"

She shook her head. "Oh, God, Cass, I don't know." She was barely able to keep herself afloat she was so exhausted. Her breath came in quick pants and she talked in short, swift jerks. "He went down — here — but I can't — find him."

Cass took hold of her shoulders. "Rest a moment. Then get out of the water. Mag will bring the other men. I'll keep trying."

"No. Oh, Cass, no. I can't leave him here."

She started weeping and Cass thrust her toward the bank. "Get out, Tattie."

"No." She freed herself and had plunged under the water before he could stop her.

He took as deep a breath as he could manage and went plunging down himself. The water of the pond was dark, stained with leaves and weeds, not very clear, and as he went down and down he realized that weeds had grown up from the bottom during the years. Their slippery branches clutched at him. In despair he thought that one small body, caught among them, was going to be very difficult to find; and if they did not find it soon, it would be too late.

He stayed down as long as he could, groping, feeling, trying to see, then came up with lungs bursting. Tattie was on her back, floating, her eyes closed, her breath coming in great gasps. She had, he saw now, stripped to her shift. That explained the floating dress. "Tattie," he called, "please. You're exhausted."

She shook her head. "No. I've got to keep trying."

"How long has it been?"

"I don't know. Oh, forever, Cass. Hours!"

"It couldn't be. Mag just came . . ."

"Mag heard me screaming, I suppose. I don't recall." She shuddered, turned over and went down again.

The next time they were both above water neither of them had enough breath to talk. They both lay hoarding it, panting, trying to take in enough air to dive again. This happened over and over again until Cass lost track of time. He went down, saw Tattie go down, stayed under as long as he could, came up only when his lungs were ready to explode. He knew she was doing the same. Would the other men never come?

Not once did they lay hold of even so much as a small jacket, or a little hand or foot. Edward had simply disappeared. He was down there somewhere, caught on the bottom of the pond. Cass knew that when they did find him, now, nothing could be done for him. What was the limit of time? Six minutes? It had been much longer than that; it had probably been longer than that before he got to the pond himself. But one could not give up hope.

Once when they were both floating, resting, Cass begged Tattie again to get out of the water, rest a little while. She turned imploring eyes on him. "Rachel trusted him with me. I can't!"

Finally help arrived — Nathaniel, John Cameron, Jeremy. "Get

Tattie out," he shouted to them. "She is nearly drowned herself."

Young Nathaniel plunged in and though she struggled with him, her strength was almost gone and she could only struggle weakly. At the bank, Jeremy helped and they dragged her out and she lay where they left her, her head buried in her arms, flat against the earth, sobbing.

Cass pulled himself onto the bank also. Others were arriving, Jacob, Mag, and to his horror, Rachel had come. Young Nathaniel was treading water near the boat. "Where did he go down, Major?"

"Only Tattie can tell us that," Cass told him. "About there, someplace."

He got up and stumbled over to Rachel, took her hands. "My dear, you must not stay here. We shall find him."

Her hands were as cold as if they had been dipped in ice water and her lips moved stiffly as if they, too, were cold. "When thee finds him," she said slowly, "it will be too late. He is drowned, is he not?"

"Rachel . . ."

"There is no need to hide it from me. It would be cruel. How did it happen?"

"I don't know. There has not been time to learn. Tattie was riding him in the boat, probably. She will tell us when she revives. Will you not go back to the house?"

"And leave my child in that water?" She drew her hands away from his. "How long has it been?"

He could only shake his head. "I do not know that, either. Tattie . . ."

Her lips firmed and a spasm of anger twisted her face. "Tattie had no business taking him in the boat without permission."

"She had promised him — and we knew it."

"She did not ask. Cass, go back! Thee must find him!" She flung herself away from him and fled to the water's edge, would have thrown herself into the pond except that John Cameron's strong hands stayed her. Cass gripped her tightly when he reached her.

"Rachel, listen to me! We shall do everything we can. You

know that. If you mean to stay here, you must be sensible. You will hinder us, otherwise. Sit down on that rock over there and stay out of the way." He knew it was cruel, but they could not be hampered by her. Though she seemed frozen, she understood and nodded.

Jacob, John Cameron, even Jeremy, had stripped off their linsey shirts, their moccasins. "You are not going into the water, Jeremy," Cass told him.

The little man winced. "I expect someone would only have to rescue me, at that," he said. "But I wish I could help."

"You can." Cass's mind was beginning to work practically now. "Nathaniel," he called, "right the boat and push it to the bank. Jeremy, get in the boat and keep it steady where we can hold on to it when we come up. It will rest us more than swimming to the bank."

Jeremy got into the boat and rowed it toward the center of the pond. "About here, Cass?"

"More toward the deep end, Jere. That's right." He turned to Jacob and John. "We had better work in pairs. John, go in now with Nathaniel while I rest awhile. Then Jacob and I will take our turn."

Mag, after one look to make certain Tattie was safe, had brought a blanket to cover her, then she had gone to sit beside Rachel. She was quietly talking to her now. Cass could not hear what she was saying, and from the way Rachel looked he doubted she was hearing it either, but he was grateful to the old soul. Whatever she was saying, it came from her troubled heart and her wish to comfort. Rachel sat on the rock, her hands folded in her lap, her face blanched and stony. It was a terrible thing for her. Though she had tried to hide it, Cass knew Edward was her favorite child. How would she ever survive losing him this way?

They had to learn, if they could, where the boat had overturned, where the boy had fallen into the water. He approached Tattie who, hearing him, turned over, pulled herself up into a sitting position. He touched her shoulder, sitting beside her. "Tattie, try to help us, now. Tell me, as nearly as you can remember, what happened. Where did the boat overturn?"

She pushed her wet hair out of her eyes. "I had promised to take him on the pond some day." She spoke dully, as if the effort to speak hurt her. "He said you knew — said his mother knew."

Cass nodded. "We did. I recall the day he mentioned it."

"He kept bothering me to take him today. Said it would soon be winter and the pond would freeze." She clutched his hand suddenly. "Oh, Cass, if only I hadn't listened to him. If only I had been firm."

"Darling!" He wanted to take her in his arms, comfort her. He pressed her hand. "You couldn't know. Edward could be very persuasive."

She bit her lower lip, began talking again, holding very tightly, however, to his hand. "I told him finally I would take him. Cass, I did warn him to sit very still."

"I'm sure you did." He kept his voice low and hers was barely above a murmur.

"He obeyed for a time. He was as good as gold, Cass, sitting so straight and still, and he loved it so. We went round the pond several times and then I said we must stop. I told him I had work to do. He begged for one more time round the pond, but I told him no. I knew he would keep on and on, never wanting to stop. I told him I would take him again very soon, before the pond froze. He seemed satisfied with that. I rowed the boat to the post and had got out to make it fast, telling him to keep his seat until I could help him out. Suddenly he stood, snatched up the oar and pushed it against the bank and sent the boat out into the water again. He thought it was a wonderful joke on me and he stood there laughing and laughing. 'I'll row myself, Tattie,' he said, 'I can row as good as you.' I was so frightened — but I called to him to sit down and to row straight to the bank at once. He shook his head, and then . . . then he whirled around — for what reason I do not know. But of course the boat tipped over as he whirled about, and he was thrown into the water . . ."

A shadow fell across Cass's feet. He looked up. Rachel was standing before him, her face contorted and tortured. "It was from his own disobedience, then?"

Tattie looked up at her also. "Rachel, I cannot tell you . . ."

Rachel swung about, looked at the still, brown waters of the pond. "From his own disobedience," she whispered. "Cass, I told thee . . ."

His heart twisted by her anguish, Cass leaped to his feet, put his arm about her. She pulled away, biting the knuckles of one hand. "Thee said it was manly of him. Thee said it was a good quality. Thee said all boys were like that. And I trusted thee. But I knew my own boy better. I knew he must obey. His father said he must be taught to obey . . . he must never be allowed to disobey."

"Rachel . . ."

"I should not have listened to thee. The boy's father knew best. And Tattie had no permission . . ." Her hands went to her face. "I shall never forgive her. I shall never forgive thee."

Cass dropped his arm. He had thought her incapable of such distraction. She had controlled herself when she had heard of her husband's death. She had controlled herself when her mother died. But young Edward's death had broken down every control. Maybe it was better, Cass thought. He led her back to Mag. "Keep her with you," he said.

They were searching, then, in as near the right place as possible. There was no current in the pond; the child's body *must* be somewhere near the place he had gone down.

By teams of two they continued to dive and to search for several hours, Tattie, when she had recovered a little, taking her place with them. Wirt Powell came, and Tate Beecham, and all the women, drawn as if by a magnet, their own children clutched fearfully close. It might have been one of them.

They had finally to conclude they were not going to find the child in this manner. It was Jeremy who called Cass to the boat and talked with him. "We are going to have to make hooks, Cass, and drag the pond."

Cass nodded. "I think so too, Jeremy. But how can Rachel bear to watch that being done?"

"I will take her to the house. She will go with me, I think. And I promise to keep her there. I have some laudanum drops in my room, Cass. They will quiet her and she may sleep."

"God bless you, man. Do what you can for her."

When Jeremy had persuaded Rachel to leave with him, Mag and Cass were also able to persuade Tattie to go to the mill. Cass told her what they meant to do. "Nothing can save the boy now, Tattie. All we can do is recover his body. You have been a fine, noble girl, but there is no need for you to help with this. You have done all that could be done."

"Except," she said bitterly, "refuse to take him on the pond at all."

"You must not let what Rachel said trouble you, Tattie. She is distraught. It is not even in character for her to speak so. When she has overcome her grief . . ."

"It is when one is angry, Cass, or when one is deeply hurt, that one speaks out the truth. Rachel will never forgive me."

"Tattie, you never meant to harm her boy. Someday she will understand that."

"No. God knows I loved the boy. I was in the water almost as quickly as he was . . . I did what I could . . ."

Jacob, John, Nathaniel, all the men, had gone to make the hooked line and Mag had gone into the mill to get a warm bath and dry clothing ready for Tattie. They were alone on the bank of the darkening pond. Cass drew her into his arms, where she felt small and cold and very young. It was as if she were the little guttersnipe again, dependent upon him, needing him, turning to him. "My darling, my darling," he said softly, "I know you did what you could. And I know you loved him. Haven't I seen you with him? Singing to him? Telling him those fanciful stories he loved? Haven't I seen you today, almost drowning yourself trying to save him? Don't I know your brave, fine heart, almost better than you know it yourself? Never blame yourself, my love. Never!"

She leaned against him, both of them soggy with the pond water, their clothing dripping, their hair lank and streaming, and when he tipped up her face he thought he had never seen her look more beautiful.

She sighed when his mouth touched hers. "Cass, I am so tired — so very tired. I love you so much."

He tightened his arms and leaned his head against hers. He rocked her gently, as if she had been young Edward's age. There was no heat, no passion, in the way he felt at the moment. There was only a great, deep, solacing sweetness, a great tenderness, in his feeling for her. The tie between them went back so far. She was his child, his young one, his darling love. He kissed her closed eyes, smoothed the wet hair. "I love you too, my Tattie. Go in the house now. Let Mag take care of you. We shall find young Edward."

Just as the sun went down, the big hooks of the long rope hung on something, tightened, and as the men drew it slowly in, the child was brought to the surface of the water. In his hands were clutched the fronds of the weeds which had entangled him, and the great bush itself was still clinging to him, as if unwilling to let him go.

Cass carried him home to Rachel who, still asleep from Jeremy's drops, did not know he had returned. He took him upstairs and laid him gently in his own bed, covered him warmly, as if the little boy might know he was cold and wet, and went to wake his mother. She would never forgive him, he knew, if he let her sleep through this night.

She sat beside the child all night, refusing to allow anyone else in the room.

She sat beside him all through the next day, the door still locked against anyone who knocked.

On the morning of the second day she emerged from the room, drawn, pale, almost withered looking, but composed again. "Is it arranged?" she asked, when Cass went to meet her.

"Yes," he told her, "the men have . . ."

"I don't want to hear about it. Let it be today, then."

He stood by her side as the child was laid in the ground, in the small, pine-ringed burying place. There were three other graves in it; one tiny one, which housed the stillborn child of Nellie and Tate Beecham; one very large one, which old Tench Johnson occupied; one not so large in which Mary Hewett slept. Now young Edward Cabot would lie beside them all in eternal repose.

Daniel Choate, the white-haired, kindly old clergyman, prayed at the graveside and above the sound of his voice a bird sang in a nearby tree. Over and over it sang the same small song, a petulant, repetitive three notes which ended always in an upflung question. Why? Why? Why? the question seemed to be. Cass wished it would go away. He wondered if Rachel was hearing it too, if the bird bothered her. She gave no appearance of hearing or seeing anything. She stood erectly, dressed meticulously, the gray dress she wore a new one she had just completed. Not a strand of hair was out of place and her cap was perfectly pinned. Her face, however, seemed to have shrunk, to be all enormous, dark, shadowed eyes. She did not once lean on Cass, or seem even to notice that he was beside her, and she had not said another word to anyone since telling him to let the funeral be today. Sheba, Molly, the women of the settlement had tiptoed around about the house, frightened by her unnatural silence. They would have been weeping, they knew. No one had seen Rachel Cartwright shed a tear. In the face of her stony composure the woman did not know what to say, or what to do.

As Daniel Choate's voice quavered on, the acrid, resinous odor of the pines bit Cass's nostrils. He hated pines. He wished he had not left these standing. They were the most mournful tree on the face of the earth, and piney land was always sour, acid soil. This little spot was fit only for a burying place.

Across the open grave Tattie stood with old Mag. Mag, Cass saw, had made a valiant effort at a respectable appearance. For once she had left off her striped stockings and her legs, mammoth as ever, were decently wrapped in black. Her hair was as neat as it could ever be got, and Tattie must have pinned her cap for her. It was straight. Tattie was almost as pale as Rachel, but where the older woman's composure was unbroken, Tattie was weeping steadily. She made no sound, made no effort to hide the tears, letting them flow in a stream down her face. My Tattie, he thought. Warm of heart, quick to storm, to quarrel, to fight—just as quick to weep when the tears were ready. He wished Rachel could weep.

At the house when it was over, Rachel still did not speak. She laid off the light shawl she had worn over her shoulders, touched her hair briefly with one hand, stood musing a moment, lost in thought, then went upstairs to her children whom Sheba had been tending. Cass watched her straight back lightly climb out of sight. He was afraid for her. He wished she would do anything but keep this dreadful silence. He wished she would rant at him again, or even at Tattie. Anything would be better than this awful, frozen stoniness she had imposed on herself.

Feeling weary, worn (he, too, had loved the boy and felt his own grief), he went to tell Molly to serve supper. Molly looked at him out of frightened eyes. "Miss Rachel . . . she all right?"

"I don't know, Molly." He shook his head. "It will take time, I suppose. Take her a tray upstairs."

He hoped she would have recovered, a little at least, by the time he had to leave her to go to the convention.

CHAPTER 26

It was a bleak, cold day, with a yellowed sky threatening snow. The room of the log house was crowded, the floor cold beyond all heating, only those delegates sitting near the fire sufficiently warm to keep from shivering. Perhaps, Cass thought, it was the tension as much as the cold which had every man hugging his coat about him. No man here present misunderstood the importance of this assembly.

Thomas Todd, clerk, was calling the roll of the seventh convention — Tuesday, November 4, 1788. His voice droned down the list: Alexander Bullitt, Abraham Hite, John Edwards, Isaac Morrison, James Wilkinson, Caleb Wallace, John Allen, Thomas Marshall, Benjamin Logan, Samuel McDowell, John Brown, Harry Innes, John Jouett, Christopher Greenup, George Muter, Cassius Cartwright. Brought back to reality, Cass answered his own name firmly. All the important men in the country were members of this convention and, he thought, the only one of the old pioneers, the sole, solitary survivor of the transition from settlement to statehood, was Benjamin Logan. All the others were, by comparison, johnny-come-latelies. Where was Boone? Still wandering the woods. Where was Harrod? Lost, no one knew where for certain — murdered by Indians, by his partners in a mining venture, escaped to the Delawares — no one could tell. Where was Clark? Sulking, it was said, in his tents, drinking himself into oblivion.

They were, he thought, looking about the room, like armies

drawn up on a field of battle, the extremists, led by Wilkinson and John Brown, Innes, Sebastian and Wallace, on one side; the conservatives, led by Judge Muter, Thomas Marshall, John Allen, Joseph Crockett, Cass Cartwright, solidly on the other side of the room. The line was drawn down the middle.

Judge McDowell was once more elected to the chair. Routine business, certain letters, certain papers, were read, hastily approved and ordered to lie on the clerk's table. Now, Cass thought, with a mixed feeling of dread, fear, anxiety, eagerness, exultance that they were ready, were organized — now the battle will be joined. It had been decided that they would, themselves, plunge into the heart of the matter, throw down the challenge. By moving immediately into the fray they thought they might throw their opponents off balance. On his feet, his long jaw outthrust, Cass moved that the resolution of Congress concerning Kentucky's admission as a state be referred to the committee of the whole. In effect this motion meant that the convention should decide at once what its powers were. There was an immediate second, and the motion was open for discussion.

At once and as expected, General Wilkinson was on his feet. Elegantly arrayed, rubicund, his small height impressive in its military erectness, his large, dark eyes lambent in their benevolence, he waited for the attention of the entire body. "Gentlemen," he began in that deep, fine voice, so perfectly modulated that it sounded like that of a trained musician, "gentlemen: This motion of Major Cartwright's will have the effect of determining the powers of this convention. I deem it the ardent desire of this convention to pursue such measures as may promote the interest and meet the approbation of their constituents. I further deem it the duty of this convention to act in a spirit of harmony and concord, on which the prosperity and happiness of all depends. But I should like to call to the attention of this assembly that it is a convention, a body, called into existence through the action of the last convention, and that it must of necessity have the power contained in the general resolution of that last convention's final action. This convention, therefore, has whatever powers are necessary for the well-being of the district, and under such powers is obligated, by its very election, to pursue its business accordingly." He spoke, for him, briefly, but the periods rounded beautifully, flowed mellowly.

Judge McDowell carefully managed the discussion, correctly allowing speakers, in turn, from either side. Joseph Crockett spoke to the point that the only power this convention possessed, by virtue of instruction to many of the delegates, was to proceed to apply again to Virginia for statehood with whatever addresses they cared to make.

Listening, weighing the tempers of the speakers, it was Cass's responsibility to call, at the proper time, for the question. It had been decided to allow only a brief discussion, and when four speakers, two from each party, had had the floor, Cass asked for the question to be put. Wilkinson had called a group of his men around him and they were huddled together. There was a surprised flurry among them, but before they could recover, the question was put, and so easily that it left even the conservatives gaping, the motion carried. The resolution of Congress, that Kentucky again petition Virginia for statehood, was referred to the committee of the whole.

They were a long way from being out of the woods, but Cass felt exuberant. This was victory number one. The business of the convention, now, was to discuss the petition to Virginia. James, he knew, would make a stumbling block of every article to be contained in it. Every hour of discussion held a threat, but at least a resolution that this convention continue in full power had been avoided.

One by one the articles to be included in the petition were taken up. Doggedly each party fought, discussed, finally agreed, until just before noon a point was reached where the chair could appoint the committee to draw up the petition. Wilkinson had given ground all morning reluctantly. The final note of irony was his own appointment to the committee to prepare the address to Virginia. It had been planned this way. He could do no damage in the company of John Edwards, Thomas Marshall, Judge Muter, John Jouett and John Allen. It was a stacked committee. The convention adjourned until noon the following day. In caucus,

Cass warned the jubilant conservatives, "We have yet to get the petition passed. We have a long way to go yet."

They had proof the next day that Cass was right. General Wilkinson would not be so lightly dealt with. The roll was barely called when he was immediately on the floor, with a motion that the previous convention's recommendations concerning the navigation of the Mississippi be referred to the committee of the whole. God, Cass thought desperately, we hadn't counted on that.

It was an adroit move. It would reopen all the old passions; in debate it would inevitably sway many of the members still smarting from their economic injuries. It would also revive the personal glory of James Wilkinson; it would remind the members that James Wilkinson knew what he was talking about; that he, alone, had been able to take shipments down the river; that he, alone, knew how best to help the country in this predicament; that he, alone, could open the river eventually to them all.

Judge Muter tried to steer the motion into committee. The navigation of the Mississippi, he said, was not the proper concern of this convention. Its only concern was with statehood.

James Wilkinson was on his feet again. "Gentlemen, anything which pertains to the welfare of this district is the proper concern of this convention. We represent the people, and it is the people who are being deprived of their natural and lawful rights to navigation." He allowed himself to become oratorical, bold and righteously indignant. "Spain has objections to granting the navigation in question to the United States; it is not to be presumed that the Congress will obtain it for Kentucky, or even for the western country — her treaties must be general. There is one way, and but one, that I know of obviating these difficulties, and it is so fortified with constitutions and guarded with law that it is dangerous of access and hopeless of attainment under present circumstances. It is the certain but prescribed course which has been indicated in the former convention, which I will not now repeat, but which every gentleman present will connect with the formation of a constitution, a declaration of independence and the organization of a new state which might safely be left to find its way into the Union on terms advantageous to its interests and prosperity." At this point he looked meaningfully at John Brown, seated near him. His voice deepened resonantly, importantly. "There is a gentleman present who has information of the highest importance," he continued, "on this subject of the navigation of the Mississippi."

Here it comes, Cass thought wildly. This was the thing they had been most afraid of. If John Brown publicly, openly, allied himself with Wilkinson now, if he laid before the convention those conversations with Don Gardoqui, a resolution to accept the terms of Spain would be before the convention before you could sneeze. Cass glanced hurriedly at Mr. Marshall, at Judge Muter, at John Allen. Their faces reflected his own anxiety and concern. What could they do? The man had the floor. They could not interrupt with a motion to adjourn. They had faced this danger in their pre-convention meetings. They had said, then, that if it came, they could only depend upon the instructed delegates to stand firm. They had said, if necessary they would rally the people with petitions to the convention. Cass nodded to Joseph Crockett, who it had been decided, would ride and do the rallying, and quietly, unobtrusively, Crockett slipped out of the assembly room. Now was the time.

The general had paused for the impressiveness of his next words to have full effect. "I call upon that man, now, to speak to that point and to tell us of his conversations with a man of high influence."

Smiling, the general parted the tails of his coat and took his seat.

John Brown rose slowly to his feet, his hands holding to the back of the bench in front of him, his body bent slightly forward. "Mr. Chairman," he began, his voice very low, a note of hesitation in it. "Gentlemen of the convention. I do not . . ." He paused, and Cass saw him wet his lips. "I do not believe myself at liberty to disclose what has passed in private conversation between myself and the Spanish minister, Don Gardoqui, respecting Kentucky." The words came haltingly, almost painfully. Then gathering more conviction, he continued. "I will venture to inform you, however, that provided we are united in our councils, everything we can wish for is within our reach." Abruptly he stopped talking, avoided looking at Wilkinson, sat down.

Cass's mouth dropped. It was unbelievable! John Brown had badly let the general down. Had James had the nerve to call on Brown without warning him? Had he hoped to take him off guard, call on him publicly, compel him to divulge the conversations with Don Gardoqui? Had someone, Mr. Marshall, Judge Muter, talked with Brown? Last night, this morning, undermined his belief in Wilkinson? Something — something had swayed him! If the general had expected to push John Brown into a corner, he had just learned that John Brown would not be pushed. He was counted a man of courage, of integrity, of honor. Perhaps his own plain common sense had told him not to let James Wilkinson use him. Whatever it was, it was a terrific defeat for Don Jaime. Cass looked across at him. He was looking at John Brown as if he found his action incomprehensible. Disbelief, shock, anger, amazement, crossed his mobile features and he half rose from his seat. Then he got hold of himself, erased the open message of his emotions from his countenance and composed himself. Inwardly Cass chortled. Look to your guns, now, Don Jaime. Your priming misfired that time! But there was sweat on his own face, he found, when he licked his lips and found them salty.

Don Jaime promptly looked to his guns. Only momentarily baffled by John Brown's defection, he took the floor to uphold his own motion. He asked permission to read a manuscript which he held. "This, gentlemen," he said by way of preface, "is a memorial which I prepared last summer when I was in New Orleans and it is addressed to the Governor-Intendant, Don Esteban Miró. I flatter myself it will relate to our common problem in better words than I can now summon and it will tell you what I, in my great concern for this country, essayed to do to solve it."

The chair gave permission for the manuscript to be read.

Leaning back on the hard, short-backed bench, Cass listened carefully, watched carefully, also, as the general read. James was like an eel, wiggling from one position to another. It was always dangerous to be careless with him, as he had learned from disillusioning experience. What his motive was for reading this paper was not evident, but every word of it had better be heard with attention.

Soon it occurred to Cass that the general seemed to complete the reading of some pages in a remarkably short time. Other pages took him almost twice as long. He's skipping, Cass thought. He is not reading the entire thing. Then he noticed another thing. Benjamin Sebastian was sitting next to James. As the general finished each page he handed it to Sebastian. Well, there was nothing wrong with that. Someone had to hold it.

In all there were some twenty pages, and it took Wilkinson some thirty-five minutes to read them, for occasionally he had to dilate upon some point. When it was concluded, everyone present knew that General Wilkinson had descended the Mississippi in the summer of 1787, that upon his arrival in New Orleans he had informed the governor of the object he had in view, of obtaining commercial advantages both for himself and for the western country; that he had represented the great advantage which the Spanish government might derive from cultivating an amicable intercourse with Kentucky; that he had addressed the fear as well as the hopes of the Spanish nation — that he had told Governor Miró that Kentuckians had a right by the law of God and nature to the use of that river, that the time might not be remote when they would claim as a right what they would now accept as a privilege. In conclusion the general said that Governor Miró had requested him to commit to writing his sentiments on this subject, with which request he had complied by way of this present memorial.

Apprehensively Cass waited to see what he would do next. Would he move that the "right" this memorial spoke of be incorporated in action? There was certainly no harm in the document, *as read,* he thought, other than the threat of that right.

But Wilkinson did nothing but accept the gathered sheets of his manuscript from Benjamin Sebastian's hands and take his seat. Ought they, Cass wondered, to ask that the manuscript be laid on the clerk's table, to be incorporated in the records of the convention? It might be very interesting.

In the pause of silence which followed the conclusion of the reading Cass stood. He did not formulate his words into a motion. "Gentlemen," he said, "might we not ask the general to furnish the clerk with the manuscript he has just read so that it may be incorporated in the records of this convention?"

James Wilkinson cleared his throat. "I regret," he said, "that I have only this copy of the memorial, but I shall be happy to make a clear copy of it and give it in the clerk's hands, not later than tomorrow."

But the question was raised. This paper was not properly a part of the convention's business. The general had merely asked permission to read it. It was not, therefore, the obligation of the convention to retain it in its files. That was true, Cass thought, but he wanted mightily to get his hands on that document. He was pondering whether to object, when a motion was made that the convention "highly approve the address presented by General James Wilkinson to the Governor-Intendant of Louisiana, and that the President be requested to present him the thanks of the convention for the regard which he therein manifested for the Interest of the Western country."

Unanimously the convention's gratitude was voted and immediately it adjourned itself until noon of the following day.

Thursday, November 6. The committee to prepare the petition to Virginia was not yet ready to report. Madison and Mercer counties had been committed to ask for "a manly and spirited address to be sent to Congress to obtain the navigation of the river Mississippi." These men were in no way connected with the extremist party — they represented, rather, the conservative opinion on the way to go about obtaining the free navigation of the river. Wilkinson, however, now moved that the address be prepared, and succeeded in having appointed to the committee himself, John Brown, Harry Innes, Benjamin Sebastian, as well as two conservative members, Thomas Marshall and Judge Muter. This was the last channel through which the convention could be maneuvered at all, and no one begrudged him the slight victory. He could certainly do no damage in an address to Congress.

There was a brief flurry of excitement when John Brown moved "that it is the wish and interest of the good people of this district to separate from the state of Virginia, and that the same be erected into an independent member of the federal union."

So — you are still for illegal and immediate separation, but you won't go along with Don Jaime on his Spanish scheme, Cass thought.

There was no need for any excitement. The chairman ordered the motion to lie on the table of the clerk, since there was already a petition for statehood before the house.

Friday, November 7. The convention met for roll call. A letter from Mr. James Speed was read and tabled. The convention then adjourned so the committees could continue in meeting.

Saturday, November 8. Wilkinson made another adroit move. Immediately after roll call he asked for the floor, obtained it, and moved that since this convention seemed so divided in its opinions it be adjourned in order that the delegates might learn the wishes of their constituents.

Quickly the motion was defeated, but it made Cass and his party realize that they were still in danger. Wilkinson was tough, there was no doubt about it. Nothing escaped his attention; there was no loophole too small for him to seize upon. He was not going to be easily licked.

Sunday, November 9. The convention lay over at rest. Joseph Crockett returned from Fayette county with a petition praying the convention to vote *only* for legal separation. It was signed with five hundred names. Seeing it, Cass thought they now had a little more ammunition for Monday. The petition to Virginia would be certain to be ready, be read, and some action on it taken. Wilkinson, he thought, would be certain to challenge it, even though he had been on the committee to prepare it.

Monday, November 10. The chairman reversed the order of business and the address to Congress was read first. The general read it of course, and of course he had written it. No one could mistake its florid style. Cass grinned as he heard the rolling peroration. "Fathers! Fellow-citizens! and Guardians of our rights! As we address you by the endearing appellation of fathers, we rely on your paternal affection to hear us; we rely on your justice . . ." and so on for many, long pages.

Without discussion the address was adopted to be enclosed in a letter to the President of Congress.

Immediately, then, the petition to Virginia was read . . . not by Don Jaime. It was handed to the clerk, Thomas Todd, who droned it out in an uninspiring voice. It was not, Cass saw, the work of James Wilkinson's hand. In all likelihood it had been greatly influenced by the legal mind of Judge Muter. It was a manly, straightforward address, a request that Virginia provide for Kentucky's separation and that she use her influence with Congress to the end that the new state be admitted into the American Union according to the late recommendation of the Congress of the old Confederation.

Girded for the argument which they thought inevitable, the conservatives looked at each other, nodded, ready to take the floor. To their amazement there was no argument; there was only a brief discussion, and the petition was accepted, a resolution passed to send it to the speaker of the house of delegates in Virginia.

What had happened?

Cass looked across the room at James Wilkinson, feeling a little dazed. James met his eye and astounded him with a wry smile and by drawing a finger across his throat. He was giving up! Cass felt a chunk of admiration and of tenderness in his throat. Gad, but he liked the man. Rogue he might be, villain he probably was, devious, shrewd, clever — too much of all these things for his own good. They were on opposite sides of the fence and Cass would fight him to the bitter end — but, he confessed to himself, he would never cease to regret the necessity, nor would he ever cease to miss the man's gaiety, wit, humor and charm. To the end of his days, he knew, there would be a small, private place inside himself which General James Wilkinson had touched, brightened, then left desolate.

A hand touched Cass's shoulder, and a head bent toward him. It was the sergeant-at-arms. "Major, you are wanted outside."

Jeremy waited in the hall for him, his pinched, lean face blue with cold, his hunched body swathed in coats and scarves, his eyes grave. Cass saw also that he was swaying with fatigue. "Jeremy! You're frozen, man! Come with me to the taproom. Let me get something hot inside you."

Jeremy managed to shake his head, but when he tried to speak he could only make a croaking sound. Cass led him into the taproom, unwrapped the layers of coats and scarves, drew up a chair for him. Provoked, he scolded. "Are you frostbitten, Jere? What in the name of Christ brought you out in this kind of weather?" Sudden fear struck him and he stiffened. "Indians?"

Jeremy bent over the mug of hot rum the serving girl brought and took a deep swallow, holding it, letting it roll slowly around in his mouth and down his throat to warm it. "Rachel," he said in a whisper. "She drowned herself in the millpond yesterday."

CHAPTER 27

His first emotion was shocked horror. "No!"

Jeremy warmed his cold-stiffened hands on the mug of rum, gulped it down and gave the empty mug to the girl to refill. He wiped his mouth with his coat sleeve. He could talk better now. "Mag found her about the middle of the morning. Her body had drifted down and was caught in the big wheel."

There was swift remorse then. "I should never have left her, Jeremy—come away to this convention. I should have stayed with her. I knew she had not yet recovered from young Edward's death."

"If," Jeremy said, taking another swig of his rum, "you are going to feel guilt, Cass, feel it for your real sin. You should never have married her."

Cass gave him a quick glance. "I thought you liked Rachel."

"I did. I admired her and respected her. I had a very deep affection for her. But she was out of her place and her time here on the frontier and you were responsible for bringing her here."

Cass remembered his own indecision at that point guiltily.

"The seeds of this tragedy were inherent from the beginning," Jeremy continued slowly. "Kentucky, or any other frontier for that matter, requires a tough character, a tough frame of mind, in its women as well as in its men. Rachel had only gentleness and goodness. She had not the earthiness nor the lustiness of a Mag, or a Hannah Fowler, or an Esther Whitley, or a Jane Manifee, or even of an Ann Logan. The women who come with their men into this country must have a coarse fiber of strength within them, a tough, resilient fiber. Rachel did not have it. Her fiber was soft, tender, and at the core, unbending. With her own kind of man, which Edward Cabot evidently was, she had her own kind of strength — a force and spirit which armed her for the blows of fate. Without him, and no man could have been more different than you, she was robbed of that force. That is what you must feel guilty about if you mean to load yourself down with remorse. Once here, however, the deed done, it was too late. A woman on the frontier must take up her own load, bear it almost wholly alone, for a frontier man must ever be about the business of his country. I doubt," he continued dryly, "if your presence at home would have made any difference. There had long been an arid desert between you and Rachel."

Cass bent his head. "Jeremy, you are merciless."

"No. I am merely truthful. 'There is no armour against fate,' Cass. If it was fate that you should marry Rachel, it was fate that she should die by her own hand."

Cass took a long breath. "Poor child, poor child."

He felt the same kind of grief he had felt for young Edward, as if innocence had been undone by its own virtue; the same kind of helpless, quiet sense of loss. There was nothing in it of the deep, rending, empty grief a man would feel for the woman he loved with a full, yearning, passionate love. It was so long over, that kind of love, that not even the face of death could resurrect it.

"Is the convention nearly through its business?" Jeremy asked.

"In effect, yes. It will probably adjourn today." He smiled at the wispy, little man. "The people won, Jere. We've licked him."

Jeremy's eyes lit up. "Good. Good. I told you I had faith in the people."

Cass rose. "I had better pack my things and start home at once, Jeremy. But you are much too worn out and frozen to make the journey back immediately. Stay here a few days — rest and thaw yourself out. Come with me to my room, though, now and we can talk further while I get ready."

In his room, Cass went about picking up his scattered belongings, throwing them into his portmanteau. "Who is at the house with the children?" he asked, packing his shirts. "Mercy? Melie?"

"Tattie. She went down immediately and took charge of the children and the servants."

Tattie!

He held a shirt in his hands, the linen smooth under his fingers. There was one small frayed spot at a cuff edge. He was conscious of its roughness, slid his hand over it rubbing it idly. He gazed out the window at the winter-bare landscape, noticed, barely conscious of noticing, that the ground of the square was thawing, was becoming mushy with brown, miry mud. Tattie.

He did not try to hide from himself what Rachel's death meant for him and Tattie. With one clean stroke, out of her deep unhappiness, out of her misery, out of the tangled threads of her own destiny, she had raveled out the tangled threads of theirs. He felt a genuine sorrow at what she had done. He had never ceased to have an affection for her that made him care about her welfare. If he had neglected her by his absence so often, it was what every other man in the country who held any place of prominence had to do. If he had ceased to love her with the deep intensity he had felt in the beginning, it had only been a relief and release for her. If he had come to love another, he had tried to be honorable about it. If he had been unfaithful in thought, he had at least been faithful in act. Feeling regret for Rachel's death, he could, at the same time, and honorably, know that it opened for him a new life. There would come a time when Tattie's rightful place would be in the big house, beside him, mother of Rachel's children, and mother of his. "There is no armour against fate." It was best, he thought, to leave it at that.

He laid the shirt in the satchel.

CHAPTER 28

It was four more long years before Kentucky was finally admitted into the union as a state—June 1, 1792, the fifteenth state of the United States of America. Vermont had slid in a little ahead to make the fourteenth. But there were never again the crises and great danger which had fermented the sixth and seventh conventions. If Wilkinson, Cass thought, was actually in league with the Spanish at New Orleans, he must be having considerable trouble saving face with them those years, for he could bring all of his friends to the trough of water, but he could never force them to drink. In the end the forces of law and order, the patient respect for legality, the feeling of Americanism, won.

Don Jaime was not in Kentucky at the moment of victory. He was back in the United States Army, a corps of which had been sent by the new President, George Washington, to the western country. From Fort Washington, which in time became the city of Cincinnati, the little general, no longer a general but a lieutenant colonel now, wrote as grandiloquently as ever to his friends. "Disgusted," he said, "by disappointment and misfortunes" and because of an "ignorance in commerce" he was glad to "resume the sword of my country." "My views," he stated further, "in entering the Military Line are Bread & Fame—uncertain of either, I shall deserve both."

Mr. Thomas Marshall was one of those who had recommended Wilkinson for the appointment. Having been a neighbor of President Washington's in Virginia, his word carried weight. "Why?" Cass asked him, hearing about it.

The elder man chuckled. "Because, my friend, I thought it an excellent idea to get him out of Kentucky, and I deemed that he could do no great damage under the disciplines and controls of the regular army."

Cass laughed. It sounded like good reasoning to him. But he did not envy the army officers who would have him to contend with.

Cass's own life, by the time of the statehood of the district, had fallen in extremely pleasant lines. Tattie was his wife and had already presented him with twin sons. She could, and sometimes in the heat of anger did, sling a pot across the room at him. But she also could, and always did, love him warmly, wholly, and excitingly. The new brick house was finished and if it was usually untidy, often actually dirty, it was nevertheless a place of realities and of life being lived lustily. If the children went about most of the time rather unkempt, resembling somewhat the guttersnipe Tattie herself had been, they went about nonetheless in certainty of love and regard, hardy, full of mischief and fun, their bright young minds tutored by both Tattie and Jeremy in the sensible learning that would stand them in good stead. He often thought his life had become richer than he deserved. Jeremy, who could always bring him down with a solid thump, reminded him at such times, "We always get what we deserve, my friend, because we get what we go after."

James Wilkinson's town, Frankfort, all his own holdings in it lost for debts, became the capital of the new state. But slowly the dream of incorporating his own town faded from Cass's mind until if he could have incorporated it, he would not have. He liked Cartwright's Mill exactly as it was. When Green County was cut off from Lincoln County, in the same year Kentucky became a state, the county seat was established at Glover's Station, and the new town became Greensburg, and Cass felt no regret.

During all the years of his life he followed James Wilkinson's career, through its ups and downs, with more than passing interest. It was James Wilkinson who, as the army officer in charge, accepted the transfer of the entire Louisiana Territory at New Orleans after Thomas Jefferson, then President, had bought the territory from France. James Wilkinson was later appointed Governor of Upper Louisiana, which eventually became the Missouri Territory. He sent out expeditions from St. Louis to map and explore the southwest, among them the expedition of Lieutenant Zebulon Pike, and the expedition of his own eldest son to explore the headwaters of the Arkansas River. He was involved in the Burr conspiracy. He was often the stormy central figure in courts martial brought against him, but he was never actually convicted of any of the charges.

To Cass, everything the man did had the single theme at the center — Washington of the west. He thought he could see, always, that great dream of empire and when, in his old age, he had a letter from the man, from Mexico, he felt certain of it. "This land lies in wait," Wilkinson wrote, "for a man of astuteness and cleverness. Had I the funds I could easily become that man. There are vast sums to be made from colonization in Mexico, along the Rio Grande and in the area they call Tejas. The Spanish are willing to make great grants of land. I am about seeing into this venture at this time. I am writing every man I know. Do you send me a small amount, Cass, and I can invest it for you in Mexican land which will, in time, pay you a rich return."

It was 1825. Cass himself was sixty-six, the little general sixty-eight. The bright, deluded mind, ever turned to the expediency of serving his own ends, ever seeking his dream of conquest and empire, was still bemused by the notion of fame and fortune — in Spanish land, with Spanish gold. The eloquent pen was still flowing, the rhetoric just as polished, the periods just as rounded. But the hand that held the pen was faltering. The man was dying.

He was buried in the cemetery of the parish of the Archangel San Miguel in the City of Mexico.

Reading his published memoirs later, Cass thought he had written his own epitaph. "With a sanguine temperament and ardent affections, feeling has prevailed more than judgment in directing my career, and fame has presented allurements more inviting to me than fortune, without which, in the present times, virtue and merit much more exalted, must become a frail dependence."

The glory road had ended.